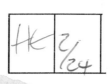

'Koo, Lulu and Beth, three very different women, wake up in a strange hotel room with no recollection of how they got there! From this intriguing beginning, *Summer Dreams at the Lakeside Cottage* sees them take charge of their destiny and explores just why all three are running away from their lives. Warm, humorous and full of friendship; an ideal holiday read'   Georgia Hill

'I loved joining Koo, Lulu and Beth on their hen adventures – this is an uplifting and wonderful story about the power of female friendships, love and self-discovery'   Donna Ashcroft

'A warm, funny, uplifting writer to celebrate!'   Katie Fforde

'A lovely, heart-warming story . . . I was hooked!'
                                                    Christina Courtenay

'A delightful tale of friendship, family and love'   Jenni Keer

'Thoroughly entertaining. The characters are warm and well drawn. I thoroughly recommend this book if you are looking for a light-hearted read. 5 stars'   Sue Roberts

'Uplifting'   *Woman & Home*

'A pleasure to read . . . A summer breezes treat'   *Devon Life*

Erin Green was born and raised in Warwickshire. An avid reader since childhood, her imagination was instinctively drawn to creative writing as she grew older. Erin has two Hons degrees: BA English literature and another BSc Psychology – her previous careers have ranged from part-time waitress, the retail industry, fitness industry and education.

She has an obsession about time, owns several tortoises and an infectious laugh! Erin writes contemporary novels focusing on love, life and laughter. Erin is an active member of the Romantic Novelists' Association and was delighted to be awarded The Katie Fforde Bursary in 2017. An ideal day for Erin involves writing, people watching and drinking copious amounts of tea.

For more information about Erin, visit her website: **www.ErinGreenAuthor.co.uk**, find her on Facebook **www.facebook.com/ErinGreenAuthor** or follow her on Twitter, Instagram, TikTok or Threads **@ErinGreenAuthor**.

By Erin Green

Summer Dreams at the Lakeside Cottage
Christmas Wishes at the Lakeside Cottage

A Christmas Wish
The Single Girl's Calendar
The Magic of Christmas Tree Farm
New Beginnings at Rose Cottage
Taking a Chance on Love

From Shetland, With Love series
From Shetland, With Love
From Shetland, With Love at Christmas
Sunny Stays at the Shetland Hotel
A Shetland Christmas Carol

CHRISTMAS WISHES
AT THE
LAKESIDE COTTAGE

Erin Green

REVIEW

First published in 2023 by
HEADLINE REVIEW
An imprint of HEADLINE PUBLISHING GROUP

1

Cataloguing in Publication Data is available from the British Library

ISBN 978 1 4722 9509 5

Typeset in Sabon by CC Book Production

Printed and bound in Great Britain by
Clays Ltd, Elcograf S.p.A.

MIX
Paper | Supporting
responsible forestry
FSC
www.fsc.org   FSC® C104740

Headline's policy is to use papers that are natural, renewable and recyclable
products and made from wood grown in well-managed forests and other
controlled sources. The logging and manufacturing processes are expected
to conform to the environmental regulations of the country of origin.

HEADLINE PUBLISHING GROUP
An Hachette UK Company
Carmelite House
50 Victoria Embankment
London EC4Y 0DZ

www.headline.co.uk
www.hachette.co.uk

Dedicated to L. S. Lowry (1887–1976)

'And I like large parties. They're so intimate. At small parties, there isn't any privacy.'

F. SCOTT FITZGERALD – *The Great Gatsby* (1925)

Chapter One

Saturday 23 December

Lowry

'Here we are, folks. By far the worst case I've collected today but sadly nothing we haven't seen before,' I announce, barging into consulting room one with a wire cat carrier, just before three o'clock. My uniform is mud splattered and dusty – I had to scale a garden fence to perform the rescue – my stubby ponytail threatens to escape its hair bobble and my stomach is rumbling after a long and weary early shift. I'm tired and disheartened as I heave the occupied carrier on to the vet's freshly wiped consulting table. 'It'll make your blood boil, but the sooner you examine her ... the better she'll feel.' I don't await Vet Colley's instructions; I've worked alongside him for many years. Passing my clipboard of notes to young Jenny, the veterinary nurse, I continue with my running commentary as I unhook the carrier door and gently fish out the emaciated animal within – the poor thing has all but given up her fight for life. 'Found abandoned in a rear garden, no food, no sign of water or proper shelter. The neighbour reports the homeowners left a couple of weeks ago and simply left her behind and, well ... look.'

The cat doesn't flinch or fight, her head hangs low, her matchstalk frame poking through dirty matted fur. She hasn't the energy to struggle; she barely has enough to breathe.

'How do some people sleep at night?' mutters Vet Colley. His shoulders drop and his brow furrows as he views the neglected cat.

'Who knows. But we need to do what we do and in time . . .'

'In time? Lowry, can you not see what we have here?' he says, beginning to examine the poor creature with a featherlike touch.

'In time, with our care and attention she'll be another survivor,' I say, fussing the cat's ear to offer some comfort. 'We work wonders around here.'

'Well, given that you're supposed to be heading off on annual leave, she won't be *your* little wonder, Lowry,' calls Jenny, tapping the computer keyboard to create a new file from my paperwork. Jenny's right. My shift officially ended an hour ago, but home time means nothing in my world. Here at RSPCA Salford is where I belong – amongst the litter trays, the feeding bowls and faded knitted blankets – answering emergency calls from distressed but kindly neighbours. Regardless of my shift rota, I'll happily spend hours sitting on a scrubbed floor beside a basket tending to a tiny mite disadvantaged by those who promised to love and take care of them. Because animals never renege on their promise of unconditional love shown to us. Sadly, some humans fail miserably, pushing the boundaries of moral decency.

'Mmm, but I'm needed here . . . I'll arrive when I arrive,' I say, as Vet Colley gently prises open the cat's mouth, displaying needle-sharp teeth.

'She's barely older than a year, poor thing,' he says, securing his stethoscope in his ears and listening to her chest.

'Lowry,' sighs Jenny, shaking her head, her eyes not leaving the screen, 'if Roger finds you're still here . . .'

I don't answer – a shoddy attempt to ignore her kind warning. Big Boss Roger can go whistle for the time being; my duties and moral judgement come before family matters. Having encouraged my love of animals since childhood, my mum's hardly going to complain; I'm simply doing what I do best. If anything, they should be praising me for having prepacked my suitcase, which is already sitting on the rear seat of my tiny car beside a selection of gift-wrapped Christmas presents – enabling me to leave straight from work.

'Lowry,' Vet Colley says, his gaze fixed upon his delicate patient, 'this little girl's in safe hands – get yourself off and enjoy the Christmas holidays before . . .'

Bang on cue, the consulting room door opens and his booming Mancunian tone doesn't need any introduction. 'Are you still here? Lowry, your shift finished an hour ago. A six o'clock start means a two o'clock handover. Off home – now!'

Caught again! I turn to address my long-suffering boss, his bulky frame holding the door wide open. His size and exasperated glare are softened by his attire, this year's Christmas jumper depicting a comical reindeer with a red flashing hooter.

'I was just . . .' With the best will in the world, I've no remaining argument left to answer him. This happens every time I have holiday entitlement owing: I drag my feet until I'm forced to take the required days or lose them to 'the system'. I appreciate Roger's concern, but he needs to understand me a little better too; without a partner or children, my work is my life. He worries about my working hours and, sometimes, even I can see his point about staff wellbeing and work-life balance. But after a decade of knowing me, having watched me work my way from a weekend volunteer, as a shy nineteen-year-old, through training and exam study to become a qualified animal inspector, he should accept that an extra hour won't kill me. Though looking at Roger's unwavering expression and fierce stance, he might.

Helen

I'm five minutes earlier than my allotted three o'clock arrival time, so I'll happily wait here in the car, as not everyone appreciates such courtesy nowadays. I've parked alongside the cottage's drystone wall, complete with a picket gate, and am delighted by the prospect beyond. An authentic country cottage with a bulky thatched roof, with possibly a second apex protruding towards the rear, a quaint kitchen garden either side of its cobbled pathway and a picturesque porch above a moss-green door framed by the bare branches of wisteria, which must look stunning during the summer months.

It's only taken me two hours across country to arrive from Todmorden, a pleasant and relaxed journey accompanied by Radio Four, my trusted companion. The snow repeatedly predicted by the weather lady has held off so far. Fingers crossed, the relatives arriving in the coming hours will get here stress-free and before the night draws in. Those who've decided to delay their arrival until tomorrow or the day after might have to do battle with the snow. Why some folks can't organise themselves and commit to specific arrangements is beyond me. Though they've never been any different, so more fool me for expecting change. Still, that's family, and we love them for being unique.

The surrounding Cumbrian countryside wouldn't have been my first choice. I've previously opted for quaint rental cottages nestled much further afield, but this location means less travelling time for all concerned and, more importantly, it's ideal for Rupert's Boxing Day plans.

Despite the chilly temperatures, I climb out of the car for a closer look.

Rupert's already paid the full rental price, so technically the cottage is ours for the next six days – despite only needing it for five of those days. Unless the owners prove to be the picky sort who'll charge for my extra five minutes stating I'm trespassing.

The metal catch on the gate has a satisfying springclose action once you pass through and release it. So lovely. There's a solid unevenness underfoot as the cobbles aren't the modern flat-topped sort but originals with a rounded mossy surface, probably laid a century ago.

I'm admiring the craftsmanship of the leaded windows staring boldly from the frontage, with the upper windows cutely peeping from beneath the thatch overhang, when the front door springs wide open.

'Hello, I'm Josie . . . housekeeper for Lakeside Cottage. Helen, is it?' asks a spritely lady, dressed in a pleated tweed skirt, sensible walking brogues and a well-weathered but bright smile.

'Helen, yes. That's me. We're quite a large party so we thought it best that I arrive first. It saves ushering "the gang" through each room and them getting underfoot while you explain the essentials.'

'A wise decision. Our parties are usually quite large, given that we can accommodate sixteen guests in our nine bedrooms. On occasion, some guests have become quite tetchy during the handover tour with the named keyholder – which is only for their benefit, enabling them to have full use of the facilities.'

'Of course. Our party would be no different, despite there being only adults,' I say, grateful to Rupert for accepting my early-arrival suggestion. We've been caught out many times before when renting a holiday retreat, and it's never ideal to start a family gathering on the wrong note.

'Welcome to Lakeside Cottage!' Josie gestures towards an artistic name plaque fixed to the rustic brickwork. 'I'll give you a run-through of the what-nots, and please feel free to ask questions. The rental charge covers everything you see within and around the cottage, so please use as you see fit. An added bonus for large parties, such as yourselves, is that we haven't any neighbours for half a mile in either direction. Though the village of Hawkshead and all its amenities are just a short walk along the lane, so it doesn't feel desolate or too remote.'

My heart melts; it's just what we Carmichaels need – solitude and space to create special festive memories.

'Thank you. We intend to celebrate the Christmas of all Christmases, if I'm honest,' I say, gleefully stepping into the hallway and closing the door by its tiny metal latch, noting the other sturdy bolts and locks fitted below, for additional security. My next spot is the substantial coat rack on the opposite wall, another much-needed facility when our family come to stay. Funny how my self-imposed role as the organised matriarch reappears given an opportunity, but as I always remind them, we each have our talents. Mine are acceptance and organising – make of that what you will!

The hallway is a fair size, vast in fact: a wide staircase is directly before me, with a rustic newel post matching the beams overhead and polished floorboards. Tasteful decoration in a classy mustard with gold detailing highlights many original features such as the picture rail and the doorknobs complementing the four panelled doors leading off.

'You've chosen the perfect location then. Firstly, I always point this out as guests usually ask: here's our guest book with a pen, feel free to include your thoughts and memories, which add to the history of the cottage. It's worth a little read on a quiet cosy night – it's quite humorous in places.' Josie gestures to a side table, on which rests a fancy ceramic dish filled with keys and a beautiful padded book complete with a pen, as mentioned.

'Thank you, I might have a little read myself,' I say, purely to be polite because I'll be rushed off my feet, if previous family holidays are anything to go by. This time especially, given the jam-packed itinerary for our five festive days.

'There are four sets of keys in the dish; if you could ensure they're returned at the end of your stay on the twenty-eighth, I'd appreciate it.'

There's no point mentioning our planned departure on the twenty-seventh – the keys will be there waiting for her either way. From what Rupert's said, it wasn't worth quibbling about the cost of the extra day. He was happy to pay the full price to secure such a beautiful property, in an idyllic location.

I listen intently as Josie outlines where I'll find the house-keeping manual, the instructions for every electrical item in the cottage and the bin collection rota. Local hospital details, doctor's surgery and local takeaway numbers are also provided – the owners really have thought of everything and Josie diligently delivers the details. 'A list of emergency numbers, including my own, is pinned inside the pantry door.'

God forbid we need those.

'In here we have ...' Josie opens the first door on the right-hand side revealing a huge lounge which extends the full length of the cottage. I recognise the smell of beeswax from my childhood which I assume has been used on the traditional furniture. There's an impressive stone fireplace and granite hearth dominating this end of the room, around which I imagine the family, snuggled cosy and warm, enjoying a Christmas tipple.

'Wow, look at those views,' I gasp, instantly drawn to the windows along the side of the room. As if by magic, a large lake appears in the distance with a backdrop of purple-headed mountains beyond, gently caressing a wintry sky.

'Impressive, hey? More so in the summer, but nevertheless very relaxing whilst having a quiet moment to yourself,' says Josie. 'I never tire of looking at the landscape – no two hours of the day are the same.'

'And the owners, do they live here for part of the year?' I ask, wondering how they could bear to be away.

'Oh no. They live in Shetland, actually. They make regular visits from time to time but never on a permanent basis.'

'How lovely. They've obviously got good taste.' Again, the decoration is high-end and traditional; there's nothing tacky or pretentious, just simple lines and decent quality. Very much a luxury home-from-home, with pale carpets, rich maroons and the odd splash of silver detailing on the satin cushions and brocade curtains. Their choice of interiors matches mine exactly, if I could afford to own a cottage such as this.

'There's a log pile just outside the rear kitchen door, which saves the faff of chopping wood, though some guests like to try their hand once they locate the axe in the outhouse,' says Josie, adding, 'They usually manage to chop one or two logs then appreciate what's provided.'

'It'll keep them entertained, I suppose.' I can see our lads doing exactly that, goading each other in a brotherly competition which will inevitably end in tantrums or a dash to the local A&E, much as it did when they were youngsters.

'Anyway, the dining room is opposite,' says Josie, swiftly exiting and leading the way across the hallway and opening the door to the left of the entrance. I poke my head and shoulders inside to view a massive oak dining table with 'Two, four, six, eight … sixteen?' I say, proving I can count, before realising there would hardly be fewer in a cottage accommodating sixteen guests. The leaded windows overlook the front garden, which is still lovely despite it being a little bare at this time of year.

'Then behind the dining room, we have the snug. Ideal for quiet conversations or just a quick episode on the TV while everyone else watches the lounge's main TV.' Josie opens the panelled door revealing a very modern room, with two squashy marshmallow-styled sofas and a low-lying coffee table, abstract prints framed on each wall and a plasma TV in the corner with numerous board games stashed beneath.

'Useful space,' I say, sensing we might need a rota system to ensure fairness if troubles break out amongst the siblings.

'There's a record player directly opposite under the staircase, which seems a strange place to house it but even with the volume turned low it can be heard throughout the cottage. There's plenty of vinyl albums and singles, stored in the cupboard below.'

'That might come in useful for some background music,' I say, instantly preparing for all eventualities.

'And finally, through here, we have the kitchen. What I call a proper farmhouse kitchen.' We exit the cosy snug to enter the rear kitchen. Josie isn't wrong in calling it a farmhouse kitchen – it is massive! A red tiled floor, a scrubbed table in the centre, surrounded by deep countertops, various pots and pans hanging on wall hooks, a blackened hearth and a bright yellow Aga, which overshadows the modern cooker slotted in beside.

'I've cooked in here many times and loved every minute of it – a proper cook's kitchen, in my opinion,' says Josie.

'Now, that's one thing we do have in our party, a true cook. Martha will be in her element, but she's certainly not expecting this. She assumes she'll have to slum it for a few days in a kitchen that isn't up to her standards, but this … well, she'll be happy with double-frontage fridges,' I say, excited to see her initial reaction.

'Wait till she sees the scullery, the food stores and the utility room – all located along the passage; there's everything she'll be needing for a jolly Christmas. We've provided a couple of complimentary festive food hampers in the stores. Each contains a few essentials so you can enjoy a snack and a little relax before you need to venture to a supermarket. There's a local Co-op a little way into Hawkshead, they stock most goods.'

'To be fair, Martha is bringing everything she needs for the week ahead. She's like that – nothing's left to chance. She's been preparing food for days, but it's great to know we won't go short with a Co-op on our doorstep.' A quick scan of the kitchen suggests there's every imaginable gadget lined up along the counter tops – so everyone else will have what they'll need.

'It goes without saying the rear garden, coal shed and outhouse are easily accessible,' says Josie, pointing to the rear exit, a solid, wooden split stable door.

There's a sense of security and safety regarding solid wooden doors. The threshold beyond is unknown until the actual moment it's revealed. After which there's only ever forward motion, without the option to retreat and revert to a previous time – much like our journey through life. This rear door allows you to view the prospect beyond before deciding to venture through. Now that I like.

'Nice door,' I say, admiring how practical it would be in warmer months.

'It is. Very practical too as we've acquired a stray tabby; guests have started to feed her. She's no trouble, other than being a little minx, but not everyone likes seeing a cat curled before the Aga.'

'I can imagine.'

'Anyway, you can't get lost wandering out the back. The garden is terraced and sectioned, though sadly the fence on this right-hand side hides a gorgeous view of the lakes, which is a shame. It'll need dismantling and re-erecting come the spring.'

I'm impressed. Which is amazing since I didn't locate or book this particular rental cottage; it was found by Diane, Rupert's fiancée. And praise where praise is due, I think she has proved herself top-notch. I really hope Rupert approves too. Though you never know with that old bugger.

'Ready to view the upstairs?' asks Josie, with a chuckle. I assume I look overwhelmed because that's how I'm feeling at the thought of nine bedrooms.

'Lead the way but if it's anything like down here then our family will have no complaints. I can't believe this property has ever been rented out as everything looks pristine – does no one ever ruin or break anything?'

'Sometimes, but it's rare. The owners insist on offering an unforgettable experience with high-quality fittings and fixtures, and in return the guests respect their surroundings – we've had very few issues,' says Josie, retracing our steps towards the central staircase. 'There's one master suite and a selection of doubles, singles and twin rooms with various bathrooms.'

'My second task, which makes me sound like mother hen, is to allocate the bedrooms, so I'm hoping there won't be too many arguments.' I'm hoping to ensure Diane's daughter, Lowry, has a decent room – it'll be a nice welcome to our family.

'I doubt you'll hear any complaints. Most guests remark on the comfort and quality of our mattresses and bedding,' says Josie, as we slowly ascend the staircase. The top stair gives a distinct yet homely creak as we reach the airy landing.

Chapter Two

Lowry

For two hours, I follow my trusted satnav from the familiar city streets of Salford to this vast wilderness of the Lake District. My only companions are a family-sized bag of chocolate limes, open and scattered on the passenger seat, and my Christmas tunes playlist, from which Noddy Holder sporadically wails his festive greeting. My chin is inches from the steering wheel as I lean forward, peering into the darkness as my aged Mini creeps along this narrow, desolate lane. My bulky work jacket is uncomfortably bunched about my ears and the seat belt is stretched to the max. I'm grateful that the snow threatened in the earlier weather forecast hasn't occurred but the bitter cold is testing my car's heater. I don't think my little brown Mini was built to contend with conditions such as these. Though at forty years old, and well looked after, she's plodding along nicely through life, just like me.

These final few minutes of the drive are the most daunting – everything looks the same in the dark. Having successfully navigated winding single-breadth lanes since leaving the motorway, I fear I might now be lost. I'll be stuffed if I have to turn around as I haven't seen a passing point or a driveway for ages – nothing but ancient hedgerows or shimmering lakes on either side. Despite my earlier fence-scrambling experience, my typical day consists of trudging along busy high streets, through housing estates and industrial areas to answer emergency animal calls. I'm not used to windswept environments, wild terrain or idyllic seclusion in search of 'a rambling cottage befitting any festive rom-com movie' – my mother's description, not mine.

I've no one to blame but myself. I should have left work earlier so that I could drive during daylight hours but no, my heart was set on settling the new arrival, the abandoned cat, into her pen as my final festive job. On second thoughts, it's probably the two other emergencies that I offered to assist with that have truly delayed my arrival, despite Roger's repeated insistence that I should go home for the holidays.

Given my late departure, I didn't bother to change from my unflattering uniform but headed straight out; I'll freshen up on arrival – then my holiday can truly begin. I might be reluctant to take my holiday entitlement but boy, what a few days this should be! Five festive-filled days in which my mother, Diane, has chosen to celebrate Christmas and marry the new man in her life come Boxing Day. Not that I've met my soon-to-be stepfather, Rupert Carmichael, but that's the downside of living miles away from my parent whilst I retain my childhood roots in Pendlebury, with a vocational job where weekend shifts are essential and unplanned overtime necessary.

Not that I'm entirely to blame – the speed with which their whirlwind romance has developed in a mere twelve weeks has made my head spin! Mum's about to have her dream wedding after a lifetime of waiting for Prince Charming. For this alone, I'm truly happy, delighted – all those wonderful life-affirming adjectives – but still, blimey O'Reilly, they didn't hang about in setting a date! That would be like me being married by Easter! Now, that would be a whirlwind romance – correction, a miracle romance given that I've not had so much as a Christmas kiss in the last, oh, now, let me think … two? Three? Dare I say … four years? My brain enters a time warp as I recall the details of my break-up with Tommy Collins, trying to avoid igniting my emotions or reopening the wounds this late in my journey. I'll need more than a few minutes to compose myself otherwise. If I ever arrive, that is. Does this well-trodden lane, probably created aeons ago by a horse and cart, for a horse and cart, go on for ever?

Lights ahead! Quaint picturesque cottage lights to be precise.

I slow the car to a crawl, peering up at the chocolate-box cottage complete with what appears to be against the starry night sky a quintessential thatched roof. A centrally positioned doorway beneath a titchy porch canopy with mellow light spilling from large windows on either side. This must be it: Lakeside Cottage.

I draw the car to a halt behind several other parked vehicles edging the lane, not totally convinced by the satnav's announcement of 'your destination is on your left' and somewhat grateful that my satnav didn't ad lib with, 'But you're daunted by the prospect of the festivities so would you like to return home?' I expect the festivities are in full flow; my mum and Rupert were planning their arrival for four o'clock, after a trusted relative did the honours of collecting the keys at three.

The amber glow pouring from both the ground and upper windows suggests every room is occupied, which equals a fair number of people. I'm not entirely sure how many are invited for the five-day stay, though Mum did say Rupert has children from a previous marriage so I'm expecting other adults, probably around my age.

Given my track record, I'm probably the last to arrive. Being an only child raised by an only child and single mum whilst living with her ageing parents – family gatherings weren't a necessity in our Pendlebury semi. But those days of 'just the four of us' are long gone.

I can't sit here all night. As I get out of the car and lock the driver's door, a niggling thought occurs: what if I'm at the wrong address? My stomach lurches, my palms instantly sweat and my knees weaken. I'm stalling for time because be it a lame security dog hiding in a factory, chasing an escaped budgerigar through dense shrubbery in a local park or locating a pet python in an abandoned maisonette, I've never previously had any trouble with directions. Yet at the idea of meeting my mother's intended and his family, I'm bricking it.

I leave my suitcase and Christmas presents in the car to collect once I'm shown to my room, unhook the picket gate and traipse along the cobbled pathway. Even in the darkness, it all looks very lovely and typical of my mum's ideology, given her fraught and often painful wait for a real-life fairy tale to finally come her way. Having raised me single-handed, she deserves every wonderful moment over the next few days.

I'm hoping that the 'Diane and Rupert' depicted in perfect calligraphy on the snow-white wedding invite are the happiest of couples with many years ahead of them. Hopefully my anti-social nature can cope amidst the Carmichael company, otherwise I'll be nipping to the seclusion of my room to escape the crowd. Horror of horrors, if I'm expected to share . . . please let me have a bedroom of my own.

'Lowry,' I tell myself as I approach the front door, 'enjoy it. She's not asking a lot, just a few days amongst newly gained relatives before she jets off on a sunshine honeymoon.'

After which I'll return to my work – without Roger wittering on about my annual leave – and peace of mind, knowing that my mum is living her best life.

The front door's tiny bevelled window casts a mellow light on my tired features, for which I'm grateful; despite my twenty-nine years, I feel ancient. I'm in need of food, a warm bed and a soothing hug – much like the abandoned cat back at the Salford rescue centre. On second thoughts, it's wrong of me to make that comparison; I haven't been neglected or received cruel treatment, unlike that poor creature.

From the tiled doorstep, I can hear muted tones of lively bustling inside, a combination of wedding prep and festive fun. I take a deep breath before pulling the ancient bell chain. I hear a delicate tinkle, sense the ripple effect as others cease their activity to listen before someone is nominated to answer the door, probably my mother since I'm so late: it's nearly eight o'clock.

Through the bevelled window, I watch a male figure appear in the hallway; his rapidly approaching form is distorted into abstract blocks of colour: marl grey, peachy pink face, navy top with denim.

The door is wrenched wide open, releasing a snippet of a Christmas tune, and a hulk of a guy, matching my mother's maturity, whom I assume is Rupert stands on the coir matting in his burgundy slippers. I'm about to speak, officially introducing myself as Lowry Stephens, Diane's daughter, before apologising profusely for my late arrival, when he cuts in first.

'Finally! You've taken your bloody time – I called you three hours ago! I can't see how that's classed as an emergency response. Anyway, here they are … No, I don't want to keep them, I'd prefer you to remove them from the premises and be done with them.' His gruff tone sounds somewhat condescending. At this point, he holds the door open with one slippered foot whilst reaching down beside the doorway to retrieve a cardboard crisp box, which he swiftly passes to me. The top is neatly closed with the flaps tucked under and over each other, creating a slight gap in the top. I instinctively take the box and feel some weight inside.

'Thanks. I really appreciate it despite the late hour. Here, drop that into your charity tin and … well, a Merry Christmas to you.' He slips a folded note between my forefingers, which are wrapped around the box, and hastily closes the front door, pushing me backwards from the doorstep. The hallway light is dowsed as his retreating figure enters a room on the right. I hadn't uttered so much as a syllable.

A faint meow sounds from the cardboard box.

Are you kidding me? Is that the man my mother is about to marry? Or am I at the wrong cottage? Right now, given his abrupt manner, I'd prefer it to be the latter rather than the former. Christ, Mum, what a bloody charmer!

In near darkness, I bend down to put the cardboard box on to the cobbled path and gently ease apart the interlocking flaps to peer inside the box: two squirming kittens – one black and white, the other a brown tabby. 'Where's your mother?' I ask, brushing aside my concerns for my own parent. The only explanation: this is a joke. A family initiation of sorts based purely on my job role – humour all the way. It has to be. I'm no stick-in-the-mud. I'll happily play along with a barely funny joke but when the timing is skewed it ruins the intended humour. And secondly, which irresponsible pet owner has allowed their tiny kittens to be used in this welcoming skit?

I stand and quickly rap on the wooden door expecting a blaze of hallway light to snap on and a gathering of jovial faces to crowd about the door. No answer. Ha ha, very funny. This is certainly not how I thought I'd be greeting my mother tonight. I give the bell chime a second yank. Nothing. I rap again, but ten times harder. Still no answer. It's not that there's a din coming from inside, but muted sounds of activity drift through the aged glazing as shadows and silhouettes pass each downstairs window. Surely someone can hear me?

It's no good, they're not responding. Or they're pretending not to hear me for added effect. They obviously think their little joke is a warm introduction to the gathering when the reality of the situation is a desperate need to get these two babies reunited with a warm, snuggly belly and oozing teats.

It's the lack of understanding that annoys me: tiny kittens shouldn't be manhandled but left to suckle. Oh well, I'll happily slap a smile on my mush and find another route into the cottage to reunite these babies. This suddenly feels like a busman's holiday!

I stand, pick up the kitten box and venture left, past a large window and around the corner of the cottage in search of a rear entrance. I'll admit, I'm het up, but it'll pass once I'm inside. A simple 'Hi, welcome to the clan, Lowry!' would have been appreciated though. Bloody good job I left my suitcase in the car given that my hands are full and I can't see to find my footing on the uneven ground. I assume everyone inside is thinking, 'What larks!' and I don't wish to come across as the grumpy gal, but seriously, what a greeting for a festive holiday!

Within seconds, I round a second corner to discover a rear garden lit by more illuminated windows and, thankfully, a quirky stable door with the top section swung wide. Ironic – I'm not the first to be relieved to find an open stable door at this time of year, bearing gifts. The family won't be expecting me to appear this way but hey, the joke can be on them. I'll ensure Rupert gets his cash back too. Surely my mother didn't hatch this plan?

Resting the box on the door's lower portion, I nosily peer inside. My spirits leap: the delightful view that greets me typifies the true heart of any home. The cosy but large kitchen, emitting a miasma of tantalising aromas, is a pleasing substitute for the warm welcome I should have received five minutes ago at the front door!

'Hellooo?' I holler in a cheery sing-song voice, overcompensating with festive cheer in an attempt to play down their surprise trickery.

Martha

I prop the pantry door wide open with a big sack of spuds, allowing the kitchen light to flood into the walk-in parlour, easing my task. I've never seen a jumble like it – those pesky lads, what are they like? Give them the simple job of unpacking the groceries and I end up having to realign and shuffle every packet, tin or box on each shelf. As if I haven't enough to contend with at the minute. But if I don't organise our food stores, I know what'll happen: I'll waste precious time searching for vital ingredients, missing the short-life dates and wasting food unnecessarily when I intend for every morsel to be eaten before we leave here on the twenty-seventh. Have they no idea of the basics of kitchen management, not to mention food hygiene?

From the hallway behind me, a medley of festive tunes drifts from the record player – it's been years since I saw or listened to vinyl. I thought underneath the staircase was a daft place to house a record player, but actually it's the perfect position in a property this size. It might sound twee but it's the ideal way to conjure the Christmas spirit, igniting memories of previous family Christmases. And, if this year proves to be my final Christmas in service with the Carmichaels, then I'll cherish all the memories I can muster.

I swiftly retie my apron strings before grabbing the assortment of fresh seasonal vegetables and stashing them in a free-standing wire trolley providing space for all the other festive goodies. I'm grateful that it's only the festive food I need to worry about and not the catering for the entire wedding reception too, unlike a previous occasion.

For goodness' sake, why are the bottles of port shoved in here! I know full well that the Carmichael boys have been raised to show respect for their father's wine cellar since they

were knee-high to a grasshopper. Many's the time I found
the older two, Emmet and River, as teenagers, slumped in the
cellar tittering and wittering, having shared a bottle of Rupert's
finest. And then had to smuggle them past his study door to
their bedrooms and serve them countless black coffees and
bacon sandwiches to hasten their sobriety. As for Teddy, the
least said about him necking a bottle of malt whisky having
failed his GCSEs the better; not a night I wish to recall, given
the whole shebang with ambulances and stomach pumps and
that bottle of unidentifiable tablets. But it's all water under the
bridge now – all three lads towered head and shoulders above
me in the supermarket earlier today and I didn't have to lift a
finger. Though I fear each of them dropped a little something
extra, treat-wise, into the trolley, just as they did as youngsters.
If Scarlet had been present, no doubt she'd have pushed her
luck too – taking it to the extreme, as she always does. She's
definitely more work and worry than the three lads put together,
but Rupert doesn't see it – never has, never will. Daddy's little
girl – Lord help us when she arrives tomorrow. Why people
couldn't coordinate their arrival dates is beyond me. Probably
their egos preventing them falling into line with the rest of the
family. I hope Diane knows what she's let herself in for.

I'm lost to my task, tutting and head-shaking as I correct their
shoddy efforts at stacking shelves which represents at least two
of the three shopping trolleys' worth of food purchased en route
from Todmorden this afternoon. I'm praying that the fridge
freezer works sufficiently and copes with the contents stashed
inside. Thankfully, I unpacked the chilled items myself, so I
know everything is stored correctly in the fridges, unlike this
pantry. I'm sure they do it on purpose, guaranteeing I don't ask
them to help out more often. Or has my guidance over the years
been thoroughly wasted – going in one ear and out the other?
Love them to bits and all that but give me strength! If they

were mine; they'd be in here right now correcting their slapdash efforts rather than lounging around in various rooms awaiting the festive excitement to begin. Though I'm probably better off without them under my feet; Lord knows I have enough to do . . . I glance at my hands busily aligning each item. The left works as it always has, the right trembles ever so slightly, as if vibrating like a tuning fork. Not that it's noticeable to others. I've learnt to hide it well but it has a tendency to show itself at the most inappropriate moment depending upon my stress level, tiredness or general busyness of life. I pause for a moment as my right hand quivers, ignoring my inner voice telling it to 'be still', and visualise my mother's hand doing the exact same thing; in fact, this moment could be a déjà vu from her time in service at the stately home.

Not that I've visited a doctor, I don't need telling there's no specific test. I remember with Mum, it was more her continual decline which ticked the boxes in asserting her condition and eventual diagnosis, though by that time anyone with eyes in their head could spot her tremors a mile off. It was almost as if she'd been living with the condition for years before others were happy to officially label it as Parkinson's. Slightly arse about face in my opinion, but that's the nature of the beast when you're dealing with certain illnesses. Though I did always feel Mum was happier before she had it confirmed, as if that glimmer of hope that she might not have it was enough to give her peace of mind – if that makes sense.

How I've managed to hide it so far is a miracle. It's not as if they don't see me around the clock, so to speak, given that I have a live-in position, albeit in the garden annexe at Cloisters. Though the lads have always called it the 'granny flat' – some might see that as derogatory but I quite like the fact that I'm accepted as their adopted 'gran'. It's slightly different now that they're older, all coming and going with their own lives, but still I must see each of the lads at least twice a week as they drop by unannounced for meals. They know me too well to do otherwise. I've always said, 'There's always enough in the pot for one more and if not, we'll serve everyone extra bread and butter.' It's rare that I have to rely on the bread basket to fill their stomachs but still, it's an open invitation at mealtimes as far as Mr C's concerned.

I know what's ahead, having witnessed my mother's decline. Unlike the Carmichaels. Though how I'll break such news to these caring folks is another worry, but one I can't dwell on now, so I switch my thoughts.

The very idea of having a family of my own gives me the collywobbles: the responsibilities and demands, not to mention the dramas. It pains me to say it but this way, working for the Carmichaels for as long as I have, I get the best of both worlds.

'There. Done!' I back out of the pantry, ignoring my trembling right hand, satisfied with my task. It might not be the fully equipped hi-tech kitchen that I'm used to, but I can't complain. I have everything I need in a rental property of this size: an Aga has never failed me yet in life, there's a decent well-scrubbed table and I've my faithful copper pans which I made Emmet bring in his Range Rover, though he had to unpack a box of additional blankets which someone – namely Helen – thought was essential. Give me strength! My faithful saucepans are critical for a festive period with this family, but we won't be needing additional woollen togs in a cottage such as this! Though given my ample, or as some would say well-endowed figure, I never feel the cold – but then no one should ever trust a skinny cook.

I check my watch, hoping the family are hungry given this late hour. My speciality lamb and rosemary casserole needs to simmer a little longer before serving but it'll be worth it – especially as I couldn't help being a bit heavy-handed with the splosh of red wine.

'Hellooo?' comes a tuneful voice, causing me to jump.

I take several sidesteps across the red tiles to peer around the bulky fridges to the kitchen's rear door. And there she is. Not our Scarlet but Diane's lassie, Lowry. Oh my, she's the spitting image of her mother, with identical hazel eyes and prominent cheekbones.

'Come on in, Lowry. Here, let me get the door catch for you. Though I'd imagined you'd have come in via the front, or did those lazy buggers not hear you knocking? Here, let me,' I say, fumbling with the metal catch to release the lower portion of the door and holding it wide open. 'Do you need help with your belongings – is the box heavy?'

'Hi, sorry. Thank you. Yes, Lowry,' she says, looking somewhat puzzled. 'Oh no . . . these are the kittens.'

'That's nice. You've brought your pets with you?' I step aside as she enters and places the box on to the tiled floor.

'Not mine. Yours.'

'Ours? I believe there's kittens in the outhouse but . . .' I watch as Lowry lifts the interwoven flaps to reveal two squirming kittens. 'Oh, I see. No prizes for guessing who packaged and parcelled those hoping to remove them from the cottage. The she-cat has brought them inside twice since we arrived this afternoon. Your mother doesn't seem too bothered but Mr C, eek . . . he's not one for sentiment or cute fur-babies. Ahh bless, just look at 'em.' I cease talking as the kitchen light catches the RSPCA initials embroidered on Lowry's jacket. What a clanger to make!

'The she-cat is where?' asks Lowry, looking up at me – her gaze filled with tenderness, though her stubby blonde ponytail is in need of retying. I subconsciously touch the nape of my own cropped cut, grateful not to have the flowing locks of my youth. Impractical at my age and in the rising temperatures of my domain.

'In the brick outhouse.' I gesture outside.

'I'll be back in a second,' says Lowry, collecting the cardboard box and taking it back outside. Bless her. Mr C has a heart of gold where his family are concerned but sadly it has its limitations when it comes to the wider world. Having survived in the family longer than any other female, I pretty much know the man inside and out. Though I wouldn't put up with half his nonsense; regardless of his age, the man's in love with being in love!

I stand back from the door and watch Lowry's shadowy figure gingerly cross the patio to the brick outhouse, or cubby hole, as I'd call it. Outhouse makes it sound like an outdoor lavvy, and it's definitely not – I've checked! Diane has spoken proudly of Lowry in recent weeks, so I'm not surprised that her girl is on-point and ready for action. I'm in awe of anyone with such a single-minded focus in life; she seems to be my kind of gal. Within minutes, she's back, having reunited the wee family.

'Sorry, I hate to be a stick-in-the-mud but . . . you know,' she says, as I close the back door. 'Hopefully, the mum will do what she needs to despite their brief absence. She's not wearing a collar and name tag but that means nothing.'

I'm humbled by one so young, but Lord alone knows how she ended up with that box.

'As I said, she's brought the kittens inside twice since we arrived. Mr C's not one for animals; he'd never hurt them but . . . Anyway, how was your journey?'

'Good, thank you – literally straight from work, as you can see.' Lowry tugs at her collar, before adding, 'I'll freshen up once I've said hi to my mum.'

'Yes, of course. How rude of me. I'm Martha by the way – cook, cleaner and bottle-washer for the Carmichaels, but enough about me. Diane was in the lounge last time I saw her. This way, lovey – let me take you through.' I'll ask later how she came by the kitten box; for now, I'm sure seeing her mother is her priority, before a hot shower and my boozy lamb casserole.

Helen

I cross the landing checking that each vacant bedroom is prepared for those who are yet to arrive. Behind each of the nine panelled oak doors sits a sumptuous bedroom: doubles, twin and singles – to which I have carefully allocated occupants. A task I volunteered for, knowing that Diane couldn't possibly get the combinations right first time without causing offence or igniting unnecessary drama. Admittedly, some beds will remain uninhabited but that's not a bad thing under the circumstances. Large families always have their internal conflicts swirling just below the surface. I doubt Rupert wants any mayhem or drama before the wedding.

I've shown each occupant to their room on their arrival, so my plan hasn't been scuppered yet, but it'll only take one person to upset the apple cart. I stand in the centre of the landing, which is stylish and spacious for a cottage of this age – big enough even for a bulky couch and a sturdy bookcase. I look at each closed door in turn, checking off on my fingers who is located where. At the rear of the property, Lynette will have a single room and Scarlet a twin room to herself; Teddy has a single, and Emmet and River are sharing the large twin room, despite appearing distant with each other in recent weeks. Moving forward along the landing, Rupert and Diane are in the master suite, with its huge canopied bed and an extra-large bathtub. At the front of the cottage, Martha is the sole occupant of the double room with the breathtaking landscape of rolling hills in the distance, and Lowry has the same. Though I've made sure Lowry has the more spacious and feminine room with the white shabby chic dressing table and matching stool. I nearly changed my mind and assigned Scarlet to that room, but she gets spoilt enough when she comes home. And finally, my sister, Janie, and I are together in the last remaining twin room. Eight bedrooms sleeping eleven occupants, when they eventually all arrive. Which leaves one double room spare, in case anyone isn't happy with my arrangements. Fingers crossed everyone will be satisfied. Though why I do this to myself is another matter – volunteering for tasks when others rarely offer becomes somewhat tiresome. At least this way, I'm guaranteed a decent night's sleep, if nothing else. I don't know if I'm strong-willed or utterly foolish to do what I do for the sake of the entire family. A braver woman might have sought sanctuary elsewhere and rebuilt her world focusing upon new passions.

A shriek of joy and excited voices drifting from downstairs stops me mid-thought. I assume Diane's daughter has just arrived.

I lean over the banister rail to listen, trying to decipher the high-spirited greetings from the compilation of Christmas tunes. I'll bide my time. I'll wait until the initial hullabaloo has died down; it's always the best policy with the Carmichaels as the poor woman will be swamped with names and faces in an instant. Life's taught me that you're rarely remembered when introduced in a chaotic manner.

What was I going to do? Ah yes, inspect the landing's storage and linen cupboards for fresh supplies, but that can wait for now.

I swiftly return to my bedroom, quietly closing the door for a final few minutes of peace. Our Janie isn't arriving until tomorrow so I've claimed the bed furthest away from the door, knowing I always retire hours before she does. I've staked a claim to my half of the dressing table too; with our Janie's spread of lotions and potions there won't be space for my few essentials, a perfume bottle, hand lotion and a comb, unless I do. Not that she'll care. She'll brush aside any remarks with her customary 'Ooh, don't be petty, Helen – just help yourself to mine and be done' but that's not the point, is it? I have my own belongings and wish to use what I wish to use and not borrow from my younger sibling based on her lack of personal boundaries. I pull out the dressing table's padded stool and plonk myself down before the three-winged glass. I might as well tidy my appearance whilst I'm here – first impressions and all that jazz.

Feeling each of my forty-nine years, I ponder my reflection. I'm relieved to have waved goodbye to my younger self who was never happy with what she saw staring back. A woman who regularly appeased others with her hairstyle and general appearance. Now, I please myself, pure and simple. I've embraced the natural tones in my hair, and I've learnt that an exquisite cut ensures it falls in a flattering manner with little effort or fuss. Maintaining a decent but basic skincare routine all my life has finally paid off – I needn't seek advice from specific professionals, unlike some I could mention, but allow my natural skin to shine. Finally, I smile at my own reflection. A genuine appreciation for the woman seated before me – only I know everything she's been through, and survived. I quite like her. I've arrived at that point in life – comfortable in my own skin. How I wish that had happened decades ago. I quickly tease a comb through my styled hair, allowing the shades of marl and silver to blend harmoniously, add a spritz of perfume to my wrists and I'm good to go.

'Helen!' calls a male voice. I turn on hearing my name yelled from downstairs. River won't expect me to holler back, they know me too well. Screeching and shouting around a home has never been my style, so I'll answer the call by returning to the group in my usual calm manner. I stand. I breathe. I smile. Time to welcome another new face.

In reality, I suppose the 'spectrum of love' failed me. I was experiencing that all-encompassing, ten-out-of-ten, head-over-heels-in-love commitment whereas Rupert was harbouring something much less towards me and, obviously, much more elsewhere. Not that I feel that now, as the intensity of my feelings has mellowed. Though I'll confess to the occasional bout of something . . . be it unnamed. Thankfully, my love has matured like a good wine into something that is priceless and should be cherished – it could quite easily have soured to taste like vinegar, igniting a deep shudder from within.

Having crossed the landing, I pause on the top stair, which squeaks underfoot, and take a final deep breath before descending at my own pace, knowing this introduction is simply the latest of many. I can do this. I've done it before and I can, and will, hold it together and do what is required of me in the name of the family.

I find River, my nephew, lingering in the hallway outside the open lounge door, waiting for me. His stocky frame, blond stubble and unruly haircut gives him an unkempt and roguish appearance, not to my liking and I fear copied from my own son, Emmet, in recent weeks. Though River looks more like his father with each passing year, which is frightening.

'Lowry,' he mouths, gesturing through the doorway, from which jubilant greetings can still be heard. 'Diane's girl.'

'Thank you, River,' I say, squeezing past him to join the happy throng. I'm greeted by a series of rear views, each in various snapshot positions of half standing to awkwardly shake hands with the young woman before settling back down into their seats. Diane is centre stage, standing before the roaring fire, her arm proudly draped around her daughter's shoulder, attempting to conduct the family introductions to a bewildered young woman dressed in a mud-splattered uniform. Martha stands a little way off, no doubt wanting to return to her kitchen but not wishing to cause offence by rudely disappearing. She's virtually one of the family, though without enduring a blood tie, marriage or divorce with Rupert. A wise woman, I might add. I hate to think how many times I've witnessed this formality only to have the wrong name temporarily assigned to the wrong person due to the frantic manner in which the information was presented to a newcomer. It takes some fathoming out on first hearing, but with only half the relations here, this simplified version is a mere morsel of what's to come.

'Lowry,' says Diane, politely turning her daughter around to face me. 'This lady is Helen Carmichael ... Rupert's ex-wife. His first wife.'

'Hello, Helen, nice to meet you,' says Lowry, extending her hand. Her skittering gaze steadies and calms, offering me her full attention.

'Hello, my dear. Lovely to meet you at last. We've heard so much about your good work,' I say, not shaking her hand but gently enclosing it in both of mine to give a warm reassuring squeeze.

'Thank you. I got caught up at work so apologies for arriving at such a late hour,' she explains. Her bright hazel eyes appear eager to please those present.

'No worries, you're here now,' I say, releasing her hand to address the elephant in the room. 'We're an unusual family, Lowry – a bunch of allsorts and blended in the strangest ways, so please make yourself at home and let's not hear any more apologies. You couldn't offend if you tried!' I know that final line might have been a step too far but she looks as nervous as a kitten. 'Anyway, I'm sure the names and faces will blur in an instant, but let's run through them again, shall we?'

I notice Diane unfurls her protective arm allowing me to stand closer to Lowry, my head inclined inches from hers. 'I'm Helen ... Rupert's first ex-wife. That guy there is Emmanuel, our number-one son, known to us all as Emmet.' I gesture towards my one and only child, nonchalantly helping himself to a Scotch from the sideboard's decanter rather than paying attention to our new arrival. On cue, Emmet turns to glance over his shoulder, giving Lowry a view of that stubbled chin which I dislike so much, though his dark curls are still adorable. The awkward bugger doesn't bother to say hi but gives a weak smile, intent on pouring his whisky. 'And this chap is River, son number two,' I say, gesturing towards the doorway, where he's remained. 'He's my nephew and younger brother to Emmet.' Lowry politely smiles in River's direction before a puzzled furrow appears on her brow, as I continue. 'Yes, somewhat confusing, but true. It'll all make sense in the coming days.'

'Hi there. Great to meet you, Lowry,' says River, his rugged manner much warmer than that of my solemn offspring, who I note has resettled in the armchair from which he has rarely moved since his arrival.

'Likewise,' she says, glancing at me for a further explanation but I won't offer one – I never do. I don't go into the minutiae of our past, skimming over the details during introductions, because how can you live in the present moment or greet a happy future if you're always peering into the heartbreak of the past?

'And here we have our beloved Martha. Now, she is our saviour in many ways. She puts up with our constant battling, sorts out our niggles and feeds us until the cows come home! Not a blood relation, but I think I'd miss you first and foremost, Martha.'

Martha laughs, as always.

'We met in the kitchen, didn't we, Lowry?' says Martha politely, as is her way. Though seriously, I mean every word. If anything happened to Martha, or she left our family fold for whatever reason, though I know she'd never be anywhere other than organising this brood, I'd possibly pack up and ship out too. She's been my rock for these last three decades. 'My angel who bakes' is Rupert's endearing name for his long-suffering hired help. I suspect he thinks more highly of her than that, given she's survived all his nonsense unscathed.

Lowry's nodding, as if taking in the details, but I know it will take time for her to connect certain facts.

'This young man is Teddy, son number three, and the best-looking, hey, Ted?' I say, cheekily trying to lift the mood a little as my Emmet slugs back his whisky, a signal that he's unimpressed by the proceedings.

'Hi, nice to meet you,' says Teddy, dutifully glancing between his older siblings from his position on the couch. His slender frame, clean-cut jaw and trendy haircut suggest his tender years in comparison to his siblings. I'll throw in the towel when he opts for facial stubble.

I place a hand on Lowry's shoulder gently turning her, as her mother had earlier, towards the furthest armchair, 'And this gent is Rupert Carmichael, head of the family and soon to be your stepfather. Though he's not as wicked as he likes to make out, so don't stand for any nonsense if that's how he appears to you,' I say, my voice trailing to a whisper but I mean every word. I sussed him out years ago. He likes to present an impression to the world but underneath that gruff exterior he's usually a big softy, with a few exceptions, of course. You'd think he'd alienate me from the clan for that fact alone, but he never has. If anything, our divorce has only brought us closer. 'As you can see we're not the most conventional of families but hey, we blend together quite nicely!' A titter of laughter sweeps around the room before Rupert speaks.

'Lowry, hello. I ... sorry we ... met earlier. I thought you were sent by ...' I'm confused by how he's struggling to deliver his sentence whilst staring bug-eyed at her dishevelled uniform.

'Yes. You thrust a box of kittens at me and donated twenty quid when I arrived on the doorstep,' replies Lowry, confidently stepping forward extending her hand. 'Here's your donation money back. I've returned the two kittens to their mother in the outhouse.' I thought she was going to shake hands, but no, she offers him a folded twenty-pound note.

'Blimey, a youngster who returns cash rather than takes it,

now there's a novelty amongst this brood,' declares Rupert, retrieving the cash. Another ripple of laughter circles the room, apart from my Emmet, who is silently watching the proceedings in that brooding manner of his. I do hope he snaps out of it by Christmas Day – turning thirty shouldn't be a time for mourning, though maybe sitting through these introductions for the umpteenth time is enough to cloud one's mood. My poor lad. Enduring his father's behaviour for as long as he has can't have been easy – especially when it casts long shadows on the lives of others.

Diane and Rupert exchange a quizzical glance. I'm not sure what's occurred but no doubt I'll hear about it later. In this family nothing stays secret for long.

'Darling, it took me ages to get everyone's name right, so don't worry. No one will be offended if you get it wrong,' says Diane, clucking like a mother hen. 'It took me a fair while, didn't it, Helen?'

I smile graciously. If any newcomer knew how long it has taken the rest of us to come to terms with the family history, they wouldn't blush at a few misplaced names.

'Anyway, introductions complete, for now. The others will be arriving tomorrow. How about we crack open a little fizz and let these festive few days begin – otherwise they'll be over before we know it,' I suggest, looking towards Rupert for confirmation – old habits die hard.

'If we're lucky,' mutters Emmet from the armchair, eyeing his brother River before emptying his whisky glass. I dash my son a warning look, then spot his father's raised eyebrow indicating his displeasure too. Whether that's because of Emmet's remark or his own undisclosed behaviour on the doorstep, who knows?

'I'll organise that. If someone would like to show Lowry to her room, I'm sure she'd like to freshen up and unpack her belongings,' says Martha, subtly addressing the basics which the rest of us frequently forget or overlook.

'Yes, sorry. So rude of me. What was I thinking? You haven't had a moment to unpack or sort yourself out. Sadly, another trait of this family – we take over your time without even realising,' I say apologetically. 'I'm sure Diane would like a few minutes with you in private too.'

Chapter Three

Lowry

'Seriously, Mum, I wouldn't have believed it if it hadn't happened to me. Literally, the door opened, he chastised me for taking so long, then thrust the box at me and stuck a folded note between my forefingers. Door closed, job done. No warmth, some manners and little compassion. Is that really who you're marrying?' I say, walking back and forth unpacking my belongings into the various chests of drawers, having collected my suitcase and gifts from the car. My mum perches on the dressing table stool, which matches the overtly feminine and delicate décor of this beautiful bedroom, looking decidedly uncomfortable.

'Don't rush to judge him, Lowry. We all have our off days,' she sighs, shifting in her seat. 'He phoned someone earlier but I didn't realise it was to do with the kittens. You know that not everybody's an animal lover.'

'Mum! Surely, you've mentioned my job in the last three months – didn't he take note? Obviously, he was expecting another female to join the clan yet he answers the door in that gruff manner. He nearly died when . . . Martha, is it?' Mum gives a tiny nod confirming the name, before I continue, 'When Martha escorted me into the lounge for the family meet-and-greet session.' I'm complaining but I can't help noting how well she looks, very well in fact: there's a rosy glow to her skin, a little more weight than is usual for her slender figure and a contented smile. We're so alike with our tawny blonde hair, hazel eye colouring and complexion, I recognise my future self in approximately twenty years' time.

'Let's forget about that and put it aside, Lowry.'

'OK, as difficult as that is. Previously, you mentioned a family business, so what trade are they in?'

'Doors. Interior doors ... though they do exterior ones too, but mainly interior ones.'

I point at the bedroom's wooden panelled door. 'Like ... doors?'

'Yes. Any sort you can think of, they do it. I've been for a tour around their factory and the warehouse, it's massive. He employs each of his sons; the daughter's not much interested – she's got her own thing going on. He employs Helen part-time too. I can't remember who heads which department or has what role but it's a proper family concern under Rupert's guidance. Which extends to their workers' families too; they employ many relatives as it builds loyalty within the firm. They're very successful with a long history going back a couple of generations. Rupert was an only son so it came directly to him, and now his boys are partners too – he's hoping they'll take it forward after his death.'

'That's not morbid at all, Mother,' I jest, sidestepping the implications for her if that happens any day soon.

'Not really, it needs careful consideration for the future. You hear of family companies failing and going under once the next generation start bickering in the boardroom, each demanding their own portion of the company and attempting to divide lucrative contracts fairly – when it's never fair, is it?'

'How would I know? I've neither siblings nor a family business to worry about when you pop your clogs.'

'Lowry! And then there's his daughter: Rupert wants Scarlet's interests to be looked after properly by her older brothers.'

'That's nice.' A financial safety net in life, if nothing else.

'When she marries, Rupert would dearly like the son-in-law to join the family firm as a means of connecting and protecting her company share.'

'If she marries, Mum – surely the woman has a choice in the matter?'

'Yes, of course, "if" ... but you know it is "when", don't you? How many women consciously choose to stay single for ever, mmm? I didn't, did I? I'd have loved to have been married and provided you with two loving parents, but it just wasn't how it was for me, sweetie.' Mum inclines her head, and her perfectly coiffed hair keeps its pristine shape as it falls sideways. She's obviously waved bye-bye to her usual mobile hairdresser, possibly saying hello to the expensive stylist used by Helen, the ex-wife.

'I know that, but Rupert shouldn't assume that Scarlet wants exactly what he wants. It's hardly been a two-happy-parents scenario in his house either, has it? Let's face it, children see stuff and it shapes how they see their own future.'

'Children are tougher than you think,' snaps my mum, raising her eyebrows at me, clearly offended by my remark.

'I agree, but certain things affect them, you know. I'm not saying I couldn't or wouldn't raise a child by myself, but I'm not sure I'd choose my own upbringing for a child.'

'Thanks a bunch, Lowry. Your grandparents helped us immensely – they put a roof over our heads,' she quickly adds. 'Some women have to contend with providing that too.'

'I know. They did when I was tiny, but as the years went on, Mum – they also became very needy of your time. Hardly an easy life, was it?'

'I did what I could when I could. They're gone now so there's no point dredging up old times.' Mum's hazel eyes glisten, requiring a double blink. She won't admit it but I saw the strain she was under, shouldering the burden of daily life – juggling a full-time job and wrangling with a headstrong teenager whilst caring for two elderly parents. It's not as if she had siblings to rely on either.

'Don't get all uppity, I'm just saying. I saw how difficult it was, for you and me ... I think I would choose a different situation. Which brings us nicely around in full circle to the wedding.' I quickly change topic, fearing our conversation is rapidly going downhill.

'Tell me you're excited! You are excited, aren't you?' she asks.

'Excited for you, of course I am! I've waited so long for you to meet a decent man, who'll bring enjoyment into your life, and affection and company – even more so since I've flown the nest. I'm just not entirely sure Rupert deserves you after his doorstep performance! What would Grandad say?'

'Seriously, Lowry, give him a chance. He's a wonderful man ... and a fabulous father.' Her face is aglow, her smiling cheeks plump and there's a glint in her eye, which she doesn't need to blink away – confirming all I need to know.

'OK. I promise to put the initial incident to the back of my mind. Though how many children does he actually have?' I place my final pile of folded clothes into a drawer and softly close it before returning to the bed.

'Three lads and a girl, each with different mothers,' she says, biting her bottom lip on finishing her sentence.

'Four by four?'

'What?' Her brow puckers instantly.

'Four babies by four women – four by four,' I say, flipping the lid of my suitcase closed and quickly zipping it, wishing I hadn't made such a flippant remark. 'Obviously, he's been married before to Helen. And the others?'

My mother looks sheepish. 'This sounds so bad but yes, to all of them,' she says, swiftly continuing, 'but when there's children involved you try and do the right thing, Lowry.'

'You're bride number five!' Hell no! Another red flag is unfurled while I'm still folding and packing away the previous one.

'I didn't want you to get the wrong impression before meeting him.'

'Well, you should have answered the door then!' I can see she's crestfallen but I don't want to gloss over the importance of her happiness. I'm not going to kowtow to an entire family just because this guy's obsession, fetish even, for weddings provides my mum with a great day out and a beautiful gown and deletes 'miss' from her status. 'Look, as long as you're truly happy, then I'm happy. I'd just have liked to have been bowled over by your husband-to-be on meeting him. I promise I'll try to get to know him over the coming days.'

'He's excited to have a stepdaughter, Lowry – he's never dated anyone with children of their own before. He misses not having his own girl around as much as she was when she was growing up. I've only met her the once, very briefly. Scarlet's a proper daddy's girl.'

'You haven't spent much time together then?' I say, stashing my empty case under the double bed. I'm eager to shower and freshen up before dinner but recognise the importance of hearing the basics of my soon-to-be relatives.

'No. She's out of the country a lot, mainly flitting here, there and everywhere for her modelling work. I've spent more time with his sons. Nowadays, it seems you girls fly further afield, from your parents, than the boys ever do,' says Mum, her voice softening with each word. 'Lovely lads ... they look after their mums.'

'Mums? Surely they each only have one?' I say, straightening the duvet, erasing the suitcase impression and ignoring what could be taken as a barbed comment.

'They do, but you heard Helen say "this is a blended family" – they look out for one another. Now that sounds nice, doesn't it?'

I nod, but getting used to this blended family format might take more effort than I was banking on.

'And there was me thinking the hardest part would be keeping a straight face when I have to actually call someone Rupert,' I say, in a comedic tone trying to lighten the conversation. 'What a name!'

'I thought exactly the same when we first met, but you get used to it – it grows on you after a while.'

'Obviously. Or rather it has on at least five of you!'

'Now, stop it! That's naughty,' she says, failing to suppress a giggle.

'Who else are we expecting?' I ask, eager to hear guest names.

'Sandra and Sally will be coming for the actual day – how could I not invite them? You know we go way back to our primary school days. I was bridesmaid at both their weddings.'

'But that's it? Your two best friends and no one else? No work colleagues from Jacob's manufacturing?' Mum shakes her head. 'Are you serious? After all the years you've been there. What about your Thursday night ladies' group – surely you invited them?' Mum repeats her headshake. 'I thought you kept in touch with lots of people.'

'I do. But I wouldn't expect anyone to travel halfway across the country to attend my wedding on Boxing Day when most people are happy to be at home with their own families over Christmas.'

'You've got a point there. Maybe that's the downside of having a festive wedding, or the plus point if you're picking up the tab.' A thought strikes me. 'You aren't paying for all of this, are you? Tell me you're not. You've both contributed, haven't you?'

'I'm not. Rupert has been most generous. You worry too much, Lowry. Like I said, he's lovely when you get to know him. I've paid for my gown plus yours and Scarlet's bridesmaids' dresses ... but everything else Rupert has seen to.'

'But you've been allowed a say ... to choose what you'd like for your wedding?'

'Of course. Lowry, what do you take him for?'

Her words linger in mid-air, as if driving home my assumptions as unreasonable rather than highlighting his response to me on the doorstep.

'Well, I'm collecting info with each introduction and incident, Mum – that's all I can do.'

She looks exasperated by me, which isn't a first in our relationship. I think it's pretty much our default setting when I don't immediately share her viewpoint. 'Enough about Rupert, tell me about your dress,' I say, eager to see her gleeful expression return before I have a well-deserved shower.

Helen

'Emmet, will you please stop pacing and talk to me? What's the matter?' I'm not managing to disguise my agitated tone as much as I'd like. My son stops striding the length of the patio to stand beside the coal bunker, dwarfed beside the brick outhouse, and stares at me. Irritatingly, a cigarette is pinched between his thumb and forefinger, his partly curled palm protecting the lighted tip from the cold breeze. The patio's light dowses itself, thrusting us into darkness; Emmet waves a hand to turn it back on.

To our left, in front of a drystone boundary wall that's barely chest height, is a DIY built-in barbeque surrounded by numerous empty ceramic flowerpots, awaiting warmer days. Thankfully, there are no neighbours, just open scrubland leading the eye towards a horseshoe of mountains.

'You seriously don't know?' he scowls, his temples creasing deeply.

'Well, yes. Of course I know. You behave like this and I feel the need to ask rather than blurt it out in the open. I don't want to keep nagging at you but . . . surely we can get through the next few days focusing on something other than . . .' My words falter and fade, as I'd expected them to, as they always do. It hurts me to see him like this. Admittedly, I'm so used to 'bottling up and battling on' that I'm not good at asking questions of my own son to unearth the cause of his sadness. Maybe I should have been more expressive during my desperate times? I might have healed properly, be elsewhere leading a different sort of life, if I'd faced my demons a little more.

Emmet's dark gaze stares at me from beneath an unruly mop of curls. How can a grown man revert back to a small child before my eyes? He might as well be that shy little five-year-old being told off for putting a hole in his new school trousers than the strapping man I've raised and fed for nearly thirty years.

I don't want to say her name but I will, for his sake. I can't keep pretending she doesn't exist, much as I'd like to.

'Annabel was special to you, I get that. You don't have to tell me it hurts like hell, I know. There were days I didn't know how to breathe and had to talk myself through each action, step by step. But believe me, Emmet, it eases with time. And then what you're left with is the experience and realisation that what you thought was the ultimate adventure in your life maybe wasn't quite what you had . . .' I see his shoulders droop, which kills me inside. 'And you quickly realise there's something else out there waiting for you, something more precious than you could imagine. Someone who sees and appreciates the real you and . . .' I need to cease talking, wind this up, otherwise I'll go too far and say the wrong thing, like I have on many previous occasions, and he'll sink further into himself. Tread carefully, Helen. 'She'll have been through similar and hopefully will never dream of treating you like . . .' Like Annabel did, I want to say, but he'll think I'm having another dig at his raw wounds. '. . . others did.' I fall

silent, relieved that I kept myself in check, which I can usually do
with other relatives but not with my own flesh and blood, sadly.

Emmet takes a drag on his stubby cigarette, blowing a plume
of grey smoke high into the air above my head. I watch as it
billows over the patio's stone steps leading to the garden's upper
terrace and disappears. This huge rear garden would be a major
attraction of the rental cottage in any other season but not now,
the depths of winter. I'd suggest we take a seat on one of the two
benches on opposing sides of the lawn, but the path of higgledy-
piggledy stepping stones is barely visible, and my feet would be
soaked in the long grass. But who cuts lawns in December?

I'd like a closer look at the trellis archway dividing the
remainder of the garden, densely covered in an attractive purple
leaf which appears to be flourishing despite the time of year. But
I won't, now's not the right time.

'I really wish you wouldn't smoke,' I say, knowing my request
will fall on deaf ears like it repeatedly has since his uni days.

He rubs the cigarette out on the coal bunker's brickwork and
picks something from the tip of his tongue before speaking.

'Oh Mother, anything else I need to change?'

My index finger rises, just as it did in his childhood. 'That's
not fair. I rarely comment, Emmet. I see where you're at and I
understand why, but surely you recognise some things need to
change. The whisky earlier – how many did you have? You paid
very little interest when Diane was introducing young Lowry.
Then you refused a glass of fizz when Martha tried to jolly us
into a brief celebration. It comes across as rude, Emmet – and
that's simply not you.'

'Sorry, it wasn't my intention. The daughter seems pleasant
enough. I'll apologise to Diane and Lowry if you wish, and try
harder during dinner. But for God's sake, Mum, how many more
times will we be expected to play happy families? It's wearing a
bit thin for most of us. Thank God Diane's of an age where she

won't be wanting any more children, otherwise we'd be having all that nonsense again.'

I don't answer. I get where he's coming from but loyalty to his father doesn't permit me to say what I truly think, even to my beloved son. I've never been one for badmouthing the other parent, unlike some I could name.

'I hear you. Diane's lovely and they seem to get along very well with many shared interests. Maybe we should have a little faith that this will be his last wedding.'

'Shared interests? You're right, Mum. She's very nice … in fact, I might say too lovely. But I'm yet to see her play golf, drink a Guinness or jubilantly celebrate with each member of the boardroom over an increase in sales figures from last month's orders.' Emmet raises his eyebrow in a questioning manner, just like his father always has. I get that Rupert piles the pressure on him, but that's always the case for the supposed heir in a family-run business, isn't it? It's a pity his siblings aren't a little less workshy and step up to shoulder some of Rupert's expectations, easing the pressure on Emmet.

I give a nod, reinforcing his thinking.

'If anything, she doesn't fit with the mix, does she?'

Again, I don't answer. I almost anticipated this remark weeks ago when their swift engagement was announced.

'Come on, be honest, Mum. You're the classic wifey material, Janie was the wild child, Lynette was the plain-Jane bride and Fena was an interesting fancy who caught his eye whilst he was travelling in Japan. Diane's different,' he says, counting us off on his fingers. I hate that the children do this but they're not far wrong in their assessment of their father's array of wives. There are no two pairs in his game, though maybe a slight similarity with me and Janie.

'As I said, maybe she'll be the final Mrs Carmichael … the grounded one to whom he can remain loyal until old age and then pop his clogs in the loved-up way that he wishes.'

'Phew, Mum, he's only fifty-five! You know as well as I do there could be another three brides before he meets the Grim Reaper.'

'Emmet!' My raised index finger had had no effect earlier but this time it does; he falls silent, staring at me from beneath that unruly mop of curls. I get where he's coming from but hate to appear disloyal towards either Rupert or the Carmichael sisterhood.

Martha

Bang! Bang! Bang! I stand in the kitchen doorway bashing a wooden spoon against a giant saucepan, drowning out the record player. It might seem incredibly uncouth and informal for such a family gathering but without our usual dinner gong in the hallway of Cloisters, Mr C's main residence, what am I supposed to do? Holler like a fishwife on a market stall? That would wind Helen up a treat – she despises shouting. She's a gentle soul who enjoys a calm, well-organised environment. I've witnessed many mistake her quiet nature as spiritless, but she's no doormat; to have endured the feat asked of her – I'd call her courageous.

Whereas me, I'm dependable, which I frequently remind folk of by serving up grub at each meal. They'd all be underfed if it wasn't for my culinary skills. Instantly, I hear a cacophony of doors opening and closing, hurried footsteps and staircases creaking as everyone darts for their chosen seat at the table. From childhood, the boys have always raced each other to the table to nab prime position alongside their father.

A satisfying sight for me given that I've single-handedly laid and decorated the table, creating festive centrepieces from feathery ferns plucked from the garden, decanted the wine and put a couple of bottles of fizz on ice. I just need eight hungry people to be seated around the dining table and my job is complete.

Within seconds, there's a blur of bodies heading to the dining room and I can hear chairs being moved and repositioned. We don't usually serve dinner at nine o'clock at night but given the late arrival and the fluid itinerary of this evening in comparison to the following few days, I'm not complaining. I cease banging the saucepan and listen intently, knowing I'll overhear the conversation and reaction.

'No, you don't. I'm there!' shouts River.

'Thanks a bunch,' retorts Teddy.

'Grow up, the pair of you!' scolds Mr C.

'This is lovely, Rupert,' says Diane, joining the dinner party.

'Very nice,' comes Helen's tender voice. 'Martha always does a lovely table, whatever the occasion.'

'Not there, Lowry. Martha always sits closest to the door, as she's up and down fetching and carrying from the kitchen. We help where we can, or at least where she allows us to,' says Diane. I smile; she's not wrong. I regularly refuse their assistance where food or service is concerned. I am fiercely protective over my domain and no one, not even Mr C, would dare to step out of line.

The family make me laugh, though I don't let on. It's unusual for hired help, staff ... whatever you wish to call me, to join the family on such occasions; most would sit and eat alone in the kitchen. But the Carmichaels have been my family, my only family, for the past three decades. High days, holidays and Sunday lunch follow this well-practised tradition. Quite a contrast from the daily routine when Mr C usually eats alone, unless he's entertaining a guest or two. Sadly, unbeknownst to them, my routine will have to change – and soon, if I'm to make the most of my health. I hope I don't develop the same shuffled walk that my mother had; it was debilitatingly slow despite her best efforts to stay mobile for as long as she could. I recognised early on in her diagnosis that she couldn't keep up with running a large kitchen – certain aspects of cooking are time-critical and serving lukewarm food is never the aim. It was only a matter of time before her injuries started, first stumbling and then actual falls, and she did herself damage, falling on those hard tiled floors. I lost count of how many times she was taken to A&E. Though I suppose the hands instinctively reach out to brace your falling frame only to snap back and damage delicate ageing wrists.

Satisfied that they're happy, I return to my hub to dish up before making my entrance carrying platters piled high with mashed potatoes and vegetables, depositing each along the table for the diners to help themselves. I quickly double-back for my large casserole dish, which I position at the vacant table setting nearest the door, where I'll be sitting. This will be the smallest meal I serve in the coming days – with three more guests arriving in the next twenty-four hours I'll have my work cut out. I begin ladling the lamb casserole into dishes, which the family pass along the table, oohing and ahhing as the delicious aroma ignites hunger pangs. The action of serving out wholesome food takes me back to those golden years when the children were tiny tots and the mothers were still at loggerheads with each other. Mr C was always in the thick of a situation; being newly married or recently divorced seemed to be his revolving state of affairs. And all the while his interior door business fed and clothed each babe in turn and continues to this day to provide everyone with a steady income and employment.

'I'll say grace, shall I?' says Mr C, the second I settle in my seat, having served my own portion. 'For what we're about to receive, may the Lord make us truly thankful.'

From under my fringe, I sneakily glance around the table at the heads respectfully bowed. Mmm, he can say that again, and not solely in relation to the grub on the table. Mark my words, he might want to offer thanks for not having *all* his ex-wives under the same roof this holiday.

I always rest easy once the dessert is served. I'm not a lover of sweet treats, so I forgo the Charlotte Royale, filled with tart raspberry mousse and served with double cream. They rarely force my arm as it enables the lads to have larger portions – even now they're grown, they still eat as if they have hollow legs.

'Tomorrow, I'd like a group of us to head out in search of a Christmas tree – something suitable for the lounge. I realise it's a rental property, and we're only here for a few days, but still, I'd like a traditional festive feel with decorations and the presents piled underneath – especially given the other celebrations,' says Helen, glancing between Mr C and Diane as she speaks.

'Don't bother on my behalf,' cuts in Emmet, referring to his birthday on Christmas Day.

'It isn't purely for you,' says his mother sharply.

'Cheers. There's nothing like a mother's love, is there?' quips Emmet to River.

'And that was nothing like my mother's love,' replies River, looking at Teddy.

'Nor mine. Your maternal standards are slipping, Helen,' Teddy jokes, encouraged by his older brothers.

'That'll be the day!' mutters Helen, receiving a swift look from all three boys. I don't think there was any malice meant, but the lads continue eyeballing each other long after her remark.

I settle back contentedly, listening to the flow of family conversation, which has become fluid after the initial introductions and the wine at dinner, much like a soothing lullaby. Mr C is in his element with his family seated around him, his boisterousness fuelled by the anticipation of his upcoming nuptials. Diane seems quiet, tired perhaps, after a long day of travelling, and possibly nervous about the family gathering. Emmet is brooding, lost

inside his own head – 'gone fishing' as I like to call it – though if
he nips outside many more times for a quick smoke his mother
won't be best pleased. Helen hates the habit immensely. I don't
encourage him, never would, but these last few weeks . . . months
even, it's been his coping mechanism. Between his break-up with
Annabel and the pressure his father puts on him, it's no wonder
he's withdrawn into himself. Young Teddy and River are the
same as ever. River's loud and proud, dominant in every action,
sentence and gesture in comparison to gentle Teddy, who rarely
argues and respects his elders, possibly more than he should. And
Lowry, freshly changed after her late arrival, seems level-headed
and very independent. Unlike this brood. She'll be in for a shock
when Scarlet arrives . . . I'm not banking on those two getting
along, if I'm honest. Chalk and cheese, in every way.

'Lowry, so what is it you do?' asks Teddy, turning to speak
to his neighbour.

'I work for the RSPCA attending emergency calls to collect
or rescue injured animals in the Salford area. I take them back
to base for assessment and treatment by the in-house vets and
attempt to provide suitable care and attention where needed.'

'And in your spare time?' continues Teddy, as we all nod in
admiration.

'In my free time, I tend to help out with the dog-walking
sessions, cleaning the animal pens and socialising some of our
more distressed animals.'

'Are they difficult to rehome then?' asks Helen, finishing her
dessert.

'Sometimes. If a dog's been in the shelter from a pup, it won't
understand how to react socially or behave within a family
home.'

'I suppose, if they've been ill-treated, they'll need time to
overcome such experiences,' adds River, butting in on the conversation, which is typical amongst the brothers.

'Absolutely, though sadly some never regain that trust. And you, I believe you all work together?' asks Lowry, widening the conversation to include the entire family.

'"Work" being the goal but not necessarily the outcome, hey, fellas?' asks Emmet, raising his brows at his father at the head of the table.

'You can say that again, Emmet. We're not all grafters around this table, are we now?' says Rupert, staring in turn at his younger sons.

'I am,' protests Teddy indignantly, prodding at his own chest. 'Bloody great – I get tarred with the same brush regardless of my efforts.'

'That'll be me then ... the time-waster, the incompetent workshy one ... let me think of my other titles. Mmm, shoddiness personified, and my weightlifting abilities. There, I think I've covered them all, Lowry. These guys do all the work; I do nothing, apparently,' grumbles River, clearly narked by the list of insinuations.

'Weightlifting?' repeats Lowry, obviously intrigued by its inclusion.

There's a ripple of laughter around the table, except from River.

'Yeah, apparently. I wait ... while everyone else does the lifting. One of these days I might take my skills elsewhere, then we'll see who's laughing!' he retorts, glaring, in a comedic fashion, at both his father and older brother.

'Promise, promises,' says Rupert, reaching for his son's shoulder.

'You've been saying that since your first day, River,' quips Emmet, pushing his empty dessert bowl away.

'Don't try buttering me up,' retorts River, shaking off his father's hand.

'As you can see, we get along just great, Lowry,' says Emmet, with a smirk.

Teddy remains silent, cautiously watching the interaction play out.

'Anyway, we make interior doors – take care, or you might find yourself working alongside us,' says River, grimacing.

'As we say . . . don't knock it!' says Emmet, raising his glass in her direction. Rupert begins to laugh, as does River.

'You'd have to put up with crap lines like that all day, every day, if you did, Lowry. I'd stick with what you're doing, it definitely sounds more fulfilling,' adds Teddy.

'Please don't start with the endless knock-knock jokes; it's not clever and they're not funny,' groans Helen, shaking her head. 'Can we get back to discussing the Christmas tree excursion?'

My cue to make the coffee and fetch the mints, I believe. I slowly push my chair backwards, rise from the table and quietly return to my own festive haven. I feel safe in my kitchen, where I'm not on show; others usually enter my domain with a request, so they rarely notice if I'm having a good day or bad. Though this stage, with the mild shakes and unsteadiness, is nothing compared to what it might become in time. That's if my mother's pathway with PD is anything to go by. I've read so much about each person having a unique experience with this illness, any illness, in fact.

As I reach the kitchen door, a unanimous groan erupts from the dining room, an annual occurrence in response to Helen's desire for the perfect family Christmas outing or her exclamation of 'I think homemade decorations are delightful!' I get where she's coming from but every year it falls flat – arguments, squabbling and one time, no actual tree. Maybe she should be honest enough to explain the significance of her festive vision, to which they're supposed to live up.

Chapter Four

Lowry

I quietly open the kitchen's stable door, just after half ten, in need of a brief escape from the overheated dining room and the constant chatter. The cold night air feels delicious as I inhale deeply, allowing it to tingle my innards, chasing away the stuffiness. I'm not good at being constantly surrounded by people; even a few hours is a bit much. Do they ever stop talking? I've hit that stage where my brain hurts from all the information it's gathered yet I'm still trying to be sociable and pay attention. Sadly, their conversations centre on treasured family memories which they all laugh at, forcing me to politely listen, waiting for an invitation to join in or for a new topic to come up. It appears my introduction is over, their initial interest has waned.

I pull my jumper sleeves down over my hands, scrunching my palms to hold my cuffs in place, before stepping outside into the darkness. The night sky is an array of twinkling stars, which seems artificially bright in comparison to my usual view during a night shift in Salford, but then there's hardly any light pollution here. It seems absurd that our love of glaring bulbs down here should affect what we see of the stars above.

I nip across the patio and dart up the tiny flight of stone steps to stand before an expanse of lawn and a large trellis archway with the bulky outline of an ominous monster. I daren't step any further as the grass is overgrown and lollopy – my feet will be sodden in seconds. My elevated position makes little difference to my view as I peer skywards, except for removing me from the glare of the kitchen's light. Under the glittering array of stars, I feel tiny and insignificant, despite my good intentions in this world. That's probably my saving grace in life, my empathy towards any creature in need or distressed. How many neglected animals are suffering unnecessarily in search of warmth and shelter?

'Please make sure they survive the night – all she's asking for is a chance,' I whisper aloud to the universe.

'Sorry?' comes a male voice from my right.

I start, turning in panic to look all around me. I hadn't realised that anyone else was out here enjoying the peace, but there's no one in sight. I take a few tentative steps on to the sodden grass to peer around the back of the outhouse, where a broad figure sits on the bench, the glowing tip of a cigarette cutting a vertical arc in the darkness.

'Emmet, is it?' I say tentatively, peering into the shadows. He can see me clearly, backlit by the kitchen window.

'Yeah, but come again?' I can barely make out his silhouette in the gloom and certainly no actual features. Stranger still, I sense he's frowning intently – that's been his expression for most of the evening. The cigarette butt points at me like a strange red star. Not a habit I'm keen on, with the billowing smoke and acrid smell. Not that I've ever tried it, but still, each to their own.

'S-sorry?' I stutter, pretending not to understand.

'Just now, what did you say?'

'Nothing,' I lie, too embarrassed to admit it, let alone repeat it or explain why.

'I could have sworn that you mentioned "surviving the night" . . . no?'

I shake my head, feigning ignorance.

'No?' He sounds disbelieving, and after a lengthy pause, he adds, 'Forget it. How are you finding us?'

Relief. I now feel utterly ridiculous for denying it in such a sneaky way. Why did I not come clean? Because he might poke fun? Or tell the others? Worse still, I bet the universe paid more attention to my lie rather than my request.

'Fine, thanks. You seem a tight family . . . which is nice.'

'Do we?' His surprised tone could cut glass.

'Yeah. I'd have loved to have had siblings.'

'Pets instead, was it?'

'Something like that,' I reply, wondering why I'm still talking into the shadows.

'Mmm,' comes his reply, and a plume of grey smoke lifts into the night sky.

'I've never known anything else. Unconditional love from pets and three adults – that was my childhood.'

Emmet doesn't respond, just the glowing cigarette tip continues to move in a wide arc, up then down.

Our silence stretches for aeons. I'm not getting a warm vibe from this guy, it's more like an electric fence at high voltage. I don't wish to pry – I'm trusting my mum's opinion about this family. I sincerely hope, for her sake, that this whirlwind romance truly delivers her a happy-ever-after. And if it doesn't, I'll do what I can to rescue her from the aftermath.

This scenario reminds me of a frightened German shepherd bitch I needed to corner and collar, hiding in the shadows of a run-down warehouse. Once my eyes became accustomed, I could see her bulky outline; she was cowering, yet throughout the rescue I was expecting her to launch at me, all bared teeth and terror, if I moved too fast.

I'm suddenly conscious of my uninvited presence. What must I look like standing here in damp canvas pumps, clutching my cuffs for warmth half-bent to peer into the shadows, invading his peace. The option to casually sit down alongside him for a buddy chat passed minutes ago; it would be weird to sit down

now without his encouragement. Worse still, if I choose to settle
on the other bench, on the opposing side of the lawn, its distance
will suggest a stand-off. I remain where I am, with my lie swirling
above my head, much like his exhaled smoke drifting towards
the trellis archway. I don't wish to tread on any toes, force myself
on people who aren't interested or make others feel they have
to accommodate me. I'm here purely for my mum, no one else.

'Anyway, I'll leave you to enjoy your smoke. I'd like to check
on the kittens before heading inside.'

'Cheerio, enjoy,' comes his voice.

Within seconds, I'm down the steps, back across the patio and
peering in through the door of the outhouse, which I'd wedged
open earlier with a discarded house brick. I'm relieved to be on
familiar territory, dealing with an animal; interacting with Emmet
was like getting blood from a stone. I'm aware that Emmet is still
sitting on the other side of the back wall, ciggie in hand, blowing
smoke at the trellis, so I lower my voice for fear he'll hear me.

'Tsssssk, little kitty, only me. Let's see how you're doing.' I raise
my mobile, illuminating the nearest corner of the outhouse and
revealing a bed of brown sacking. The cat's eyes shine emerald
green as her inquisitive nose lifts in my direction. Poking from
between her paws, snuggled against her saggy belly, two fluffy
kittens sleep.

'Now, that's what I call tight,' I whisper, not wishing to disturb
her. 'I'll grab you some food and water – back in a second.'

As I head for the kitchen door, Emmet strides into view,
arriving at the same time, his ciggies and lighter clasped in one
hand.

'Oh sorry,' I say, not looking where I was going.

'After you,' he replies, gesturing with his free hand towards
the stable door.

'Thanks.'

'Is she OK?' His voice sounds softer.

'Fine, thank you. In need of food and water, that's all. I'm hoping Martha will have a little something going begging.'

I open the kitchen door, greeted by a wave of festive tunes. Coming in behind me, Emmet gives a snort. 'Believe me, Martha always has a little something but begging won't be necessary. She's a feeder – be it humans or felines.' Bang on cue, Martha enters the kitchen backwards, carrying a tray of dirty glasses – each one rattling against its neighbours. 'Isn't that right, Martha – you're one of life's feeders?'

'You'd have not survived infancy if I hadn't feed ye, that's for sure! What is it you need, lovey?' Martha asks me, ignoring Emmet's deep laugh and depositing her tray by the dishwasher.

'Possibly some meat scraps and a dish for some water,' I say, looking about to help myself.

'I spied a dog bowl under the sink – this cottage literally has everything a family could need. Here,' says Martha, swiftly retrieving the silver bowl. 'There's a few pieces of cooked lamb in the fridge which I kept as a little extra, knowing the lads always come mooching at supper time.'

'Perfect. May I?' I point towards the fridge, unsure of her kitchen rules. Martha nods, awkwardly hauling herself up from her kneeling position courtesy of the kitchen cupboards.

'Sorted?' asks Emmet, lingering at the hallway door.

'Yes. Thank you,' I say, eager to get on with my task.

'Good. And don't worry, I'm sure she'll survive the night, even if she can't make amends for bugging the hell out of my father!' says Emmet, swiftly leaving the kitchen.

My mouth drops open – he heard. A dark horse, if ever I've met one.

'Is he on about the she-cat or your mother?' asks Martha, clearly confused, filling the bowl with tap water.

'The cat. My mother hasn't bugged his father yet, has she?' I ask, slightly concerned at the suggestion.

Martha shrugs. 'Are her kittens very old?'

'A few weeks, no more. I can't believe Rupert would dispose of someone else's kittens having just arrived at a property,' I say, retrieving the plate of cooked lamb from the fridge. 'He's only renting this cottage for ... what? Five days?'

'Mr C is a law unto himself, my dear. He can't and won't be told what's happening under his own roof, whether that be a rental or not! He wasn't best pleased when the cat trundled in carrying a kitten as soon as we arrived. Less so when he put her outside and she returned ten minutes later with the other one.'

'Despite her being stick thin?' I ask warily, knowing the cat's expanded waistline counts for nothing whilst she's nursing.

Martha shrugs again, while I shake my head in disapproval. I'm wanting to like this guy but sensing it could prove difficult.

'Don't let his gruff exterior fool you – the man's a pussycat where women are concerned,' says Martha, loading the dirty glasses into the dishwasher.

I quickly dice the lamb into smaller pieces, interested to hear more about my stepfather-to-be. 'Have you been with the family long?'

'Long?' Martha turns around abruptly, the sudden action causing me to look up from my task. 'I've welcomed every one of his bairns into this family, catered for all but his first wedding, witnessed every declaration of love and as for the various decree nisi ... well, I could write a book on the happenings of the last thirty-one years! I'd call that long,' retorts Martha, her eyes wide, her eyebrows lost within her fringe.

'Sorry, I didn't realise. I get now why you're classed as part of the family,' I say, swiftly backtracking to avoid causing offence.

The kitchen door swings open and the man himself enters, much to my embarrassment, plodding in wearing his slippers and carrying an empty coffee mug.

'Martha, any chance of a brew?' He wiggles the mug in her

direction. His tone is deep and somewhat gruff, similar to our initial doorstep meeting.

As quick as a flash, Martha turns from the dishwasher and takes the empty mug. 'Sure. I'll bring a fresh one through.' Rupert is turning to leave when Martha pipes up, 'I was just saying I've been with the family for over three decades, through thick and thin.' I notice she didn't address him directly, though she has previously referred to him as Mr C. He abruptly stops, turning to Martha, then slowly turning towards me. I'm watching his every move and mannerism for clues about the life my mum is about to enter.

'Certainly have, old bean. I don't know what we'd have done without you. The women in this family have been shocking cooks; the children might never have survived past infancy. I'd probably be four stone lighter and wouldn't suffer from angina if it wasn't for this one! I always say, Martha's my angel who bakes!' Rupert gives a knowing nod, as if confirming his belief to himself, before leaving the kitchen.

Martha waits for the kitchen door to close properly before whispering, 'A pussycat, believe me. It's regrettable about the angina and his waistline – I opt for healthy options where possible but the man likes his puddings!' She flicks the kettle on and returns to her dishwasher task.

I'm not so sure, but I don't comment. Life has taught me that your reaction to animals is indicative of your true colours. And my priority, before heading to bed, is a hungry cat curled on sacking in a brick outhouse.

Helen

Emmet slams the front door behind us as I eagerly stride ahead into the darkness beyond the white picket gate.

'Isn't it beautiful?' I say, as he catches me up.

'It is, but it's far warmer inside, Mother. Wouldn't a ginger wine before the log fire be a better way to end the day?'

'No. I need some fresh air, it's been nonstop since I arrived. What with organising the bedrooms ... your bedroom is fine, isn't it? I wasn't sure if you'd want to be doubled up with River but you usually get along so well. I didn't want it to look like favouritism if I gave you the spare double room, though it's there should you want it.' I'm more tense than usual with all the planning and organising, but then it isn't a normal Christmas, is it? Not with Emmet's big birthday, on Christmas Day, plus a wedding the following day. During the last twelve weeks, I've wondered if Rupert is perhaps unhinged. Who in their right mind contemplates marriage number five when the previous four have not endured the test of time?

It still irks me to think they couldn't have selected a different time of year, though to be fair Rupert has been married in all three of the previous seasons, so winter makes a change. Not that this wedding symbolises the end of his seasons, but it's there, it could do. Admittedly, there are worse surprises than hearing your ex-husband's embarking on his fifth marriage. Not that I don't wish them both joy and much happiness but can I really bear to witness another cycle of wedding bells and honeymoon photos before a possible divorce looms on the horizon?

'I get it. And I couldn't let you wander by yourself at this time of night in an unfamiliar area. I've even brought a torch that Martha found in the scullery – we can do without an emergency to cope with too.'

Arm in arm, with the sweeping torch beam a stride before us, we take a left turn from the gate and stroll past our line of parked vehicles. I bet it's a pain not having a driveway, but it's a blessing to be without neighbours given that we've filled the grass verge with an array of vehicles: Emmet and Teddy's mud-splattered Range Rovers, Rupert's polished Jaguar and my Audi.

I presume the old brown Mini is Lowry's. Though there's Janie, Lynette, Teddy's mum, and Scarlet to arrive yet so the line-up will extend still further.

Strolling with my son feels nice. What I wouldn't give for the return of his tiny chubby hand clasped in mine. Back then, I never dreamt his palm would ever outgrow mine.

'I've no idea where this leads to,' I say, pointing ahead along the darkened lane. 'I assume there's access to the lake, possibly a designated nature reserve or wildlife area close by.'

Emmet doesn't answer. He's willing to accompany me but he's not in the mood for chitchat. I understand, he's got 'stuff' swimming inside his head. I remember how distraught I was after my break-up with Rupert. It's the rejection, the very idea that someone has chosen not to be with you despite the love you're offering. Whether it be a conscious decision or a knee-jerk reaction to a moment of passion. The realisation that every effort you've made giving of yourself and your life doesn't make them happy – that simply eats away at you for months, years even. As for the love, well . . . does that ever truly die? I remember recalling all our happy occasions and wondering if it had all been an act? It certainly wasn't on my part; the happy snaps in the photo box capturing sandcastles and tentative baby steps were genuine for me – I was loving our young family, being a mum and a wife. Rupert's focus was clearly elsewhere.

Call me foolish, but I've waited long enough for Rupert to come to his senses about us. Haven't I proved my loyalty and devotion throughout these years! I've stood on the sidelines waiting for him to come to the realisation that what we had back then was what he needed all along. My God, when I think of all that I've put myself through in the pursuit of love . . .

'Look at the height of those mountains,' says Emmet, bringing me back to the present. 'It's amazing what time and pressure can create.'

'Pressure, hey?' I say, following his gesture towards the darkened horizon where the purple topped mountains from earlier have been replaced by dark looming shapes interrupting a starry sky.

Emmet explains about tectonic plates and their shifting movements – his tone is lighter now he's absorbed in a topic. Whilst listening, all I can think is how big the Carmichael mountain would be if our time and pressure had resulted in visible structures. Some families know nothing of heartache or destruction whilst ours has experienced everything. The heartbreak, arguments and the repercussions of every decision have been borne by the innocent few. How different would my son's thirtieth birthday celebrations be if Rupert hadn't strayed? Would Emmet be settled, with plans for a family of his own? The majority of his close friends have the normalities of a home and a committed partner, if not a wife. Sadly, not my boy. Who probably deserves it more, because I . . . we didn't . . . couldn't provide that for him. He deserves to know the security and love that a family can bring – not that that would erase what he experienced as a child but it might enrich his life as an adult. It's the reason I made an effort with Emmet's ex, Annabel, for so long. I tried so hard to find a connection, some common ground or shared interest on which we could build a relationship, but she wasn't interested in a rapport with me. After two years, she was struggling to maintain one with Emmet. I knew it was over long before he did.

'Mum?'

'Sorry. I was in a world of my own,' I say apologetically, feeling guilty that 'stuff' is now filling my head.

'Let's walk across here – it looks like there's a jetty by the water's edge.' I look where he's pointing and spy the outline of posts protruding in the distance.

He diverts the torch and we stride from the tarmacked road on to the grass verge and through a large gap in the bulky hedgerow leading us into an open pasture, thankfully without livestock.

'Careful. Mind your step.' Emmet squeezes his elbow closer to his side, locking my linked arm more tightly against his frame.

'It looks quite picturesque with the clumps of reeds . . . and is that a rowing boat tied up?'

'Looks that way. Though I don't suggest we take a midnight excursion, Mum. They'll never think of scouting a lake in the dark, now would they?'

The pasture is rough and uneven underfoot but the serene landscape ahead is enticing. I wish I could take a decent photograph as the misty hues of blue and grey would look fabulous framed and hanging above my mantelpiece.

'This will be the lake we can see from the lounge windows,' I say, trying to place myself in relation to the cottage, which I can hardly make out over my left shoulder. We stand on the bank, reeds and rushes on either side, scanning the vast expanse of chilly water, which is gently rippling here and there. I bet it's teeming with life beneath the surface, much as I have been these past thirty years.

'Do you miss her?' I ask, not sure I wish to hear his answer.

'Sometimes. I'm getting used to her absence – each week has been easier than the one before – but still, it was her choice not mine in the end.'

'You're hurting less?' I don't wish to pry, but I need to know. I longed for him to find someone he loved, pushed for him to share his life and probably encouraged him to commit faster than he usually would. And then it was over. Resulting in nothing but his lingering sadness. Gone. Lost. Empty.

'I wouldn't say less, I'd say differently. I can now admit there was something missing for me. I understand her reasoning a little more than before, which helps but doesn't actually help, if you get my drift. Annabel was right – you can't wait around for ever while a guy figures out if it's you he wants to commit to. She wanted me to know that, feel that, even if we didn't marry immediately. I didn't know that deep down – and for me that's the missing piece.'

I get it – which makes me feel guilty. I should have hung back, like I had before, but with his age, his maturity, I was eager, too eager, to see him settled. Though if it wasn't right from the off, with the right foundations, I had no business willing it along that path. I wasn't 100 per cent about her, I simply felt he was. I won't meddle next time. I'll leave them to their own devices. I won't push, drop hints, make suggestions, plant ideas – nothing of the sort. I'll trust his instinct next time. Though given what he's going through right now, and it's been messy with all the financial commitments he's had to unravel in recent weeks. Next time, if someone special appears in his life, and hoping his father's life story hasn't put Emmet off seeking a loving connection in life, I'll respect his decisions and mind my own business.

'Don't you think there's any chance of your pair ...'

'No.' His tone is stern, as if the word is spat from his lips before his emotions can suggest otherwise.

'OK. It won't always be like this you know ... One day ...' I say, knowing I sound ridiculous to him. Emmet gives a snort, but I continue, '... one day the right person will come your way when you least expect it.'

'Right now, that's the last thing I want to hear,' says Emmet, unlinking his arm from mine, only to wrap it around my shoulder and pull me closer.

'One day,' I mutter, vowing to remain silent and enjoy this moment because just like my boy's tiny hand in mine, I won't ever know when it's the last time.

Martha

After the kitchen is tidied, with the dishwasher performing yet another speedy wash and the majority of the cottage having either retired to bed or nipped out for a quiet walk, I slope off into the snug with a large mug of cocoa and two books. It's rare that I get a chance to relax after a long, busy day so I'm grabbing some precious R&R time for myself, while I can. I could easily go to bed, get cosy beneath a warm duvet and read before turning out the light, but I opt for this sacred little space. I'm sure it'll prove popular in the coming days, so I'll bagsie it now.

The padded cover of the 'Guest Book' announces its role in fancy gold script, with an accompanying pen tucked inside. I'm not one for sentimental twaddle regarding bricks and mortar, so I'm half expecting to spend all of two minutes reading a steady flow of gushing comments by strangers. I couldn't have been more wrong! I was immediately intrigued by its memories from the opening page.

Thank you for choosing Lakeside Cottage, Hawkshead, for your holiday stay. We offer a blend of home comforts coupled with hospitality in an atmosphere of timeless elegance, within comfortable and stylish rooms and alongside unrivalled lakeside views of Cumbria.

We want you to enjoy every precious day of your stay so we pledge to you our service is guaranteed to meet your highest expectations. Should you require any additional help or information during your stay at Lakeside Cottage, please do not hesitate to contact our local host, Josie Adams (contact details are listed in the kitchen).

Please add notes or memories of your holiday to our

guest book, as it provides a true history of the many and
varied lives passing through this beautiful cottage.

Wishing you and yours the warmest of welcomes,

Mr and Mrs Campbell, Shetland.

The owners deserve to do well, whoever they are, given their
kind words and warm welcome. Though I probably shouldn't
have expected anything less from people who have created such
a beautiful 'home from home' experience. Some twenty minutes
later, I'm still flicking through the comments when I notice the
quivering jitter of the page caused by my right hand as I read an
entry by Lulu James, from Kettering:

I came, I went and I bloody well conquered! I've left my
fingerprints in numerous rooms and created fabulous memories in others. May you have the best bloody holiday of
your life at Lakeside Cottage – I certainly did. Plus, I went
home with the greatest souvenir of my life!

Which sounds marvellous after some tame entries about
quality bedding and mattresses! I'll have to remember to add
a line or two at the end of our stay, or at least encourage the
others to. I set the guest book aside, conscious that my free time
is diminishing, and that quivering page only acts as a reminder
for other matters.

I crack open the hardback cover – not one of mine but
discovered on the landing's bookshelf, where it caught my eye
in passing. A beautiful clothbound edition of *Lyrical Ballads:*
a collection of poems by Wordsworth and Coleridge, very apt
for our location. Not my usual reading matter but definitely
something that I can enjoy, mull over and wistfully ponder
whilst bringing together the extensive menus I've created for
this holiday season.

In addition to applying the decorative flourishes to the wedding cake, I'm making a birthday cake for Emmet's big celebration. How and why everything comes together on the same weekend is beyond me – family planning, dear people, in all senses, is needed from the next generation!

I skip the first poem, patchily remembered from my school days and somewhat loathed for its lengthy narrative, which I feel no urgency to revisit tonight. I grab my cooling drink, take a sip and slowly begin the second poem, 'The Foster-Mother's Tale', though it doesn't state which poet crafted the stanzas.

I inadvertently stop reading as particular lines catch my eye or my heart – having been nothing less than a foster-mum to these four bairns. It wasn't my original plan, but it's how life evolved. Loving other people's children is an art, something of a vocation, with definite boundaries, within which I've artfully manoeuvred myself – stepping up to the plate when necessary and swiftly retreating when required. Unseen gestures, undiscovered love bountifully applied like balm to chapped skin . . . recognised when absent but unnoticed when carefully applied. I worry about them, the boys more than Scarlet. Phew, there's no flies on that one; she'll cope in life and deal with it head on, but the boys . . . they're softer, more easily damaged by this world.

I reread the poem, noting that the word 'perilous' jumps off the page, grabbing my attention – how accurate can one be regarding the specifics of a relationship? Like a spell at sea, I've weathered each storm – taking orders from a captain who wasn't trained or worthy of the mission. Who knows if Mr C's truly planned and prepared for this next one; only time will tell. Likewise with my situation – I've only ever known this role.

My peace is suddenly destroyed by a clattering in the hallway; a hullabaloo of voices, cackling laughter and much swearing brings my poetry reading to an abrupt end. I dash to the door, popping the poetry book on the coffee table – if those pesky

lads are messing up my clean kitchen I shall have their guts
for garters!

'What in heaven's name are you both doing at this late hour?'
I say, exiting the snug to find both River and Teddy attacking
the lounge door. Teddy has the interior door clamped between
his thighs while River's arm pumps a screwdriver like a piston,
trying to raise the hinge pin from its nestled state.

'We're removing the downstairs doors to make it easier for
folk to move around the place,' declares River, glancing over his
bulky shoulder. 'There'll be too many bodies and not enough
free-flowing routes to ease the congestion between rooms. It'll
make life easier, Martha. Trust me.'

Mmm, famous last words! I stay schtum and watch. I'm
hoping their unhinged actions don't prove to be an omen for
the forthcoming wedding. I've witnessed enough 'uncouplings'
within this family to last a lifetime!

'You do what you like with the lounge and dining room but
you touch my kitchen door and I'll be getting your father down
to you in an instant, do you hear me?' I snap, too loudly for
this hour.

Teddy and River both stare at me, before their faces crease
into laughter as my tone ignites teenage memories regarding that
particular threat.

'Martha, it's OK. We know what we're doing!' hisses Teddy,
through his laughter.

'Exactly. We're quite capable, even without Emmet to super-
vise!' adds River, causing Teddy to burst into laughter again.

'I warn you – I'll get the broom handle to you both if needs
be. Ruining the place whilst everyone's back is turned!'

'You'll be thanking us tomorrow, when the others arrive. We
can lean the doors against this wall and put them back before we
leave. Save your health and temper, Martha – look, it's done now,'
says River, as the hinge pin is finally released from the coupling.

'I'll give you "health and temper" – ruining my bit of peace,' I say, turning on my heels to return to the snug. 'And don't touch this door either; a snug's not a snug if I can't put a decent piece of oak between your racket and my sanity!'

Chapter Five

Sunday 24 December

Lowry

Urgh! I can't sleep, despite being tired. My phone screen reads seven minutes past three, which is ridiculous o'clock to be awake and thinking. My bed's comfortable, the duvet snuggly and the pillows are like a billowing cloud – which creates an issue. I'm wrapped up warm, as snug as a bug in a rug, and that poor cat is outside nursing two tiny kittens in a brick outhouse. My conscience won't allow me to sleep peacefully with that knowledge rattling around my brain.

I frequently hear a barrage of excuses from owners when they leave their cats outside in weather such as this: 'He has a fur coat,' 'They're used to this weather,' 'She loves hunting at dawn' – but I don't buy any of them. Cats love luxury, they've perfected the art of self-care; they could probably teach us humans a thing or two!

Hopefully she's scoffed the diced lamb and has enough water remaining till morning. But what if the promised snow has fallen? What if the temperature has plummeted below freezing?

I might nip downstairs to check. It'll take no more than a minute and then I can sleep, satisfied that she's OK.

I push the warm duvet aside and my arms instantly goose-bump – it must be freezing. I don't usually react to such things; I'm an RSPCA 'toughie' who's out in all weathers, come rain or shine.

In the darkness, I open the wardrobe, feeling along the clothes hangers for my long woollen cardigan to slip over my fleecy pyjamas, I'll catch my death otherwise. In my haste, the moulded hanger tilts, causing the cardigan to fall and crumple at the bottom of the wardrobe. I crouch, my hands ferreting around the cavernous space to retrieve my clothing. An unused space begging to be filled with a pile of folded sacking providing a quiet spot for a nursing cat perhaps? Swiftly, I collect my crumpled cardigan and cover my goosebumps.

Once a plan is hatched in my brain, it usually remains unchanged. Whether I'm chasing an escaped pet rabbit along the grass verge beside a dual carriageway, locating a lost python underneath floorboards or capturing a dangerous dog with an extendable grab collar – my first idea is usually the best. Though in this case, I'll need to provide an indoor litter tray too.

I slowly open my bedroom door, trying desperately hard to remember if the door hinges creak. My bedroom is positioned at the front of the property, neighbouring four other rooms but just a short distance from the staircase, unlike the rear bedrooms along a corridor. Silently, I creep barefoot on to the moonlit landing, carrying my canvas pumps, which I daren't put on yet, and pull my bedroom door to before turning left.

I hesitate on reaching the top stair, as various wheezing and rattling snores drift through numerous closed doors. Talk about noisy!

I take my first step and freeze in horror as a loud creak underfoot announces my wandering presence to the sleeping cottage. It's to be expected given the age of the cottage, but not helpful when you're on a mission. I cringe mid-step, nervously holding my breath for fear of a bedroom door opening to reveal a pyjama-clad Rupert demanding an explanation.

Nothing.

I tiptoe like a cat burglar down the remaining stairs, holding my breath so that I gasp on reaching the hallway, into which the front door's bevelled window lets some light.

I'm puzzled to see two wooden doors leaning lengthways against the hallway wall and notice that both the lounge and dining-room doors have been removed. Is this a family tradition which the Carmichaels failed to mention at dinner? Though my route through the kitchen will be easier if that door's been removed too.

I turn right heading for the kitchen. Sadly, that door is still in place, as is the ... I stop in my tracks on spying a strip of mellow light escaping from beneath the door of the snug. Has the light been accidentally left on or is someone else wide awake at this hour?

Not wishing to find out, I sneak past, praying the kitchen door won't give me away as I gently turn the knob. When the door swings open without a sound, I want to celebrate, like a contestant appearing on a Saturday night TV challenge, but I resist. The red tiles underfoot are freezing, causing me to wince, as I cross to the stable door where I quickly slip my pumps on before gently turning the door key.

It's bitterly cold. I should have opted for a coat, but the glistening frosting covering every blade of grass, patio slab and stone makes the garden look beautiful. Magical, even. I scurry across the patio to the outhouse, removing the wedged house brick to open the wooden door a little wider, enabling me to crouch within.

'Hello, my beauty, still snuggling your babies?' I croon, creeping inside to peer at my newly acquired charge. 'How would you like a warm spot inside the cottage as a secret resident? Yes, I think you'd like that.' I collect the box, which I'd discarded earlier, and gently lift my cat family complete with their bed of sacking into the box. I tip the remains of water out of the silver dog bowl and pick up the empty food dish, tucking both alongside the little family. 'Sorry to move you like this but it'll only be for a moment, then you can settle as you were before.'

I can't help but wonder how my other little Christmas cat is bearing up back in Salford's rescue centre. I leave the door of the outhouse wedged open with the house brick, to give the impression that nothing has changed.

Now for the return journey, without disturbing the occupant in the snug.

As swift as you like, I'm back inside the kitchen, tiptoeing across the tiles without removing my pumps, now my hands are full. I'm almost jubilant, which turns out to be slightly premature – the snug door is now wide open and the mellow light is spilling forth; the hallway's like Blackpool Illuminations. I'll never sneak past without being seen. Unless the occupant is fast asleep on the couch ... in which case, how's the door wide open?

I stop short of the doorway, venturing as close as I can without being seen. I strain my ears trying to make out another person's breathing, the tiniest of movements or even a welcome snore. Dare I peep around the edge or simply dart past, hoping they don't see me? My heart is racing, and my arms tighten around the cardboard box, hoping the cat doesn't make a move or start mewing.

I can't stand here all night. I can't hear a thing, but that means nothing. I inadvertently glance towards the record player, underneath the stairs, which is finally silent. I inch forward, peering around the doorjamb; slowly the snug interior comes into view: the arm of a couch, the full seat, the low-level coffee table ... and still I continue to move forward without spotting a person inside. Then it hits me: the room's empty, there's no one inside. The only sign of previous occupancy is a slim hardbacked book lying on the couch cushion. Where are they? I daren't wait to find out but quickly nip past, with my adrenalin pumping, taking the stairs two at a time, as swift and as silent as I can be.

Safely inside my room, I carefully unload my precious cargo into their secret wardrobe space, hoping I've given her babies a chance of survival. The she-cat nudges my hand as I tuck the sacking around them into a protective bedding.

'I'll make you a litter tray first thing in the morning, I promise,' I whisper, knowing that a cardboard box of newspaper and loose soil will simply have to do. 'Try as you might, you couldn't get past Rupert. You're a tricksy one, aren't you? Ha, that's a suitable name for the time being. Goodnight, Trixie.'

I know it's naughty – I'm not even the one paying the rental on this cottage – but no one will ever know. Hopefully, in five days' time the kittens will be stronger and healthy enough to return to the outhouse. I partly close the wardrobe door, jamming it open with my work boot.

I climb into my warm bed, knowing that three more little hearts are also as snug as a bug in a rug despite the chilly weather outside. Though the question spinning around my mind is now: who else was up and awake in the snug? And did they spot me when I nipped outside to collect my kittens?

Helen

'What have they done to the doors?' I ask Martha on entering the kitchen before breakfast. Emmet and I had seen their handiwork last night. 'They can't leave anything alone, can they?'

'River and Teddy removed them last night while you were out walking, a right faff, if you ask me,' says Martha, busy forking a grill pan filled with bacon and sausages.

'But no one ever does ask, do they?' I snipe, rattled that the opinion of others is rarely sought by some folk. 'I've a good mind to point out that this is someone else's home, not ours. Martha, is there any toast going?' Instantly, feeling guilty for asking as she's busy.

'Fresh on the table not three minutes ago,' she says, gesturing towards the dining room.

'Sorry, I'm … sorry.' I flap my hands apologetically and disappear from under her feet. Martha would never say that I was interrupting or getting in the way, but you know by her expression, that manner that silently reminds you: 'You're in my domain.'

As I enter the dining room I'm welcomed by the wintry sunshine streaming through the lattice windows – no signs of snow yet – a glorious spread of breakfast treats and a table of four men, seated amongst many empty place settings.

'Good morning! How did we all sleep?' I ask, heading straight to the sideboard to collect my desired toast, wholemeal, with butter and honey. Viewing the wide selection of flaky croissants, fresh fruit, yoghurts and cereal prepared by Martha, I feel a little guilty sticking with my usual toast. Though I do fancy some eggs. I receive a selection of grunts and moans as the fellas sip their coffees and await their cooked breakfasts. I settle myself next to my son, evening up the table's occupants. 'Well, I slept wonderfully. The beds are comfy, the heating was just right and my shower was piping hot – simply gorgeous choice of rental. Diane chose well, Rupert, dropped on to a real winner.' In more ways than one, though I don't state the obvious.

'I'd say so. She was dubious about the size of a "cottage", but with nine bedrooms, how could it be anything but large?' he replies, from the head of the table, always his preferred seat. He looks quite stately with his three sons seated on either side, though my Emmet looks the worse for wear – probably down to the booze and ciggies he's living on. Rupert has always looked respectable at breakfast, his marl grey hair damp from his shower and never a whisker in sight. Teddy's shaved and groomed as always, and River doesn't look as dishevelled as my lad, but still, he could at least comb his hair before joining the breakfast table. Why River is following Emmet's stubbled look is beyond me. Casually dressed in jeans, rugby tops and fleeces, they'd make a truly handsome bunch if they paid some attention to the basics – like Teddy has.

'Exactly. I think once we've spruced it up with Christmas decorations and when everyone arrives . . . I think this could be the best weekend we've had as a family.' There's silence. 'I was hoping for a little enthusiasm, guys.'

'Yay!' cheers Teddy, attempting to please me with sarcasm.

'Thank you, Teddy. Don't start playing the "we don't want to be here" card because I'll get the violins out. It's an impor-tant weekend in this family – Emmet's big birthday,' I glance at our son, who offers me a grimace rather than a pleased smile. 'Christmas celebrations, plus your father and Diane's wedding. Now I realise that not everyone can be here to celebrate but we do need to be supportive and welcome Diane and Lowry into the family.'

'Sure,' says River, 'though we didn't see much of her last night given her late arrival.'

'No, but today's a brand-new day, River – make an effort, please. Chat, include her in the activities, find out what she's into. The way you lot behave together we could do with some new blood around here. And what's with the doors, again?'

'It makes things easier for people,' says Rupert, sitting up tall as Martha enters carrying the first two cooked breakfasts. 'Here she is. Thank you very much, that looks wonderful.'

'You're welcome. I'll be through with the other plates in a second,' says Martha, delivering the second plate to Emmet and receiving a hearty thank you.

'Any chance I could have a couple of poached eggs, Martha?' I ask as she nips by.

'Sure.' And with that she's gone.

I return to the topic of doors. 'I don't think it does; if anything, the removed doors simply clutter up the space in the hallway.' I point over my shoulder, as if they can see through the brick wall. 'Personally, I think they'll be a hazard, when the hallway and entrance are busy. Someone's going to fall over and injure themselves.'

I'm busy buttering my toast but look up and catch the four males rolling their eyes at each other. 'And you can stop with the Carmichael eye-rolling. I'm saying my piece as a member of this family. I have a right to, just as the rest of you have. There, done.'

Martha enters carrying three rattling plates. She swiftly delivers my side plate, containing two poached eggs, and places two cooked breakfasts before the younger guys.

A chorus of thank yous fills the air, to which Martha cheerfully responds, as always, 'You're welcome,' and heads towards the open doorway.

'Anything you need help with today, Martha?' I ask, knowing full well she'll have planned it to the nth degree, but still, something might arise.

She stops in her tracks, looks at me, ponders for a split second before shaking her head. 'Nothing springs to mind, unless some folk around here pinched my ingredients from the fridge as a midnight snack?'

My mouth drops wide. I look straight at the three lads, who are busy scoffing their breakfasts. 'Fellas, you know how it is in Martha's kitchen. I'm so sorry, what do you need – they can nip up to the Co-op for you.'

'I think we'll need more cheese for the platters, an assortment of crackers and some cocoa powder so I that can remake my chocolate mousse,' says Martha, checking each item off on her fingers.

'I'm so sorry. Lads, this isn't funny – every time we stay together, you do this. She works her fingers to the bone for us and you repay her by making life difficult, on Christmas Eve of all days. No more.' I'm annoyed and irritated that the three culprits continue to eat as though I'm not speaking. Who the hell do they think they are? They're certainly not children any more and yet ... *Bang!* My hand slaps down on the oak table with more force than I was intending, making everyone jump. 'Are you listening?'

Lowry enters and stops dead, glancing about the dining room, looking decidedly uncomfortable; I bet she heard my reaction.

'Sorry, Martha,' pipes up Emmet, offering her his winning smile.

'Yep, guilty as charged,' says River, holding his hands up.

'Not me, I didn't touch anything,' adds Teddy, continuing to slice his bacon rasher.

'I'm so sorry, Martha. Write a list and they can collect it first thing. I promise.'

'Very well,' says Martha, adding, 'Morning, Lowry, help yourself from the sideboard. If you'd like something cooking, just shout, my lovely.'

'Morning. Thank you, but I'm happy with cereal,' says Lowry.

'Morning, Lowry. No eggs or bacon – there's everything in the kitchen ... unless the lads have eaten it in the night, that is,' I say, wanting to soothe away the atmosphere she's walked into.

I notice her eyes widen, and she glances at the three lads busy eating.

'Honestly, I'm fine. I'm happy with cereal,' she says, selecting a box from the sideboard.

'Did you sleep well?' I ask, wishing to include her.

'Yes, like a log,' she replies, pouring milk from the jug and collecting a spoon.

'That's good to hear,' I say, noticing the three sons are eye-balling each other yet again as Lowry makes her way around the table to the seat one down from me. Lord knows what's going on but these Carmichael lads, as big as they are, will be the death of me.

Chapter Six

Martha

I wipe down the kitchen countertops with a diluted disinfectant solution before I make a start on decorating one cake and baking another; there's no point skimping on the basics of hygiene. I can do without a dose of food poisoning giving the family the trots before the wedding.

I'm happier now that the family have all left on Helen's tree excursion, which gets them from under my feet. She's sent Teddy off to the Co-op with my shopping list and a flea in his ear, though I don't think he was actually involved in raiding the fridge last night. Boy, did Helen make me jump this morning when she slammed her hand down on that dining room table during breakfast. Woo, I thought, she means business – it's not like her to lose her cool. Helen's definitely the matriarch of the family regardless of her divorced status, and I don't blame her for standing her ground – someone around here has to. Not that Mr C doesn't pipe up when needed regarding the boys, but that's usually more business-related than around the home. He lets them get away with a tad too much in my opinion. He didn't concern himself about the inconvenience to me, did he? No. He left it for Helen to deal with, and she did.

I give a little chuckle; Helen's demanding but her heart's in the right place. She wants things done right, which is why they'll be trekking for ages until she spots the perfect tree. I remember when she conducted my interview in the kitchen of their first home way, way back in time. The agency sent me the address and advert details: 'live-in cook wanted for a young couple' ... I think they'd only been married a month and Mr C had had enough of lumpy mash, thin watery gravy and rock-hard peas so he took action. I've never seen a young wife be so nervous whilst asking basic questions. Visibly shaking she was, and short of questions to ask me, so I took up the mantle and began telling her about the experience I'd gained as a child watching my mum be the head cook in a stately home in Derbyshire. Trained by the best I was, positioned at her elbow. Until she lost her confidence along with her good health. Then it was a different story: she wouldn't carry trays, point-blank refused to hand out teacups as the accompanying rattling could notify an entire ballroom of a bad day, and as for her beautiful cake decorating – that went completely due to her lack of dexterity. I can still hold an icing bag but I've previously had to scrape off a birthday message once or twice and reapply before it was entirely readable.

I rinse my cloth under a hot tap and gaze out the window; the outhouse door is slightly ajar, which reminds me of Lowry, bless her soul. I hope that she-cat's nurturing those kittens and hasn't rejected them after Mr C's rash behaviour yesterday. Bless Lowry for standing up for what she believes in. Though I couldn't do her job, getting called out all hours of the day and night to tend to distressed animals. It must be upsetting seeing how some folks live and treat poor defenceless creatures. I'd spend half my time in tears. It makes me so angry when I see photos showing cruelty and neglect taken to aid prosecutions. I couldn't harm a fly – though if these pesky Carmichael boys pinch a midnight feast from my fridge again, I'll be making an exception to my moral code.

I hang the damp cloth on the door of the Aga to dry and scrub my hands before making a start on the birthday cake. I can decorate the wedding cake while Emmet's sponge is baking.

Some folk have their obsessions about stationery, books or shoes, like young Scarlet. Mine is food: baking, cooking or eating – a lifetime of enjoyment which is proudly displayed on my hips. I'd never trust a skinny cook, so I don't expect others to. I've planned for weeks for this weekend, noted every detail and organised my food shopping accordingly, but that wasn't foolproof, was it?

Flicking open my notebook, I browse my own instructions for Emmet's cake. As much as he's fighting the mere mention of celebrating his big birthday, it has to be done. Bless him, though he won't care to admit it, he's been struggling these past few months since he and Annabel went their separate ways. I don't think it matters if it's your decision or theirs, it still bloody hurts when the realisation comes. Like a sledgehammer to a crystal vase – there's little chance of a repair job, try as you might to glue the pieces back together. Not that I've had recent experience but I remember my younger days when I had dreams of a partner and a family of my own . . . before I gained this one, that is. He'll be fine in a few more months, but right now the pain is visible with his every breath.

It takes me minutes to collect the necessary equipment, the scales and baking tins – I'm so impressed that this rental cottage caters for every feasible task whilst staying here. I can't imagine they ever have any complaints from guests.

I gently close the door of the modern oven, which has its uses alongside the Aga, and set the cooking timer for two large sponges before fetching out the wedding cake safely stashed in the food stores. My heart was in my mouth all through the car journey from home; I kept peeking inside the cake boxes at each comfort break in case the layer of royal icing had cracked during transit, but thankfully Emmet drove like an angel.

I fill my icing bag dollop by dollop with white icing, scraping the bowl clean and hoping I've made enough to decorate the two-tiered wedding cake before me. I can see the finished detailing clearly in my head but my hands will have a mind of their own once I start swirling this nozzle around. The worst-case scenario will be scraping off the freshly applied detailing and redoing it if I'm not happy; I'm learning to accept such things. I spin the revolving cake board several times, hunting for the perfect spot at which to start.

The kitchen's back door opens revealing Teddy, breaking my concentration. I stop studying the cake.

'Hi, Martha, I managed to purchase every item on your list,' he announces, coming in laden with numerous shopping bags. Instantly, I know he's done his usual trick.

'Three bags? Added a little of what took your fancy whilst navigating the aisles, did you?'

'Some, but I could have bought a lot more,' he says defensively, depositing the bags on to the floor in front of the huge fridges.

'This will be worth seeing,' I mutter, pushing my immediate task aside and excusing his interruption.

I stand and watch as Teddy unpacks his goodie bags, holding each item aloft to receive a nod or my questioning in relation to my original list. He's not much changed since childhood, always placid and even-tempered, unlike the older two – though I've always been a believer in 'show me the boy of seven and I'll show you the man'. He's found a style of his own regarding dress sense; he likes to look after his appearance, which does him justice. Though his independence and mindset need to follow suit if he's to find happiness in the Carmichael business. Rupert doesn't need another Emmet or River; he needs Teddy to be Teddy, bringing his thoughts and ideas to the boardroom table.

'I couldn't find an advent calendar being as it's so late in the month but I did find mistletoe!' announces Teddy, producing a bound sprig from his shopping bag.

'Never mind. I'm not sure this family needs any practice opening tiny doors on a daily basis; in fact, come to think of it, they really don't need any encouragement to kiss relations either, Teddy,' I say, shaking my head and staring at the mistletoe sprig.

'Where should I hang it then?' asks Teddy, looking around the kitchen.

'It'll cause more trouble than it's worth so directly above the newel post on the staircase,' I say. No bugger will be able to stand under it then.

'See, I didn't let you down, unlike the time I got totally wasted in Dad's cellar,' he jests, emptying the final shopping bag.

'I always look past that incident, Teddy.' He knows he made a fool of himself, but what young kid hasn't?

'Just starting, are you?' he asks, slumping into the nearest chair, thankfully positioned out of my eye line, clutching his selection box which wasn't on my shopping list.

'Trying to, but my inner critic is playing harsh today,' I say, positioning my icing nozzle against the cake.

'Mine too,' he mutters, his gaze fixed on my pristine royal icing covering each cake tier.

'Anything worth sharing?' I ask, removing the icing bag from my chosen position as yet again he interrupts my start.

'Not really, just mulling stuff over.'

'Can I?' I gesture towards the cake.

'Sure, carry on. I won't disturb you,' he says, without lifting his gaze.

I give the cake board one final twist and decide on a new starting point on the blank canvas. My mind switches to auto-pilot as one hand guides and swirls the nozzle while the other gently applies pressure to the bag's contents. I stick with my tried-and-trusted designs, delicate but nothing overly complicated, as befits a wedding cake. Not that I haven't had lots of practice over the years; hopefully this will be Mr C's final one, fingers crossed.

I muster the will to begin icing, knowing that a steady hand is essential to create my usual flourish. Woe betide my reputation if I scrawl their wedding date like a child under the watchful eye of my audience. Why couldn't his shopping errand have taken him another twenty minutes?

'Bloody hell, Martha, you do that with such ease,' whispers Teddy, aware that I need quiet but obviously not willing to remain so.

'Pure practice, my lad.' My focus is intent on the icing nozzle.

'You could do that professionally, you know.'

'Thanks, but I already have enough employment hours each week without wanting more.'

'Don't you ever wish you'd chosen a role elsewhere?'

'Not really. I've enjoyed my time with this family. It's provided an income, a home and a family for me – what more could I want?' I fight back the emotion for fear it'll crack my voice, alerting him to my future plans.

'A life outside of this . . . We're hardly the easiest of families to cater for. And, as for the nonstop drama . . . that couldn't have been written into your contract all those years ago.'

I acknowledge his remark with a gentle nod. 'You're not wrong, but then my contract never predicted four tiny bairns tugging at my apron strings either. And I wouldn't change that for the world.'

I stop, twirl the cake board around to get access to the next blank section and begin piping again.

'I can't see it getting much better for me. Emmet's settled in his position, River is too, despite his constant moaning in the boardroom. Dad's content to slacken the reins of responsibility in their direction yet offers me very little in that respect. I can't see much changing until the inevitable occurs and that could be another twenty years away. I don't reckon I can wait that long working in their shadows.'

I lift my gaze from the cake, flicking him a look over the top.

'Seriously, Martha, I want something a little more challenging, where I can make a difference in other people's lives. Otherwise I'll sink into the routine and end up leaving it too late to risk going elsewhere.'

'And what would you do?' I ask, biting my bottom lip as I attempt a tricky design by layering on top of the previous details without leaving drying time.

'Who knows, but I won't find it if I don't look, will I?'

'You won't. But what happens if your best life is right under your nose and you don't realise?' I ask, playing devil's advocate, as lovingly as I can.

Teddy shrugs. 'I don't know. But what if my best life is else-where and I stay where I am, lingering on the sidelines and never seeking my true vocation?'

Brave answer, young man.

'Have you talked this through with any of the others?' I ask, not wishing to air a view, knowing even such innocent involve-ment might come back to bite me on the arse.

'Nope. They were all wrapped up in finalising big contracts before the Christmas deadline. Or the wedding, in Dad's case,' he explains. 'Whereas me – I simply closed the accounts files and set them aside for the festive period. They'll be untouched awaiting my return in January. Nothing will have changed, my desk will be as I left it.'

'I see . . . Any ideas about what you're seeking?'

'Change, I suppose.'

You and me both, lad – though mine might prove to be filled with bittersweet moments of deep regret. If I stay in service too long I might not have the time or health to enjoy the little nest egg I've put aside.

'That old chestnut – now, I've witnessed a lot of that during my years. I think you need to be a little more specific, Teddy.'

'Change of direction. Change of industry. Even a change of product – I reckon I could sell anyone a door in my sleep, the sales patter goes through my head morning, noon and night. I'm not even in sales!'

'Couldn't you ask Emmet for a transfer into his sales department – try your hand with him for a while before deciding to step aside? It might offer some resolution or a definite answer.'

'Maybe. And you?'

'Me?' I'm shocked by his question.

'Oh yeah, I forgot . . . you'll always be here – Dad's "angel who bakes".'

'Mmm,' I mutter, realising he is joking; many a true word said in jest. I wonder if he'll remember this moment later on.

Teddy sits back, chuckling to himself before standing tall, his chair scraping terribly on the tiled floor.

'Hmmm, sales department – I could do. Thanks, Martha.'

'You off?'

'Yeah, if I run, I might catch the rest of them scouting for Helen's Christmas tree.'

'Are we forgetting something?' I say, eyeing his selection box. 'How old are you?'

'Martha, who doesn't love a selection box at Christmas? A variety of Bournebury chocolate, the leading chocolate brand, all to yourself?'

'Yes, you used to stuff yourself silly straight after breakfast so there was always the danger you'd be sick before your Christmas dinner,' I recall with a smile.

'Do you want first dibs?' he asks, eagerly opening the packaging, instantly becoming that seven-year-old with cute blond curls and an impish grin. 'I'll even let you have the Crunchy Bournebury Brittle, if you want it.'

'Ooh, your favourite – I am honoured!' I won't deny him;

the offer is enough. 'I'll have the Chunky Nougat Nut instead, if I may?'

'Sure. Catch.' Teddy scoots the nougat bar across the table in my direction. I smile as he eagerly rips into his favourite bar with the enthusiasm of a schoolboy at the tuck shop. I put down my icing bag and do likewise, purely for old times' sake.

'Zipped tight, right,' I say, before taking my first bite. I'll continue my task once he's joined the others in gathering their tree and decorations.

'Too right, our secret,' mumbles Teddy through a mouthful of chocolate.

I don't watch him leave but I sense his shoulders are lighter on exiting than they were on entry. Such engagements weren't written into my contract thirty years ago, but it's moments such as these that warm my heart, knowing my worth in this family.

Lowry

'Come on, slowcoach,' calls my mum over her shoulder, as I lag behind the family pack. I'm wrapped up warm in my winter togs but I wish I'd stayed at the cottage with Martha. Or gone shopping with Teddy. Or even stayed in my room with Trixie, whom I pretended to visit in the outhouse after breakfast, only to sneakily collect soil for her makeshift litter tray. I can't even see the cottage or its neighbouring lake any more, we've walked so far, surrounded by dense woodland.

The smell of the damp earth, the scattered beams of sunlight and the birdsong are failing to distract my thoughts – unusual for me given my innate calling towards nature.

When Helen invited me to tag along, in search of a suitable Christmas tree, I imagined we'd be driving in convoy to a designated commercial site supplying festive goods to the public.

Not trekking through local woodland, peering at fir trees and deciding if we could nab that one or not? Again, if this is the usual behaviour of the Carmichael family, I'm a little concerned for my mum's future happiness.

When I was a youngster, our home might not have had the largest tree at Christmastime but it was always a real one, and most definitely legit, having been purchased from the local farm shop. We never hoiked a specimen from the roadside and claimed it as ours, which I have a distinct feeling is what's happening here.

I don't quicken my pace, surveying the party ahead: Rupert and his eldest sons plod over the rough terrain, each scouring left and right and pointing sporadically before holding a heated discussion. Helen trots behind them in a leisurely manner, admiring the surrounding flora whilst noting every move the men make.

'Are you OK?' asks Mum, linking her arm within mine, having waited for me to catch up.

'Yes, though I'm a little dubious about this outing. I thought we'd be visiting an actual farm to select and purchase a tree.'

'We-ell, maybe we will . . . later,' she says sheepishly, her gaze avoiding mine.

'Why's Emmet carrying an axe then? Unless my life is in danger and I'm being blindly led deep into the forest to be offered up and scarified in some crazy initiation ceremony.'

'Lowry, you do say the strangest things,' she mutters, shaking her head in disbelief.

'Do I? Or is this slightly weird?' I say, stopping dead in my tracks and forcing my mother to a standstill too. 'Because I think if Rupert can afford to rent a massive cottage, feed and house an entire blended family for five days without accepting a penny from the likes of me, who he only met yesterday, plus arrange a wedding off the cuff . . . then I think he can afford to buy a bloody big Christmas tree the way most people do, Mum.' I stare at her, forcing her gaze to meet mine. 'Seriously, we're technically trespassing and poaching a Christmas tree ... Afterwards will we be sourcing a turkey the same way or has Martha sorted that task already?'

'Now you're being daft – we aren't trespassing, this is the countryside. And of course she has. Martha collected the turkey from the butcher's only yesterday,' retorts Mum, irritated by my sulky remarks.

'How would I know? I never dreamt I'd go poaching with the new relatives, but hey, here I am! Happy holidays, folks, welcome to the Carmichael clan! Is this their idea of looking after you in the best possible way?'

'Helen loves this annual tradition, so please don't ruin it for her. She does so much for the family.'

'Why can't we ever have normality?'

'Lowry, we've always had normality.'

'Uh-uh, we had your version of normality, not mine. I was the only child in my primary class to live with my grandparents, the only kiddy whose mummy went to work each night once I was tucked up in bed. Admittedly not the only child with an absent father, but the only one who still knows nothing about her origins.' Cruel and unnecessary of me to throw in that final remark, usually stashed deep within my emotional arsenal, but you can't claim 'normality' when you're keeping secrets from your daughter. Mum won't argue back or share any details, despite my constant questioning at all ages. Her perpetual silence has created an invisible barrier between us which she seems unwilling to destroy by sharing any details about my father. And people wonder why I prefer the company of animals – uncomplicated creatures with no desire to deceive, deny or delay any sign of affection. 'Wouldn't it be easier to just tell me and be done with the topic? You can draw a line in the sand and start married life without this ... between us.'

'I'll remind you ... you were a child who had three adults

devoted to her upbringing, a little girl who was surrounded by unconditional love at every stage. Need I say more?' Nice sidestepping, Mum. And she wonders why I dislike this secrecy she's created about who I am. The truth allows light into your life, while secrets and lies linger much longer, casting darkness and shadows far into the future, blemishing happier days. Such as now. I shouldn't be mentioning my parentage on the weekend of her wedding! But it's present all the time, a shadow from the past ruining what could be between us. Regardless of the topic, I know she can hold back the smallest uncomfortable details if they don't fit the narrative she wishes to portray. And that fact unsettles me, every time.

'I just want normality for you, Mum, and this . . . this isn't normal.' I gesture fleetingly between us and then towards the Carmichaels ahead.

'Says who?'

'Me. I say.' Raising my hand, as if in a classroom.

'Hopefully by Tuesday evening, you'll have realised that normality doesn't exist in family life – each one is unique and somewhat different.'

'Tuesday evening? That's very specific.'

She gulps, a guilty look appearing on her face.

'Mum?'

'We jet off to Mauritius straight after the wedding reception – a quick outfit change, then off to Manchester Airport to catch an evening flight.'

'On the actual day! I thought you were flying the next day . . .' A thought dawns, forcing me to pause before continuing, 'I'll be left here amongst the family?'

'Yes. But Lowry, you'll know them by then and it'll be fun for you youngsters to spend time together.'

'Or I could just slope off too and enjoy a day or two at home before returning to work,' I say, starting to formulate my own plan.

'Lowry, please don't. That would be rude after they've made such an effort to welcome you.'

We've been standing chatting for some time and the others have clocked that we've stopped and have turned around to watch our interaction. Our body language must be screaming disagreement, if our expressions aren't.

'Diane, is everything OK?' calls Rupert, from the head of the pack.

'Happy now?' my mum hisses at me from the corner of her mouth before dragging a smile up from her boots and turning to answer her beloved. 'Yes, darling, with you in a second.'

'I want the very best for you. And so far, I've seen a beautiful cottage, heard about numerous marriages, come face to face with many offspring and apparently there's more expected to arrive tomorrow. Yeah, Mum, this is normality at its finest.'

'We need to walk otherwise they'll think—'

'Bugger what they think – you're not their mum! Or does that automatically happen once the vows are made?' I sound like a sulky teenager but I can't switch back to adult mode, as easily as I'd like.

'Give it time, you'll see.'

I don't reply. Instead, I warmly smile at the family ahead, all expectantly waiting for us to resume our happy outing.

I distance myself from my mum's company at the first possible chance; I don't want to run the risk of arguing again, and spoiling a pleasant memory ahead of her nuptials. Teddy walks ahead with Helen, having caught us up after running his shopping errand for Martha.

Walking amongst the winter foliage, with the smell of damp soil rising from underfoot, provides a grounded sense of reality. These aged woodlands have witnessed so much history and now I wander past, representing just a brief moment in their existence.

'How's it going, Lowry?' asks River, as we gather around a copse while Rupert and Emmet size up a particular spruce.

'Not bad. You?' I say, struck by his uncanny resemblance to Rupert, with those piercing blue eyes, though his tone isn't quite as harsh.

'So-so, to be fair. I wish this pair would hurry up and decide so we can return to the warmth. I'd much prefer to be indoors, enjoying a decent malt and watching festive movies, than choosing which fir to decimate so we can carry it back and decorate it with shiny paper chains.'

'You're not one for the outdoors then?' I ask, rather taken aback given his rugged appearance.

'Er, nope. What's to like? It's damp, dismal and dreary standing here amongst bare foliage with a low winter sun and no alcohol. You'd assume by my name that I'd have an affinity to nature and be at one with the woodland?'

I nod.

'Nah, you couldn't be further from the truth. My mum was a bit of a wild child in her youth so she chose a name to reflect her perceived values at the time. With Emmet's name being so biblical and wholesome, I was landed with the unconventional hippy label – neither name fits our personalities to be fair; he's hardly righteous.'

'What's in a name?' I mutter, remembering Juliet's quote from my school days.

'Ah, yeah, exactly – you may ask,' he says with a smile. 'Though yours is hardly common.'

'I like it though. My grandad suggested it – after the artist, but I couldn't draw a stick man if I tried.'

'I'm not as content with mine.'

'Haven't you a middle name you could go by?' I ask, trying to sympathise.

'Sure I have. How's Onyx grab you?'

I can't hide my instant reaction, a grimace. 'Are you sure your mother likes you?'

'Exactly. River Onyx Carmichael – it's got a certain ring to it, don't you think?'

'Sorry, but that's just cruel,' I say, stifling a giggle.

'Do you want to guess how bad the bullying was at school?'

I start to belly laugh, before managing to say, 'Your life would have been a living nightmare at my school.'

'It comes to something when a teenage boy wishes he'd been called Moses or Gabriel, to align with his older brother's biblical name. Ey up, finally, there's action,' says River, turning swiftly as the sound of an axe slicing bark fills the air. Everyone's conversation ceases as we stand watching Emmet perform under the attentive gaze of Carmichael Senior, who's holding his son's coat. I'm shocked at the crispness of the chopping sound; it seems surreal, like a sound effect created by Disney.

The swift arc of the axe being drawn back and swung high before it plummets towards the gaping wound appearing at the trunk's base is mesmerising. The spruce gives a wobble each time contact is made. I can't help but wonder if it hurts? Does it cry out, but we can't hear it?

Emmet continues in a steady rhythm, driving the axe blade through the trunk, his hands clasped tight around the wooden handle. His body weight sweeps through with each movement. His broad shoulders are set square, and his jaw fixed; he's determined to slay this giant.

A buzz of excitement begins deep in my stomach as I watch him repeatedly drive home at the one spot, creating a pale chasm within the bark. A glisten of sweat develops on his brow, his shirt darkens along his spine and beneath his arms, his dark curls are plastered to his forehead. Without warning, Emmet stops and stands tall, allowing the axe head to lower to the ground before drawing his hand across his brow. His brooding gaze connects with mine, and for a split second all else fades. A flicker of something, a thought or maybe a question, flashes through his mind as his eyebrows twitch, and I tear my gaze away. A vibrant humming in the pit of my stomach flares uncontrollably as my cheeks blush profusely. What was that?

'Are you alright?' asks River, looking bemused as I turn to face him.

'Sorry?' I'm lost in my own head, recalling the flicker of Emmet's brow.

'I said, are you alright?'

'Fine, thanks. Yeah, just fine.' The chopping sound resumes, each blow echoing through the copse and reverberating deep within me.

River eyes me cautiously before glancing towards his elder brother and I see a knowing smile slowly appear.

'What?' I say narkily.

'Nothing. All good in the hood, as they say.'

I pull a quizzical expression, suggesting he's the one out of kilter, in a feeble attempt to cover my own confusion.

Chapter Seven

Helen

I'm thrilled with our efforts to forage for natural decorations from the hedgerow and nearby woodlands. The spruce is far bigger than I intended but these things are hard to judge purely by eye. We all thought it was about seven foot, judging by the height of the three lads, but sadly not. They'll need to chop a considerable amount off the top for it to stand correctly in the lounge. I can't complain about the abundance of holly we found; it's obviously a good berry year, given the plumpness and quantity on each sprig. And the stark colour contrast between the foliage and fruit is so satisfying.

'Where is all this going to go?' asks Teddy, dumping his bundle of holly in front of the hearth.

'Across the high mantelpiece in here and in the dining room, woven through the staircase banister, above the doorframes in the hallway ... There won't be any wasted, don't you worry,' I say, gesturing as I explain.

'For a moment I thought you might not have a plan, Helen,' teases Teddy, neatening the holly pile with his foot.

'You mistake me for someone else, dear Teddy,' I say coyly.

'Shout if you need me. I'm nipping out the back to super-vise the dissection of the spruce,' he says, darting out of the lounge before I can set him to work. I have no idea where Diane or Lowry are, though I suspect they're having a heart to heart about this morning's disagreement. Lord knows what that was about, but it didn't look like an easy conversation, for either party.

'Helen, Dad asked if you'd come and take a look at this tree stump,' says River, entering the lounge as I'm standing before the front window, musing about the mother and daughter.

'Regarding what?'

'How much stump needs clearing of the lower branches and whether you want the stump end split to absorb the water.'

I sigh. These lads will be the death of me.

'We're only here for four more days, and we'll be removing all the decorations before we leave! Tell your father it doesn't matter given the time frame.'

River disappears, and I stir myself into action by readying the corner where I propose to put the tree. There's plenty of free space in this room but I'm liking the corner position by this front window, where it will be a focal point next to the hearth, slotted in beside the plasma TV, which I hope won't be on that much during our stay. Family conversation and interaction should be the name of the game; it's not as if we haven't seen every festive film a million times over.

'Are you not ready yet?' asks Rupert, entering the lounge with Emmet ahead of the tree-carrying party.

'Not quite. If you can grab the other end of the plastic sheeting, it'll be easier to lay it in this corner to protect the carpet from any water spillage,' I say, indicating the folded sheeting I found in the scullery. It takes minutes to lay it against the skirting board in the far corner, the metal tub will pin it securely in place and the piled presents will hide it from view. 'Can you busy yourself attempting to stand the tree upright, and make sure you set it properly amongst plenty of bricks, while I fetch a pail of water?'

'It'll be in front of the TV screen if we stand it there, Mum,' says Emmet, eyeing the positions of the plastic sheeting and the low-level plasma screen.

'You know I hate it when the Christmas tree is shoved in a corner unseen and forgotten,' I say, determined that the annual tree should be visible for maximum enjoyment.

Emmet shrugs. I assume my point is duly noted so I exit the lounge leaving them to their task.

'Martha, have we a bucket or a pail at hand?' I ask, nipping through her domain en route to the scullery area. Martha's standing before the Aga, stirring a pan of something delicious-smelling.

'Down the very back in the utility room, there's several – all of them clean,' she replies over her shoulder.

'Thank you.' I follow her instructions and find a clean metal pail just as she'd said. I go through to the scullery, taking a moment to admire the large butler sink and flagstones – I do love an original feature in a cottage and this place is full of such treasures. With the pail in the sink, I open the cold tap and wait while it fills sufficiently, remembering that I do have to carry it back through without slopping it on the carpets. I love it when plans come together and the family unit work together to forge happy memories.

'Hello, Helen, you haven't seen my mum, have you?'

I turn around to find Lowry in the scullery doorway.

'No, sorry. Everything OK?'

She shrugs, a somewhat glum expression on her face.

'It's difficult, not knowing how things are for her and not having spent time together before the wedding. I wanted to make . . .' She pauses, then shakes her head before lapsing into silence.

'I get it. You wanted to make sure all is well before she commits to Rupert. And you haven't had the best first impressions, have you?'

Lowry's expression breaks into a smile. 'No, not really. It's ridiculous but I wanted to fall in love with him too, for my mum's sake.'

'I understand that. I felt that way about Annabel, Emmet's last girlfriend. I so wanted to like her, wanted to be bowled over by her and enjoy her company and marvel at the relationship she was building with my son, only to find . . .' I lower my voice at this point, for fear anyone else hears my confession. 'Only to find that she irked me with her neediness and, dare I say it, her hold over him. That's sounds awful, because he was head over heels for her but me, urgh! Not that I wanted to see my lad's heart broken but he'll survive, and maybe next time . . . I too will be lucky enough to enjoy her company.'

'That's it exactly, Helen.'

'What do you need to know? I can tell you most things about Rupert.' Lowry inclines her head as if I'm joking. 'Seriously now, I'll be honest. No one's perfect, but the man doesn't show his good side to many people and you might not see it before the vows take place. Honestly, ask away.'

'Will he look after her . . . properly, I mean?'

'Without a doubt. The man might have had four divorces but his heart is in the right place; he's been fair every time. Admittedly, some marriages have been more war-like than others' – I widen my eyes to stress that little point – 'but each marriage has ended with the children being the priority and the mother always having what she needs. Again, some want more than their fair share, but Rupert has always negotiated towards a satisfactory conclusion for all parties. Surely that's obvious given that he is now on amicable terms with all four women – that is no mean feat!'

Lowry is taking in every word. Bless her for worrying and for being brave enough to venture there. I'd like to think my Emmet would do the same for me, though as I've never met another man I was even remotely interested in after Rupert, such a situation has never arisen.

'I've had more than enough Christmases where my heart hasn't been in the festive mood and I've been on autopilot simply to get through the proceedings for the sake of my child. Rupert has always included us, both of us, that is – not just demanding his boy for the festive period, as some men might. Money has never been a worry: Rupert has always been generous with his allowances and his responsibilities towards Emmet and myself. We made a commitment to each other in planning our boy, and we've never shirked that responsibility. I can't complain, other ex-husbands wouldn't have done as much over the years.' Though I suppose his sense of guilt may have spurred that on a little, though I don't say this to Lowry, it might seem bitter. 'Either way, I've never had to go without. Personally, there have been many lonely days when I'd have liked to experience love for a second time. Not the foolish type of love belonging to my younger days but a mature love filled with honour and respect.' I fall silent and blush, hoping I haven't been too honest.

'Thank you, Helen – that's put my mind to rest in some respects. You've been very helpful,' she says, squeezing my forearm in appreciation.

'Good. As I always say, you only need to ask,' I say, checking the cold-water tap is fully turned off before heaving the filled pail from the sink.

'Are you sure you can manage that?' she asks, gesturing to the pail.

'Yes, thank you. I'd best hurry back – leaving the blokes to their own devices for too long always ends in trouble. You'll learn that sooner rather than later.'

'I'll remember that, Helen.' She gives a little giggle. I begin a slow walk with the water pail, and Lowry follows my steady steps right the way to the lounge door, where we separate and she flies up the staircase, probably heading to her bedroom or in search of her mother.

'Sorry for taking so long but – my God, what the hell have you done to the tree?' I shriek, staring at the square chunk cut from its lower branches made to measure around the TV plasma screen. 'You think you're so damned funny, don't you? Well, news for all – you're not! You've ruined it!' I hand the water pail to Teddy and leave the room, much to the hilarity of the four men belly-laughing at their own juvenile antics. I swiftly follow Lowry up the staircase, much sooner than I intended, in search of my own solace.

Martha

It's taken the best part of my day but I'm delighted with the end result – Emmet's celebration cake looks great. He'll be grateful, but I baked it for Helen, if the truth be known. I appreciate the effort she goes to all year round for others; it's the least I can do to show a mother her son is also treasured by the rest of us.

My plans for the future keep whirling around my mind each time I'm left alone; I'm struggling to suppress the ideas when others aren't around. I have a little nest egg, nothing grand or substantial but enough to ensure I can take the trip of a life-time before I'm unable to. I've seen the world with this family, honest I have. Be it the annual beach holidays to the Maldives or Bahamas, the winter skiing in Austria or Italy, and even the luxury cruise liners – when you'd think they'd leave their own cook behind to babysit the homestead at Cloisters. Of all the trips I've been on with the Carmichael family, the only holiday they were forced to cancel was Hawaii, when Mr C's father passed. The only place I ever dreamt of visiting. I'm not certain what it is that appeals to me about it, because the first two things anyone ever says when Hawaii is mentioned is the amount of construction work and the extortionate price of everything. I'll admit I was shocked to hear about the towering buildings and commercialism, but I still yearn to go there, just once in my life.

To see the beauty of Wailua Falls, the volcanoes and rainforests and taste the local cuisine will be my dream come true. My expectations might be high, and the cost higher than imagined, but I know I can't work all my life – even though I've enjoyed it as much as I have – and then go to my grave without a single regret. I'm sure many would assume I regret not having a life partner of my own, or children, but I've had the best of both worlds here with the Carmichaels. Those four bairns have brought as much love and enjoyment into my world as if they were my own flesh and blood. And as for a spouse, well, Mr C's been testament that not everything works out in life just how you'd like. Maybe I've saved myself time and heartache in that department, unlike him.

I can't grumble: many people spend a lifetime investing energy and effort into a family only to find themselves alone in their later years, regardless of their hopes and dreams. I count myself as one of the lucky ones, unlike my mother – so I'm going to learn from her example. She worked herself into the ground in service at those stately houses and for what? To end her days with just me to tend to her needs, without a word of thanks from the big house, not even a funeral wreath on behalf of the estate. I won't be making the same mistake, though I already know this family wouldn't dream of treating me in that manner when my time comes.

As I fill my icing bag with blue icing to prepare for the finishing touches, I hear an impatient rap on the front door and instantly know who has arrived: Janie Carmichael.

I could have done with just ten more minutes to finish the cake, but unless I'm very much mistaken I'll be needed on hand to help ease the tensions. I probably have five minutes before my services are required so I do my best to inscribe a loving birthday message, adding a decorative flourish or two along each side of the cake to enhance the overall appearance. I stand back to assess my handiwork: a birthday message scrawled in blue icing – not my best script. In fact worse, nothing but a shaky, quivering mess. I'll need to scrape off the blue lettering and clean up the white icing beneath before making a second attempt.

'Martha!' I hear Diane's call before she enters the kitchen, and have only a brief moment to straighten my pinny, hide the offending cake and lose my empty icing bag amongst the dirty crockery piled by the sink.

'Coming,' I say, drying my hands as we meet in the doorway. 'I've put the kettle on ready for tea, Diane.'

'Thank you, Martha. I believe another guest has arrived . . . she's currently in the lounge. Should I . . .?' Diane's all of a dither, which is to be expected as she hasn't met this ex-wife before.

'We'll go through, shall we?' I say, as respectfully as I can muster.

'Yes, could we?'

I lead the way, knowing that we need to make an appearance purely for politeness but nothing more will be asked of us in Janie's presence. Diane lingers outside the open doorway, clearly visible to those within thanks to the removal of the door. Rupert and the boys are in various stages of resettling in their seats after greeting Janie interrupted their enjoyment of a James Bond movie.

'Look at these beautiful garlands of holly – I assume Helen's been busy again. Oh Martha, still here? Surely you've come to your senses by now, old gal?' squeals Janie, looking spritely with her maroon-coloured spiky crop and taking centre stage before the hearth, dressed in red leather trousers and a thoroughly modern top that reveals a bare right shoulder.

'Hello, Janie, looking lovely as always,' I say, nearing to give and receive the usual kiss on each cheek, as is our custom. She was always one for kisses, very demonstrative from the first time I met her.

'How are you bearing up keeping this lot in check?' asks Janie, looking past me at Diane, who looks fearful of the newcomer. 'And this must be Mrs Carmichael-to-be. Congratulations, my dear ... I hope you prove more successful than the rest of us, though Helen and Martha here have a proven track record so a few helpful tips might be available. But still, I sincerely wish you the very best of luck! Though if it all falls through, refuse any job offer he might make, then come and do daily shopping sprees and boozy luncheons with me!'

I baulk at her words but smile – this is classic Janie. If anything, she's mellowed over the years. I remember the time she'd run around the house in bikini bottoms and nothing else, when visiting the newly-wed Helen and Rupert.

'She means it in good faith, Diane,' I say wrapping my arm around Diane's back, hoping she takes no offence from the one-time 'wild child' of Rupert's previous brides. Diane's gaze flickers towards Rupert for reassurance, which he offers in his typical manner, which is considerably lacking in what a woman sometimes needs.

'Janie, this young lady is Lowry ... my daughter, my only child,' says Diane, gesturing towards the couch whilst recovering from Janie's brash introduction.

'Lovely to meet you, Lowry. I'm sure they've all welcomed you to this mismatch family but let me be the first to say, family ties mean that no matter how much you might want to run from your family, you won't outrun this bunch! Believe me, I have tried!' says Janie, which provokes a roar of laughter from the other family members, including a titter from myself.

'Janie! How well you look,' exclaims Helen, dashing into the lounge, her arms open wide to greet the second wife. 'How was your journey?'

'Dreadful drive through all those tiny narrow lanes. I'm surprised I got here in one piece and that the car wasn't scratched to smithereens with all those hedgerows and twiggy branches,' replies

Janie, embracing Helen in a bear hug and returning the peck on the cheek. 'I was just saying, beautiful decorations, Helen – they're very *au naturel* – though I don't think much to your tree.'

'Stop, please don't mention it! I'm ashamed of it. The lads butchered it in my absence,' says Helen, waving a dismissive hand towards the giant spruce with its cut-out section snugly fitting around the edge of the plasma screen. The men smirk at each other behind her back.

'Have you missed me, sister?'

'Actually, I've been very . . .' begins Helen.

'Sister?' gasps Lowry, her mouth dropping wide in astonishment as she stares at the two women standing before the hearth.

'Bugger, that's a bomb drop!' mutters Emmet to River.

'Don't you just love it when that penny drops!' replies River to his older brother.

'You two are sisters?' mutters Lowry, gesturing between the two, before glaring at Mr C in the armchair. 'You married sisters?' No one answers her, as we wait for the final penny to drop, which takes a little longer than usual as Lowry slowly turns towards Emmet and River, staring in disbelief.

'Yep, we're technically brothers but also cousins. My mum did mention River was her nephew when you first arrived, Lowry – don't you remember?' explains Emmet in a gentle voice.

'It's true, I did. I always do. He's my nephew but also a stepson,' adds Helen.

'And he was once my husband but a brother-in-law before that role,' offers Janie, biting her bottom lip in a comedic way and pointing at Rupert. 'Sooo naughty of us, but if Helen can forgive and forget . . .'

'I never forgot!' interrupts Helen, raising her index finger towards her younger sister.

'OK, I was pushing my luck there, but if Helen can forgive . . . then . . . well, you know.'

'And you think that's acceptable?' Lowry is on her feet, staring at Mr C, and her expression is one of horror.

'Now there's a question never put to him before!' says Emmet, with River and Teddy nodding fervently in agreement like the front row of an audience. I don't know what to do: make my excuses and leave the lounge, bundle the young woman out of the room or remove Diane, who appears to be frozen to the spot in shock. And as for Mr C, his expression says it all – total disbelief.

'Lowry . . . please don't!' cries Diane, her hands flying to her chest as if in self-protection. Lowry blushes profusely, before slowly lowering herself back into her seat, startled by her own outburst.

'I admit that I-I-I have m-m-made numerous m-m-mistakes as a young man,' Rupert stammers, looking between his three lads, and I'm not sure if he's talking to them or viewing the evidence of his behaviour. 'And I regret creating issues that have loomed over this family due to my actions. I love each member of my family dearly and hold them all in high regard.'

Issues? I've never heard him refer to such things before – that in itself, hearing something new, seems strange after serving this family for so long. Maybe this is Diane's influence shining through.

'I think this particular matter needs to be discussed privately, Rupert,' says Helen, glancing around the lounge and reaching out towards Diane to offer comfort, which is gratefully received.

'I'll fetch the tea through, shall I?' I say, knowing it never fails to soothe this family when the nerves are rattled. It also provides thinking time for those involved in the actual drama.

'I'll lend you a hand, Martha,' says Lowry, jumping up to follow me from the room.

I hold the kitchen door open for her to dart through. Lowry's cheeks remain flushed and her expression startled. The young woman is visibly shaking.

'Sit down and give yourself a minute, Lowry,' I say, drawing a chair from beneath the table. I busy myself with teapots, leaves and trays, suspecting she's in a state of shock.

'Martha, help me to understand, please. He married Helen, they had Emmet and then he divorced her and dated her younger sister, Janie – married her and then had River and then ... divorced her too? Is that what happened?'

I turn, looking over my shoulder to confirm her thoughts. I don't think I need to tell her the lines were a little blurred and the timings more overlapping; that's the nature of an affair.

'My word, you hear of this sort of thing but you never think it actually happens in families,' she says, adding, 'Surely there are social rules that we each live by which say dating sisters is out of bounds, marrying sisters is totally off-limits?'

'Is love not blind?' I say, repeating the well-worn phrase I've heard used over the years.

'Surely not that blind. What on earth did Helen's parents think? Divorcing one daughter to be with another, phew, no way!' Lowry puts her head in her hands, muttering, 'And this is the man my mum wishes to marry?'

I can't comment; it wouldn't be right or my place. I mash the tea leaves and arrange an accompanying plate of biscuits.

'I'm taking this through, are you coming back in?' I ask, knowing it'll be easier that way. If this china rattles much more as I carry the tray, I'll have Helen asking me outright what's wrong! Seriously, I sound like the percussion section of an orchestra!

Lowry shakes her head, before standing. 'I need time to think. I'll be in my room if anyone asks for me.'

'Here, take a cuppa with you,' I say, putting the tea tray down before pushing a mug into her hand. 'Shout if you need me.'

Chapter Eight

Lowry

I open the wardrobe door, plonk myself cross-legged on the floor and sip my tea whilst watching Trixie nursing her kittens. Despite her poor condition and dull-looking coat, she's a sight to behold in her makeshift nest: a contented mum doing what nature does best – without human interference. Or creating, what did Rupert say, 'issues' within other people's lives?

'Bloody hell, that was a confession and a half! Long looming shadows more like, which have stretched to encompass many people. Worse still, he now wishes to involve my mum in this jumble of a family,' I mutter to the mother cat, purely to air my view. 'No such worries for you, hey?' Trixie noses her young, encouraging them to suckle, though from where I'm sitting they appear to be gutsy little kittens. I could happily sit and watch this scene all day, and back at the rescue centre I often do; it beats dashing home to an empty flat to watch a night of repeat dramas or the soaps on TV.

There's a sharp rap on my bedroom door, followed by a male voice: 'Lowry, it's Teddy.'

I gently push the wardrobe door almost closed, allowing a small gap to remain, leave my mug of tea on the dresser and ready myself to address my guest.

'Hi, Teddy, can I help you?' I say, poking my head and shoulders around the door.

'I wondered if you were OK, if you were coming back

downstairs,' asks Teddy, thumbing over his shoulder. 'I promised your mum I'd fetch you down.'

'Thank you, but I'd like a little time to think, if that's OK.'

'Are you sure, Lowry? We're not a conventional family, never have been and I doubt we ever will be . . . If I can help, I'm happy to,' offers Teddy. His blue gaze seems steady and honest.

I allow the door to open a little further, not as unwelcoming as I first appeared on answering.

'Sure you don't mind? I might seem a little intrusive with my line of questioning.'

'Mmm, I do hope so – it wouldn't be much fun otherwise,' he jests. I open the door even wider, stepping aside to accept Teddy's kindly offer. 'There's a sofa here where we can pitch,' he says.

'Well, I have two decent chairs in here; it'll offer a little more privacy than the landing, if you're happy to sit. Help yourself, the starting clock will begin as soon as I am comfy,' I quip, feeling embarrassed to have caused a situation that's made him feel obliged to reassure me.

I settle opposite, pause and then launch into my questions.

'Has your dad ever apologised before for causing such issues within the family? Sorry to harp on, but having listened to the introductions – it impacts on everyone, doesn't it?'

'No, never before. Though he's never been asked such questions so . . . forcefully by someone outside the family. It's the cause and effect of his actions, isn't it? Marrying sisters and having a child with each isn't the norm. Helen rarely mentions it but the effect on her as a woman must have been profound. She must have been distraught when she found out, because let's be honest, I can't imagine they'd have come clean before an affair began, so they must have got together behind her back. And that's never fair on anyone, is it?'

'Never. It must be soul-destroying and worse still when you

think of typical sisterly relationships,' I add, feeling really uncomfortable.

'Exactly. River's always been honest about his own misgivings about their behaviour and Helen always refers to him as her nephew. I don't think she can bring herself to acknowledge the stepson angle, despite the divorce.'

'I've never understood the stepchildren label anyway,' I say, waving the idea aside.

'We siblings never have either, we're simply brothers and sister. Which now includes you.'

'Mmm, lucky me,' I jest, not sure if I could offend Teddy. 'And what about your mum – when did she come on the scene?'

'Not long after River was born. There's only two years between me and him, and two years between the eldest two too.'

'He wasn't slow off the mark, was he?' I mutter more to myself, quickly adding, 'Sorry, that sounded so judgemental of me.'

'I'm pretty judgemental myself, and he's my father, Lowry. If anything, he's taught me how not to act as a man, if you get my gist.'

I nod, not daring to speak.

'And then there's Scarlet ... she's a fair few years younger than me at twenty and most definitely a daddy's girl – she puts us lads to shame with her devotion to our father.'

'Her mother is called ...?'

'Fena. We often joke that she's the stunner who caught Dad's eye when he decided to go travelling to clear his head after his third divorce. Scarlet has that striking mix of genetics which gives her a captivating appearance ... which I believe she uses to her full advantage.'

'She's a model then?'

'Hair and beauty, yeah – you'll understand why when you see her raven black hair – down to here it is.' Teddy does a blokey cutting action halfway down his upper arm. 'She's my sister, but she's a stunner . . . looks-wise.'

Looks-wise? I hear his final comment and interpret it to mean there's some noticeable flaw or absence in the personality department.

'It's a lot to take in so . . . anything else you'd like to know?'

I ponder before asking; I don't wish to appear rude or judgemental, like earlier.

'Can I ask what's the issue with Emmet . . . he seems a little distant?'

Teddy takes a deep breath, shifts in the wicker seat before answering. 'He's getting over one of life's hurdles, shall we say, a break-up. He's taken it hard, not bounced back as we all thought he might and right now he seems intent on testing every bottle of Scotch within easy reach. He's smoked like a chimney for years, which bugs the hell out of Helen – she hates smoking.'

'Me too. I really don't see the attraction.'

'I agree, but it's been his coping mechanism since uni, so I can't see him changing any day soon, not on that front anyway. The Scotch he'll drop when he sees fit – he hasn't got a problem, if that's what you're asking.'

'And River?'

'River's River. What you see is what you get where he's concerned. He pleases himself most of the time, but there's a brotherly rivalry, as you saw with the door removals last night. That's usually Emmet's trick but River got in first, with Emmet being off top form.'

'And his birthday?'

'Yep, rubbish timing, hey? Helen has arranged celebrations for his thirtieth but he'll not thank her for making such a fuss at the minute. I'm sure he'll want to celebrate at some point, just not now. We'll take him out on the lash one weekend when he's ready.'

'You lads get on well, then?' Teddy's proving easy to chat to, and if he cares to ask me questions, I'll probably answer him as honestly.

Teddy nods, a beaming smile adorning his features. 'We sure do, given the circumstances. Did you ever want three brothers and a sister growing up?'

'Honestly? Nope. I was happy with what I had: my mum, grandparents and a houseful of pets. There was no squabbling that way. A child only knows what it lives.'

'Nice deal. How're the kittens getting on in the outhouse?' asks Teddy.

'Fine. The mother accepted them back after their brief separation, which was a stroke of luck,' I say, trying hard to stop my gaze drifting towards the open wardrobe door.

'He would never harm them, you know – Dad's not like that.'

I don't answer, for fear of dobbing myself in, and secondly, I know that the briefest of separations could have been disastrous for the kittens, had their mother refused to accept them back.

Rap a tap, tap!

We both turn towards the closed door, like guilty teenagers caught red-handed up to no good.

'Hello? Come in,' I call.

The door slowly opens and my mother appears. 'Ah, you're busy, I see. I wanted a word if you were free,' she says, sending a weak smile in Teddy's direction.

'I think we're done, aren't we?' says Teddy, turning towards me.

'I think so, but if I think of any other questions, I'll come and find you,' I say, grateful for his time.

'You do that,' says Teddy. My mother lingers by his chair awaiting his exit, forcing him to promptly stand. 'Diane.'

'Thank you, Teddy,' murmurs my mother, as he passes her heading for the door. From her expression, I think I'm in for it, though my mother rarely picks fault with my behaviour. 'Nice chat?'

'Yeah, pretty much. They're all trying to ease my nerves in one way or another,' I say, fighting the surly tone which even I can hear. My mother settles in the vacant chair. She's looking decidedly pensive. I'll wait; it's clear she's got something to say.

'I didn't appreciate your reaction earlier, Lowry. I know it comes as a shock hearing the full details of Rupert's life but can I ask that in future—'

'Future? Are you suggesting there's more enthralling episodes to come? Because if I'm currently at the dramatic dum-dum-dum stage of this to-be-continued soap opera I'd prefer not to be left in suspense a minute longer!'

'Lowry!' Her teeth are gritted, her hackles are up. 'Look, I had my reservations at first, but these are his past relationships – Rupert's been single for at least twelve years.'

'You've had weeks to digest this information. I've had less than a day and you're expecting me to fall into line because it'll save face amidst the Carmichael family. I'm not part of the Carmichael family –'

'Yet.' Her voice is low, barely audible.

'No, Mum. I'm a Stephens. I'm not taking his name – you are! Which is why I'd quite like to feel comfortable with the match prior to your wedding day, if that's not too much to ask. And as for my reaction, I'm sorry, OK? Sorry that I had higher expectations of your husband-to-be. Sorry that I didn't pack my game face for a Christmas weekend and a family wedding. Topped with my sincerest apologies if your shocked daughter embarrassed you in front of a delusional family who think this blended crap is the modern norm. It's not! Blended families fight, squabble, argue and some openly but very honestly despise each other. They don't sodding embrace each other as if living in some kind of cult! But one thing they've got over me – they at least know who their father is!' There, I've said too much. I knew I would.

'Well, if you're going to be like that.' She's out of the wicker chair quicker than a cat on a hot tin roof, heading towards the door before turning abruptly. 'I'm doing the best I can, Lowry. These are the circumstances of the man I love – I didn't play a part in creating them but I can play my part in easing the drama.'

'What, like Helen does?'

'Helen is lovely. She's given her heart and soul to this family – you'd do well to take a leaf out of her book.' She raises her index finger at me like she used to when I was a child.

'She certainly has. But where's it got her, Mum? Decades as a divorcee organising Rupert's entire brood. Is that what you want?'

She sighs heavily; she's run out of words. Lost for explanations with which to defend the indefensible. It feels a bit like my visits home in recent years, which have been filled with strained silence for fear I'd ask the same old question.

'I'll see you downstairs. Please join us – when you're ready,' she says before departing.

Helen

'What's the news then, sis?' asks Janie the second we're in the snug, the door securely closed and each of us settled on opposing sofas. Janie has her usual festive coffee, with a tipple of Irish cream added for good measure, which she tries to convince us is a single shot but a double is more likely. I settle for my usual black coffee, a sensible single shot from the kitchen's chrome gadget.

'You know Rupert. Meet, get engaged and book the wedding in twelve weeks.' I raise my eyebrows for effect.

'Hardly a shotgun affair, given their ages, but still, why now, after all these years he's happily plodded along with this blended arrangement and now . . . well, number five – who'd have thought it. She seems very nice though.'

'Diane's lovely, she's fitted in very well. Lowry seems to be stressing a little, but it's understandable; she only met us yesterday.'

'No pre-meet and greet then?'

'Nope, which is unfortunate. Diane had the advantage of meeting us one at a time over Sunday lunches, afternoon tea and specific visits arranged by Rupert literally from the moment they met, but Lowry has been thrown in at the deep end. I never know how to broach the question of our connections. I always say the nephew line, hoping the penny will drop, but it obviously didn't in this case. I believe Teddy is having a quiet chat now, in the hot seat for twenty questions, that kind of thing.'

'I hope she takes full advantage of his generosity; I know my River would never offer his time so generously. Emmet might, if he were in a better place. Is he still . . . you know?'

'Pining, full of woe . . . oh yes. I can't wait for him to snap out of it, this thing with the whisky and his ciggies is wearing a bit thin now.'

'Oh Helen, the lad's hurting.'

'I know, but for how much longer? She wasn't the nicest person, treated him shoddily from what I saw and rarely made an effort with his friends or his interests . . . hardly supportive, was she? But I'm holding my tongue. You can't say too much about these things, just in case.'

'In case of what?'

'In case she returns.'

'I doubt it, Helen. I think Emmet has more self-respect than to allow that to happen after what he's been through. She waltzed off, out of the blue, leaving him in trouble with the mortgage, and as for those credit card debts she dumped on him – well, it's taken months to sort out but I can't imagine she'd have the nerve to show her face. Rupert's helped him out, of course, but even so Emmet must have had many a sleepless night mulling over what she'd done. Nah, a return isn't possible.'

'She knows it's his big birthday this weekend – she might chance her luck,' I say, wishing I were as confident as my sister. 'Act the innocent, so to speak.'

'I wouldn't think so, lovey. Anyway, what about you?' asks Janie, swigging her coffee.

'Home alone each night waiting for my son to call, that's my usual routine.'

'And it's been that for far too long. I've got a new friend . . . Darius. Worldly-wise and as keen as mustard. We've been out the last three weekends and we click' – she snaps her fingers in front of her face – 'just like that. It's as easy as being alone being with him. None of those awkward silences, clashing of topics or difference of opinions . . . seriously, it's like talking to myself half the time.'

I wince. Is that really what she wants?

'What's wrong with that? It's lovely. No treading on eggshells about religion or politics or attitudes toward one's children . . . we've hit it off and I'm simply enjoying myself. Oh, come on, Helen. A girl's got to have a little fun when you get to our age. I've done the wife and mother thing – and look how well that turned out! River's well and truly off our hands, and Rupert has always carried out his duties regarding the lad, so he'll never go far wrong, will he? So why not? Me time, that's what is needed now.'

She's got a valid point, but where does one start nowadays? If my son's having such difficulties finding a nice girl at his age, what are the chances of me finding a decent gent at mine. Phew! More chance of Rupert not showing up come Tuesday's wedding and standing Diane up at the altar. That would never happen – Rupert is always early for his weddings.

'I know what you're thinking, what's the point? Relationships are more hassle than they're worth – but trust me, Helen, you need some fun in your life and the waxing schedule is far less hassle than it used to be.'

I don't answer her but sip my drink instead. Trust? Not a word that exists in my world. She's got a bloody nerve even uttering the word. If I can't trust my own sister, my own blood, to be left alone with my husband, while I nip to the shop for a few items without coming back to find them at it on the lounge floor of our holiday caravan, with our baby asleep in his cot! Don't talk to me about trust . . . I'll never trust anyone in my life again. Ever.

I put my coffee cup down and curl my legs beneath me, not that I'm trying to create a barrier between us but some wounds remain raw regardless of apologies.

'What's the plan for the wedding? I take it there's an itinerary in which we each must play a part?' asks Janie, swiftly changing the subject.

I give her a look, as if she doesn't know better than to ask.

'A two o'clock wedding, full regalia of bridal party and groomsmen, bouquets, a procession of wedding cars and a simple reception at a local pub. Though one small difference – they've each written their own vows, apparently.'

'It figures – that would have to happen one day. What do they say, "If you keep doing what you've always done then you'll keep getting what you've always got"? Never a truer word spoken.'

'Janie, you are awful.' I can't help but smile, even though she did me wrong in her younger years. She's never been any different with her minxy ways, yet we've always found a way through the mire.

'It's not worth attending one of Rupert's weddings if you can't have a giggle at the extravagance he puts on, knowing the old bugger's going to mess it up in, what . . . three years, is that the longest marriage?'

'Three years and two months to Fena, though Lynette's came close, just three months less.'

'Phew. Lynette. Is she coming?'

I tilt my head and give a coy smile. Here we go!

'Ahh, I thought she'd have bailed on this one.'

'She's never bailed before on family gatherings so I don't see why she would now. Her room is ready and waiting for her arrival this evening.'

'Bloody great. She can bore us all to death with her constant dull-as-ditchwater Zen rituals.'

'Don't be mean.' I know what her next line will be.

'Come off it, Helen. The only good thing about Lynette is Teddy. I can't actually believe Rupert left me for the likes of her. She's like a wet weekend in ... in ... I can't actually think of a place as boring as Lynette.'

'Janie.'

'But it's true. I've never seen the attraction – she's as plain as a plain Jane can be and yet she clocked up longer than either of us. Go figure! The man must have been out of his mind choosing that one, unless she's got skills in the bedroom, which I very much doubt given the way she acts so prim and proper. Unless it involves her ridiculous shoulder shimmy that she puts on! I ask you, Helen – what's that all about?' Janie instantly performs the shimmy move as if I've forgotten.

'You can't say that!' Funny how every woman questions a man's sanity when she views the woman he left her for. I should know: been there, done that, even questioned my own sanity and self-worth after my divorce from Rupert – numerous times. Still do, on occasion. Many occasions, in fact. But you can't go through life comparing yourself to others, nit picking every detail of your appearance or character. It would be so destructive – like a self-assassination. Especially when the other woman's your sister! Have I become the woman I always should have been? Or have I been moulded by Rupert's behaviour and other women's fancies?

'Why can't I? Believe me, he had no complaints about me in that department so she either won him over with her Little Miss Coy act or she's a bloody freak between the sheets. Though I can't see it myself.' Janie performs another shoulder shimmy for good measure, before giggling.

I'm lost for words.

'What?'

'Nothing. Anyway, Scarlet arrives early tomorrow morning,' I say, sidestepping any further discussion about Lynette.

'On Christmas friggin' Day? Couldn't she spare the time to grace us with her presence for a little longer? Not that I'm disappointed – that girl's too full of herself. Bloody me, me, me all the time. Stop laughing, it's not funny, Helen.'

I can't help myself. It's even funnier that Janie may secretly recognise the connection between herself and young Scarlet. She can't stand to be outshone by the younger generation.

'Seriously, she makes me feel old,' mutters Janie, knocking back her coffee.

'And that's what narks you.'

'She's like Betty Boo on coke ... and that's what narks me!'

Lowry

'Lowry, are you free for a chat?'

I look up from the TV to see Rupert standing in the lounge doorway, waiting for my answer. Teddy and River glance between us before returning their attention to *How the Grinch Stole Christmas*. I nod and immediately stand up, sensing I'm about to have an insightful talk.

'Shall we?' asks Rupert, indicating the snug as I join him in the hallway. I'd have thought the dining room more appropriate given he is being so formal but the snug works for me.

We settle on the opposing sofas, and immediately I feel he's ill at ease in the pastel-painted room, with its squidgy soft furnishings and abstract paintings. This hulk of a man, silent in many ways yet forthright in others, is like the sun around which this family revolves and his decisions cast long lingering shadows in his wake.

'I wanted a little chat, to get to know each other. I'm sorry we haven't spent any time together before this weekend. I appreciate that my family circumstances are more complicated than for most men my age. I wanted to assure you that I have the best of intentions regarding your mother. I'm also aware that our engagement, the announcement and wedding preparations have been very swift, but neither of us has time on our side, so to speak, not that I have any immediate health issues to be worried about, other than a touch of angina. I simply didn't wish to wait. I'm a true believer that when you know, you know. And I assure you, Lowry – I've been bowled over by your mother since the moment we met. I'm not expecting you to decide overnight whether we're to establish a firm friendship or simply be acquaintances – it might take months for us to get to know each other – but through weekend visits and open discussions I'm hoping that you'll see how happy your mother is – which is my primary concern. If I can't make her happy, Lowry – then I have no other reason for being part of your life.'

I'm taken aback; his little speech sounds genuine and honest.

'Thank you, I appreciate the sentiment. My mother is my only concern – which is why I'm here. I'd probably be covering a shift at work otherwise.' Not that Big Boss Roger would allow me to do that, but I'm fully aware of my faults and where my weaknesses lie, unlike some I could mention.

'Is there anything you want to know? Anything at all,' he says, settling back on his sofa and staring intently at me.

'Maybe a little background about you,' I say politely, hoping he realises I mean other than the marriages and children.

'Well, let's see . . . I was an only child, raised by both mother and father in Todmorden. I went to grammar school, after which I joined the family business that my father had inherited from his father. I started on the warehouse floor as the tea boy with additional duties, albeit mainly sweeping up the wood shavings. By the age of eighteen, I was allowed to assist in the manufacturing process of wooden doors rather than simply watch and learn from my elders. Year on year, I was given more responsibility until my father retired aged sixty. After that, I took sole ownership of the business, employing relatives or family friends as I saw fit. My lifelong pal from school, Gunner Jeffery, being one of them, though he has left for pastures new, as he's previously done on many occasions. He's currently working in telesales somewhere in London – I've no doubt he'll be gracing our factory floor with his presence again one day.'

I listen carefully, not just to the details but to the manner in which he tells his story. He's quite imposing, a bear of a man, though he looks distinctly uncomfortable in these cosy surroundings. He's not being overly flowery with his language, more direct, so I'm hoping it's an honest account, though I can always confirm the details with other relatives. I don't interrupt, allowing him to take the conversation in any direction he chooses.

'My own sons have joined me in the business and I hope, one day, though not too soon, that they will run the business as a joint venture. I'd like Scarlet to be actively involved or at least secure her share of the business. Helen has been involved since Emmet started school, and my other ex-wives were offered employment, though the others did refuse, choosing their own paths.'

'Janie works?' I ask bluntly, unsure if I'd misunderstood her earlier reference to daily shopping and boozy lunches.

'Actually, no, Janie doesn't – she's the exception.'

'Ah, I thought not.'

'And, now that you're part of the family – if you'd like to join . . .'

I baulk at the suggestion. 'Sorry, but I have a career which I love.'

'I realise that, but your mother has mentioned the long hours, the weekend work, the shift rotas – working with animals sounds all well and good but . . .'

I can't believe that in the space of five minutes I need to justify my decisions and employment choices with my mother's subtle opinion being used as testimony for the opposition.

'Sorry, but I love my job. I've worked hard, studied and made sacrifices to secure the role that I have. So I won't be quitting any day soon in order to join your family business.' I'm breathless on completion of this statement, through a mixture of annoyance and surprise.

'*Our* family business, Lowry – you'll be part of the clan shortly.'

'I thank you, but employment won't be necessary. All I ask is that you treat my mother well.'

'Wouldn't you prefer to be able to see her more often? Less working hours, less stress, more contact time?'

I'm seeing more than I wish. Is he trying to be helpful or just disregarding my life choices? 'Admittedly, I'd like more visits, but I also crave my independence and a worthy career into which I've ploughed a lot of my time and energy.'

'How about cutting back, going part-time?'

'Excuse me?'

'If you reduced your hours, your mother would benefit . . .'

'Is this about me and my job or your worries about filling my mother's time in case she becomes bored?'

'This hasn't come from me. Oh no. Over the weeks your mother has mentioned how she'd like it if . . .'

I shake my head; I'm lost for words. I feel snared, as if I've walked into a trap.

'I thought I was offering a solution that might make it easier for you both, but if that isn't the case . . .'

'No. That isn't the case from my side, though I can't speak for my mother. I will be discussing this topic with her, so thanks for the suggestion, but I'll be returning home to Pendlebury and my regular work just as soon as this weekend is over.' My smile is forced, my tone flat and my temper smouldering. 'If there's nothing more, I'll rejoin the others.'

'No. Nothing more. Nice chat, hope it puts your mind at rest,' says Rupert, as I swiftly stand and leave the snug.

I return to the lounge, Teddy and River look up from the TV screen for a nanosecond, observe my expression and avert their attention back to the antics of the Grinch.

I flop down into the armchair like a teenager grounded for a Bank Holiday weekend. I've missed a crucial bit of the festive film, but stare ahead blindly, pretending to watch it. In my head, the conversation continues in full flow, as if still occurring in the snug. Was that an attempt to demean my job? A character test of some sort? Or simply a wasted opportunity for Rupert to intro-duce himself? He didn't even apologise for last night's incident. More importantly, what has my mother been saying? I re-label the film in my head as *How Rupert Scuppered my Christmas at the Front Door*! Ironic, given the business he's in.

Chapter Nine

Martha

'Have you spoken to Lowry yet?' I ask, dusting the kitchen tabletop with flour.

'Not really. I believe Teddy answered a medley of questions earlier,' says River, cradling a beer bottle as he watches me prepare the pastry for the salmon en croute. 'Because my mum's arrival wasn't embarrassing in the least, was it?'

'River. You know how it is,' I say, placing my chilled pastry parcel on to the sprinkling of flour.

'I do, but I've witnessed the same reactions time and time again. What this family needs is a PowerPoint presentation to explain the basic outline of our family tree to people before they meet us. With bullet points, colour photos, a neatly drawn timeline, perhaps a couple of upbeat quotes scattered throughout ... even a compulsory glass of whisky to assist with the shock factor, and then the formal introductions can begin,' jests River, though I know he's not really joking. 'Maybe with an accompanying leaflet which they can take away and study. Should I suggest it at dinner?'

I dust my rolling pin with flour and begin the rhythmical action which I find so calming, for me and for bystanders.

'It's quite overwhelming for anyone, but understand Lowry's position ... she's concerned for her mum,' I say, watching his forlorn expression.

'But will it ever be any different, Martha? I've had girlfriends who have cringed, mates who constantly take the mick and now a soon-to-be stepsister – did you see her face? She was mortified.'

'And?' I ask, sensing there's more.

'And I'm the result of that union – it doesn't always feel great being *that* child,' he says, shifting his stance before crossing his arms, beer in hand. 'No one asked me if I wanted to be the end result of my mother's affair with her brother-in-law.'

'Are any of us asked, prior to birth what we'd like? I can't remember being asked if I wanted to be the only child of a young widow, but such is life.'

'Come off it, Martha – my situation is hardly normal. Helen's my aunty and my dad's ex-wife though I treat her like a stepmum, Emmet's my brother and cousin, my dad's my dad and ex-uncle, my mum's my mum and technically my ex-uncle's ex-bit on the side! Now come on, that is cruel! You try convincing a new date that you're stable, a decent fella and likely to stick the course if things go well. Seriously, I'm stuffed in the family stakes.'

'River, your day will come. The right girl . . .'

'Phew! Are you seriously going to use that line on me?'

'Yes, I am. None of that will matter to the right girl – her concern will be you, she will cope with the rest.'

'What? Like Lynette did? Like Fena did? Like Diane . . .?'

'Like Diane will!' I flick my gaze up to meet his. It's clear what he's thinking.

He shakes his head vigorously, before speaking. 'Nah, I give it six months. She might have survived the last twelve weeks with him being charming and gallant, showing her around the family, making swift plans for this wedding, but mark my words, it's the next twelve weeks Diane needs to survive. The honeymoon will be over, normal daily life will resume and . . .' He stops talking as Emmet walks through, heading towards the kettle.

'Don't stop because I walked in,' teases Emmet, lifting the kettle and heading for the sink.

'I won't . . . I was just talking about Dad's morals.'

'Oh those. There's a cheery subject,' says Emmet in my direction, with a twinkle in his eye, as he fills the kettle. I say nothing. As children, these two were like chalk and cheese, they both hated what the other one had, wore or was playing with, yet in recent times, River's appearance, dress sense and sometimes his mannerisms emulate Emmet's. Though River will never have that brooding stare, and his unruly blond hair will always contrast with Emmet's dark curls.

'Have you seen them lately?' asks River nonchalantly, receiving his brother's full attention in a split second, minus the jest. 'Or are you just living through the aftermath of his decisions too?'

Emmet slowly turns off the gushing tap, returns the kettle to its electrical point and flicks the switch on without saying a word. But he's thinking; his actions are deliberate as he ponders the question with a conscious awareness that all eyes are on him. He leans against the pantry door and eyes his brother squarely.

'Both actually. Annabel wanted more, yet there was something missing for me. She wasn't going to wait around having realised I had doubts about us. I couldn't trust myself to commit in case I was making a mistake, just like the old man has four times over,' says Emmet, as River goes to interrupt him. 'Don't say five, because that's plain rude. But yeah, I wonder. Wonder what it is that Dad's searching for? What's so significant that he'll spend a lifetime chasing it? What was it that was missing for me? Have I made a mistake already but don't yet realise it? Will the phrase like father, like son turn out to be true? So yeah, if you're asking about the impact, the aftermath, I think it is highly likely that we – me, you, Teddy and Scarlet – have a lot to think about if we're not to follow the same route. But surely that's no different from the nature or nurture in other families. Is it instinct that held me back from Annabel or learnt behaviour copied from my parents – I'll never know, will I?'

'But doesn't that scare you, Emmet? To think you could be fifty-five and on wedding number five? Followed by ...'

'Don't!' instructs Emmet, raising his chin as he speaks.

'OK, but you know what's coming, right? That scares the shit out of me – a lifetime of ... what? Wasted energy, lost causes, packing suitcases, saying goodbye to kids? I don't want it.'

Emmet gives a slow nod, and stepping forward, he clasps his hands on his brother's hunched shoulder and holds tight before speaking. 'Let's hope you find what you want and need pretty soon and then you'll be so grateful for what you've found in your twenties – you'll have a little more empathy for the man who's been searching his entire life.'

Their gaze is locked: Emmet's steely but steady, River's strained and searching, before the moment is broken when Emmet pulls River towards him for a rough blokey hug and a resounding backslap.

A lump jumps to my throat, so I lower my head and continue to roll the pastry, though I've overworked it already thanks to that little scene.

'Phuh, don't give me that brotherly love act! I'm a pain in the arse to you, you're forever saying so,' says River, in a cocky tone, though he's clearly moved by Emmet's embrace.

'You are, but you're still my kid brother,' says Emmet, unmoved by his own actions but aware of River's. 'Now bugger off before Teddy thinks I'm picking favourites.' Emmet returns to the boiling kettle and River quickly slips through the kitchen door, almost instantly doubling back to explain the commotion erupting in the hallway: 'Lynette's just arrived!'

'Thank you, I'll be through in a second,' I say, knowing there's enough of a welcoming committee to give me five minutes of wiggle room before I'm needed.

Emmet's silent, his shoulders square and his back rigid, as he makes a tray of teas.

'Are you alright?' I ask, knowing he's not.

'You know me, Martha – I'm always alright, it's the rest of 'em you've got to watch.' On his final word, he gives me a glance over his shoulder – those twinkling eyes have returned.

'Just checking,' I say, knowing my mince pies aren't going to win any prizes or much praise this year. My rolling pin skews from the pastry and sends a knife spinning off the scrubbed table to land on the tiled floor. 'Bugger it! Of all the things to drop it's a sodding knife. Sorry, Emmet, could you pick that up for me? I can't pick up myself as it'll bring bad luck.' I've enough bad luck coming my way without tempting fate.

'What utter codswallop!'

'Mark my words, we can expect a male visitor who'll change our luck and believe me, I've got enough catering for those here already.'

'Is that so?' mutters Emmet, retrieving the offending knife.

Lowry

I sit on a cushion by the fireside, my back leaning against the arm of my mum's sofa seat, enjoying the festive family movie. Having enjoyed a glass of wine, some moreish party nibbles and witnessed for the umpteenth time a mother's desperate cry of 'Kevin!', this now truly feels like Christmas. The festive decorations look exquisite, even the tree, now beautifully decorated with baubles, tinsel and garlands of red and gold found in a box stashed in the upstairs linen cupboard, despite the hideous modification created by the blokes; it's a bit distracting, albeit quite funny. Thankfully, the piles of gift-wrapped presents, which Helen instructed us to fetch from our rooms, distract the eye slightly.

'Lynette's here,' whispers my mum, when Rupert and Teddy

suddenly stand, press pause on the TV's remote control and drift towards the hallway.

'I'm staying put,' says Janie to us, holding her wine glass aloft – which looks incredibly full given she's drinking Irish cream. 'Would Lynette want a welcoming party? I think not.'

Mum and I both stand, making an effort to show interest in ex-number three. I believe I'm doing quite well with the names and the faces, but it helps that they're very different in appearance. Helen is a classy kind of woman, Janie appears to be the energetic, young-at-heart one, and from comments I've heard, I'm under the impression that Lynette is ... suddenly standing before me and exactly as I've imagined. Slim build, verging on too-thin, dressed in simple black slacks and a plain mustard sweater, blonde hair pulled into a harsh ponytail which must pull on her hairline, not a fleck of make-up, very much a soap-and-water woman.

'Hello, you must be the lovely Diane I've heard so much about. I'm Lynette,' she says; her voice is warm and syrupy. My mum doesn't answer but simply stares at the newcomer, quite taken aback. Lynette doesn't hesitate to softly pat her arm, adding, 'It's quite overwhelming, I completely understand. And you must be Lowry, such a beautiful name. How are you?'

'Lovely to meet you, Lynette. How was your journey?' I say, covering for my mum's embarrassment.

'Such an easy and relaxing drive until I hit these teeny-weeny little lanes – then I wasn't so brave, especially when another car came the other way. But I'm here now and that's all that matters.' Lynette does a happy little shoulder shimmy-cum-shrug as she speaks. She seems so natural, so unspoilt.

'Janie, so sorry I dashed past without even saying hello. How are you? You're looking very well.' Lynette stands before Janie's seat, all smiles and compliments.

'Jogging along as I always have, Lynette, you know me. And you?' says Janie, making no effort to greet her.

'Much the same as ever, still doing my thing with nature and practising the art of Zen – loving life, basically,' says Lynette, performing her tiny shimmy again.

'Great,' says Janie, downing her drink and peeling herself from her chair. 'I'm grabbing a refill. Is it a fizzy water or a slimline tonic for you, Lynette?'

'Neither, thanks, I'm enjoying flat water only nowadays, no bubbles,' says Lynette, so freely.

'Tap water it is, and without ice – see, I do remember!' says Janie, preparing to leave the lounge. Lynette instantly turns around to continue her chat with my mum, and over Lynette's shoulder, I swear I see Janie perform the tiniest little shoulder shimmy as she goes.

'Martha, that spread was amazing!' squeals Lynette, surveying the empty serving platters and dinner plates littering the dining table. 'Salmon en croute is one of my favourites.'

'Thank you, Lynette. It's always a pleasure to serve – there's never any leftovers,' says Martha.

'Not even for a midnight feast?' asks River cheekily, glancing along the table towards Emmet.

'Especially for such nocturnal habits! Cheese is one thing but main course delicacies shouldn't be touched, thank you very much,' jibes Martha, carefully getting to her feet to clear the crockery.

'I'll give you a hand,' I say, jumping up before others can offer. Beside me, my mum reaches out a hand under the table to gently tap my thigh, as if to say 'No, don't.' 'I want to,' I whisper, trying to be inconspicuous.

'That's very kind of you – many hands make light work,' says Martha, piling up the nearest crockery, creating quite a rattle of china whilst doing so. I follow suit and collect the plates nearest to me, then follow Martha from the dining room towards the kitchen to unload.

'I'm not used to being catered for by someone else, I'm more of a muck-in-and-help kind of person,' I say, apologising for offering to assist. 'That certainly was delicious, Martha. Can I ask were there any scraps of fish left over for the . . .?' I ask casually, only to find a Tupperware box of fish flakes slid across the countertop towards me.

'The cat?' says Martha, with a coy smile. 'I simply couldn't throw out the bits when I was cleaning and trimming the main portion of salmon.'

'Thank you, she'll love it. It'll give her a boost – nursing depletes their own health so much,' I say, clutching the box tightly, eager to escape the family dinner.

'Why don't you nip outside while I finish off here. They won't miss you for a minute or two,' says Martha, pointing at the rear door before heading back towards the dining room.

'Perfect. I will.' Or not, if I can sneak past you. I watch her disappear into the hallway and know I have a few minutes before she returns. I quickly unlock the back door, leaving it wide open to give the impression I've gone outside, then I nip into the hallway and dash up the staircase, two at a time, clutching the Tupperware box. I cross the landing in large strides, trying not to make a sound to alert the family below, and enter my bedroom. On opening the wardrobe door wide, I see Trixie is awake with her kittens playfully climbing over her curled back.

'Here you go, sweetie, a nice little treat.' I tip the pieces of fish into the small feeding dish before popping it under her nose. She doesn't hesitate, gulping them down before the kittens have even the chance to show any interest. 'Sorry, but I've got to go.' With my fingers crossed, I quickly retrace my path across the landing, down the staircase and into the kitchen, hoping that Martha is still piling plates in the dining room. I head straight for the back door and leap outside, managing to re-enter just as Martha comes into the kitchen. 'Brrr, it's cold out there, but she loved the fish,' I say, acting as if I'd been in the outhouse all the time.

'Bless her, I'm surprised she's stayed out there. It's getting colder by the hour,' says Martha, unloading the dirty cutlery into the dishwasher rack. I notice she misses the rack's slotted holes several times whilst placing each item be it a fork or a knife.

'She's warm and cosy – don't you worry.' I pop the empty Tupperware box by the sink and head back to the dining room, praying my kindness towards animals cancels the little white lie I've just acted out to fool Martha.

Helen

I open my carol book at the required page, 'Silent Night', and stand shoulder to shoulder with the sea of strangers filling the wooden pews. The church organ gives a tuneful flourish and we, the congregation, find our voices.

Before us, an arched window of stained glass appears blackened against the night sky; the large alcoves and archways of the church are packed with candle stands, whose soft mellow light flickers strange shadows on to the pale church walls. The altar is dressed in linen cloths resplendent with gold edging and topped with the chalice and a large gold cross.

I really didn't think I was going to make the Midnight Mass service but thankfully Emmet was kind enough to walk with me from Lakeside Cottage to the local church. The late-night stroll along the deserted lane, leading into the village, was quite beautiful. I expected us to part company on nearing arrival, but no. Emmet escorted me almost to the church door when he saw the steep climb of the pathway, before I alone joined the throng of attendees entering church.

It's a solitude I find nowhere else. And I treasure being able to disappear in a safe and secure environment with like-minded parishioners and follow my traditional routine, despite our family gathering back at the cottage. It's a most welcome distraction, which will sustain me over the coming days. A time for reflection, self-awareness of our actions and, hopefully, a little more humility in our hearts given the time of year.

Not that I'm overly anxious about the coming days but the family can be so unpredictable, and the very prospect of drama sends me into a dither. Then, to add to the nerves, there's the mayhem of a wedding on top! What were they thinking choosing a Christmas wedding? As if we haven't enough to contend with during the festive period, with it being Emmet's big birthday. Though maybe I'm to blame for the original timing of that, but when you're young and newly married, you don't give much thought to the annual consequences of a warm spring night in March!

My brain continues to whir whilst my voice harmonises with everyone else's. Pity there's not a choir to accompany us, though our efforts are joyful and enthusiastic, if not entirely tuneful.

Where our Emmet's waiting Lord only knows. He's probably continued to walk into Hawkshead for a look around. Or nipped into a local pub, though I doubt there's anywhere open at this late hour. I was pleased to see in the local newspaper that the service is actually at midnight and not the token half-ten arrangement I usually attend back home in Todmorden. I like the gesture, as it encourages the elderly and families to attend, but to still call it midnight mass seems slightly puzzling.

Finally, we reach the third verse, the organ ceases, the congregation shuffle and are seated en masse, as the vicar takes his place.

I wonder if he'll be conducting the marriage? Probably – I can't image these smaller villages have a choice of clergy nowadays; my understanding is that small parishes regularly merge for services and share one incumbent. Not that I'm a weekly attendee, but I do like to go to church to recognise certain dates in the calendar. I only wish the rest of the family would join me, but it was never Rupert's thing and the children have followed his guidance, though not in all areas, thankfully.

'And so we pray,' the vicar announces, via his head mic, as we instinctively lower our heads and I close my eyes, as is my habit.

'Me again, asking as always for guidance in the coming days. Ensuring that I can cope with the difficult moments that might present themselves, either through the weakness of others or the numerous misunderstandings that occur when we unite as a family. Please watch over Emmet; he's brooding again, and relying on stuff to get him through. Guide River with his wily ways – it will only ever lead to trouble. And young Teddy, always wanting to copy his brothers . . . let him know that he, as he is, is enough. And Scarlet, when . . . actually *if* she arrives over the weekend. You know what she's like, with her impulsive nature and fiery temper. Please let us have clear warning if any emotional bombshells are about to drop. Bless Martha, may she always be present and patient, or at least available to help me retain my sanity or marbles should I lose them. I sincerely wish Rupert and Diane all the love and happiness in the world; surely the man has to get it right one time in his life? Diane is such a sweetie; and her daughter, Lowry, allow her to feel part of the family and see a glimpse of our normal side and not the crazy mixed family that we sometimes display over dinner, or lunch, or any other time of the day. And for the others, please dilute our Janie's wild-child antics just for one weekend. I appreciate we're like chalk and cheese as siblings go, but I'm not sure I want to bail her out of her usual scrapes with Lynette. From whom you need to save us all, if she's still living up to her reputation as the family martyr. And Fena, who sadly won't be joining us, but still, bestow on her a wonderful Christmas wherever she is. Amen.'

I give a heavy sigh before opening my eyes. A wave of relief flushes over me; I didn't forget anyone – now that's a novelty, in itself.

It feels like meditation, addressing my thoughts and worries in one simple action which I'll admit focuses my mind. I wait for the vicar to continue his service – this feels lovely. I'm glad I made the effort after a hectic day.

Chapter Ten

Monday 25 December

Lowry

I peer over the staircase banister and breathe a sigh of relief on seeing there's no light escaping beneath the snug door. Everyone's in bed, no chance of being caught tonight. I don't need to tiptoe as I make my way into the kitchen, across the tiled floor and unlock the back door. My unlaced pumps are decidedly unattractive teamed with my fleecy pyjamas and long cardigan thrown over the top, but I need to empty and refresh the soil from the litter box to ensure that no mishaps occur in my bedroom.

I leave the back door ajar, cross the patio and head for the shrubbery on the left-hand side to discreetly empty the dirtied soil, so that others don't step in or smell it. My breath billows before my face it is so cold. I locate the tiny trowel where I'd left it this morning, and hastily lift fresh soil into the cardboard box. The earth is definitely harder to dig than before; I have to chip away at the surface crust before scooping each trowelful into the makeshift litter box. I don't mind. As long as she's comfortable for the time being, I'll do what's necessary – even if I am freezing my arse off out here. I smile. Crouching in a shrubbery border beneath a starry sky on a chilly night is pretty tame compared with some of the bizarre things I've done to ensure animals are happy and healthy in the course of my career.

'What are you doing?' His voice makes me jump out of my

skin. I drop the trowel on to the dirt and look up, expecting a police officer with a flashlight, but no, it's Emmet.

'You scared me. Having a smoke, are we?' I say, dodging his question.

'No, actually. I was just sitting out here. So what are you up to?'

'Nothing. I'm not up to anything,' I say, feeling around for the abandoned trowel.

'Collecting earth in a box – why?' He glances towards the outhouse, in his usual brooding manner.

'Please, just leave me to do it.' I feel utterly stupid. Is it just because I've been caught in the act, needing to lie yet again, or because it's Emmet who caught me? I still blush each time I recall my reaction to him swinging that axe and felling the Christmas tree.

'Lowry?' He bends down, his hand reaching for my forearm as I busily chip at the earth, having located the trowel.

'What?' I turn to face him, and a fresh smell of toothpaste surprises me: I expected tobacco.

'I'm not the enemy, you know,' he says, retracting his hand.

I sink back on to my haunches and sigh, before speaking. 'I know, but I'd like to get back to the cottage without the interrogation. OK?'

'OK, deal.'

'Thank you.' I don't know what else to say.

'How are the kittens doing?' He stands up and backs away from my crouched figure. I must look incredibly silly frantically digging.

'Feeding well and sleeping lots, as kittens should,' I say, trying to soothe our terse interaction.

'That's good to hear. I was sitting on the bench and heard the back door open,' says Emmet, thumbing over his shoulder towards the lawn area.

'It was locked though,' I say, knowing I'd turned the key.

'It was. I left using the front door and came along the side path, bringing the keys with me.' He digs into his jeans pocket and swings a keyring from his forefinger.

'I see, wise decision.'

'I'd hate to be locked outside with everyone snoring inside, now wouldn't I?'

I nod. I've finished my task so I thrust the trowel into the ground ready for tomorrow and stand tall, my box of soil in hand.

'Look, let's call it a truce? I didn't mean to make you jump or frighten you. Come now, have a nip of whisky and we'll let bygones be bygones. What do you say?'

'I should really be getting . . .' It's now my turn to gesture over my shoulder towards the cottage. Then, as an after-thought, to the brick outhouse, reaffirming where he believes the cats to be.

'Ahh, come on. We're supposed to be getting to know each other as family. How's being shitty with me going to aid that cause?'

Typical Carmichael, laying it on thick. He'll take it as a snub if I return inside and might even mention my nocturnal digging at breakfast.

'Go on then, a quick one,' I say, dropping my earth box by the kitchen's back door. 'Do I need to fetch a glass?'

'You sure do,' he says, making his way up the stone steps and on to the frosted lawn.

'It's a bit cold to be stuck out here, isn't it?' I say, cradling a large whisky, my feet lifted on to the bench and an arm wrapped about my knees, cuddling myself for warmth. If I'd realised it was this cold, I'd have refused his offer.

'Possibly, but it's better than being inside, staring at a darkened ceiling until sleep decides to come my way. Cheers!' he says, lifting his glass in my direction.

'Cheers,' I mutter, taking a sip, instantly reeling backwards as my throat burns. 'Phuh! That's strong!'

'Is it?' he mutters.

I watch as he downs it like milk.

'Is this your usual poison?' I ask, taking the smallest sip, wishing I had a single shot.

'I don't usually drink as a rule, but with the holidays, the family gathering – it's there, isn't it?'

I get where he's coming from; sometimes it's easier than not. Though I fear it might take me a couple of hours to finish this glass given I'm consuming it in the tiniest of sips.

In the distance, a church bell chimes three times. I'd thought it was later than that. Ridiculously, I look up, as if I could see the church spire from here.

'Happy birthday! I should have said it earlier,' I say, as the significance dawns on me, raising my glass towards him.

'Thank you. Merry Christmas to you,' he says, returning the gesture before glancing up at the night sky.

'Is it the pits being born at Christmas?'

He laughs. 'Pretty much. As a kid, you always get a joint birthday and Christmas present. As an adult, no one has any spare money to go out and celebrate with you, plus the family expect you to spend the day with them, which overthrows your actual day. It would be nice to have an ordinary birthday day which is entirely mine.'

'You should have a second birthday like the King does,' I say.

Emmet shakes his head. 'I can't imagine a birthday in June.'

'Would that be exactly halfway through the year though?' I reply, knowing calendars play tricks with odd days here and there.

'Who knows.' He starts to laugh, softly at first but it soon increases. His terseness is melting away.

'What's so funny?' I feel slightly stupid; I'd thought I was offering a solution.

'After a weekend with this lot, you'll know why I wouldn't wish to have a second birthday and make more family occasions, but bless your heart for trying, Lowry.'

'Mmm, on second thoughts . . .'

'Exactly. Do you really think you could stomach many more Janie-shaped surprises?' His tone is bemused. 'And believe me, she has many more stashed in her closet.'

'Err, nope. Less so the telling-off I received afterwards from my mother for embarrassing her. One of those can-I-have-a-quiet-word chats in which I instantly revert back to a sulky child. At what age does that stop happening?'

'Never!' His answer is blunt and non-apologetic in its delivery. 'Though at least it doesn't follow you to work and the board-room – because that is the ultimate cringe, I can tell you. River has a story or two of when Dad's given him a dressing-down in front of his department – not pretty.'

'Maybe I've misunderstood then . . . I got the impression that everyone gets on well and this is truly a blended family, at home or at work. That's what my mum has been led to believe too.'

'Do you think one man with three of his four ex-wives plus his soon-to-be-wife sharing a cottage for an idyllic festive holiday, plus a wedding celebration, could ever please everyone or truly create family harmony?'

When he puts it like that, it sounds totally absurd to even try. He's easier to chat with now his guard seems to be lowering.

'It's all an act then?' I ask, turning to face him despite not being able to see him clearly.

'I wouldn't go that far. It's more that it's a polished routine, with each of us putting up with the niggles and disharmony that we usually steer clear of for the rest of the year. Have you got close relatives or cousins, stepsibling?'

'Nope. I'm an only child of an only child, so our family consisted of four members, us two and Mum's parents. We could have a family gathering in a fairground waltzer car. Though my grandparents have passed now.' Why did I choose a fairground attraction as a fitting meeting place for my loved ones? The example sounds a little heartless.

'I'm sorry to hear that, but if it's any consolation, you'll feel a whole lot better about your situation after this weekend. That is pretty much guaranteed whilst staying amongst my family, however hard we try to accommodate being pleasant to each other.'

'It's complicated, isn't it?'

'You can say that again. As I said, one man, four women and their four offspring – complicated, and bloody expensive. And now, there's two more – not meaning to offend or anything.'

'How does it work the rest of the year?' I ask, gingerly taking a sip of whisky and grimacing.

'We lads work together, my mum runs the sister company selling exterior doors, Janie drops by for a family visit now and then, Lynette rarely and Fena never, as she lives in Japan. Scarlet spends her time staying here, there and everywhere when she's in the country – she hasn't got a permanent base.'

'I see. But you lads and your father see each other on a daily basis?'

'Yeah, at work. Unless our schedules don't match or meetings prevent it. Teddy still lives at Dad's, though I don't know for how much longer after tomorrow.'

'Tomorrow?'

'The wedding. I've a feeling he'll be moving out to give Dad and Diane more space and some privacy to start married life.'

'Yes, I see.'

Emmet smiles, which seems out of character for the brooding figure I've witnessed in recent days. Is this his birthday mood or simply his away-from-immediate-family mood?

'Dare I ask how long the others have lasted?'

'Marriages? Ooh, no, I wouldn't ask if I were you – just take it that this is the happiest I've seen him in a long time. I might have been just a kid the last time he tied the knot but he didn't seem this committed back then. I think Diane is different . . .'

'I just want the best for my mum,' I say, twisting to sit along the bench, knees up with my feet planted on the seat section, leaning sideways against the back support. As if on cue, a gentle fluttering of snow begins to fall like confetti. 'Look, it's snowing.' I raise my free hand, catching the sparse offerings.

'It was forecast for earlier. Anyway, I'd have quite liked the same for my mum but she's so set in her ways she won't even contemplate the idea of a quick coffee with a bloke, let alone a date or anything more.'

'She's never dated?' I return my focus to our conversation, as the snow continues to fall from the dark skies, providing a magical backdrop.

'Nope. Not since my father. I can't see that ever changing.'

'Does she still have . . .?' I want to say feelings but I daren't in case he snaps back into his terse mode.

'No! Bloody hell, no way! The arrangement between them is entirely amicable – it always has been because neither of them wanted me raised in a war zone so they made the effort to build bridges. Which has come in handy ever since as a child-friendly, co-parenting template for each of the other wives, but no. Good God, no! My mother wouldn't switch places . . .' Emmet stops talking. 'Shit. Sorry, that came out wrong, but you know what I mean. I'm sure she's healed from the hurt; she's moved on in many ways and she's happy with her lot.'

Happy? I'm not so sure. Why would the first ex-wife put up with entertaining, hosting, organising four other women plus their offspring if she didn't have some lingering attachment? Tucked away and deeply hidden perhaps, probably pushed to the back of the emotional cupboard with a pile of life crap balancing on top, just like that rip-roaring heartbreak caused by your first ever true love! It's there buried, deep inside each of us, underneath a huge pile of everything else!

The snow is falling much faster than before and a distinct cover of white is beginning to settle on everything, including us.

'Anyway, I'd best be getting back inside before I freeze. Thanks for the whisky, it was gross but it might help me to sleep,' I say, uncurling my legs and sneakily tipping the remaining drink on to the grass.

'You didn't just chuck . . . oh, forget it. Thanks for the birthday wishes. Night,' says Emmet, sipping his drink.

'Night.'

I don't hang around but dash from the lawn down the stone steps to pick up my box, then across the patio to the brick outhouse. I squeakily open and shut the outhouse door several times, suggesting that I entered and left, before nipping in through the kitchen door and darting up the staircase.

Brrr! I'm frozen to the bone and can't wait to dive back under my duvet, though my bed will be decidedly cold by now. As I cross the landing, the softest click of a door catches my attention from the right-hand side. Did it come from along the corridor? Was someone else out of bed? I pause, expecting someone to appear from their room, but nothing. I go straight to my bedroom door, firmly close it and return the little box to the bottom of my wardrobe.

Chapter Eleven

Helen

From the year dot, I've always insisted that we spend Christmas as parents, regardless of the circumstances. I wasn't prepared to have Emmet's birthday and Christmas Day both ruined in one go due to the absence of his father. Rupert knew where I stood on that front, and full marks to him, he has always laid the ground rules down for the women in his life as to where he needs to be on Christmas morning. And this morning is no exception, despite it being Emmet's thirtieth birthday.

'Happy birthday, my darling!' I cry as I enter the dining room, which appears more brightly illuminated after the heavy snowfall outside. I spy my boy seated beside his father, surrounded by a smattering of opened cards and small gifts, complete with a beautifully iced celebration cake. Bless Martha, she never lets us down, ever.

A silver tray of champagne glasses, filled to the brims, are ready and waiting for a celebration. And I know Janie will down her glass in one, on an empty stomach, when she arrives. 'I've a little something put aside for later, just between us.'

'Thanks, Mum,' says Emmet, receiving my kiss to his cheek with good grace. 'Here, have a glass of bubbles.' He hands me the nearest glass, filled to the brim with golden champagne.

'Cheers, my darling. It seems like yesterday that I said to your father ...'

'Oh great, this story again,' says Emmet to Teddy and River, sitting opposite.

'It'll put you off your bacon and eggs that's for sure,' says Rupert, raising his greying eyebrows at Diane, seated on his other side. She looks fresh, no signs of the nervous bride, yet.

'Urgh!' groans River, 'I'm glad my mother doesn't recount tales of her bodily functions every year.'

'River, I'll have you know I had to endure . . .'

'A forty-seven-hour labour,' whispers Emmet.

'Forty-seven hours of labour,' mutters Rupert.

'Forty-seven hours,' groans River.

'Forty-seven hours for this boy,' says Teddy, simultaneously with the others, in a crescendo of male voices.

'I'm glad you think it's so damned funny. I'd like to see you fellas try and push a watermelon out of your arse!' I say, riled that they're making fun of my greatest memory, more so when my remark sounds more like something our Janie would say. I kiss Emmet on the forehead before heading towards the breakfast buffet. I was not the same woman after I first held that tiny baby on Christmas morning, his scrunched fists flailing as he screamed in temper at being disturbed from the warmth.

'Happy birthday to me, folks!' adds Emmet, grabbing his champagne flute and downing half of it.

'Makes you feel all warm inside, hey, Emmet?' jibes River, following suit with his glass. It's good seeing them reconnect without the stress of work.

'You lads have no idea. And you're simply showing your immaturity, acting up when I'm trying to wish my boy a happy birthday . . . but I don't care, you'll learn one day!' I say, selecting slices of wholemeal toast from the offerings laid upon the sideboard.

'Oh great, have I just missed the annual forty-seven-hour reminder?' asks Janie, sauntering into the dining room in a fetching velour lemon leisure suit, her hair and make-up on-point, as always.

I ignore her remark and continue to spoon marmalade on to my side plate.

'Sure have. How long did you endure, Mum?'

'Ah, about seventeen minutes, sweet. You wouldn't wait so you were born on the kitchen floor, then the ambulance crew arrived in time to mop up the mess. How was I supposed to know it wasn't indigestion?'

I roll my eyes at Janie's remark, knowing it's safe because my back is towards the breakfast table. There's nothing admirable about giving birth on a kitchen floor because you thought yourself too bohemian to read any baby literature during your pregnancy. I call it irresponsible for yourself and for your unborn baby, but hey, what would I know? I read everything.

'River, don't look so shocked. How was I to know?' says Janie, settling at the table and reaching for a glass of bubbles. 'Happy birthday, Emmet – may all your dreams come true! Cheers!'

'Thanks, Janie,' says Emmet, tucking into his cooked breakfast.

There are times when my sister simply steals my thunder. And, despite me swallowing my feelings each time and not mentioning it, it really pisses me off!

I leave the sideboard and sit at the table, as far from my sister and as near to my son as I can be, and begin buttering my toast.

'The plan for today is celebration for Emmet first thing, pressies opened once everyone is out of bed and breakfast has been cleared – I suggest we gather in the lounge to exchange gifts before enjoying our usual feast just after the King's speech. I'll check with Martha that that's doable but I'm sure she'll say . . .'

'Helen, give it a rest for one day, sweetie. I'm exhausted just listening to you rattle on about precision timings and itineraries – phew! It's bloody Christmas for Pete's sake,' says Janie, waving a coffee spoon in my direction and swigging her bubbles.

'Good morning! Happy birthday, Emmet, and such a beautiful

flurry of snow for your very special day,' says Lynette, arriving bang on cue, as we sisters snipe at one another. 'It's only a little something but I made it especially.' She pops a small gift beside his hand, wrapped in brown paper tied with string, and affectionately rubs his shoulder.

'Why, thank you, Lynette – but really you shouldn't have.' All eyes watch as Emmet opens his present, each of us wondering whether it'll be a typical Lynette gift – something life-enhancing and pure Zen which will prove to be utterly useless to him and gather dust on a shelf for evermore.

Emmet reveals a wooden dice with scripted font on each face.

'It's an affirmation dice. We all have times when we need a little guidance,' offers Lynette, along with a sympathetic expression. Thanks a bunch, Lynette; he'll assume I've been talking out of line.

'Th-thanks, it's lovely,' says Emmet, twisting the wooden cube in his hand to read each side. 'I'm sure it'll come in handy.'

'Each morning you roll the . . .' continues Lynette, oblivious that she's overselling it.

I look away – a bloody affirmation dice, as if my son needs any of her boho New Age thinking to get through the day. What a waste of time.

'Utter bloody nonsense,' whispers Janie, and I can't agree more. Lynette continues to explain how to use the dice, despite it being blindingly obvious. Bless Emmet, he politely gives her his full attention.

'Roll it,' she urges, much to my annoyance.

'Er, it's fine.'

'See what your message is for today, your big birthday,' encourages Lynette, still hovering at his shoulder.

Emmet rolls the dice, purely to humour her. It travels a short distance on the oak table and they both lean forward to see.

'"This too will pass,"' announces Lynette eagerly, before drawing back and exclaiming, 'Oh!'

'That's smashing, Lynette, lovely gift. Thank you,' says Emmet, ignoring the rest of us. We're all teetering on the edge of belly-laughing, including Teddy.

'Bloody good job too,' mutters Janie. 'I wouldn't want to be stuck in this moment for a second longer!'

'Not too swiftly – you want to enjoy your special day, don't you?' says Lynette, backing away towards the buffet.

What a ridiculous gift to give a grown man. She's so locked into her own free and simple lifestyle that she has little awareness of others. I hate to think what Teddy will receive for his thirtieth birthday, maybe a week's silent retreat in a faraway commune or a fortnight in a monastery.

No one says a word as Lynette browses the breakfast selection, mmming and ahhing to herself over the freshness of the croissants and possibly the whiteness of the eggshells, steering clear of any sugar-laced muesli.

I need to reset my mood, go back to how it was before Lynette, no, Janie entered the dining room when I was thrilled about sharing my son's birthday. I must focus on the enjoyment of us being together as a family, blended or not, happy or not, because otherwise, before we know it …

The sound of screeching tyres outside causes us all to sit up, stretching our necks to peer through the leaded windows where a nippy red sports car is being erratically parked at the cottage's snowy white frontage.

'Scarlet's here!' says Rupert, his voice perkier than I've heard in recent days.

'Scarlet,' mutters River, glancing at Emmet.

'Dear Scarlet,' whispers Lynette, putting down her selected breakfast to stare out the window. 'And who's this she's brought with her?'

We all awkwardly half stand from our seats to view our latest arrival bustling through the picket gate with a male figure traipsing through the snow two steps behind her, loaded up to the gunwales with her designer baggage.

Martha

'Scarlet, welcome ... Here, let me take that, and that,' I say, reaching for two cumbersome bags clutched in her hands as I hold open the cottage door for her timely entrance from the snow-covered pathway. She's dressed up to the nines, full hair and make-up, clad in a gorgeous woollen wrap coat of pillar-box red, very fetching against her flowing mane of raven-black hair.

'Ooh, isn't this quaint? Very chocolate-box amidst the snow-drifts, don't you think?' says Scarlet, handing over her goodies without a welcome or acknowledgement. I don't take offence; she doesn't mean it, most of the time. She peels off her long coat and throws it at the staircase, not aiming for the newel post, and it lands covering the four lower steps. I'll hang it up in a second – she won't. She certainly looks bright and bonny, with a bit more flesh on her bones than the last time I saw her.

'The family are in the dining room, just through here,' I say, gesturing towards the doorway, knowing that everyone is listening and waiting.

Scarlet makes a beeline for the family.

'Hello, Daddy! You'll never guess who I spotted waiting for a taxi outside Windermere train station?' she cries on entering, as I lean her bags against the two interior doors removed by the lads. I'm suddenly conscious that a second person is trudging along the pathway, beneath a mountain of luggage, and it's only when he arrives in front of me that I recognise him.

'Gunner Jeffery. How lovely to see you again, after all these years,' I say, not missing a heartbeat to hesitancy or shock and remembering his much-loved, self-styled and long-defunct army title. Was it yesterday that the kitchen knife fell to the floor? Lord knows what Mr C will make of this unexpected guest.

'Martha, Martha, Martha – always a sight for sore eyes. How the devil are you?' comes his throaty tone.

'I'm very much alive and kicking, thank you. And you?' I ask politely, stepping backwards to allow him the wide berth necessary to get through the doorway, given his rotund waistline and heavy luggage load. In the decade since I last laid eyes on this fella, he's doubled in size and his blood pressure is clearly through the roof, going by his ruddy complexion.

'Never better. Is that old mucker of mine still even-tempered and marrying attractive women?' he jests, looking around the hallway, as if that's where Rupert would be found.

'It appears that way, Gunner Jeffery,' I say, closing the front door and indicating the free floor space in which to drop the suitcases. I'm hoping the family have heard my conversation and are prepared to welcome the unexpected. Thankfully, there's one spare bedroom, if required.

'I bet she's as gorgeous as the previous ones and hopefully a stayer!' He gives a throaty laugh at this final comment, and I want to cringe, knowing Diane will be able to hear him through the dining room's naked doorway.

'There's a full breakfast prepared if you care for some eggs and bacon.'

'You never let me down, old gal. What is it Rupert always calls you, "my angel who bakes"? Bakes, cooks, poaches, grills, slices and dices – isn't it? Nothing ever changes around here does it ... apart from the missus, hey?'

I smile politely, gesturing towards the dining room. 'If you'd like to go through.'

Jeffery follows my instructions and I hear strained-but-surprised welcomes chorused by those at breakfast. I turn to find Lowry standing stock-still partway down the staircase, looking between me and Scarlet's coat strewn in her path.

'Scarlet has arrived, along with Mr C's oldest and dearest school friend, Gunner Jeffery,' I say, collecting the expensive coat thrown on the staircase and clearing her descent, before adding, 'You might wish to go through for an introduction or to the kitchen first to enjoy a quieter breakfast.'

Lowry mouths, 'Thank you,' and follows my lead along the hallway.

I re-enter the kitchen, having taken fresh pots of coffee through into the dining room and collected the dirty crockery. I pile the crockery up on the counter, grateful not to have dropped the best chinaware on the walk from the dining room to the dishwasher. One day in the future it'll happen, though I pray I won't destroy the Carmichael family heirlooms, piece by piece, as my physical condition deteriorates.

I wasn't surprised to find Scarlet hanging on to her father in that little-girl manner that she always adopts. I always thought she'd grow out of it but apparently not: she's virtually on his knee.

'How's your bacon?' I ask Lowry, who's seated at the table, contentedly hunched over her plate and enjoying every mouthful as far as I can tell.

'Delicious,' she answers, looking up briefly. 'Have things quietened down?'

'They have. Though I'm sure there'll be one or two hushed but heated conversations regarding our unexpected guest, Jeffery,' I say, grabbing my oven mitts to check on the progress of the turkey roast.

I didn't need to look at Lowry to know her ears pricked up.

'Problems?'

'You could say that. Though I'm not one for gossip.' A shrill scream drifts through from the dining room – Scarlet, no doubt.

'Nor me. But do tell.'

Closing the Aga door, I give her a sideways glance. I like her, she's natural, honest and – given the attention she's shown towards that she-cat and her kittens – a decent addition to this family.

'He's a close school friend of Mr C's, who I haven't seen for nigh on a decade – though I could hardly not recognise him. He's definitely put on some weight, though haven't we all in that time?' I say, correcting my line of thought. 'Jeffery's settled at the far end of the dining table, wheedling his way in on a Christmas invite which I don't believe was extended to friends, however close they once were.'

'And Rupert won't be glad to see him?' asks Lowry, finishing her last mouthful.

'Nope.' I pause before adding, 'I'm not sure Janie will be either, given the antics during their younger days – if you get my drift.'

Lowry's eyes widen before she speaks. 'Like that, eh?'

I give a tiny nod, before saying, 'I can't imagine the lads being too happy either. River's always been protective of his mum . . . just as the others are. It's a Carmichael trait, you know, look after your nearest and dearest – which is how all this blended family stuff has evolved. Mr C never turned his back financially on an ex-wife; no, he might have done wrong in many ways but he's always managed to cope with paying the necessary bills for everyone.' Be it a decent property of their choosing or an annual allowance, he's paid the price.

'I assume Gunner's a nickname?'

'Exactly. He says it as if he's got a double-barrelled first name, Gunner-Jeffery,' I mutter, allowing my true feelings to leak. 'He likes to remind everyone he once had a promising army career, but I think it's more a warning – spend too long in his company and he'll take a potshot at you!'

'Oh, I see,' says Lowry. 'Has he never married?'

'No, but that doesn't mean he hasn't been busy auditioning a load of potentials. Ouch, how catty do I sound?' I say. 'He might not be guest number thirteen but still, his unexpected arrival might put Mr C's back up.'

'And children?' she continues.

I shake my head.

'Oh.'

'Which is part of the reason Mr C always welcomes him into the family fold. After which Jeffery usually screws up and rapidly disappears for a suitable amount of time to allow memories to fade. Then he returns like the prodigal son, but in friend form. Mark my words, it never takes him long to kick the hornet's nest.'

I hope I'm not talking out of line, but Lowry might be more worried about her mother's future after this arrival. If I can reassure her a little, I will, despite it making me sound oh so gossipy and slightly catty.

'And Scarlet – is she always this loud?' asks Lowry, standing up from her seat and bringing her dirty plate to the dishwasher, as yet another ear-piercing squeal erupts from the dining room.

'This? This is nothing. You've got to remember she's been the only girl amongst his sons. He sees the boys virtually every day at work or at home but Scarlet . . . well, he had to get used to only ever seeing her on high days and holidays as Fena lived on another continent.'

Lowry closes the dishwasher door and sighs.

'This is so very different to what I know or what I wanted for my mum, Martha. I half expected to be smothered by Rupert trying to reassure me how good life will be for her after the wedding yet he's hardly said a word and all I'm seeing is . . . well, relationship chaos, to be frank.'

I bite my lip; I get where she's coming from. It looks bad, awful, in fact, but I know in my heart of hearts that Diane will be cared for. 'She will be secure for the rest of her days, even if this doesn't work out, you know,' I say, hoping to soothe her worries.

Lowry leans against the countertop and sighs. 'I wanted more for her than financial security; she already had that.'

Chapter Twelve

Lowry

'Phew, thank the Lord that's over for another year,' says Janie, settling in the nearest armchair, cradling her festive 'coffee', which looks incredibly similar in appearance to pure Irish cream. 'Her excited screaming does my head in. You'd think that three brothers, a father and three ex-wives would be enough of a welcoming party, wouldn't you?'

Entirely rude of me, but I'd skirted the dining room, hoping for a quiet chat with my mum before the others joined us in the lounge. I flash a suggestive look at my mother, indicating I'd like a word, and go to stand up.

'Don't rush off – it'll be your turn next,' says Janie, holding her coffee mug aloft.

Bang on cue, I hear a shrill female voice demanding, 'Where is she?' from the hallway. 'The lounge I suppose. Let me through. Teddy, shift yourself.'

'Always the diva, hey?' comes Teddy's reply.

Mum glances up at me as I continue to stand, unsure what to do. Continuing with my plan to leave will look as if I'm snubbing Scarlet, whilst sitting back down feels like I'm complying with Janie's orders. Hobson's choice, again.

I don't have much chance to decide as a lively young woman bounces into the lounge, blocking my escape route. Her raven-black hair sways as she strides in, her hand extended in my direction and a forceful expression on her beautiful features.

'Hi, I'm Scarlet Carmichael-Sato – I assume you must be Lowry. Nice to meet you.' She does the thing I hate women doing, taking me in with a sweeping glance from top to toe and back up to meet my startled expression. I wish she hadn't done that.

Her steady gaze doesn't waiver now; mine is all over the place, taking in her features, mannerisms and seeking acceptance after her instant reaction to me. There's nothing wrong with anything she's said in her introduction, but I don't like the forthright manner in which she stands before me, blocking my route. Her overbearing energy hits me like a tsunami – this girl has confidence by the bucketload.

'Quite correct, Lowry Stephens . . . soon to be stepsister, half-sister – whatever the correct social term may be,' I say, unsure where that little reference came from.

'Phuh! I don't do such nonsense myself, though the lads might,' says Scarlet, waving away my remark with her long red nails, like swatting a fly.

Janie smiles to herself and takes another swig of her 'coffee'.

I sit back down on the sofa as if the introduction to Scarlet had physically bowled me over, depleting any energy I had had before she entered the room.

'Diane, how are you?' asks Scarlet, having finished with me. 'Please don't make me wear an ugly dress for the wedding. Daddy tells me he hasn't seen it but please . . . I beg you,' she squeals, her hands flapping in excitement at shoulder height as if conjuring a magical bridesmaid's dress. 'I'd prefer to wear a torn binbag!' Personally, I haven't asked many questions, knowing I'll wear whatever Mum asks me to, given that it's her one and only chance to be a bride.

'Ooh, Scarlet, as if I'd do that to either of you. We'll take a minute together later and I'll show you if it'll put your mind at rest,' my mum reassures her, glancing in my direction to include me in the arrangement.

'Ooh, I can't wait – I know exactly what I've been hoping for,' she says, sweeping both hands down her curvy figure in a tight-fitting action, with an added little wiggle. I instantly shift my gaze, embarrassed, and come eye to eye with Emmet, whose right eyebrow gives the tiniest lift in my direction, as if seconding my thoughts. We appear to be on the same page regarding that little gesture.

One thing's for certain, she's got the perfect healthy body – womanly and curvy in all the right places. I assume with her being a model, I won't be fighting over the last portion of dessert with Scarlet.

'Daddy! What's happened to the tree?' cries Scarlet, spying the decorated tree trimmed around the TV. Helen shifts her stance beside the hearth but keeps schtum.

'We picked a spruce with very full branches ... so the lads cut out the offending section – quite ingenious really,' explains her father. Again I glance at Emmet, who is stifling another fit of laughter. He seems quite playful when he's not silent and brooding.

'How ridiculous! Boys, surely you've watched *Home Alone* enough times to know what happens?' wails Scarlet, between her belly laughs.

'Scarlet, when did you last eat?' asks Martha, as always preoccupied with filling everyone's stomach.

About four years ago, if the modelling stereotype is anything to go by, I think to myself, staring into the hearth's roaring fire. I daren't look up in case I catch Emmet's eye for the third time.

'Earlier,' she replies. 'I'm not hungry, but if there's any more fizz open then ...'

Martha gives a nod and exits the lounge to collect the necessary.

'How's it feel being thirty, Emmet? You old git!' asks Scarlet, launching towards her older brother, wrapping her arms about his waist and snuggling in to receive a hug.

I don't listen to his reply. It's quite clear she's the baby, the spoilt one, the one who rarely hears the word 'no' and never utters the word 'sorry'. I remain in situ, almost frozen to the sofa cushions, wishing I could sneak out for a quick chat with my mother about the situation and ask a few more questions about this bridesmaid's dress. I've a funny feeling that anything chosen to suit Scarlet's hour-glass figure will definitely not suit mine!

Helen

'Sorry to be cryptic but I simply wanted a moment alone with you,' I say, closing the snug door as Emmet settles himself on a couch. 'Happy birthday, my boy – I can't believe how the time has flown.' I delve into the gift bag and retrieve his present, complete with bows and shiny paper, which I know he wouldn't have wanted in front of the others.

'Cheers, Mum,' he says, taking my gift and standing to deliver a peck to my cheek. I'm hoping he likes it; I chose it carefully but there's always that niggling doubt when it's for a special birthday. I'd hate to disappoint him – I feel we've let him down on so many previous occasions. His fingers tear at the gift paper, shredding it just as he always did as a youngster, to reveal a jeweller's square box.

Emmet's gaze hesitantly flickers up to mine before he opens it.

'Mum, you shouldn't have!' But I hear the delight in his voice and know it was the perfect choice. He can afford to buy a new watch whenever he wants, but one which is gifted holds a lifetime of memories.

'I wanted you to have something special, and your father bought you a watch for your twenty-first so I wanted to mark your thirtieth in the same way.'

'Mum, that's grand – it really is!' The watch is off its padded band, clasp open and he's noticed the simple inscription on the back:

To Emmet, happy 30th birthday, love always, your Mum xx

Emmet is sliding it on to his wrist, and his face is a picture. Just what I ordered! Call me selfish but I didn't want to share this moment with anyone but him.

'I'm hoping it's a perfect fit – I measured the links on your other watch, and the guys in the shop were fabulous about altering it. Oh yes, perfect!'

Emmet pulls back his sleeve, and two golden faces greet me from the other couch.

His arms wrap around me in an instant, and I simply want to bottle this feeling of having my son to myself on this his special day, just like bottled perfume which I can revisit and rejoice in as and when. I know the past few months have been difficult for him, but brighter days are nearing – he just needs to keep plodding on.

I crouch before the tree and select a gift, knowing that all eyes are on me as I play Santa Claus.

'Teddy, this is for you,' I say, clutching his present and stepping carefully between the gift piles to reach his designated spot beside the armchairs. 'I'm hoping you like it, but if you don't, please say. I kept the receipt.' I'm always listening out for what I can buy them but am never 100 per cent sure until they've opened it and I've seen their reaction. A bit like life really; you think you know what you want until it is truly yours, then bugger, it's not all it's cracked up to be.

'Thanks, Helen, I'm sure it'll be perfect,' he says, taking the offered gift. I'm nervous buying for the lads, they never ask for much and as a result by default they wind up with a whole load of socks and hankies. The girls on the other hand ...

'Thanks, Helen,' calls Scarlet, waving her new clutch bag in my direction. 'Just what I asked for.'

'You're welcome,' I say, knowing I can breathe now she's happy – we won't have tears on Christmas Day. Always a downer for me, but sadly a regular occurrence where Scarlet is concerned. I try so hard to get it right, seek out the right gift, find the right place to purchase at the right price. When present-opening ends in tears, like last year with that hair-styling set she'd asked for – well, having to fetch the Kleenex for her dampens all my Christmas spirit. Some years I've been tempted to wrap a new box of tissues up for her as a standby gift.

I glance around the lounge. This is one of my special moments on Christmas Day, once we've seen to Emmet's birthday celebrations. I've always insisted that he has two separate presents, none of this joint present malarkey which other relatives try to fob him off with.

After handing out the remainder of the gifts, I sit down, relax and enjoy us all being together, beside the Christmas tree, knowing that we each have everything we need – right here.

I glance towards Diane and Lowry and am pleased to see they each have a neat pile of gifts and happy smiles. Their gifts might not have the personal touch that will follow in years to come when we know them better, but I warned the lads they would each need something as a welcome to the family. I presume there were some spare gift tags lying about, because a small gift pile has magically appeared for Gunner Jeffery, whose ruddy smile says it all – even I didn't manage that task. Bless Martha, she includes everyone at the shortest notice. She's nothing but kindness, through and through.

'Thank you, Helen. Just what I needed!' squeals Janie, her feet pounding the floor excitedly.

'What have you got, Mum?' asks River, leaning over the arm of the sofa, attempting to view her gift.

'Never you mind,' I snap, wishing to maintain the decorum of our gift-opening ritual.

'Tell us!' demands Emmet, leaning against the fireplace, unwrapping his own pile of socks and hankies.

'A fifty-pound voucher,' says Janie proudly.

'For Boots or John Lewis?' asks Scarlet half-heartedly, busy with opening her own present pile.

'Ann Summers, if you must know!' declares Janie, discreetly tucking the voucher into her bra for safekeeping. 'A little treat for *moi*, methinks!'

There's a sudden silence in the lounge, with much eye-rolling and eyebrow-twitching amongst the younger generation. As I said, I listen out whenever each relative drops hints throughout the year about their wish list and I love it when I get it right, but does Janie have to share every detail of her private life! I believe she might have had one or three festive coffees too many.

Present opening always hits a moment of 'done', when the thank yous fade, the interest in others' gifts wanes significantly and everyone's eager to crack on and remove the packaging from their favourite gift. That moment comes earlier than usual this year, thanks to Janie's input. I'm fearful that Emmet will nip out for a ciggie break, which would halt the flow of the proceedings, so I'm grateful when Martha stands up from behind her pile of gifts to ask, 'Shall I fetch the fizz?' Another long-standing family tradition, though the number of bottles required for a decent glass or two has increased as the years have gone by. I remember when one bottle was enough, for me and Rupert – which we rapidly finished and spent the rest of Christmas Day in bed, pre-baby of course!

I quickly look around, noting who's present as Martha

disappears to collect fresh glasses. Lynette duly follows her, to lend a hand. Diane, Lowry, Rupert, Janie, River, Teddy, Gunner Jeffery, Scarlet and oh, my Emmet . . . who hasn't nipped outside for a quick ciggie. Hooray!

Chapter Thirteen

Lowry

'I have my reservations, Mum ... and I have a right to say.' The words are out of my mouth before I can think. I'm pacing back and forth across my bedroom floor like a sulky teenager hoping to get my point across. I'm also fearful of the hidden cat meowing while my mother is here, sitting on the delicate padded stool of the dressing table.

'But you're getting along with everyone so well,' she says, as if that's a suitable answer.

'Kind of. On some level ... though Martha's my favourite and she's not actual family,'

'She is really, though,' retorts Mum, before asking, 'And the others?'

'Janie's a bit ...' I razzle my hands before me to fill in the missing words, 'and I'm not convinced that's milky coffee she's drinking either. Helen seems lovely, and the guys have each spoken to me at various points; nothing too surprising there.'

'And Lynette?'

'Oh yeah, I forgot Lynette. Well, that's just it – Lynette's so nice she fades into the background, doesn't she?'

'She's a sweetheart – no malice towards anyone.'

'But still, what's with the shoulder shimmy every time she speaks?'

'Lowry, we all have our little traits, you know.'

'Not like that we don't.'

'You're very distant . . . and sometimes verging on defensive – rightly or wrongly. Helen or Janie, or even Lynette, might feel that's not helpful in a family situation.'

'I'm defensive? I wonder where I get that from, Mother?' I don't want to push the issue; it is Christmas Day after all. 'I'm simply going to call it – I think you're going to get hurt.'

'But Lowry . . .'

'But Lowry nothing, Mum. Postpone the wedding, please!' I stop midstride and stare at her, awaiting her response.

Her mouth drops wide and her expression is shocked.

'Now surely that's not necessary?'

'I get it, Mum. This is the first time you've had a proposal. The first engagement you've ever had, the first wedding, booked at record speed, and it almost came off but this scenario, which-ever way you look at it, is utterly crazy. He has a track record, he has four children by four different women, and he still has those four women tagging along in his life! That alone is crazy talk in looney-tune town, Mum. He has paid every bill, bought every property, stumped up every monthly allowance for his indiscretions over the years and yet you want to marry this man and become the final wife? The next divorce, the finale to his wedding spree? I ask you, Mum, what the hell are we doing here?' I dial down my tone, as I feel the dramatics starting to unfurl.

I stop talking altogether when a bulbous tear runs down her left cheek. I didn't mean to make her cry, but if these hurtful facts prevent her from being next in line for a decree absolute, then so be it!

'Lowry, you don't understand,' she mutters, dabbing at her tears. I'm distracted by a faint scratching noise from the ward-robe.

I quickly answer, to cover the noise. 'Then try me . . . tell me . . . explain to me, Mum. Because believe me I've spent nearly two days in this cottage trying my hardest to see what the attraction is. He hardly speaks. He hasn't paid me much attention or tried to get to know me. And we hardly had the best start, did we? I get that you might feel safe and secure with him. I realise that you might for once in your life feel loved. I wouldn't want this situation but I can even see the attraction of knowing he isn't cruel, can we use that term, towards his ex-wives . . . they haven't had to scrimp and save as you did whilst raising me. But for the love of Christ, call the wedding off – live with the guy for a year and see what happens. In a year's time, if all is well, I'll happily admit I was wrong and walk you down the aisle to become his wife but this . . . this is rushed, and I think it's rushed for a reason.'

Mum sighs, her shoulders lifting and lowering in a dramatic fashion. This isn't what I wanted the day before her wedding, or even on Christmas Day itself . . . but if I don't say it, then who will?

'Lowry, please try to understand,' she says, giving me a mournful look.

'Seriously, Mum – I'm trying.'

'Rupert is kind, caring, he's formidable regarding his businesses . . . he refuses to ignore family members and their dilemmas – ask the lads, they've each been supported by him in recent times. I've found my match, Lowry, and I don't get why you can't see that. I'm happy with Rupert, so please let me be.'

What would I say if it were me? If I had a relative reading me the riot act when in my heart of hearts I knew that the man I was with was 'the one'. Would I listen? Take note? Follow their advice? Or be defensive by doing my own thing, knowing what I knew?

'I don't like this, Mum.'

'I know, sweet. I can see it from your side. Honest, I can,' she says, wiping her cheek with the back of her hand. 'I promise you, that after tomorrow you won't have to worry about me. I know because of the moments we have shared together – believe me, he is the most genuine man I have ever spent time with – which is why I love him so much.'

Aargh! She brought the 'L' word into it, which I was trying to avoid as it gives more weight to her argument. But there it is, thrown into the conversation like an emotional hand grenade.

'Do you?'

She nods, adding, 'With all my heart.'

'And he's told you that too?'

Again she nods. 'Not as often as I say it to him – you know what men are like – but yeah, he has told me that he loves me.'

We remain silent and staring, as if transfixed by each other's beliefs. I have one ear cocked towards the wardrobe, listening intently for any movement or the creak of a door opening.

'You haven't sold the house, have you?' I ask tentatively.

'No, Lowry. You know I haven't.'

'I don't know that for sure. You've kept everything pretty hush-hush, only sharing what was necessary as each week went by.'

I'm stumped. I've come to the end of the road, no more argument or explanation to give. If this is what she wants, then so be it. My only job is to be there to support her if this goes belly up in the next eighteen months.

'Would you like to see your dress?' asks Mum, breaking our silence.

'I was hoping for a surprise on the day but tell me it isn't all . . .' I glide both hands down my torso like Scarlet had, minus the wiggle.

'Yours isn't, but hers is.'

'Good. We're very different.' I mean it in a nice way, not wanting to sound too catty.

'It wouldn't do for us all to be the same – and she calms down over time.'

'She needs to,' I mutter to myself before adding, 'What's with Gunner Jeffery too? Are you buying the accidentally spotted him outside a train station routine?'

'Rupert doesn't appear riled by it – so why not? I bumped into Rupert coming out of a multi-storey car park, remember? I swiped his bumper clean off – look where it's got us!'

I shrug, not knowing what to say without sounding facetious.

'I tried to choose a dress style you'd like, nothing flouncy or twee. Your dress is elegant and classic, I'm sure you'll like it. The dressmaker said it should fit like a glove as long as the measurements you gave are accurate,' she says, holding up crossed fingers. 'They both look lovely. I wish you'd try it on.'

I shake my head. I've had no involvement in the rest of the planning, so is it too much to ask for a surprise on the day regarding my dress?

'I trust you. Come on, we need to get back downstairs otherwise we'll set tongues wagging.' I wrap my arms about her shoulders and give a bear-hug squeeze. I know I'm being overprotective, rudely questioning her feelings and Rupert's integrity, but this is my mum. I've only got the one, unlike some I could mention.

'We should hurry otherwise that she-cat might step out from its hiding place and confirm my suspicions,' she says, giving me a knowing look as we head for the door.

I say nothing, knowing my reply might sound defensive.

Martha

'And that, Martha, was the mother of all meals!' declares Rupert, pushing his chair back from the table, as we all are, allowing room for our expanding waistbands. I give a gracious nod accepting his compliment – what else did he expect? It's me,

Martha; my cooking never fails this family, ever! This year is no exception. Earlier on there was not a mouthful remaining on any plate, serving platter, ceramic dish or gravy boat; not a single Brussels sprout survived – just twelve dirty plates with cutlery waiting to be cleared. And now twelve empty dishes, spoons and cream jugs are the only evidence that I'd made a mountain of profiteroles, Emmet's favourite, for dessert. 'In the tradition of the Carmichaels . . .' Mr C hasn't even finished his sentence when a barrage of voices start shouting their desired tasks.

'Washing up.'

'I'm not drying up – I did it last year!'

'Bagsie clearing the table.'

'No, Teddy – you got to do that last year!'

'What's your problem, Scarlet?'

'Snooze you lose, Scarlet!' calls Emmet playfully along the table, knowing he can play his 'exempt card' on this annual tradition.

I sit back and enjoy the family frivolity. This is the only one of two days in the year on which I never lift a finger after dinner, the other being April first, my birthday.

'You just watch!' hollers Scarlet, jumping up from her seat and grabbing the dirty dish nearest to her. Oh Lord, this will end in crockery breakage if she continues in that way.

'That's not fair, you sneaky mare!' retorts Teddy, jumping up at his end of the table to do likewise.

'Here we go!' calls River, rolling up his sleeves, indicating a washer-upper preparing for duty. Not that he'll wash every pot by hand given that there's a fully functioning dishwasher at his disposal, but he's supposed to, according to the rules of the family tradition. And I will be brought a large brandy and encouraged to put my feet up and take no notice of the hulla-baloo that occurs should they start to argue about who was the designated dryer-upper, a job that no one ever volunteers for because that unfortunate soul misses out on the next hour of festive celebration as they remain in the kitchen alone until the task is complete. Though I have occasionally assisted when taking my empty brandy glass through – I felt so sorry for Lynette last year; she looked like a bedraggled Cinderella.

'Martha, where would you care to take your brandy?' asks Emmet.

'I do believe the snug is calling my name,' I say, knowing that the little poetry book is still on the coffee table. I might indulge in some lyrical ballads while the kitchen is tidied and set right for my next shift.

'Madam, if you'd care to alight from the table, I shall bring your brandy through in one moment,' says Emmet, imitating a butler, with a flourishing hand gesture towards the snug. I notice that Lowry and Diane are staring at the mayhem being played out around them. I'll leave it to others to explain the rules. I push my chair backwards, take my leave and make my way to the quiet delights of the snug.

But where is my book? I'm sure I left it on the coffee table. I check underneath in case it's been knocked to the floor, check the sides of each sofa cushion in case it's been pushed down out of sight, and finally settle myself, knowing that my brandy will soon be appearing and I don't want to break with tradition and not be ready and waiting when Emmet delivers my treat.

The few spare minutes allow me a chance to dream a little about Hawaii. Back home, I've already collected a stash of glossy brochures from the travel agent, studied every page for infinitesimal details about the resorts, stunning locations and sights of interest. The question is how long will I need to stay to do everything I want to – the longer I stay, the more it will cost, and the more my accommodation costs, the less I'll be able to do activity-wise. I need to find a sweet balance so that when I arrive back home, wherever that might be, I won't regret skimping on my trip of a lifetime. Such regrets would only cast shadows on my happy memories, and I can't have that.

'Here you are, a double and a bit!' announces Emmet, entering with a bulbous brandy balloon on a tray.

He graciously lowers the tray for me to remove my drink.

'Why thank you, Emmet … would you care to join me?' I say, as is our custom.

'I thought you'd never ask!' he replies, swiftly nipping out into the hallway to collect his own drink before re-entering and closing the door behind him. He flops on to the opposing sofa, his glass held high, ensuing he doesn't spill a drop.

'What have you there?'

'I nearly emptied the Irish cream, but I knew someone would have a fit if I did, so I've opted for ginger wine – a very large one, but still.'

'Cheers, Big Ears!' I clink my glass against his.

'Same goes, Big Nose!' replies Emmet, with a definite twinkle in his eye.

We both take a huge sip, drawing in the air and savouring our annual moment. I'm grateful for him continuing our customary tradition of an after-dinner tipple. Despite it being a difficult year, I was determined to be here for his big birthday. I'll happily relinquish my role knowing I reached this milestone – nothing lasts for ever, does it? I wonder where I'll be this time next year. In a tiny apartment far away from Cloisters? Possibly alone? This thought scares me after so many years spent amongst the Carmichaels. Maybe I could get a rescue cat for company, like the stray that Lowry is feeding. Though taking on added responsibilities might not be a good idea if I deteriorate as quickly as my mother did. I wouldn't wish to end up neglecting a loving animal because of my own encroaching health issues.

'We've done this for how long now?' asks Emmet, as if he doesn't know.

'Fourteen years ... which I can't quite believe.' Mr C wasn't opposed to his son drinking at such a young age, despite me being cautious at the time.

'Phew! And just like that – time flies!'

'It certainly does, Emmet.' I note his relaxed manner. His body has sunk into the sofa cushions as if we've been sitting here for an hour or so rather than a few minutes – something is different about him today, and it's not just related to turning thirty. Like the snowy weather outside, something has changed – like a sprinkle of magic that can brighten the soul.

'What?' he asks, as if reading my thoughts.

'Have you packed up smoking?' I ask, taking a long shot. He hasn't passed me in the kitchen to nip outside as he did yesterday or the day before.

His eyes widen. 'Maybe. Maybe not.'

'Bloody hell! What's brought this on?' I ask, though I suspect I can guess who.

'I suppose you've got to grow up sometime.'

If he thinks he can fool the likes of me with such talk, he's barking up the wrong tree. I can see the attraction: his brooding, masculine energy pulled towards Lowry's kind and caring nature. I fix my gaze on his dark eyes, raise my brandy glass to my lips and slowly sip.

'What?' he says for a second time in so many minutes.

'Pull the other one, sunshine – it has bells on it!'

Chapter Fourteen

Helen

'River, we haven't even started and you're cheating already!' I holler along the table, attempting to bring order so the house rules can be explained to our newbies. And probably argued over by our regulars.

'It wasn't me, it was Gunner Jeffery!' answers River, playfully elbowing the older gent alongside him.

'If you can't behave as a pair and be nice to each other then we'll separate you now,' says Janie, wagging a finger in her son's direction. I'm still regretting our sisterly partnership last year so have opted to team up with Lynette for our Christmas night annual board games tournament. I'm sure we'll score as many points and I won't have to battle against Janie's tipsiness during the final rounds. Janie's surprise partner this year is Scarlet – I'll be jiggered if the pair of them can finish any round successfully given they're both half-cut already.

The dining room has been transformed into a games room, the sideboard is covered in party nibbles and calorific treats plus the usual selection of wines, spirits and Janie's Irish cream liqueur. The record player volume has been turned up a notch to fill the cottage with festive tunes, much to Rupert's dismay – he's sick of hearing the needle being replaced every hour.

Rupert is busy drawing up the official score sheet, of which he takes charge despite having to multitask by partnering Diane, as to be expected this year – though our house rules clearly state they need to separate next year and be on opposing teams. Talking of winning teams, it's nice to see that Martha and Emmet haven't joined forces, given that the pair thrash the rest of us most years with their aptitude for rolling dice, answering general knowledge questions and making up of bizarre words to place on triple word scores, which just happen to be in the dictionary each time they're called out for cheating. I'm not sure our Teddy will be up to Martha's winning standards but a change is as good as a rest for one year. I note that Lowry looks positively aghast at the prospect of completing the pile of board games to the left of Rupert's seat.

'Don't look so frightened, lovey – you'll be amazed how swiftly we can get through these with our adopted rules – it'll only take three hours,' I say, trying to ease her anxiety.

'And you'll probably eat your body weight in Twiglets and cheese straws during the tournament,' says Emmet, to his seemingly nervous teammate, placing his hand encouragingly on her upper arm. Lowry's fraught gaze instantly softens. The array of snacks always appears far too much at this stage of the proceedings but it will prove to not have been in three hours' time. Likewise with the alcohol – the sideboard isn't big enough to accommodate food and drink for twelve people.

'And that's usually the winning strategy, so take full advantage of it, Lowry. Otherwise Martha and Teddy will meet you in the finals,' calls Scarlet, downing the remains of her large glass of rosé before ambling over to the sideboard to refill her glass.

'We aren't declaring our strategy, actually,' announces Martha, bumping her shoulder against Teddy's. 'They who dare simply win!'

'Enough of all this talk psyching each other out, let's get on with it – we'll be here all night otherwise,' grumbles Rupert. 'First round is Speed Scrabble.'

There's a unanimous groan from the majority of the teams.

'May the best team win, hey, Martha?' says Emmet, sending her a winning smile along the table, then flashing a warmer grin towards his nervous teammate.

'We sure will!' replies Martha, matching his grin.

What is going on between those two? I know the brandy ritual usually goes to their heads but they seem to have the devil in them since leaving the snug. I hope against hope that Martha isn't harbouring a secret on his behalf. If I find out that she's been in touch with his ex and is instigating something, I'll be gutted. I get that Martha thinks she knows what's good for my son, but on this occasion she'd be failing him badly. If anything, I'd quite like Emmet to meet someone more on his wavelength, someone more down to earth ... more ... I look across the table and notice how engaged and animated he is in discussion with Lowry. She is blushing, ever so slightly but it's there – a slight flush to the apples of each cheek and creeping up her throat. I swiftly glance around the table – is anyone else noticing this? Everyone seems busy with their team efforts; only I seem mesmerised by what's playing out before me.

You can usually tell when a games tournament is nearing its end – there are empty seats around the table where knocked-out teams have lost interest and drifted off to focus on filling their stomachs or boozing in the kitchen. At least one argument will have broken out, forcing someone's temper to flare and igniting a stroppy walk out to join the drinkers elsewhere to get their version of the defeat into the public domain whilst others continue to do battle. Though this year, the usual hasn't happened; we're still all present, no one has left the table – which I'm delighted about.

My eye passes over each duo along the table. Scarlet has thrown a strop, unsurprisingly given that she and Janie were too tipsy during the last round to attempt playing our quick-fire version of Trivial Pursuit. If Scarlet incorrectly states that

Melbourne is the capital of Australia one more time, even I'll be asking for a refund on that boarding-school education, which Fena demanded as early as her twelve-week scan. Janie's slurring her words terribly, while Lynette's attempting to ply her with black coffee, though her never-ending kindness is being rejected. Teddy's fallen silent as he's lost a multitude of points, which has undermined Martha's strengths. Rupert wasn't paying attention due to his dual roles, so he and Diane have failed to collect points as they should, while Lynette and I have made only a half-baked attempt to win – neither one of us has the competitive streak of a true-born Carmichael. River and Jeffery have proven to be a winning combination, and Emmet and Lowry ... my interest lingers on that couple. Emmet's on fire with his jokes, whimsical banter and a much more relaxed manner. Lowry's the smiliest I've seen her since she arrived; maybe her concerns for her mum have been answered. They're laughing and joking, and why wouldn't they be – they're top of Rupert's leader board – but there's ... a contented air about them, as if they've known each other for years and not just these last two days.

'I'm bored,' announces Scarlet, getting up from her seat to walk carefully along the row of chairs, discreetly holding on to the back of each as she passes. 'Can we have some other music on?' No one answers her; we let her please herself.

Here we go, the beginning of the end for our tournament fun.

There's silence from the hallway, and then the music booms into life; the volume is turned way up high.

Every fibre of my body cringes on hearing the song's intro, knowing what to expect before it happens. I wish I'd nipped into the kitchen to refill my drink when Scarlet left the room because now she's going to make an entrance, and I don't care to watch. Who in their right mind would sing this to their father and brothers? Bloody Scarlet, that's who!

Lowry

I hear the distinctive *ba-booms* fill the air but continue to focus
on our battleship grid; with our sixteen-point advantage on the
score board we could win outright if we secure this victory. But
my concentration is broken and my eye is drawn to the open
doorway as a sultry figure appears, pressing her spine against
the wooden doorframe and seductively shimmying up and down
it like a dancers' pole. Her accompanying pout and fluttering
eyelashes only reinforce the opening of a performance which
I hope will cease immediately but fear may continue for the
duration of the song.

I jerk my gaze from Scarlet's writhing figure to fixate on the
gleaming wooden table, and silently vow not to look up until the
tune has ended. I don't want this image in my head. Sadly, my
peripheral vision isn't as controllable. How I wish I'd nipped to
the toilet at the first recognition of the Christmas tune.

Scarlet continues as if she were on stage headlining a variety
show by making her way to the head of the table and leaning
seductively against her father's armchair. Her red lips continue
to pout as her index finger traces the outline of his shirt collar.

Oh, dear Lord, please take me now, right now, this moment,
and put a stop to what's about to happen . . .

In a sickly-sweet voice, Scarlet – clearly the worse for wear –
begins to coo the lyrics of 'Santa Baby'. I hate to be a bitch,
but . . . it is one thing to croon this festive favourite in a group of
ladies at the Christmas works do or a hen night but in the middle
of a family Christmas get-together, when our ability to escape is
reduced by alcohol consumption and our greed for turkey.

It is taking all my effort not to raise my gaze but momentarily
I fail miserably, as Scarlet's curvy frame begins to sidle around
the dining room. Her hips are moving faster than Shakira's ever

did, her lips are pouting more than Mick Jagger could dream of and Jessica Rabbit wouldn't stand a chance against this beauty in a lash-fluttering competition. I won't mention her well-endowed cleavage, which is definitely on show, for fear of revealing my own insecurities.

Worse still, her cooed lyrics and sultry looks appear to be directed at her father and three brothers. Emmet's frame freezes rigid beside mine – gone is his relaxed manner; his jaw is clenched and his gaze appears fixed on our battleship grid. My brain spins into an internal monologue whilst trying to control my eyeballs. Wrong, just simply wrong in every way, Scarlet. This is the kind of thing you jokingly sing to your other half whilst half-cut and washing up the Boxing Day crockery, not in a room full of adults, when your DNA profile is linked to virtually every male in the room!

Dear God, please stop her, end this monstrosity of a performance which she will surely regret first thing tomorrow morning or when she sobers up, whichever comes first. And which the rest of us will be unable to erase from our memories for a lifetime. Never again will I hear this song without recalling this moment, if I live to the ripe old age of 103. I fear for my sanity having this image in my head. Surely this is verging on incestuous?

There's a sudden change of pace as she delivers a slutdrop dance move in the middle of the dining room. I hardly think it appropriate in front of family, but even less so right in front of Gunner Jeffery's seat – his eyes are agog. I bet this picturesque cottage has never seen anything like this before! The owners might be able to withhold the deposit if this performance sullies the atmospheric vibes and can't be eradicated by the housekeeper come the end of our occupancy.

River seems to be thoroughly mortified by her dancing; Teddy is blush red and staring as if in a trance at the tournament's score sheet; Rupert appears to be bursting with pride and awe at his only daughter's spontaneous performance and . . . I sneak a peek in Emmet's direction to find him wide-eyed, pupils dilated and watching me.

Bang, we eyeball each other. Neither one looks away or flinches. Instead, his eyelids close a fraction, just an almost infinitesimal amount, suggesting he's not impressed either and that he too wishes he were dead, on his thirtieth birthday. I raise an eyebrow in reply; we're on the same page. I suddenly want to burst out laughing; of all the things that we could have agreed on – it is this!

Scarlet sidles closer to Gunner Jeffery's chair, to gently trace her index finger around his paunchy jawline, which I can't imagine Janie will be best pleased about, given Martha's earlier comments. Or her father, for that matter. I can't imagine that my mother approves of this little treat on the eve of her wedding – I imagine there will be lots for her and Rupert to discuss tonight prior to the light being dowsed.

Oh my God, she's literally climbing on to Gunner Jeffery's lap; surely not suitable for family viewing? I will need a stiff nightcap to rid myself of this visual 'show and tell' of 'how to get more presents out of Daddy, or even his oldest friend'.

I daren't look at anyone else, knowing that Emmet is watching my every move. I don't want to cause him or me further embarrassment, having maintained our composure for so long to ruin it at the end. Though I'm not sure Emmet's realised the worst is yet to come, while I am mentally ahead of the game and know that in a few minutes, and it is getting nearer with each damn second, Scarlet is going to end her sultry song and they, the family from which I'm excluding myself, are going to have to react and potentially applaud the dancing just delivered to them regardless of how cringeworthy they actually found it. I will not be clapping, cheering or wolf whistling, which I suspect a certain gent in the room might actually do. Though if silence descends and no one reacts apart from the recipient of the nearly-but-not-quite lap dance, I may need an escape route. I might pretend to wipe my nose, cough or even feign a life-threatening coronary at that precise moment, as my body and morals forbid me from encouraging such behaviour in public. And especially on Christmas Day!

That's when I realise that Martha is missing – how did she escape? When she hears of this incident, she should be eternally grateful that she wasn't violated like the rest of us. I swear I'll lose the plot laughing if Emmet should stand up in the middle of this performance to grab a whisky. Though I might be brave enough to request he pours me one too!

Finally, thankfully, the music stops. Scarlet falls silent and I dare to lift my head to read the room. Teddy and River are still avidly staring at particular spots about the table, while Rupert's brow is twitching like a two-stroke engine firing into life with a certain realisation. Gunner Jeffery is grinning like a Cheshire cat up at Scarlet, who is discreetly dabbing her glowing brow with a napkin. While my mother has a face like a bulldog chewing a thistle and Helen is clearly inspecting the intricacy of a house spider's tiny cobweb in a corner of the ceiling. Lynette looks like a waxwork dummy, Janie's swigging her Irish cream straight from the bottle, and Emmet is watching me.

'Phew, that was such fun … Anyone else getting up for a number?' asks Scarlet, joyfully giving a final ass wiggle in Gunner Jeffery's direction as she moves away from him.

My mouth drops open, causing Emmet to snort before he stirs in his chair to announce, 'Well, I don't know about anyone else but I need a stiff drink. Lowry, can I get you anything?'

'Please.' I'm about to make a request for a double whisky but Emmet has left the dining room in three strides, even possibly left the building for a much-needed smoke.

Chapter Fifteen

Martha

I jump as Emmet dashes into the kitchen after the music has stopped.

'Tell me that wasn't Scarlet?'

'Martha, I'd dearly like to but I can't. She did the whole she-bang like a hooker on Hollywood Boulevard – the only thing she left out of her act was the Betty Boo knee bends.'

'She didn't do that drop-down thing?'

'Oooh, she did – much to Jeffery's delight. I've a feeling Diane's not impressed.'

I watch as Emmet goes to the cupboard, grabs a couple of wine glasses, then heads for the fridge to retrieve a chilled bottle.

'And on your thirtieth too – hardly an image you want to remember, now is it?'

'Scarlet, my dear, darling little sister, the gift that keeps on giving, year after year,' he says, emptying the bottle's contents into the large glasses, the cold wine frosting each glass instantly.

'Are those both for you?' I ask, unsure what I'm witnessing.

'The other is for Lowry. You should see the look on her face – she might need medical attention if she doesn't get drunk in the next few hours.'

'Poor lass, it must be quite a shock to meet you all in one go!'

'Some family, hey? Let's be grateful that Fena won't be gracing us with her presence, or there really would be fireworks,' he says, tossing the empty wine bottle into the recycling bin.

'Don't let Scarlet hear you saying that,' I scold, though I get where he's coming from. Fena has flair in more ways than one. What's more, she's not frightened of showing it. There's no prize for guessing where Scarlet gets her sultry moves from because it certainly wasn't Rupert.

'What are you having, Martha? A tipple of port or a rum and black?' asks Emmet, grabbing a third glass from the cabinet and holding it aloft for me.

'Now you're talking. Are you making it?' I say with a giggle; he's a real charmer when he wants to be.

'Sure will. Doubles all the way!' says Emmet, shaking the glass playfully.

'Go on then, I'll have a port.' Though I really shouldn't as alcohol hardly helps my tremors.

Mmm, what's cheered him up? I watch as Emmet brings together a very generous port and lemonade with ice and a slice. I shouldn't admit it but he has wheedled his way into being my favourite, despite that brooding manner, his sharp tongue and dubious stare. River's too fluid with his morals and opinions, too hit and miss with everything he does, as if the passion that ignited a thought burns out before the thought comes to fruition. And loveable Teddy, always the baby in my eyes, following the other two lads, wishing to be like them in every way yet never managing to see his true self beneath the shadow they cast.

'Cheers, Martha!' says Emmet, handing me the hi-ball glass. 'Careful not to gulp it.'

'Not likely given the measure you've just poured,' I say, raising my glass in his direction as he collects the two wine glasses.

'Are you coming back through?' he asks over his shoulder, before disappearing towards the dining room.

'In a second. I'm just popping some mince pies into the Aga to warm through,' I say, sensing the games tournament has been abandoned after Scarlet's untimely interruption.

Why she acts like that is beyond me. It's not as if she's not the centre of attention anyway, but to prance about in such a provocative manner … and who for? It makes me cringe just thinking about it.

'Can you believe that girl?' asks Helen, appearing in the kitchen doorway. 'A bloody embarrassment, and in front of Diane and Lowry too. She ought to save that kind of dancing for her nights out with her girlfriends.' I don't answer for fear of being quoted if this erupts further; instead I look up and nod in all the right places. 'The boys are just as bad, almost encouraging her by turning a blind eye and not a single word uttered in protest. I should have spoken up, if Rupert wasn't going to. When is she going to grow up – you can't stay the baby of the family for ever, can you?'

'No. Though their silence was most likely sheer embarrassment,' I answer, secure in my opinion.

'Urgh! Sorry, I bet everyone has come through here and had a moan,' says Helen, opening the fridge door to collect the other wine bottle.

'Not quite, but give them time,' I say, cheerfully knowing that my role within this family has always been to listen to others. What will happen when the tables are turned and they have to listen to me for once? How will I actually break the news officially, or when? When I start to drop the crockery? After my first fall? Or when my shaking hand is noticed by someone? Phuh! I've more respect for myself than to wait until then, which is why this festive holiday has to be the best of the best, as I'm pretty certain it'll be my last Christmas in service. Each day brings me one day closer to that daunting task. All I hope is that I don't receive a tsunami of pity. Uh-uh, pity – can't bear it, not now, not ever! I'm all for being empathetic and recognising a situation for what it is, being realistic in life, but pity does you no good in the long run.

'Thank you, anyway . . . today was a beautiful spread, Martha. Rupert will be thrilled that everything went to plan and that Diane's first Christmas with us has gone so smoothly – which is always down to you. I can't thank you enough for Emmet's birthday cake either – you are a gem.'

I don't interrupt, I know she means every word. For all Helen's elaborate planning, there's always a stressful moment when she appears to become unhinged – much like the lounge and dining-room doors. This year, the mutilation of the Christmas tree to fit around the TV screen nearly toppled her. The true thanks I get is being part of this family all year round; it's nothing for me to put my baking skills to the test for the annual occasions. I don't know what I'd have done without this family – probably give up my holidays to work in a soup kitchen or volunteer at a local hospital; anything would have been better than what I fear would be my fate without a family.

'I assume the games tournament is finished?' I ask, closing the door of the Aga.

'Abandoned, more like. Emmet and Lowry were still winning by a mile, though Lady Luck's probably been scared away by Scarlet doing her thing.'

Helen pours herself a very large drink, nearly brimming the top of the largest of the glasses, and settles at the kitchen table. My drink remains untouched opposite her.

'Emmet's looking brighter,' I say, busying myself with collecting plates and icing sugar, ready to dust the warmed mince pies before serving.

Helen sighs heavily. I glance over. She goes to speak, then thinks better of it. I know what she's about to say, so I wait until she's ready. I know my answer, whether she'll want to hear it or not.

'Martha, do you think he's livened up since Lowry arrived?'

'I believe he has,' I say, giving her a knowing look.

'Now that coupling I quite like,' she replies.

Lowry

'Can we talk?' asks Mum, tiptoeing along the snow-laden step-ping stones to my position on the nearest garden bench.

'Sure. I was just getting some fresh air before going to bed.' I sit up, straightening my posture, readying myself after our previous chats. I'd been enjoying the silence of a winter garden after dark, where a blanket of snow covers everything apart from the odd twigs and stumps that poke through, refusing to be hidden. The chilly night air has chased away the over-whelming fug brought about by the roaring coal fire in the hearth and a tipple too many.

'A good idea. We're calling it a night too,' she says, brushing the settled snow from the remaining seat, much as I had ten minutes ago, before sitting down. 'Anyway ... have you had a nice day?'

'It's been interesting,' I say, surprised by her choice of question. 'Though I might need help forgetting Scarlet's performance. I half expected Gunner Jeffery to whip out his wallet and tuck a twenty in her garter! Is that the sort of goings-on that I'm to expect?'

'Of course not, Scarlet's only playing,' says Mum, pulling her fleecy jacket tighter around her slender frame.

'Is she? Is she really?' I mutter, trying to erase her dancing, his leer, her wiggles and his enjoyment. Urgh! 'And you?'

'Yes, lovely day. Anyway ...' She pauses, takes a deep breath before continuing. 'I'm not proud of what I'm about to say, Lowry – so I'd appreciate a little patience while I find the right words ... if you get my drift. I know you're mad at me – which doesn't m-make it any easier for me to e-explain but ...' She struggles to form each word, much as she had when breaking the news that Grandad had died.

What's she on about? Has she called tomorrow's wedding off? Has Rupert?

'I was just eighteen … and hardly worldly-wise regarding dating or boys. I'd been seeing Craig for a few months; he was a year older, lived two streets away and drove a battered Ford Capri. Anyway, one thing led to another and we ended up sleeping together after a Saturday night date.' Is this it? Is she's actually going to say? Or is this going to be another conversation she bails out of partway through? I press my lips together, vowing to keep schtum. I daren't ask a question. I daren't interrupt, or even catch her eye, which isn't difficult given that she's staring off towards the far side of the garden as if I were sitting on the other bench, positioned behind the outhouse. 'Looking back … we all do silly things at that age, thinking we're so grown up.' She pauses. Her brow quivers, her chin too, while her gaze remains fixed as she relives moments from nearly three decades ago. She suddenly comes alive, making me jump out of my skin. 'He dumped me the next weekend. Young love, hey – not all it's cracked up to be, is it?'

'Er, no,' I mutter, fleetingly remembering my own experiences, unsure if she's finished her story.

'And that was that,' she adds, as if that's a satisfying ending to her storytelling. I'd have much preferred and 'they lived happily ever after'.

'But it isn't, is it?' I say, irked that she'd even say that.

Her shoulders offer the smallest of shrugs.

'No. Don't give me that, Mum,' I say mimicking her shoulder gesture. 'This is the beginning of my story, so I'd like to know what followed. It's taken long enough for you to tell me this much; I'm hardly going to accept half a story when not knowing has overshadowed my entire life.'

She gives a heavy but controlled sigh, as if she really wasn't prepared for me to ask for specifics. I'm not sure who's being ridiculous here – me for wanting to know or her for thinking I wouldn't.

'He wasn't interested when I said you were on the way. Simply told me to go away as it probably wasn't his anyway, even though he knew that I'd only ever been with him.'

'And you accepted that?'

'What else was I supposed to do? I told my parents and they immediately hugged me, assured me that everything would be fine and said our family didn't need the likes of him. And that's how it was from that day on, just the four of us.'

'Did he never come around? Speak to you?'

'No, never. He saw me in the street once, when I was quite far gone, about seven months or so. He was all dressed up with a young woman on his arm but he carried on walking by as if he never knew me.'

'Oh, Mum. And he didn't say anything?'

'No. Not a word. He just looked me up and down as we passed – nothing more.'

'And when I was born – what then?'

'Nothing.'

'Didn't you tell him? Like officially?'

She shakes her head.

'What, never?'

'Why would I, when he'd shown such little regard for either of us.'

'Bloody hell. I'd have been kicking up a fuss – the whole bloody town would have known about it.'

'That's not me, is it? Our family quietly got on with raising you; we didn't need anything from the likes of him and his family. They had no claim on your affections, your time or your childhood. You had everything that we could provide – Grandad especially. You know you were the apple of his eye.'

'I see. And you never saw him since?'

'Once. I was taking you to primary school one morning. We were in a rush, late, I suppose. You were clambering from the rear seat of the car, all pump bag and duffle coat, and I was dashing around the boot trying to hurry you along, kindly, and he was standing on the opposite kerb. Watching. I don't know why he was there, what he might have been doing – dropping a kiddy off himself or simply waiting – but I didn't speak. We carried on along the path into school and he was gone by the time I came back through the school gate, heading for home. I never saw him again.'

'Wow. So why have you never told me this before?'

'Why do you think?' Her voice cracks with emotion. 'It hardly puts me in a good light, does it? Not the best impression to give a daughter.'

'You sound like an angel compared to him, Mum. Seriously, don't worry about that – I've met a few Craigs in my time, believe me. Hey, Craig. That name's got a whole other meaning now.'

'As your father's name,' she mutters softly.

'Hardly a father, Mum. That's stretching the term a little, don't you think? But still, yeah, I won't ever hear that name now without associating it. And his surname?'

She bites her lip.

'Don't worry, I'm not going to search for him and cause a big hoo-ha – I would just like to know the full details for my own benefit. Simply to know.'

'Talbot.'

'Craig Talbot – it feels strange even knowing that much.' His name ricochets around my mind like a ballbearing in a pinball machine hitting vital moments in my life. A lingering shadow falls away from my shoulders, allowing me to feel lighter.

If his reaction had been different, my surname wouldn't be Stephens. My signature would be different, my qualification certificates would bear a different name. I might have siblings, cousins and another side to the family; our family photo album would include others and we wouldn't all fit inside a waltzer car!

'Are you OK?' asks Mum, her voice barely audible.

'Yes, thank you. Honest, I truly am. I'm content knowing the basic facts; there's no more mystery about where I came from – that can now disappear. I feel fine. Thank you.' Her brow quivers as if she's unsure; she doesn't understand the importance of simply knowing, but she will in time. 'Come here.' My arms reach around her in an all-embracing hug that will never take away the pain of how badly she was treated but goes some way to recognise what she's gone through.

'Thank you for making that so easy to say – I was half expecting a different reaction from you, Lowry,' says Mum, as we separate.

'I don't see why. I've only ever asked the same question time and time again.'

'Mmm, maybe I should have done this sooner.'

'Mmm, maybe.' I leave it there. What more is there to say? Tomorrow is a brand-new day, her special day, on which to begin a new chapter of her life.

Helen

'What are you even doing here?' snipes Janie, holding on to the banister rail, having consumed several drinks too many. Her tone is hushed but harsh as I peer through the crack of our bedroom door, barely able to make out the figures on the landing.

'I have every right! I'm his best buddy,' retorts Gunner Jeffery testily. 'A wedding should be a family celebration regardless of the number. And I class myself as family.'

'I don't mean that . . . I mean . . . us.'

I eke the bedroom door open by another inch, straining to hear a little more. I can see they're standing at the top of the staircase, passing like ships in the night en route for the main bathroom. If Janie catches me I'll be in for it, but standing here in the dark, pressed close against the door, I'll have a chance to dart across the room should the conversation suddenly cease and Janie come this way.

'Janie, that was years ago, I've long forgotten about our dalliance. I thought you cared, when you clearly didn't.'

'I cared. Don't make me out to be some cold-hearted bitch, Jeffery.'

'Why call it off then?'

'Because . . .'

'Because what?'

'Jeffery, really? You want to rake over old coals at this time of night? We've got to survive a wedding tomorrow, and spend all day in each other's company, and you want to explode a few emotional landmines the night before, hey?' says Janie, sounding terser than I've heard her for a long while.

'It would have worked, you know. We could have been . . .'

'No. It wouldn't. How could I settle down with his best friend?'

'He was married to your sister and that made little difference to you, did it?'

I wince. Ouch, that has got to hurt! I have to restrain myself from darting out from my hiding place on to the landing to thank Jeffery for hitting the bullseye. I often wonder if folk recognise the pain and hurt that particular incident caused me, and obviously they do, if they still refer to it in private. Funny how I believed I'd fought that battle alone all these years, when others possibly had my back after all. Pity no one spoke up at the time. And rarely since.

'That was a low blow . . . and you think I haven't regretted my actions, is that it? You think you know me so bloody well, Jeffery Braithwaite – that you can stand there on the moral high ground preaching to the likes of me! Goodnight!' Her tone is edged with anger and her footsteps too. I dart away towards my twin bed in the corner, and fling myself under the duvet.

The bedroom door swiftly opens, but she doesn't flick on the light as I expect. Instead Janie moves towards her bed in the darkness.

'Bastard! Thinks he can undermine me with a comment or two,' she mutters. I'm not sure if I'm supposed to answer or be asleep, so I stay quiet, eyes closed and ears listening. There are the typical sounds of undressing, the duvet being yanked back, the mattress creaking as she settles herself.

I can tell by her inaudible mutterings that he's wound her up but she needs to let it go, otherwise she'll never sleep. Which is what I need to do.

I turn over, pulling the duvet up to my chin, and begin to drift off, knowing that tomorrow will be another long and intense day. Bright smiles are required, happy conversations, and a private little cry in the bathroom, if needs be.

'I didn't mean to hurt you, honest – I was simply jealous of what you had. Sorry.' Janie's voice is barely audible, but her whisper cuts through the darkness.

I'm about to answer when I realise that Janie thinks I'm truly asleep. I lie still, holding my breath for fear of letting on and interrupting her, but she says no more, or at least I hear no more.

Chapter Sixteen

Tuesday 26 December

Lowry

I wake just after two o'clock, search for the cold side of my pillow and attempt to snuggle down, returning to sleep. But one name fills my mind: Emmet. I turn over, pull the duvet around my shoulders and close my eyes. Like many a stray or abandoned dog I've attended to, Emmet's bark is clearly worse than his bite.

I bet he's outside. My eyes snap open and I check the time again. Seven minutes past two. Nah, he'll be inside by now and fast asleep, like we all should be. It's an important day; I need my sleep. I flip over on to my stomach, close my eyes and prepare to count sheep. He might not be!

I sit up and listen as if I would hear him breathing if he were outside on the bench by the outhouse. I can't. I can hear only the silence created by the snowfall. I fling the duvet back and hop from my bed, darting to the window to draw the curtain aside. The snow is thicker than earlier, though it has ceased falling, turning the front garden into a mass of lumpy bumpy shapes beneath a pristine blanket of white.

He wouldn't be sitting out in this, surely?

I glance over my shoulder at the wardrobe door. Trixie seems content but would it be best if I changed her litter box now, as there'll be no chance of risking it tomorrow? I'll be busy all day supporting my mum. We might be out for the majority of it – possibly drifting back here only late at night. Though I did only change the soil last night but … it won't do any harm to be ahead of the game rather than have a litter-box smell drifting out into the landing, causing the others to ask questions.

It takes me a few minutes to grab the dirtied litter box, shove my feet into woollen socks and then my unlaced pumps, and don my long cardigan over the top of my fleecy pyjamas. Not an advisable look for any other time of day but acceptable for emptying a litter box at quarter past two in the morning.

The staircase is easier to navigate now I know only the top stair creaks, which is surprising given the age of the cottage. A swift glance through the banister rail confirms the snug is empty, so no tricky manoeuvres required there, and before I know it I'm at the kitchen's stable door and the lock is undone. A set of footprints have ruined nature's perfect finish: Emmet must be outside.

As I eagerly reach for the handle, I stop – what the hell am I doing? Is emptying a litter tray in the middle of the night a feasible pretext to accidentally-on-purpose bump into a guy who'll be sitting on a garden bench smoking and drinking? Is this what my life is reduced to outside of my job? Is this why I dislike annual leave so much? Have I no other interests, pursuits or hobbies to light up my sad little world? A second voice, feebler than the first, answers: I have, but those are a hundred miles away in Salford. And right now, when I can't sleep – yeah, I'd prefer to be chatting with Emmet. Fair dos.

I open the door before my judgier inner self has the chance to talk me back into my warm bed.

The silence is deafening, standing on the snow-covered patio. Nothing moves or makes a sound, as if the world has pressed the mute button and forgotten to reset the volume. The night sky is eerily illuminated by the blinding whiteness of the snow scattered below and even the stars are struggling to compete.

I don't wish to disturb the beauty with a second set of prints so I step into those already created, making my way towards the stone steps. The trowel is obvious despite a generous helping of snow, but the dirt patch not so much. I begin to clear the snow away, knowing the earth beneath will be frozen hard. I'd have more joy with a mini pickaxe! The *ting ting* sound made by the trowel alerts my fellow garden dweller that someone else is present.

From the corner of my eye, I see the dark shadowy figure appear from the rear of the outhouse, where the bench is hidden in the shadows. I attempt to feign concentration on my task, purely to underscore the accidental nature of our meeting, though how I'll explain what I'm doing will be another matter.

'Lowry?' A voice cuts through the darkness, causing me to look up in surprise. Not the surprise I was ready to feign in order to cover my flutter of embarrassment but genuine surprise – because it isn't Emmet, it's Gunner Jeffery! Fully clothed, standing on the snow-covered lawn, staring down at me. 'What are you doing out here?'

If there was ever a moment that I wanted to dissolve like a dirt-stained snowman wearing a football scarf in a thaw, it is now. Precisely now. Because now I need to explain what I'm doing out here at this time and chance him spilling the beans come breakfast. Would he be susceptible to a bit of female charm, given the manner in which Scarlet had delighted him? We'll never know – he definitely won't be getting dancing from the likes of me; I can't slutdrop for toffee.

'I-I-I . . . w-w-wanted to take a bit of Cumbria home with me when I return to Pendlebury. As a lasting memory of my visit. I do it all the time when I visit anywhere . . . I've quite a collection at home. From here and abroad . . .' Why am I still speaking when I'm clearly lying my arse off?

'Wow, and you even bring your own box – now that's dedication, Lowry. I would never have guessed that that was even a thing for the younger generation. Do you label and decant each sample into a container for future reference, or leave it loose so you can touch it – much like a photo album brings back memories?'

'I label everything,' I fib, forbidding my inner self from making any absurd comment about my behaviour.

'Interesting. I wish I'd done something like that. I travelled the entire world with the British Army, you know, and I didn't collect any souvenirs to show where I've been. Pity really, but you . . . well, you must take delight in your collection.'

I nod, purely out of embarrassment. I'm no longer conscious of my attire, or my unlikely task with the litter box – how am I going to persuade him not to share this little gem at the breakfast table between buttering his toast and receiving his plate of bacon and eggs? I wonder whether Scarlet would oblige with a repeat rendition of 'Santa Baby' so early in the day? Would my mother mind a slutdrop at her wedding breakfast?

'Excuse me . . .' calls a voice from above. We both look up, startled by the shout, to see Emmet's naked torso leaning out of the back-bedroom window directly above us. 'Would you mind? Some of us are trying to sleep.'

'Sure,' I say eagerly, raising a hand in apology, but oh so grateful for the interruption.

'Sorry, lad, I couldn't sleep and I thought . . . oh, never mind,' replies Gunner Jeffery, walking nearer to the cottage to answer him. Emmet slams the bedroom window with some force, causing me to stare at Gunner Jeffery, as if blaming him.

'I thought the lad might be out here having a ciggie so I came out, but obviously not. Anyway . . .'

'Yes, anyway, that's enough digging for me for tonight,' I say quickly, jumping up with just half the amount of soil I originally intended to collect.

'Is that all? Seems a piddly amount for such a large box; here, let me just dig a bit more for you. I'll feel as if I've helped a little by doing so,' says Gunner Jeffery, taking the trowel from my clutches and digging a hearty amount from the frozen earth. 'There you go now. It would be nice if you added my initials – G. J. B. – to your label for this one, just as a little memory of me.'

'Yeah, I'll do that,' I mutter, wanting to die. Who in their right mind would swallow my ludicrous story? 'Anyway, time for me to go back inside . . . I am quite tired now.'

'Yes, quite. Though I was wondering if you fancied a little nightcap . . . a small brandy, to help you to sleep?'

'No. Sorry, I'm allergic to brandy.'

'Whisky?'

'All spirits – in fact. Large red blotches all over my skin – not a good look for a bridesmaid,' I say, having left the need to tell the truth during our interaction far behind. 'Night!'

'Goodnight, Lowry – see you in the morning,' calls Gunner Jeffery, remaining where he is beside my overturned section of border.

I dash inside, pull the kitchen door to and without caring about making a noise dash up the staircase two at a time. I can feel the clumps of earth dancing in the cardboard box as I go but I don't care if I'm spilling it on to the carpet as long as Gunner Jeffery doesn't follow me to learn which bedroom I am in. I don't want a repeat of the nightcap offer.

'What are you up to?' whispers Emmet, as I reach the top stair, making me jump out of my skin. He has a baggy jumper thrown over his naked chest and is otherwise decked in just black shorts. He peers into the cardboard box before delving a hand inside. 'Soil?'

'Yeah, I knocked over the potted plant in my room earlier – I've cleaned it up but I wanted to refill the plant pot properly. Thankfully, the cream carpet's been very forgiving after a quick scrub.' I cross my fingers, hoping my white lie is offset by the true reason for the soil box.

'Very domesticated and conscientious too,' he quips, tapping the side of the box.

'Well, I didn't want your dad's deposit money being withheld because of me.'

Emmet begins to laugh. 'That's highly unlikely, over a potted plant.'

'Shush, you!' I say pointing frantically down the staircase for fear of Gunner Jeffery hearing.

'You and Jeffery, hey? I would never have guessed,' jests Emmet, leaning over the banister to check out the empty hallway.

'Mmm, I'm not his type, unlike . . .?' I stop talking, not wishing to break Martha's earlier confidence. Emmet's head spins around in my direction.

'Oh my God. You know! Someone's already told you!' he stifles a laugh, his shoulders lifting and lowering uncontrollably. 'Well, I never, and I thought we were censoring the good stuff, or at least trying to until after the wedding.'

'Surely it would be difficult not to have figured this family out by then, Emmet?' I say, half expecting bedroom doors to fly open and cranky folk to start complaining about the noise. 'I think I've been overshadowed, given his interest in Scarlet's performance earlier, so I don't stand a chance.'

'Mmm, that was pretty risqué. Being tipsy, I think she forgot herself. So where have you left Jeffery?'

'In the middle of the garden, staring after me because I refused to join him for a little drinkie.'

'Really? And would you have refused me too?'

'No.' I answer without thinking, which causes him to raise his eyebrows in surprise.

'Wow, care to have a minute to think about that?'

I offer him a fleeting glance.

'Well, it's you, isn't it? Gunner Jeffery's not you.'

Emmet's eyebrows flash a twitch again.

'I'll take that as a compliment. So yeah?'

'Yeah what?'

'A drink?'

My gaze meets his. Is he serious?

'Now I'm worried. You've got drink up here?'

'No. I'm not an alky – downstairs, I mean . . . Oh, quick, here he comes!' says Emmet, pushing me along to land on the sofa beyond the banister. Emmet crouches on the floor in front of it, staring up and over the cushioned back, his index finger pressed to his lips, as the bulky frame mounts the staircase. I sink lower on to the couch, not wishing to peer over my shoulder; witnessing Emmet's reaction is enough. His chin is lifted, his dark curls frame his forehead. He rests his hand on my lower calf as if to assure me all is well, and he doesn't move it. I freeze in surprise. The heat of his palm radiates through my pyjama leg like skin on skin.

I hear the top step creak – I'm quite the expert now.

The soft plod of footsteps signals Gunner Jeffery's departure along the corridor towards the rear of the cottage and his double room, allowing Emmet to breathe freely again. His hand still doesn't move.

'I thought he was about to join us for a minute. He paused on the top stair for ages, looking around, as if he knew we were here,' says Emmet, removing his hand and standing, offering me a hand up. 'You OK?'

'Yeah, fine.'

'What's it to be, bed or a brandy?' His eyebrows twitch again. Is he trying to be suggestive or did he simply misphrase it?

'Brandy it is.' I point towards my bedroom. 'I'll just pop this box in my room.'

Emmet nods.

On my return, he steps aside, allowing me to lead the way. I frantically signal to him not to step on the top stair, as it creaks every time.

'Admit it, you came downstairs in search of me!' he jests, cradling his balloon of brandy. His bare legs are stretched out with his socked feet crossed on the coffee table.

'No. I. Didn't.' I'm rattled that he should be so bold as to suggest it.

'What then?'

I shake my head. I don't want to explain or admit anything, just quietly drink my brandy, have a pleasant chat and then go to sleep.

'After all the secrets you've learnt about this family, you're honestly going to clam up and not share?' he asks, watching me intently.

'I've no secrets to spill.' I can feel my cheeks blushing.

'Really?'

I pull a face to indicate my answer.

'Phew! You'll never survive in this family without a secret or two.'

I watch as Emmet sips his drink, mulling over his own statement before refocusing his gaze on me.

'Spill then,' I say, encouraging him.

'Me?' He purses his lips, as if thinking before he continues. 'I wasn't as bowled over by my previous girlfriend as much as others like to suggest I was. Listening to my mum's account, you'd think I was besotted . . . but I was more just smitten, I suppose. We had some great times together, holidaying and visiting friends; maybe we could have had a future together but . . . there was something missing. You know when—?' He breaks off, as if he has forgotten he has company.

'I know.'

He stares at me intently. 'Do you?'

'Yeah. It was many moons ago now but I had a hard time figuring out that just because someone's nice, it doesn't make them right for you as a partner. I was doped by the Disney love too.'

'Disney love?'

'Yeah, Disney sells you a dream, that you grow up, meet a guy, fall in love and live happily ever after. When actually it's far more painful than that and I suppose in some ways more exhilarating too, if you find the one.'

'If?' He cocks his head, adding to his question.

'Yeah, if . . . not everyone finds who they're looking for. Surely you've got a prime example of that? Your dad has spent a lifetime searching and today, yeah, it's today, he'll be getting married for the fifth time! Most people give up before then.'

Emmet rolls his bottom lip, obviously thinking.

'I used to think he was crazy, putting himself through the hurt, pain and financial sting, but in reality he's quite brave to keep putting himself out there. I've had two serious relationships and already I'm floundering, wondering whether it's actually worth the time, energy and the total feck-up it makes of your head.'

'Is that where you're at?'

'For sure. I'm angry at myself for not seeing where it was heading, disillusioned that the basics of life are so damned difficult and annoyed that I've allowed myself to become something I'm not.'

There's a timely pause. We simply sit staring at the other, our gazes drifting around the other's features, drinking them in. I wonder if my pupils are as large as his are. Or whether his stomach feels as jittery as mine right now.

'Which is?' I say, breaking the moment.

'A miserable bastard, for one.' Emmet laughs, before sipping his brandy.

I like his laugh; there's an infectious energy when the bubbles surface from their hidden depths – like a human spirit level with a very different gauge.

'And you?'

'Me? Nothing. I haven't been in a relationship for years.'

'Dating?'

'Nope. I focus on my work. Work, home, sleep, and repeat.'

Emmet nods, and his gaze lingers on mine. I have the urge to ask, 'What?' but I don't as it's almost too obvious a question.

'And you're happy with that? You're not searching for Disney love, as you called it?'

'I'm not searching. Especially not for some happy-ever-after stuff – no. I'm more of a realist than that. I want the magic, sure I do, but without the lingering shadows.'

'Phuh! Don't talk to me about shadows. Now that's one thing my dad has created many of by doing what he's done.' His tone has changed; gone is the bubble of laughter in his voice, an icy frosting has returned. 'Long lingering shadows in various shades from grey to jet-black.' He sighs, falls silent, drinks his brandy and stares at his socked feet.

I stay quiet, not wishing to intrude into his private thoughts.

'People think the same about rescue dogs . . . animals in general, you know?'

Emmet looks up with a confused expression.

'Have you had too much of this?' he says, tipping his glass.

I smile but carry on regardless. 'They think that having a newborn kitten or pup is better than having a rescue animal. As if the shadows from the animal's previous life are going to damage their new family, their new home and their interactions, when actually animals are pretty resilient in overcoming their shadows and relearning to trust us humans.'

'I bet you've seen some awful cases.'

'I have, but it's balanced out by the kindness and love I see given too – it's not all bad.'

'And your cat ... you balanced out my dad's attitude of "get rid" with your nurturing and kindness,' says Emmet softly, his lingering gaze returning.

I nod, fearful of saying the wrong thing in two ways: in my response to Emmet's gaze or confessing about Trixie's whereabouts.

'She doing alright out there?' he asks.

'Yep. Doing nicely.'

'The kittens?'

'Those too.' I can hear that I answer him too quickly.

A wry smile adorns his lips.

'What?'

'Nothing.' He downs the dregs of his brandy, slaps his thigh and rocks himself up on to his feet. 'I need sleep. Are you done?'

'I'm done,' I say, offering the glass into his outstretched hand.

'Cheers, me dears. I'll see you in the morning.' With that, Emmet leaves the snug. I hear him enter the darkened kitchen, followed by the rattle of crockery as he places the glasses into the dishwasher.

I wait until he passes the open doorway of the snug before calling, 'Night!'

'Goodnight!'

In a second he doubles back to the doorway, his hand darts along the wall and quickly flicks the plug switch for the lamp – and I'm plunged into darkness.

'Thanks for that,' I say, not sure whether to be narked or simply playful.

'You're welcome.'

As his legs appear through the spindles of the banister, I call, 'Sleep well.'

He stops walking, bends down and, pressing his face against the wooden spindles, quietly says, 'I will. Night!'

Chapter Seventeen

Martha

If it's one thing that I've insisted on at each of Mr C's weddings it has been a wholesome cooked breakfast, plus accompanying bubbles. Today is no exception. I'll be mortified if I accidentally drop one of these champagne bottles; Mr C or Helen will quickly say, 'Never mind,' but I'll mind. I'll mind very much – it'll matter to me. I hurriedly deliver them and return to the kitchen to collect the serving dishes, conscious that the whole family, minus two, have been gracious enough to be at the table for eight o'clock, as per Helen's itinerary. Which truly defines this family: ex-wife number one scheduling the running order of the wedding day for the number-five wife! I ask you, it would only happen with the Carmichaels. Lord knows what it'll be like when the younger generation start pairing off and making arrangements for weddings, christenings and such like. Though at the rate they're going, each and every one still single, I'll be in my dotage or thanking my lucky stars if I'm six foot under and no longer able to bake. I've read about many, many cases where patients – sorry, I hate that phrase, people decline to a certain point then remain there with no chance of improvement and yet ... well, no sign of finding peace. Thankfully, my mother's demise was swift; it was a blessing in the end.

If these youngsters follow their father's example, we could be looking at a further twenty marriages and sixteen divorces between them. Oh, dear Lord, not what I want for any of them.

I could have opened my own shop baking that many wedding cakes in a lifetime; I imagined two might be quite sufficient. How wrong was I?

'Good morning. Now watch your fingers on these serving dishes, they are piping hot. Please use the cloths provided if picking them up,' I say, placing the final two dishes on to the heatproof mats lining the sideboard.

A chorus of 'Morning,' 'Good morning,' and 'Morning, Martha,' answers my greeting, as I add servers and forks to each dish, hoping no one has an accident, today of all days. I turn to find Jeffery blocking my exit from the room, having just arrived.

'Morning, Gunner Jeffery. Please mind the dishes, they're extremely hot,' I say, waiting for him to step sideways.

'Hot, you say? Just as I like it, Martha. Hot, hot, hot!' We do-si-do around each other, me squeezing past his wide girth back to the kitchen to collect a fresh coffeepot. If I'm honest, he should be avoiding the cooked breakfast and opting for fruit and yoghurt. I'm grateful that I'm steady on my feet and agile enough for such moves. My mum was at this stage for a fair while, which probably goes some way to explaining why she became a little too complacent about what the future held for her. Whereas me, I'll be more prepared, having seen her experience. I sure as hell won't be regretting working until my final days, not venturing out into the world, like she did. And what for? A cushy pension that she never claimed a penny of. Phew! No way. I've paid my dues to this family, earned my corn along the way and saved a nice little nest egg. I've been planning for my future since these bloody tremors started. I've had long enough to get over the shock, mourned and grieved what could potentially be ahead of me and got my house in order. Though how the Carmichaels will take it when the time comes is something I'm yet to find out. Let's hope I get to do it my way, with some decorum and dignity in the coming year, not slumped against pillows from a hospital bed, like my poor mother.

I wonder where Janie has got to. It's not like her to go against her sister's wishes – apart from the obvious time, that is. I've got enough to do without fussing over the latecomers, and Helen clearly stated breakfast at eight.

I grab the fresh coffeepot, check I've removed everything from the ovens and the Aga and hurry back to the dining room. I rarely eat breakfast with the family but have at every wedding. Though I did consider missing this one in case it's my presence that's the omen for their future happiness. As I pass through the hallway, the front door opens, revealing a huge bundle of holly with a Janie-shaped body hidden behind it.

'Can you manage?' I ask, holding the front door open with my foot the best I can. 'These removed doors get in the way, don't they?'

'I can, but only just,' comes a muffled reply, as Janie steps inside and dumps her armfuls of holly branches on to the hallway floor. 'Phuh, that's better! I thought I'd make some posies for the rest of us ladies.'

Unusual idea. Is it just inconsiderate or is Janie trying to steal Diane's thunder?

'Have you run it past Diane?'

'Nah. Only just thought of it on seeing a hedge full of the stuff,' says Janie, touching it with her boot and getting her breath back.

'I see. You might want—'

'This bleeding family gets on my tits! No one can do anything spontaneous without the rest of you sticking your oar in!' erupts Janie, gesturing towards the greenery splayed on the floor. In a heartbeat, I leave her to it; Janie can bugger off if she thinks I'm taking an outburst from her after all these years. I enter the dining room, put the fresh coffeepot on to

the table and settle myself to enjoy my breakfast. Everyone
else can please themselves.

'Was that Janie I heard?' asks Helen, looking up from a plate
of eggs, not her usual choice.

'It was. Though I got my head bitten off, so be careful should
you wish to enquire into her actions,' I say, as a fair warning
to all. I note Helen doesn't ask me to elaborate, but then some
at the table can see into the hallway and have probably spotted
the pile of holly.

Emmet pours me a coffee from the fresh pot and hands it to
me across the table.

'Thank you. I'll just take a moment and then I'll collect my
breakfast,' I say, knowing that he knows I'm silently fuming
inside and need to calm down. 'Nice to see your appetite is
returning, Emmet.' He doesn't answer but gives me a grin.

'What will you be having?' asks Teddy, standing up partway
through his own breakfast and gesturing towards the sideboard.

'The full works please,' I say, sipping my drink as Teddy collects a plate and begins to dish up my breakfast. Bless them, they
know me better than most. 'Thank you, Teddy.'

'You're most welcome,' says Teddy, dutifully setting the plate
before me, then returning to his own. I notice Emmet gives him
a nod and a wink in appreciation. Nice boys, the Carmichaels;
they won't go far wrong in life.

'Right, I might as well say, given that Martha seems to
think . . .' Janie enters the dining room in full flow, much to the
surprise of the other occupants, and addresses the bride-to-be.
'Diane, I'd like to make each of the ex-wives a festive bouquet
to carry at your wedding. I think it would be a nice touch but
some people obviously think I'm taking liberties,' says Janie,
intently avoiding my gaze.

I watch as Diane quickly reads the room, glancing at Rupert, who is more concerned with his breakfast plate than festive bouquets.

'I-I d-don't see why not,' stammers Diane, no doubt taken aback by Janie's manner as well as her suggestion.

Janie turns to me and gives a self-righteous smile, asking, 'Would you like one or not?' Her tone has edge, which doesn't surprise me.

As quick as a flash, River says, 'Bloody Nora, when did that wedding occur, Martha?'

My eyes widen in delight at his humour and I give a little shrug, before addressing Janie. 'Thank you for the offer, but no thank you.' Which would also be my response to Rupert, should he ever confront me with a certain proposal.

'Right, three it is then,' announces Janie, turning to leave the room.

'What about my mum?' asks Scarlet disapprovingly.

'OK, four then ... despite her absence!' corrects Janie, muttering to herself as she leaves the dining room.

'Ignore her,' whispers River across the table to me. 'She's got a bee in her bonnet.'

'Hasn't she just!' I add, purely to reinforce his message. After which I remain silent; I don't like to suggest it's been there for the best part of twenty-eight years!

'Oh, hang on a minute ... is it not bad luck for the bride to see the groom on their special day?' asks Janie, reappearing as if like magic.

'I don't believe in such things,' says Mr C, not lifting his head.

'I think they can risk it, knowing the grounds for previous divorce cases in this family,' suggests River, giving a fleeting look towards Emmet.

'Ha ha, you boys are so bloody funny!' says their father sarcastically, mopping his bread around his plate.

I watch the exchange like a Wimbledon tennis match, my head turning from side to side.

'Traditions need to be upheld,' says Janie, as if announcing the dawning of a new era.

'Phuh, as if!' declares Mr C. I notice Diane's frame stiffen – poor wench!

I believe I have insight on this subject; having witnessed the last thirty years of the same old behaviours being repeated time and time again, which Mr C might benefit from. Though I doubt he'd listen to the likes of me – I'm simply his angel who bakes! What is it they say, as one door closes another one opens? Too right, and I'll be making sure my 'new' door is flung wide open and secure on its hinges. Hopefully not locked behind me, barring me from visiting now and then, when time and temperament allows me to. I couldn't walk away from the Carmichaels for ever. Oh no. I might stop being their cook but I'd have to arrange regular visits, a couple of times a year, to stay in touch with the younger generation. Just listen to their banter! I can't be losing my livelihood and my four bairns at this stage of my life!

'Well, whether you like it or not, the bride-to-be has given me the go-ahead, so I'm going ahead!' declares Janie, gesturing towards her holly pile and leaving the room.

Why anyone would choose to start such a task on the morning of a wedding is beyond me, but that's Janie for you, impulsive and feisty as ever. Would we want her any other way? Probably not, but it would be nice if she took a day off!

Helen

I stand on the doorstep of the cottage, the bare wisteria branches trailing beside me threatening to dislodge my brand-new hat as I watch the couple pose beside their wedding car, a gleaming silver Rolls-Royce complete with emerald satin ribbons. I feel a pang of something deep within, not jealousy as such, more a sense of grief – for what might have been.

The bride looks radiant, as all brides do, in a gown of shot silk that shimmers emerald and blue, adorned with feathers at her neckline, hemline and cuffs. A faux-fur wrap is secured around her shoulders and a fan-shaped bouquet of crystal sparkles and cascading peacock feathers are her only adornments. Rupert looks dashing in another tailored suit, in navy blue, with a matching emerald cravat and pocket hankie. Such vibrant colours – 'blue and green should never be seen' was my initial thought, but then, why not? There might be a clear blue sky but it's a chilly winter's day; pale peach, lemon or white would have been a complete washout on the photographs with this backdrop of snow. I've never given it much thought – we got married in March, with a white Rolls-Royce bedecked with pale pink ribbons, a bouquet of roses and I wore white, of course.

Scarlet and Lowry stand at the rear of the vehicle, obviously out of shot and physically shivering. Their dresses both match the material of Diane's gown but in very different styles. Scarlet's straight dress has a plunging neckline with a side-split to her mid-thigh – rather more revealing than I'd expect for a bridesmaid entering church. Lowry's gown is elegant and classy, an A-line skirt flaring from beneath a fitted short-sleeved bodice. Each of them carries a small bouquet of peacock feathers. Lowry clearly took more time and attention in noting her measurements as her gown fits perfectly. Unlike Scarlet's, which is definitely a touch too tight – a pity as shot silk is so unforgiving when it puckers across the hips and waistline. Diane should have insisted they wore the same style; one day Scarlet will wish she had too.

'Excuse me, coming through,' calls Martha, gently touching my shoulder indicating her need to pass.

'What have you got there?' I ask, unsure what I'm seeing.

'Two hot-water bottles. I found them in the scullery amongst other paraphernalia – those poor girls will catch their death if they stand there for much longer,' explains Martha, heading along the cleared cobbles towards the wedding party. The woman is amazing, she thinks of everything. I watch as she scurries towards the girls, discreetly giving each a hot-water bottle wrapped in what looks like a tea towel from the kitchen drawer. Rupert would never have managed without her, and likewise, neither could I.

Martha comes galloping down the path again, no doubt en route to another urgent job.

'You are good,' I say, knowing she rarely accepts praise.

'Phuh! I won't be fit enough to be running after their requests for cold treatments after I've sampled a couple of glasses of bubbly, will I?' she says, dashing back inside.

I watch the bridesmaids standing together, clutching their hot-water bottles, and yet miles apart, not interacting, just watching their respective parent. Diane is all giggles and blushes, as the photographer gently manhandles Rupert into a pose where the couple gaze at each other through a half-open car door.

'Run, you bastard, run!' whispers Janie, sneaking up behind me to peer over my shoulder. 'Bugger off now, while Diane still has good memories of her wedding day.'

'Oh Janie, you don't mean that,' I say, not liking her unsavoury remarks on such a joyous occasion.

'I bloody do. Anyway, here's your holly bouquet; don't say I never give you anything, sis,' she says, thrusting a posy of holly twigs and red berries tied with lacy ribbon into my clutches. 'I'm giving them out in order, so yours is first.'

'Thank you. Did you do Fena one?'

'Of course, I'd never hear the bloody end of it from Scarlet if I hadn't. I'll pop it on an empty pew or a tombstone in her absence.' Janie provides a daft voice for the comedy ending of her sentence.

'How many festive coffees have you had today?' I ask.

'Not enough to get me through another of his sodding weddings, I know that much.' Janie walks off in search of ex-wife number three. 'Lynette!'

I don't know exactly what I'm witnessing. It could be the new Rupert Carmichael or a reincarnation of an older version in a larger suit and with greyer temples. Either way he's getting married again! And I'm heartbroken. Not that I ever truly dreamt we'd reconcile, pick up where we left off, but stranger things have happened in life. So going through the whole charade once again kills me! I've never stopped loving this man. Despite everyone telling me what I must do, should do, could do to move on with my life, get over him – all those cliché terms that your girlfriends come out with in between offering a shoulder and boosting you with a hug. From the moment he announced he was leaving me to be with my younger sister, my life has never been my own. At first I wanted to win him back, then I adapted to the situation when his return definitely looked unlikely, making life easier for everyone but myself. Over time, I've continued compromising my needs by busily organising everyone else. If I couldn't be the wife, then I'd find a role to suit his lifestyle. One from which I couldn't be fired, replaced or divorced. I berate myself a million times a day but still . . . never for one infinitesimal moment have I stopped loving him. Never. Maybe we were simply too young and naive to stay the course. If we'd met when we were slightly older . . . perhaps we'd have stood a better chance. Who knows?

Our son never came from a broken home, he came from an extended home, where the father lived and loved elsewhere but the mother remained stoic. I wasn't a single parent, I was dual-parenting. Emmet wasn't a solo child, he had siblings. My refusal to use terms such as 'half' siblings – and now 'step', for Lowry – simply reinforces my allegiance to the wedding vows I made thirty-one years ago. Where has the time gone? How have I endured attending four more of his weddings after my own? I know the answer but I don't want to face the truth – by staying put, keeping mightily busy and pretending that none of this is actually happening.

Rupert might be marrying someone else, he might be venturing off on honeymoon yet again, but in two weeks' time our normality will resume. I'll see him every day in the office; he'll call me of an evening to confirm a detail or give an instruction regarding a business contract. The family Sunday lunches will recommence once Diane is settled and I'll adapt to the routines of the new Mrs Carmichael, ensuring that I remain within his world. I'll get a smaller slice of his attention, possibly, but I'll still be securely within the confines of his day. I'm still almost living through the vows we made three decades ago, having reinvented their meaning – 'to have and to hold' on to 'forsaking all others', 'for richer, for poorer', and ultimately, 'till death us do part'. He has loved many and married several but, ultimately, that doesn't matter to me – I've only ever truly loved one.

What's the saying? 'If you love someone, let them go. If they return, they were always yours. If they don't, they never were.' I truly thought he'd see sense and return to me after his divorce from Janie, but nope, he'd strayed too far with Lynette by then. Did I not let go? Surely allowing one's ex-husband to marry one's sister is proof of letting go, right? But what's the official expiry date on love regarding their potential return? Months, weeks – or is it decades? I suspect the latter explains how I've been stuck in a cycle of the shock of revelation, acceptance of a new situation and eternal waiting. Maybe wife number five is the signal to extinguish that flickering candle of hope?

'Are you alright, Mum?' asks Emmet, appearing at my side, his arms wrapping around my shoulder.

'Yes, yes. They look lovely, don't they?' I say, nodding towards Rupert and Diane posing before their wedding car. I catch a pleasant waft of his aftershave as he stands close and quickly add, 'You smell gorgeous, son.'

'Thank you. It was my Christmas gift from Martha – something new. They do. I'm not sure about photos before the actual event; surely afterwards is more important.'

'He needs to make it slightly different from the other occasions; the devil's in the detail, son. Thank you to you and River for clearing the snow from the pathway earlier, it was necessary.'

'No worries, it was a pain but it saves someone having an accident. Though you've got a point. I pray this is the last time. I can't keep doing this page boy or best man role by carrying his wedding rings – I've done it three times since childhood.'

I smile. 'And what a cutie you were back then – though you threw a hissy fit about handing over the lacey ring pillow.'

'Don't remind me. I'd quite like to attend a wedding where I don't need to do a bloody speech.'

'Maybe River will do the honours next time.'

Emmet frowns. 'Don't. You'll jinx them by saying that.'

'Surely you don't believe that?'

'Nah, but this one needs to be a keeper, Mum.'

My eyebrows lift on hearing that.

'Really? Any particular reason?' My gaze drifts to the rear of the silver Rolls-Royce, where two beauties are sidestepping and jigging about on the spot.

'Stop it.'

'Stop what?' I say, feigning innocence but intrigued that he knew exactly what I meant.

'Are you coming inside for one last drink? We'll be leaving in a few minutes,' he asks, changing the subject.

'I will. Decent bubbles and a posy of prickles' – I raise Janie's gift to show him – 'is about all I can expect on such occasions.' With that, I leave the doorstep and follow Emmet into the lounge to join the others.

Chapter Eighteen

Lowry

I've never ridden in a limousine before; it feels quite sophisticated settling back against the plush leather, until the seats prove to be deeper than my legs require, giving me that childish pose of swinging feet. Not an attractive look, despite the beautiful dress and faux-fur wrap. I settle beside Scarlet, and Martha climbs in after me. How do I always end up in the middle seat, feeling squashed and rumpled? Though I'm grateful that my mum had the foresight to put Martha in this, the third car, where she can relax from her duties, and not have to endure the ex-wives' limo travelling ahead or the guys' car directly behind them. I stare ahead, my view through the front windscreen framed by the broad shoulders of the uniformed chauffeur and best man Emmet – one of their colognes smells very nice. There's a definite chill factor coming from my right; Scarlet appears completely uninterested in me despite us both being bridesmaids. My only comfort is the wrapped hot-water bottle nestled on my knees, on which my feathered bouquet rests.

'It's quite a pretty village, isn't it?' says Scarlet, gazing from the car window at the stone frontages and intricately carved gable ends. 'Though, personally, I wouldn't dream of getting married in the back of beyond when Dad's local church is on his doorstep.'

No one answers.

'I assume Diane will be moving into Dad's property, if she

hasn't already?' she continues. I'm unsure whether to answer. Scarlet's head whips around to face me. 'Well, has she?'

'Yes. A week ago, I believe.' I'm about to elaborate, explaining that I don't know the full details as we've had little time to catch up over recent days – there's been so much going on.

'Scarlet, what's your point?' asks Emmet, from the front passenger seat.

'No point, dear brother ... simply confirming details.'

'Where else is his wife supposed to live?' he continues, over his shoulder.

'He might choose to sell up and relocate,' she retorts, before adding, 'Other men do.'

'I can't see your father ever leaving Cloisters, Scarlet,' says Martha, without switching her gaze from the passing view.

'Some do,' repeats Scarlet, returning her focus to outside the car rather than those inside. 'Gunner Jeffery's thinking of relocating.'

'Is he now?' asks Martha, her head spinning around so fast it scares me.

'That seems unlikely,' adds Emmet. 'The nearest he got to moving house w-was w-when ...' His words falter and fade. I lean forward, expecting Emmet to continue, but he doesn't.

'Mmm,' hums Martha, eyeing me as if I were party to the full story and not just the snippet she implied yesterday.

'I think you're all too cruel,' says Scarlet. 'Oh, look we're here. That was hardly a long drive, was it?'

'Would you have wanted to walk?' asks Martha, undoing her seat belt. 'I believe that's the plan for afterwards.'

Scarlet doesn't answer, and I notice Emmet's jaw clenches.

'How ridiculous building a church on top of such a steep hill. It's almost hovering above the village,' says Scarlet, looking beyond me to Martha, who doesn't respond.

The chauffeur slowly draws the car to a halt behind the other two parked limousines, from which ex-wives, other sons and a close friend are appearing. I patiently wait while Martha disembarks from our vehicle, not waiting for the chauffeur or Emmet to open her door.

To my right, Scarlet giggles immaturely as the chauffeur holds her door wide, offering his assistance. I remain in the middle of the rear seat, not knowing which side to exit, when Scarlet suddenly slams her door closed behind her. Too interested in the uniformed driver, methinks.

'Lowry.' His voice brings me back to the present, away from my disgust at her lack of manners.

'Thank you, Emmet,' I say, sliding across to the left and taking his proffered hand. Hmmm, it's Emmet's cologne – very nice.

'No worries. The bride and groom haven't arrived yet,' he says, as I step from the limousine and quickly brush the front of my crumpled dress.

'I don't think they should be travelling together anyway. It's bad luck … and as for the photographs beforehand – surely that's tempting fate?' huffs Scarlet.

'Scarlet, you'll be the death of me one of these days with your comments, your attitude and your dance moves. Now please, it's your father's wedding day, so mind your Ps and Qs and let's have less of your chit-chat,' instructs Martha, taking our hot-water bottles from us and dropping them into her tote bag. I wish to second her remark with a 'Hear, hear,' but daren't, though Emmet's knowing look convinces me that he has me sussed. He knows that me and his little sister are not on the same page; getting along is going to take more effort on my part and probably none from her.

'Here they are!' calls Scarlet, as the silver Rolls-Royce and the photographer's car pull into the church's snow-cleared driveway. The other relatives and Gunner Jeffery had said a fleeting 'hello' in passing, as we four huddled by the wooden arched gateway at the bottom of the steep path, before hastily departing towards the church in search of warmth. Given the freezing chill, I pray that Sandra and Sally, Mum's best friends, have sought shelter inside too.

'I assume the photographer will be wanting photographs of the bride and bridesmaids outside the church, so I'll take Dad straight inside. Martha, are you wanting to wait here or would you like me to walk you to your seat?' asks Emmet.

'I'll wait here for a little while, just to see that all is well . . . can I meet you inside?' she asks tentatively.

'Of course, I'll meet you at the church door and we'll walk down the aisle together.' Emmet gives her a cheeky wink and receives a warm smile in return. I'm bewitched by their interaction, his thoughtfulness – that's the essence of Emmet. Whether it be assisting with a car door, a refill of your glass or accompanying a lone female, Emmet's your man – I like that.

'Dad, hurry up. It's freezing out here,' hollers Scarlet at the approaching couple. I should think she is freezing, given the sizeable thigh-split in her dress. I hurry to greet my mum, swiftly gathering and lifting the back of her gown to avoid a darkening water line from the snow.

'Come on, Dad. Let's get you where you need to be . . . up the front and waiting before the vicar,' says Emmet, shaking hands with his father. After which Rupert gives him a warm embrace and several backslaps as is typical of male affection.

'Thank you, my darling. Are you OK?' asks my mum, as I totter behind her, my feet cold and wet from the patchy remnants of snow on the not-so-cleared pathway.

'Fine. Fine.'

'That's never a good sign,' says Mum, her smile lost and her gaze boring into mine.

'Honest, I'm fine. Scarlet's proving to be a pain in the arse but Martha and Emmet more than make up for her.'

'I always think that, but don't let on,' says Mum, giving a little chuckle as we draw near the others.

I stop walking, turn to her and say what I need to say swiftly, 'Are you sure about this, Mum? You don't have to go through with the wedding – we can leave if it's simply too much.'

'Of course, I'm s-sure,' she stammers, her expression turning from shock to sudden embarrassment seeing the others are watching, though thankfully they can't overhear. 'Lowry, I want to marry Rupert. I love him.'

'OK. I hear you,' I say, patting her arm to reassure her. 'I won't ask again.'

Mum's wedding smile returns as we join the others.

'I'll be seeing you ladies in a little while,' says Rupert, gallantly reaching for my mother's free hand and raising it to his lips. 'And you, my beauty – I'll see you at the altar.' I'm in two minds whether to cringe or celebrate on hearing Rupert's words. He sounds genuine, he appears genuine, but how do I know if he's said the exact same thing to four other brides? I instantly glance at Martha, as if seeking confirmation; she isn't rolling her eyes, huffing in disbelief or appearing to be experiencing a déjà vu moment.

'You certainly will,' whispers my mum lovingly.

I sneak a look at Emmet: he's calmly watching but without squirming or any negative response. I need to go with the flow; this is happening, they seem happy, it all seems totally genuine. Could my misgivings be down to my own cynicism about love? My own hurt and loss resurfacing to influence my beliefs?

I watch father and son stride away, happily chatting, and then we begin the slow but steady walk through the graveyard towards the church.

'Lowry ... this way please,' calls the photographer, as he immediately positions my mother and Scarlet in close proximity with their bouquets held aloft beneath the wooden arched gateway.

'If you could say "happy days" on the count of three, that would be great,' instructs the photographer, his tripod and camera directly in front of us. 'One, two, three, happy days!'

For the next ten minutes, we do as instructed, holding each pose as required, though the cold has frozen my smile into a permanent shape so my grin won't relax until I thaw out. If every photo needs my ruddy-coloured cheeks airbrushing to normal skin tones, I won't be happy.

Eventually we arrive at the church porch. It seems to have taken for ever to reach the stone steps. I'm as nervous as hell as Martha tenderly wishes my mother 'all the best' and kisses her goodbye. I watch as she enters the second doorway to be greeted by Emmet, as promised, and they link arms to proudly walk inside. The photographer nips through, swiftly followed by his assistant, who's loaded to the gunwales with equipment. The vicar steps forward, holding his Bible, to greet my mum with a handshake. I'm unsure where to stand – am I supposed to walk alongside her down the aisle or behind her with Scarlet? Mum hasn't said which she prefers.

I step forward, hoping for some direction, and find myself shaking hands with the vicar too.

'My daughter, Lowry, and my soon-to-be second daughter, Scarlet,' says my mum, gesturing to each of us. I give the vicar an obligatory hi, having lost my composure in the last ten seconds since Martha left our side.

'Where am I to walk?' I ask, gesturing beside her or behind.

Mum takes a deep breath. 'With Scarlet, I think. You'll step up to give me away at the altar but for this part ...' Her eyes prick with tears; I can see that instruction was difficult for her to relay, but I'll respect her wishes – it's her big day. 'I'm so proud of you, Lowry ... I really am.'

'Ditto, Mum.' I wrap my arms around her shoulders and squeeze tight. I feel we have a renewed bond after her emotional explanation last night. She'll feel lighter not carrying such a burden into her new life. I sense that when I release her, the next few steps will happen swiftly, with no time to think or possibly even feel, so this is our moment. Perhaps it's selfish of me, but I'm conscious that this is the final moment of having my mum purely to myself. I breathe in deeply, as if saving the memory; from this point on, she won't be solely mine – I'll have to share her with the others.

Martha

I stand in the doorway of the church, craning my neck towards the front pews, trying to spy Emmet, who I can't actually see. I've no issue walking in alone but it would be nice to be escorted. Mr C and Diane have chosen the prettiest of parish churches, for sure. It has heavily beamed rafters, wrought-iron lighting rings hanging low above the standard rows of wooden pews, and is dominated by an arched window of stained glass above the dressed altar. Though I've never seen a church sitting so proud overlooking its community – I bet that steep pathway puts a few of the old folk off attending regular services. A Stannah stairlift or a mini monorail might be useful for some.

As I enter the rear of the church, I'm greeted by an elaborate screen of carved wood housing a beautiful classic clock face, its delicate hands conveniently nearing the top of the hour. Through a glass window positioned high, like an enclosed balcony, I can see six bell-ringers arranged in a circle, statue-like with ropes in hand, before each in turn pulls downwards and a peal of bells begins to ring.

'Are you ready, ma'am?' asks Emmet, appearing as if from

nowhere and offering me the crook of his arm, before handing me an order of service.

'I am, young sir,' I say, taking his proffered arm. We walk along the back of the nearest wooden pew before turning left to begin a slow walk along the aisle's red carpet, passing the large archways and stone pillars, taking in the full effect of the flickering candlelight on the holy statues. 'Isn't it beautiful?'

'It certainly is, though I'm not so sure its name is entirely fitting. "St Michael and All the Angels" – surely Carmichael and all his angels would be more appropriate for today,' jests Emmet, as we approach our ensemble of three ex-wives sitting on our left in the front pew.

'You are so naughty,' I say, giving a giggle.

'But you love it,' he retorts, steering me towards the second pew, behind the so-called 'angels' with their prickly bouquets. What I actually love is how much he's brightened up over the weekend.

I give his arm a squeeze before releasing it, and whisper, 'There's one angel missing, so let's be grateful for small mercies.'

'Yes, let's!' Emmet gives me a bright smile and goes to join his father at the altar. I settle on to the pew; its backrest is ramrod straight yet comfortingly solid – I bet it's serviced and survived many generations. I give a respectful nod to each of Diane's best friends, Sandra and Sally, sitting alongside me, both looking decidedly spruced-up in oversized hats and floral dresses, despite the festive chill. They wave back in a tentative, self-conscious 'we're Diane's only guests amongst the Carmichael clan' way – I wish there were more guests invited for Diane's sake. Though without siblings or parents, the seating plan was always going to be sparse on the Stephens side.

I glance at the crucifix high above the altar and say a quick silent prayer. I'm not frightened regarding my future, more wary of running out of time, so it never hurts to ask for a little guidance.

Mr C stands upright in front of the pews on the opposite side, wringing his hands and tugging at his shirt collar. I watch as Emmet has a quiet word before taking his place on his father's right. Emmet's definitely his right-hand man, be it at home or at work; not that the other lads don't try to be reliable, supportive and innovative – they do, but they rarely come up to scratch.

Scanning through the order of service, with its delicate calligraphy font, I recognise the elements of a traditional service: the declaration, the vows – which they've written themselves, the reading, the blessing and signing of the register. The legalities of the occasion, beautifully scripted and presented within a decorative border, complete with names and dates and with satin ribbon ties – but boy, how stark is the perception compared to the reality of this particular story. I've kept each order of service for my memory box, all similar in their elements but different: one a scroll, one a single sheet, this a booklet – each filled with hope and representing a unique bonding of two souls.

I don't mind admitting, I'm nervous; this has never happened to me before at a Carmichael wedding. During his wedding to Janie, my eyes never left Helen, in case she needed a little extra support, especially with the bairn. The wedding to Lynette was a very quiet affair, given that she was six months gone and Mr C wasn't happy that her family weren't on board with the idea of marriage, let alone a new arrival, given his past history. The wedding to Fena was very different; the wedding guests were flown out to Japan for a three-week holiday as well as the wedding. That wedding was like no other: the food, the flowers, the six or was it seven wedding gowns that Fena wore that day ... Either way, it was spectacular, with the bonus of honeymoon baby news announced within three months of them arriving home. Which is one saving grace of this wedding – I can't imagine baby news will follow these nuptials, unless it's via a surrogate. But why would anyone want more children than he already has? After today, it'll be a family of three boys and two girls – that's more than enough.

Thinking of the youngsters, I turn to see Teddy and River in the opposite pew, absent-mindedly flapping their order of service against their knees, as if separating the boys from the girls – which seems old-fashioned to me but it provides symmetry to the occupied pews. Both look handsome in their smart navy suits, creating a distinct united front of the groom's party, though if – and it's a big if – this happens again, I'm sure it will be River stepping up for best man duties; Emmet has been so vocal regarding his retirement from the role.

In the pew in front, the three ex-wives sit in silence. I think the previous few days have given them more than enough time to catch up and chat. A single afternoon would probably have been sufficient, but that wasn't feasible given the circumstances. Maybe next time. Oh, no, correction, I don't actually mean that. I don't believe there will be another wedding after this one.

A triumphant fanfare blasts from the pipe organ announcing that it must be time to stand, pulls me from my thoughts, and amidst the sound of shuffling feet the front pew obliges – Diane and the bridesmaids must be waiting at the church door.

'Please be seated,' says the vicar, after our dismal rendition of 'All Things Bright and Beautiful'. Fancy having hymns with such a small gathering – how are fifteen voices supposed to create a decent sound, even with the booming baritone of an eager vicar? They should have booked a choir to help out. At one point, all I could hear was the vicar and Scarlet's tinny screeching, as if the pair of them were competing in a sing-off. Thank God she didn't add dance moves, providing a slutdrop to finish, though in that dress she'd never make it back up in one fluid move without showing tomorrow's washing!

The vicar gestures for Mr C and Diane to join him at the altar steps; he physically turns each to face the other, asking them to join hands. Diane looks truly radiant, though I've never seen Mr C blush so much; it can't help that his three previous brides are in sight over Diane's right shoulder.

'Dearly beloved, we are gathered here today in the presence of . . .' I don't switch off exactly, just zone out the actual words. I love the sentiment but sometimes, just sometimes, I get a pang of something under my ribs. Call it indigestion, growing pains or a niggling reminder that maybe I've given too much of my own life to the comfort and benefit of others. I'll never be repeating such solemn vows, devoting my life purely to one other and having the reassurance of them doing likewise for me.

There's a noisy and untimely rattling of the church door, causing us all to turn in surprise and shock. The carved wooden door opens and is frantically slammed shut behind the tiniest and most neurotic of figures, dressed in a shimmering gold lamé gown, a huge lolloping fur and a miniature riding hat, worn at a jaunty angle on a precision-cut bob. Ex-wife number four: Fena. St Carmichael has a full set of his angels under one heavenly roof – Lord help us!

'Sorry, sorry, I couldn't find the way in . . . Scarlet, Mummy's baby!' gushes Fena, scurrying along the aisle, her rapid fairy steps mimicking a little mouse, towards the front pew. She bypasses the other exes to greet her daughter with a bear hug, seemingly oblivious to the bride and groom partway through their cere- mony. 'My sweetie-pie, don't you look gorgeous! Ooh, sexy dress, sexy lady! Mmm-mmm-mmm!' Fena's voice fills the church in a way that the rest of us in unison had failed to do. 'Martha! My lovely!' she cries, having spotted me during the bear-hug moment, and flits over to warmly hug me too. I can see a row of exasperated expressions over her shoulder, possibly not too dissimilar to the view Mr C had moments ago when turning to face Diane. Lowry's jaw has just hit the floor, Diane's radiance has faded and Emmet is shaking his head in disbelief. Oh great, guest number thirteen has officially arrived – good job Mr C and Diane won't be returning to the cottage tonight. At least the rest of us can sleep snug in our beds without impending doom occurring.

'Fena! Please?' calls Mr C, his hands being squeezed by his soon-to-be-bride in the hope his previous one would actually sit down and stop taking centre stage.

'Sorry, sorry, Rupie. Just saying hi to everyone. Hi, hi, hi,' calls Fena, waving blindly at the other guests before returning to the front pew to join her daughter, forcing the other ex-wives and Lowry to budge along in an undignified bum shuffle. 'I'm ready now! Oh thank you, a bouquet for me!'

'Thank you,' says the vicar, before clearing his throat.

I begin to fan myself with the order of service, not its purpose but very much appreciated. Lord knows where Fena's popped up from, but no doubt Helen has already mentally unpacked her luggage into Scarlet's twin room. Another mouth at the dinner table is never an issue for me – if all else fails, I'll peel more spuds. As for Lynette, boy oh boy, this is going to unsettle her chakras, for sure.

Chapter Nineteen

Lowry

'OK?' asks Emmet, as we walk arm in arm up the aisle after the ceremony, bridesmaid and best man, as expected. In the glazed ringing room, the bell-ringers can be seen methodically pulling and catching their ropes, sending a joyful announcement across the entire village.

'Sure. You?' I ask through my wedding smile as River and Teddy dutifully wait for us to pass by, in order to join the departing throng. River has strict instructions to escort Scarlet, in a similar manner behind us, but she's too busy with her mother to notice him.

'I'm good. I've been here before, remember?' he says, gazing down on my upturned face. 'No offence meant, but I'm hoping that's the last time for him.'

'Me too, and not for my sake.' I resent even thinking this way as I follow the happy couple towards the church door, but I do. I have to, because that is my mum. She and Rupert halt for a few photographs in the arched doorway, forcing the procession to pause and watch.

'The old bugger needs to settle down and enjoy his remaining years, not engaging divorce lawyers, thrashing out financial arrangements and notching up another failed relationship.'

The enormity of Emmet's words hit home; I'm neither offended nor comforted by his remarks.

'Do you think he's braver than most then?' I ask, fixing my

gaze on the happy couple ahead of us, finally striding out into the winter sunshine.

'Yeah, definitely. I know I'll have given up on love before reaching his age, if my path is anything like his.'

'I think I already have,' I whisper, navigating the stone steps, as the church bells ring out in celebration.

'Have you?' asks Emmet, glancing at me, his expression showing concern. 'I hope not.'

I hear his remark but continue, unsure how to respond. 'It's too painful to keep putting yourself out there, only to be knocked back time and time again. Dating sucks, it really does.' I take a deep breath; the chilly air tingles in my chest, bringing me back to life and reality. 'Which is why I don't date.'

Emmet sighs, glances towards the wedding party gathering together their friends for a small group photo before speaking. 'But surely that's like an abandoned pup giving up on getting a second chance of a loving family home. You're saying it might as well remain permanently in a secure cage at a rescue centre rather than take the risk of trusting humans again.'

He's got me there. I believe every animal deserves a loving forever home, whether it be their first, second or tenth attempt to be homed. It's the humans who fail, not the animals.

'We're supposed to be celebrating the happy union of our parents,' I say, not wishing to be reminded of my dismal love life. We walk in silence along the inclined pathway, lined on each side by graves, their large granite headstones tilting or partially toppled at various angles like the shoulders of an aged congregation. I glance at intervals at the faded inscriptions, the languished devotion and various dates – each a moment in time that was once painful for their nearest and dearest.

'Do you ever wonder what they'd say if they could speak?' I ask, gesturing towards the graves.

'Sometimes. But I rarely walk past graves.'

'If you listen carefully, you can hear them whispering to you,' I say, stopping at the nearest grave of one Amy Peel, nee Yates, October 1878 – January 1938, and cocking my ear towards her weathered headstone. 'Listen.'

As daft as it seems, Emmet does the same. We must look a right sight, me in my silk gown and him suited and booted. My gaze is fixed on the patch of lumpy ground blanketed by snow, which is bare of any flowers or inscribed vases. And we listen.

'Do you hear it?' he whispers.

I nod, imagining a tiny woman's faint voice coming from beyond the grave. Though I suspect it's my own inner truth surfacing subconsciously.

Start living and do what's right for you.

'Fair play, Amy Peel. She told me to do whatever makes me happy. And you?'

'Uh-uh, I'm not sharing!' I say, pulling a comical expression to hide my embarrassment at withholding.

'Are you for real?' he asks, clearly put out by my refusal to share.

'Dead real. Or as real as she once was,' I say, pointing to the gravestone.

'Lowry Stephens, you tricked me into being honest and I fell for it – hook, line and sinker. Never again, I tell you.' He's joking but he actually looks hurt. I need to either backtrack or rely on humour to resolve this incident. I choose the latter.

'That's my life over then! Come on, the wedding party are waiting.' I playfully tug at his jacket sleeve, expecting him to offer up the crook of his arm, but he doesn't. Emmet simply watches me. 'What?'

'Nothing.' His voice has lost its lightness, his gaze has emptied as if someone flicked a switch from within.

My attempt to rejoin our linked arms seems foolish now; something has shifted between us. Gone is the attractive warmth, replaced by cold metal shutters slammed down and secured. I fiddle with my bouquet, teasing the flighty feathers, by means of a distraction.

'Come on, you pair!' calls Teddy from across the graveyard, where the rest of the family are huddled for a photo. Only Martha stands stock-still, observing us.

'They're waiting,' says Emmet, his tone flatlining, as if we were strangers. What an utter fool! You'd think I'd know better from experience.

'Emmet?'

'Yeah?'

'Don't.'

'Don't what?'

'Retreat ... like a distrusting dog.'

He inclines his head as if my words hit home.

'Trust goes both ways, Lowry.'

Damn it. He's got me there!

'Come on, they're waiting,' he continues, gesturing towards the family huddle, who are now frantically beckoning for us to join them.

Helen

'I think it's rather nice in here,' I say, looking around the restaurant as Emmet pours me a glass of wine. Our wedding party are the sole occupants amongst the quirky artwork in gilt frames on each wall, traditional oak beams full of character and aged floorboards, which could easily date back a century or three. Martha's beautifully decorated wedding cake is honoured with a place of its own on a decorated table in the corner. Though when we arrived, the waitress didn't look best pleased when I mentioned that two extra place settings would be required, making us a party of fifteen. I did apologise, saying I'd happily wait, empty-handed, while additional glasses of bubbles were hastily poured.

This is definitely a first – I don't believe we've ever been together around the same table. Though we must look like such a motley crew: thigh-high splits, gold lamé fabrics, half-shaven guys, Janie's loud exclamations and Lynette's teeny-tiny fascinator bobbing about exaggerating her every shimmy. Thankfully, Diane's two friends bring a little normality to the proceedings, helping to dilute the wedding pizzazz supplied by the ever-increasing Carmichaels.

'The Queen's Head is certainly fitting,' he mutters, raising an eyebrow.

'Emmet, do you mind! Today should be about the happy couple, no one else,' I retort, defending the indefensible, yet again. Though I'd like to know what he and Lowry were discussing as they lingered behind after the service. She's certainly put a spring in his step, maybe because they're of a similar age.

'And certainly not us previous four brides, hey, Emmet?' calls Janie, showing how far along the table his remark was heard. I send a polite smile in my sister's direction, suggesting point taken. I note that Fena is engaged in a lively conversation with Scarlet and Jeffery at the far end of the table, away from Lynette, so there'll be no drama arising there. Strange how female instinct creates an innate dislike for the woman who supersedes you, even as you bravely attempt to build a relationship with the woman who directly preceded you – ignoring the fact that your very existence undermined her marriage. The Carmichael dynasty has resulted in the strangest dynamics, from which I'm the exception, being inclined to like them all. Granted, I was ousted by my sister – who I simply can't hate, though I've never truly forgiven her. Janie dislikes Lynette intensely, yet Lynette seems immune to Janie's vicious vibe – she's too busy sniping at Fena. And, finally,

Fena, who couldn't care less about anyone at present but in time will develop an intolerable dislike for Diane, because that seems to be nature's way. These underlying vibes flow between us like a Mexican wave of unnecessary emotion. Strange really; when you think about it we have more in common than we care to admit. We could unite and support one another under the same Rupert's-ex-wives brolly, yet we don't!

'I think it's very appropriate. Henry the eighth and my father had more in common than most,' says Emmet, standing to pour wine for the ladies further along the table, despite the hovering serving staff.

'Exactly. What's the rhyme they teach you in history class?' calls Teddy.

'Ha ha, that's hilarious if applied to this family,' replies River, gesturing to the four previous brides, and the fifth, looking on. 'Helen would be divorced, my mum beheaded, Lynette dead, Fena divorced, Diane beheaded and Mrs Carmichael number six will outlive him!'

'Won't she be the lucky one!' calls Scarlet, squeezing her father's left arm playfully.

'You cheeky sod, there won't be another one, not after today,' chunters Rupert, turning to admire his new bride. Diane smiles demurely but no one else answers – leaving his remark to hang low over our table like a November fog.

I'm grateful when the waitresses arrive with our starters: a choice between a goat's cheese tartlet or roasted mushrooms stuffed with bacon and black pudding.

'Urgh! I hate goat's cheese! Thank God I'm steering clear of soft . . .' announces Scarlet, her face clearly depicting her dislike before her voice fades to silence.

'Mushrooms it is then, sis!' calls Teddy, stating the obvious before confirming his own choice. I await each person's selection, conscious that our additional guests might have thrown the kitchen into a tizzy, but the offered options seem to have suited everyone. I breathe easy on seeing that even Martha and I are given a choice, not just whatever's left.

'I assume Fena is hoping to stay at the cottage?' asks Martha, cutting into her tartlet once everyone is served.

'I assume so. I'll pop her in the twin room with Scarlet, so there's no major upheaval for anyone else,' I say, between mouthfuls of roasted mushroom.

'Never a dull moment, is there?' whispers Martha. 'Because it's not like you don't know you're accidentally purchasing an airline ticket to the UK at the busiest time of the year. I do it all the time, without realising.'

'It appears some people simply arrive whenever and wherever without giving any prior notice or a polite RSVP to a wedding invite,' I add, knowing Martha is fully up to speed with the fanciful ways of a certain woman.

'Attention junky, more like – coupled with a fear of missing out,' answers Martha, eyeing me cautiously. 'A dreadful combination.' She knows she can be honest with me; we'd have never made it this far without sharing our true opinions.

'You can say that again. As long as she keeps entertained by Scarlet's company, the rest of us will be happy too.'

'I doubt Scarlet will be free to speak to anyone else now her mother has arrived – they'll be joined at the hip until tomorrow's departure.'

'If Fena chooses to stay that long!' I add, knowing from experience that her daughter is often removed ahead of time, and against her will, according to Fena's whim. 'How's the tartlet tasting?'

'Delicious. Especially as someone else made it.'

'I thought that might be the case,' I jest, knowing how hard she works to meet our needs.

'Pssst, Helen!' whispers Janie, leaning along the backs of the chairs to get my attention, trying but failing to be discreet.

'Mmm?' I say, leaning behind Martha to converse.

'Fena just mentioned they've had matching wedding rings made, each inscribed inside with 'R and D'. I reckon it stands for 'Research and Development', which is a nice touch and definitely apt with Rupert's track record,' chuckles Janie, lifting her linen napkin to cover her reaction.

I shake my head. Either Janie's stashed an extra festive tipple in her clutch bag or Fena's nose has been put out of joint by the newcomer. Sadly, I suspect it's a combination of both.

Chapter Twenty

Lowry

I sit cross-legged on the bedroom floor in front of the wardrobe, stroking Trixie, the cat. I feel guilty for taking time out for myself on arriving back at the cottage. I could have opted for the cosiness of the snug but I feared someone might invade my space so chose my bedroom instead. Thirty valued minutes in which to remove my make-up, change out of my gown and fuss over Trixie and her kittens – I'm sure Lynette would label it 'Zen time' or something like that.

As happy as I am for Mum and Rupert, it was hard saying goodbye to her, knowing that a chapter of our lives is gone for ever. I needed space, away from the hullabaloo of the Carmichaels, to allow the events of the day to settle and become solid memories, not those fleeting ones that you can't recall no matter how hard you try. I'm not hiding as such, simply dragging my feet to go back downstairs. Call me selfish, antisocial, whatever; this pause is necessary to allow the occasion of my mum's wedding day to sink in.

I'm sure there's a prearranged plan for the rest of our evening, and they'll expect me to be bright and bubbly, with much chatting and merriment amidst my new relatives. It'll prove that I'm not a scared rabbit caught in their glaring headlights, especially in my mother's absence.

'Here goes, Trixie,' I whisper, tickling her ear affectionately. 'Thanks for your calming vibes and—'

'You bitch!' The screamed insult makes me jump out of my skin, the volume filling my bedroom as if the door were wide open.

'What the hell?' I mutter, scrambling to my feet and making for the closed door, as a plethora of insults continues to flow.

I find Janie and Lynette squaring up to each other in the middle of the landing, steadily sidestepping as if doing a circular war dance. Each has her index finger raised, pointing at the other, like a wand. Both are still dressed in their full wedding attire, minus the prickly bouquets and, thankfully, Lynette's deely-bopper fascinator.

'Ladies, whatever is the . . .' I say softly, attempting to soothe. I'm ignored, possibly not even seen, given their rage. A thundering rumble of footsteps erupts as numerous relatives come running up the staircase, only for each to halt at first sight of the two women. Like the Von Trapp family, in height order from the top step downwards, Emmet, River, Teddy, Gunner Jeffery, Scarlet and Helen are all frozen in situ, with some having to peer through the wooden spindles of the banisters.

'I've told you once and I'll tell you again . . . the likes of you aren't fit to kiss the boots of the likes of me. I was never a quick jump as the babysitter on the rear seat of a Golf GTI,' bellows Janie, her features twisted into ugliness by anger.

'Oh no, I forgot, you were the one who targeted and stole your sister's husband during a two-week caravan holiday in Minehead! Real rock-chick wild-child tendencies there, Janie – I take my hat off to you!' screams Lynette. Gone is her Zen-like manner.

'Oooh,' winces Helen, her hands flying up to cover her face.

'Try as you might to keep up the holier-than-thou act, Lynette, we all know you were quick enough to take off any item of clothing with very little begging. And you have the audacity to throw insults at me? Well, at least I didn't get pregnant in the back of an untaxed, uninsured ramshackle motor borrowed from Jeffery, unlike some!'

A loud gasp erupts from the staircase audience, and Teddy blurts, 'Blimey, Mum, I didn't know that!'

'I did,' confirms Emmet, grimacing for his younger brother, 'Sorry, I didn't think you needed to know.'

'Yeah, me too,' adds River, sympathetically. 'Though I thought you knew already.'

'Great! Thanks for sharing, fellas,' moans Teddy, looking embarrassed. 'What a way to find out!'

'Me too,' mutters Gunner Jeffery, peering over Teddy's shoulder. 'She was a cracking little runner, that motor. An H plate, if I remember correctly. But the big end went and I couldn't afford to . . .' The rest of the staircase crowd turn and glare in horror at his recall. 'What? I'm only saying.'

Momentarily, I lose focus, listening to the family's exchange, only to have my attention ripped back as Janie lunges, grabbing a handful of Lynette's blonde hair, dramatically pulling her opponent forward and downwards, causing her chin to twist towards the ceiling.

'Urgh!' cries Lynette, bent double but still circling, her hands flailing wildly, grabbing at Janie.

'No! Violence is never the answer, Janie,' I cry. 'Emmet, help me?'

Lynette finally manages to grab hold of Janie's fringe, yanking hard and fixing Janie's view of just the carpet.

'Go on, Lynette – shake your tush like you do with your annoying shoulder shimmy!' mocks Janie.

'At least I have a tush to shake, unlike you! You lost connection with your body so long ago you've got the coordination of a breeze block!'

'You're so far up yourself you could lick your own tonsils,' hollers Janie, wincing in pain, distorting her beautifully made-up face.

'You never wanted Rupert in the first place – you were just jealous of your sister's happiness, that's your problem. And you still are – nearly thirty years later!' cries Lynette, keeping a vice-like grip.

'At least I didn't bore him to death with ginger tea and Zen enlightenment!' grunts Janie.

'No. You've kept us all entertained by fortifying your Irish cream with an additional half-bottle of whisky for those infamous festive coffees of yours. God help the poor bugger who picks up the wrong liqueur bottle by mistake – it'll burn their throat out!'

I'm speechless. The women continue to rotate blindly, shouting insults into the air. Neither can see properly, given their twisted hold on each other's hair. Emmet joins me on the landing, making several attempts to grab at their clenched fists, but due to their locked frames spinning, he's dodging protruding bottoms, squirming shoulders and flying insults.

'At least I didn't flirt with Gunner Jeffery in a futile attempt to make Rupert jealous!' shouts Lynette. The staircase crowd shuffle as one to look at the said friend, who's blushing profusely.

'What!' shrieks Scarlet, turning white and clutching the banister rail.

'Sod off, Lynette. We've all been there – he even tried it on with Helen once!' retorts Janie.

'Oh my God!' wails Helen, sinking unceremoniously from her banister position, as if fainting from view.

'Sorry, but what?' repeats Scarlet, turning from the ex-wives' scrum to the crumpled version of Helen below her on the staircase. 'What did Janie just say?'

'You heard, Scarlet! He's tried his luck with all of us. Sorry to bust your secret bubble, sweetie, but don't worry, you'll get over it!' shouts Janie, yanking at Lynette's scalp for good measure. 'The rest of us did! Though how you'll erase that very public "private dancing" from the memories of the entire family is anyone's guess.'

'This has to stop, ladies. It must stop! Now! This minute!' They're not stopping; if anything they are becoming more frantic. I prepare myself to wade in but suddenly become aware that I'm the only one focused on the spinning figures. Everyone else, including my helper, Emmet, is distracted as Scarlet attempts to pummel Jeffery's back with her clenched fists but is being held fast by both River and Teddy. A low wailing sound drifts up from below banister level, which I assume is Helen, unseen but clearly audible. While Gunner Jeffery is jigging about, keeping his broad back turned towards Scarlet to prevent her from landing a direct hit.

'Has anyone seen Martha? I need her to sew a button on to my blouse.' Fena saunters along the rear corridor swathed in red silk, like a warning flag, to join the fiasco on the landing. Her wet hair is wrapped in a white towel turban and her floaty silk robe, which reveals a fair amount of her décolletage, is pinched tight at the waist. 'Oh dear, such a debacle is always occurring between these . . . these women. Poor Rupie, he never has peace in his home, never ever.'

'Fena, could you?' I urge, gesturing towards Janie and Lynette.

'Urgh!' Grimacing profoundly, before her eyes widen on viewing her own daughter's actions. 'Scarlet, sweetie! Manners please!'

Scarlet immediately stops, her face now flushed puce, her eyes insane with rage as she stares at her mother.

'Did you know that he's . . . he's . . . knobbed them all?' explodes Scarlet, her arms waving before deciding on a direction in which to thrust a pointing finger down the staircase towards Helen. 'Even her!'

'Tsk, tsk, tsk,' says Fena, shaking her finger at Gunner Jeffery.

'Naughty boy, no messing with the ladies. You prove your worth for my girl or you be gone!'

'Mother!' yells Scarlet in frustration. 'That is not the answer to give.'

'Shhh now, I need to find Martha . . . her skills are needed for a wardrobe emergency.' Fena stands at the top of the staircase waiting for the current occupants to shuffle to the right-handside, like on the escalators on the London Underground, enabling her to swiftly descend. 'Oh Helen, you fall down?' is all I hear as her robed figure serenely disappears. And Scarlet resumes jabbing at Gunner Jeffery while the staircase posse of Teddy and River resume trying to hold her back.

'Teddy, River, could either of you come and help please?' calls Emmet to his younger brothers.

'I'm staying out of it,' replies River nonchalantly.

Teddy shakes his head. 'Me too. Sorry, but no can do.'

'Emmet, what should we do?' I wouldn't ask if it were stray bitches fighting in a park – a cold bucket of water or a tranquilliser gun would do the trick – but this, this is utterly shocking.

Emmet stands back, for fear of getting injured, I suspect. 'This happens now and then – the past catches up, throwing them back into the despair of years ago. There's usually more build-up than this though. The negative vibes have eluded me on this occasion, but maybe it's the whole wedding debacle that's thrown us all.'

'Debacle?' My voice nearly raises the thatched roof clean from the cottage. Despite the events unfolding in front of me and my stress in recent days, that solitary word ignites my touch paper.

Emmet freezes, eyes wide, eyebrows raised – even his hands shoot out from his sides as if shaken by the volume and tone of my voice.

'I mean . . . sorry, wrong choice of word, Lowry.'

'My arse! Have you been thinking that the entire time my mother has been dating your father or just whilst you were standing at the altar being their best man or giving your delightful speech?' I growl in defence of my kin.

'Lowry, I didn't mean debacle as in your mother . . . I meant as in Fena's unexpected arrival, the stress of doing the speech, and now this, involving these two.' He points at Janie and Lynette, who do appear to be tiring somewhat, before pointing at the staircase, whose occupants are currently frozen, scared to death by my eruption. 'And Jeffery's antics . . . and maybe Scarlet's too, if I'm on the right track.'

'Antics?' mutters Gunner Jeffery, looking about as if totally confused by the accusation.

'Yes, mate. Antics. Which I haven't heard you deny yet,' scowls Emmet.

'I've seen and heard enough. Let me through, please. This is not my drama to sort out. I'll be in the snug if anyone needs me, though I suggest you ask for help from someone else!' I say, throwing my hands into the air and striding towards the staircase. I desperately need to see Martha, for her calming energy and not her sewing skills.

Martha

On hearing the commotion on the landing above, I freeze. My pastry-covered hands tremble over the mixing bowl as I prepare a suppertime treat. After such a lovely wedding, it seems all is not well. I strain my hearing to snag the angry phrases shooting back and forth in rapid fire: Janie, then Lynette, Scarlet and Jeffery, then Helen and back to Lynette and Janie, followed by . . . oh, heaven help me . . . is that Lowry? Are they arguing on a day such as today? You'd think the champagne and fine food at the

wedding reception would have had half of them sleeping away
the afternoon before suppertime arrived, but no, they crave constant entertainment, more than is good for them!

'What in God's name is happening up those stairs?' I chunter,
wiping my hands down the front of my pinny ready to give
them all what for. I'm ready to exit my peaceful domain when
Fena, fresh from her shower, appears in the doorway, blocking
my path.

'Leave them to squabble and play the victim card between
themselves,' says Fena calmly. 'You need not worry. They will
not spill blood on the carpet, so you can rest, Martha – forgive
their trashy natures.'

'But I'd never forgive myself if . . .' I say, justifying my actions.

'Poor Rupie is not here. Allow them to sort out their difference
like children in a sandpit. I need your help – I have a button
that needs sewing on my blouse. Pure silk. An exquisite blouse
purchased from Nippori town but the button, urgh, gone!'

'Sorry?'

'My blouse, the button, it "ping" on the aeroplane. I ask the
hostess nicely but she refused, even in first class. I don't know
what service standards are coming to nowadays, Martha – I really
don't. You always oblige, always . . .'

I'm up to my elbows rubbing flour and butter, with a cottage
full of people who'll need feeding sooner than I can magic up
a chicken and mushroom pie . . . and she thinks I have time
to stop everything to sew a button on her blouse. Give me
strength!

'Fena, bless you, my lovely. A quiet sit down, with my feet
up, enjoying a little rest whilst performing a quick sewing task
is just what I need. You'll be OK finishing off this chicken and
mushroom pie ready for suppertime, will you?'

She performs a double take between my claggy hands and the
contents of the mixing bowl, and she baulks.

'I, Fena, do not cook. None of the ladies in this family cooks, Martha. It is you who is the angel who bakes, not me!'

Cheeky mare! Who does she think she is? The Queen of Sheba!

'Ahh, well. Sorry, my lovely, but the angel who bakes doesn't do sewing tasks on the same day.'

'But my blouse ... my button. Does this cottage not come with a butler or a ladies' maid?'

Typical Fena, expecting a stately home rather than a cottage rental.

'You'll find a sewing kit in the hallway drawer; I saw it there myself only yesterday.'

'I am no good with practical tasks – that is why Rupie hires ...'

I interrupt, not wishing to hear the remainder of that particular sentence. 'If you'll excuse me, I must be getting up those stairs to sort out this brood before they kill each other.' I leave her standing open-mouthed, tugging at the expensive silk robe covering her modesty – as one must with Jeffery about. Before I have a chance to move, the door opens to reveal a bedraggled Lowry, who blocks my path now.

'Martha, I've no idea what the hell is happening up there, but ...' says Lowry, as pale as a sheet and on the verge of tears, gesturing upstairs. 'Janie and Lynette have literally got each other in a headlock!'

'Is Emmet up there?'

'Yes, but he can't grab hold of them given their wrangling and sidestepping, plus he possibly has too much respect for older women.'

'Don't upset yourself, sweetheart. This is the Carmichael clan at their finest. It was bound to happen the minute Mr C's back was turned. It's always the same – while the cat's away! Leave it to me, I'll sort it. Go and settle yourself in the snug, and I'll bring you a little something through in a minute.'

'Thank you.' Lowry steps aside, clearing my path, as the commotion upstairs rumbles on.

'Martha, I can make her tea if you could just sew ...' Fena calls after my departing figure.

'No can do, Fena. Mr C writes my contract and it's not negotiable in his absence.' I don't wait for Fena's reaction but climb the stairs, stepping over a wailing Helen.

Chapter Twenty-One

Helen

I never imagined entering the Queen's Head again, literally hours after leaving the wedding reception; this was not on my agenda for today. I'm shaking from head to foot but my power walk has been fuelled by the sheer anger boiling inside me at the statement made by Janie. My God, I could scream. Is there no loyalty left in this world? It was hardly a thing – Jeffery was drunk, I recoiled instantly, and he backed off, knowing I wasn't game for any games of his. I told Janie that in the strictest of confidences all those years ago, and to think she's just . . . She'd already scuppered my marriage to Rupert at that point, so why blurt out such a detail now from when I was newly divorced and somewhat vulnerable.

'What can I get you?' asks the barwoman, all smiles, just as she was two hours ago when she bid our wedding party good evening.

'A double G&T please. Gordon's is fine – any slimline tonic will do,' I say, grateful that I'd already changed out of my coat-dress during my brief return to the cottage, otherwise I'd look a right sight standing at the bar, alone. Every customer would think I'd been stood up on a date – chance would be a fine thing. I haven't had one of those in . . .? Bloody hell, I'm so sick of that loop of self-questioning. I haven't done this in . . .? I haven't done that in . . .? If the last thirty minutes has taught me anything – correction, if today has taught me anything, it's that I need to move on! I've stood on the sidelines, waiting, watching and bloody well hoping for what? A reconciliation with Rupert! Did I seriously envisage our happy ever after until death us do part could happen with several failed marriages slotted in between our original engagement and our forever engagement? That fading hope has spanned three decades of my life, diminishing with each subsequent wedding, while he has met and married others, and fathered numerous children, to his heart's content. Well, today, it's content. I can honestly say I've never seen him as happy, apart from maybe the day our Emmet was born. Yes, I'll admit today is possibly the second happiest I've ever seen him. Good luck to them both. I hope they'll be very happy together for many years to come. Good luck and a good bloody riddance too, in the nicest of ways.

I'm done! With mothering the entire brood, keeping the peace between the other ex-wives, being lumbered with all the planning, the organising, the day-to-day running of this family, which I've happily undertaken . . . till now.

As the barwoman places a chilled, bulbous glass before me, I'm aware that she and other customers are watching me closely. I assume that little rant must have played out on my face as well as inside my head. Ah well, so be it; I won't be seeing any of these folks after the next hour.

'Thank you,' I say, before adding, 'any chance you'll take for another and send it over to me in about thirty minutes or so?'

'Sure.' She offers a brief smile as she jabs at the till and grabs the card machine. I'm sure my request isn't a first for her, though it most definitely is for me.

I quickly find a vacant table, not hidden away in a corner but fairly central in the bar area, and settle down with my G&T. I need to be surrounded by people right now, chatting couples and groups, all busy living their lives. One thing I hadn't been expecting earlier today, sitting amongst the mix of relatives, was loneliness. That gut-wrenching feeling that I've ploughed all I have into doing what I can for this family, and the end result is each and every one of them moving on with their lives while I, at the age of forty-nine, am stuck fast where I was some thirty years ago. Organising each and every one of them, ensuring they have what they need, anticipating what they might want, and attempting to create family memories which they might treasure or they might even not remember in the future.

I take a sip of my drink, reach for my phone and locate the notes app. The family can sort out their own squabbles, I've details and plans of my own to jot down – because as one door closes, another opens. Sadly, at my time in life, I can't afford to waste time wondering which doors are securely bolted and which remain on the latch, so to speak. I take a second long sip before setting aside my drink.

The entrance door opens, and my gaze is drawn over the edge of my glass as Scarlet staggers in, her tetchy manner similar to my own when I first came in. My heart sinks as she darts towards my table.

'Helen.' She stands there, staring down at me like a panting child, her hands clutching the back of the opposite chair.

'Yes?'

'I've walked out too.'

'Well, good for you.' Can I not get a minute's peace? I pick up my glass, take another long, slow sip, hoping she'll break with this formal nonsense and either bugger off or grab herself a drink, unless she's expecting me to oblige.

'I thought . . . enough.'

'Mmm.' Enough? Pull the other one, Scarlet. You've witnessed a fraction of the family tension yet you're calling it quits thinking you've braved the battle like Joan of Arc.

'And I thought . . . I'd come and hear it from you, rather than sift through the details of Jeffery's explanation.' Chair and table separate, like a podium behind which she'll be my judge, jury and executioner, if needs be.

This will be interesting. I purposely put down my glass and stare at this woman I helped to raise, in many ways. I never particularly wanted a daughter – I think I was always destined to mother boys – and my relationship with Scarlet has always been slightly tetchy, as a result. I've no intention of taking the lead in this conversation; she can ask whatever she likes. I'll be honest. I have nothing to hide. I did nothing wrong, didn't encourage him and declined his so-called charms at the first chance I got. Thankfully, he respected my refusal – deep down he knew I only had eyes for Rupert.

Her expectant expression twitches, as if willing me to speak. I keep schtum, waiting.

'Well?'

'Well what?' I ask.

'What Janie said on the landing.'

'Phooey to what Janie said. What makes you think she has half the details correct?'

'Because she's your sister and you frequently share with her,' states Scarlet, shifting from foot to foot behind her 'podium'.

'Family allegiance doesn't count for much, not in this family, Scarlet. Haven't you learnt that yet?'

She shrugs, as if untarnished by family history.

'Why are you so interested anyway?' A loaded question if ever there was one.

'Just interested, that's all ...' She squirms under the weight of her own lie.

'Oh, sit down and stop pretending. What are you having?' I gesture towards my glass.

Scarlet bolts into the vacant seat, saying, 'A woo woo cocktail for me.'

'Really?' I spread my hands wide, indicting our surroundings.

'Sorry, yes. A triple G&T then.'

A triple? Not bloody likely. I gesture towards the barwoman, catching her attention. 'I'll have my second, and the same for her please.'

Scarlet whips around in her seat. 'But you drink—'

'You'll get the same and be grateful,' I snap, knocking back the last of my drink. 'Come on then, out with it, before I make you apologise for using such vulgar language as "knobbed" in my presence.'

'You and Gunner Jeffery.'

'There was no me and Jeffery. Never was, never will be! Janie's simply stirring the pot to cause trouble because there was definitely a Janie and Jeffery fling – that was on and off for a couple of years once Rupert left her – and after that a Lynette and Jeffery fling, which didn't last quite as long, and maybe, possibly, for a very short while, even a Jeffery and . . .' I fall silent, allowing Scarlet to catch up. I watch the lightbulb moment occur behind her stare before quickly continuing. 'But I can assure you, hand on heart, there was no Helen and Jeffery. Not that he didn't try his luck one night at a party after my divorce was finalised, I might add, but nope, never Helen and Jeffery. I only ever had eyes for Rupert. Before, during and after our divorce.'

Scarlet is dumbstruck. Sadly, I've seen this expression before when answering questions from my Emmet, especially during his teenage years, when he craved a normal family, like his school chums. I'm unsure if I should keep talking or wait till she gives me a sign of consciousness. 'Ah, perfect timing,' I say as the barwoman delivers my second round and hands me the card machine to pay for Scarlet's drink. 'Thank you.'

I nudge a bulbous glass across the table. 'Cheers. Bottoms up, so to speak.'

Scarlet's fingers instantly awaken and grab her glass; she greedily consumes the contents.

'Steady up, I was only joking.'

'Why has no one said before now?' she asks earnestly, pausing for breath. 'I mean, you've never mentioned it, they've hidden it, and all along he's been ... seeking out relatives to get close to. Why not be open about it amongst the family? I wouldn't have entertained the idea but ... well, oh my God.'

She's verging on the state of panic; her hands are shaking, her eyes darting around erratically and her voice is shifting through the emotional gears towards shrill. What's so important that she's reacting like this? An image of her wiggling and sashaying around the dining room flits across my mind. Her sudden eruption of rage on hearing Janie's hurtful insinuations, Fena's conversational huddle during the reception with just Jeffery and Scarlet. A fling? Possibly, but surely there'd have to be something more than that to spark such a reaction.

'Scarlet? Have you got something to announce?'

'That's bloody obvious, isn't it?'

The thought hits me from nowhere, her puckered brides-maid's dress, her refusal of goat's cheese tart, and her 'glowing' appearance before and after 'Santa Baby'. I quickly snatch the glass from her lips.

'Are you pregnant?'

Her gawping mouth answers my question.

'You won't be needing this then!' I say, placing her gin glass at my elbow. Didn't she ask for a triple? How irresponsible.

'I just needed ...'

My index finger automatically lifts to silence her protest. 'There's no excuse. I'll get you an orange juice.' Scarlet rolls her eyes to the low ceiling but I gesture towards the barwoman, catching her eye. 'An orange juice, please.' I turn back to Scarlet. 'Does he know?'

Scarlet gives the smallest of headshakes.

'Your mother?'

She repeats her gesture. There's no point asking about her dad; we'd all know about it if Rupert knew.

'I see.' Now what do I say? What would I have wanted someone to say to me? 'Don't worry, it'll be OK – we're family,' or even, 'How can I best support you?' Ironically, one phrase I won't be using is her statement from a few moments ago: 'Why not be open about it amongst the family?'

The barwoman swiftly delivers a large glass of juice and I tap the card reader. I'll make sure she gets a decent tip on the way out.

Scarlet automatically snatches up the glass and downs it, much as she did with the gin.

'Don't you take your time with anything?' I ask, before adding, 'On second thoughts, don't answer that.' Scarlet eyes me over the rim of her glass, before putting it down.

'I just wanted time with the family over Christmas, you know what it's like, with the wedding and Emmet's big birthday, before I . . . we said anything.'

I nod; it makes sense.

'I never imagined I'd be hearing such revelations for the first time from Janie – you'd have thought my Jeffery would have told me.'

'Would you? Really? What man's going to come clean about chasing his best friend's . . .' I don't want to say 'ex-wives' – or worse, 'sloppy seconds' or even 'cast offs'; it all sounds so derogatory. 'Have you never wondered why he's never invited to family gatherings but shows up unannounced, like a stray dog returning home on smelling a decent meal?'

'How would I know he was never invited? You do all the organising and he always seems to be there – no one refuses him entry.' She's got a point, and maybe that's another advantage to me stepping back from the Carmichael coal face.

'Prearranged, was it, for you both to arrive together on Monday?' I ask. I don't want to pry but we can't sit in silence.

'I arrived back from Japan a week ago, and I simply lay low at Jeffery's, allowing us some time together before the family Christmas. I was going to tell him then, when we were alone, but I never found the right time. He wanted to do all the usual – dinners out, expensive treats – and I knew me saying would put a stop to all that so figured I'd tell him at New Year.'

'Certainly no casual bumping into each other at the train station, then? Your plans were gift-wrapped ready to sneak them under the tree without us questioning anything.' Class act for one so young. 'And now? How do you think he'll react to the news?'

Scarlet visibly swallows.

'Mixed. One part of me thinks he'll be over the moon, given he hasn't got any children, but then again . . . this was hardly the plan for his later years.'

'Not planned, hey?'

Scarlet's gaze instantly drops to inspect the tabletop.

'I'm not judging, though it probably sounds like it, but please don't come the innocent with me, Scarlet. Whatever your reasons, you've done what you've done. I think the best course is to come clean to Jeffery and then—' I'm about to say her parents when over Scarlet's left shoulder the entrance of an attractive woman, wearing a cassock-styled fawn coat with brass-button detailing, a thick fur collar and matching hat, from which a mane of blonde hair falls around her shoulders, catches my eye. I know her – yes, definitely. That's . . . Oh hell no! Her name sticks in my throat, as Scarlet, curious to see what has caused my startled expression, turns around to stare at the beauty.

'Bloody hell, you're the last person I was expecting to see,' mutters Scarlet, her expression now mimicking mine. 'Is Emmet expecting you?'

Lowry

'Knock, knock, can I come in?' I look up to find Emmet's head and shoulders poking around the edge of the snug's door. I'm comfy; enjoying a lie down whilst having a quiet read. I don't sit up.

'I suppose.' I close the poetry book I've been browsing, placing it on the coffee table where it belongs and not under a cushion, where I found it.

'I've brought us a tipple,' says Emmet, jiggling two whisky glasses, making the ice tinkle, before handing me one.

'Thank you.' I've no intention of taking back my outburst upstairs, but I'll hear him out, if that's his mission.

'May I?' Emmet points to the other sofa. I nod. I don't own it, so how can I refuse? Not that his whisky offering has softened me up, but it'll feel as awkward as Saturday night in the garden, when I stood and he sat, if I insist he stands throughout.

I sip my whisky, refusing to fill the silence. The amber liquid warms my throat without causing me to choke.

'Anyway ... I wanted to come and apologise for my error upstairs. When I said debacle, I didn't mean the wedding. I meant this bloody shambles of a family. I didn't mean you and your mum, or her wedding, right?'

I twitch my brow. I hear him but I'm not going to fall over myself to accept his explanation. His remark stung, still does.

'Lowry, please?'

'It's OK, Emmet. Say what you like, now we're family. Hey, you couldn't offend me if you tried – we're a blended family. We're brother and sister now ... we've got each other's backs. We're tight now that this bloody debacle has happened. Isn't that so?' My sarcasm's spread thicker than I intended.

Emmet sits back, purses his lips. 'You've got a right cob on you, haven't you?'

I'm not entirely sure what a cob is but assume it implies moody.

'Too right I have! Have you any idea how tough it was for me to turn up on Saturday, not knowing any of you. To join in, chat nonstop, decipher the family tree, let alone the family history, and enjoy a few festive days while trying to find my feet. Only to hear you describe it as a "debacle" when you're on home territory, so to speak.'

'As I said, I'm truly sorry for the way it came out. It was thoughtless – but it wasn't meant the way you think. Honest,' he says.

'I've come across scenes like that when I'm on duty but I'm ready and prepared when it's a pack of dogs. I can count on back-up, with vets at hand with tranquilliser darts – we can stun and separate them in minutes. But to watch two mature women lunge at each other with that much hatred, well … I'm lost for words. I'm grateful that my mother wasn't here to witness it, or she'd have spent the rest of her wedding day in tears. Hardly an image I wish to remember and on Boxing Day as well!'

'It wouldn't have happened had Dad and Diane still been here. They respect Dad's presence, which is why it only happened once they'd left. It would've been tomorrow otherwise, though on second thoughts, I believe Lynette might be leaving first thing in the morning, so maybe it wouldn't have happened at all.'

'It explains why everyone arrives in shifts,' I add, fighting the urge to say more. He looks pretty glum to be fair, and he sounds genuine. 'I'm surprised at Lynette – she comes across so …' I'm lost to even describe. I'm still quite jittery despite the calming environment.

'Pure and martyr-like?' offers Emmet.

'Yes. With her ginger tea, her Zen calm and still-water atti-tude – yet she still tried to go twelve rounds on the landing.' I put my whisky glass on the coffee table; the constant tinkling of ice cubes against the crystal is giving me away.

'You're not OK, are you?' Emmet scooches over from his sofa to the arm of mine, his right hand resting on the bridge of my feet. The warmth of his touch radiates through my thick woollen socks like a heated blanket.

'I'll be fine. I'm just not used to such behaviour.'

'If it's any consolation, they've separated and retreated to their rooms. My mum nipped out for a walk, and Scarlet left not long afterwards. There's no fear of round two erupting.'

'As I said before, I grew up in a household with two elderly grandparents, my mum and a menagerie of animals. We had our difficulties sometimes, but nothing like this. And that's pretty much who I've become – a mature version of the child I once was.'

'Phuh! I've become the man I needed as a child – that's me.' Emmet's phrase hits a target deep within me. I watch him perform a double blink, as if stunned by his own honesty. 'I mean . . . that sounds so wrong of me, but I craved daily interaction with my dad. A male role model who had his shit together at home as much as he had with his business.'

'Oh, Emmet . . .' My heart melts for the little boy he once was.

Clutching his glass, he waves away my sentiment before taking a slug of his drink. His right hand remains in situ on my feet; I'm unsure whether he's conscious of his touch or not. Do I reposition my feet, encouraging him to remove his hand, or remain still, enjoying the connection? I can't deny I'm enjoying the warmth of his touch; it feels comforting. Though my pondering might ignite a crimson blush if I continue, much like the tree chopping incident – how embarrassing was that?

'Don't get me wrong, I've gone without nothing that money can buy . . . but money can't buy everything, can it?'

I shake my head; I get where he's coming from.

'Not every lad gets three stepmothers during his schooling, do they?'

'Nope. And some get lumbered with a stepfather too,' I add, for good measure.

'Exactly. Though I'd have happily welcomed a new relationship for my mother, even if it entailed a difficult period of readjustment for me.'

'None of them have gone on to other relationships, have they? Was it part of the divorce agreement?' I ask.

Emmet sits tall, his hand swiftly withdrawn from my feet, his expression somewhat puzzled. 'Why on earth would it be?'

'I don't know. I can imagine some men wouldn't want to carry on supporting a woman who's dating elsewhere? I thought your father had provided property for each ex-wife.'

'He has, but he's not vindictive. Quite the opposite. He knows the damage his behaviour has caused. For which he's paid the price tenfold in his own search for happiness.'

I pick up my whisky glass and take a sip, mainly to prevent putting my foot in it with an additional comment.

'Look, as much as I wanted bath-time with my dad, TV suppers and bedtime stories each night, I got what I got, for which I'm grateful – so many little kids get far less. I shouldn't complain, but I dreamt of a different kind of family life and that's what I'm aiming for in life.'

'Not planning on having your ex-wives scrapping while you jet off on honeymoon then?'

'Nope. Certainly not. In fact, I'd happily—'

There's a *knock-knock* on the closed door, causing us to fall silent and stare.

'Come in!' calls Emmet, as we both await an entrance.

River pops his head around the edge of the door, and ignoring me, his gaze on his brother, says, 'Any chance of a chat, Emmet?'

'Sure.' Emmet turns to me. 'Are we good?'

'Yep, we're good.' I roll up to sit, before swinging my feet to the floor. 'I'm heading out, so you fellas might as well stay in here.'

'Catch you later, Lowry,' mutters River.

'Thanks, River,' I say, as he holds the door wide for me.

I pause at the bottom of the staircase, staring at the snug's door, which closed all too quickly behind me. Couldn't River's chat have waited? A few more minutes was all we needed to ... what? I haven't the words to describe it. He'd apologised, I'd accepted his apology. He'd explained why, I'd accepted his explanation. He'd begun to open up and I was right in the middle of accepting his revealed version when River interrupted. Damn it, no one knows what's happening behind closed doors – isn't that the truth!

The newel post becomes solid and notchity beneath my resting palm, the sprig of mistletoe swings absently above my knuckles. I can't stand here all day – they'll think I'm earwigging. I have one true purpose whilst I'm here, so I head upstairs to check on my kittens, praying I don't meet anyone on the landing.

Chapter Twenty-Two

Martha

'Do me a favour!' The anger bellows through the kitchen wall from the snug like a wrecking ball of words. The contained emotion sounds so raw, almost guttural, in its delivery that I hardly recognise whose voice it is. River's? Emmet's? Surely not!

I stop draining the vegetables as my hackles lift and my hearing becomes ultra-sensitive – just as it did when they were teenagers pushing boundaries and outbursts between father and sons became a regular occurrence.

'I thought . . .' His final words are muffled.

'Well, good for you, but you thought wrong!' It is Emmet! By Christ, there's going to be trouble now, that's for sure. I put the colander down on the draining board and dash to the hallway to find a row of stunned faces peering over or through the banister rail at the closed door.

'Don't you all just stand there – do something!' I insist, looking up at three wives, a sibling and a prodigal friend.

Teddy purses his mouth while the three women slowly shake their heads – finally united. Bloody typical!

'You think everything has to be on your terms – well, go to hell if you don't approve,' shouts River from inside.

'Approve? Do you think anyone will approve – least of all Dad!' retorts Emmet.

'I get it. You've never been any different, you've always sucked up to him as the first-born, knocking me and Teddy back from the limelight whenever it was feasible, just to stay in his good books.'

'Good books? Are you for real? How has this got anything to do with work, River? You're making excuses for your own deception, and hers!'

I can't take this, not after the earlier incident, and after such a beautiful wedding. I thank my lucky stars that the happy couple have departed, Helen has taken a walk to steady her nerves and Scarlet . . . well, to hell with that young madam and her Jeffery-inspired rendezvous.

I reach for the doorknob.

'Martha, you can't!' hisses Janie, staring through the wooden spindles.

'I wouldn't if I were you,' advises Lynette.

'Best to leave them – it'll be finished before you know it,' says Fena, still in her silk robe but with her hair beautifully styled.

'Of all the rotten scheming things in this world, you choose to treat me like this!'

'Choose? You think I chose for this to happen?'

'Hasn't this family been damaged enough by Dad's behaviour – or are you setting the standard for the next generation?'

'Like father, like son, isn't that the saying?' shouts River.

'You bastard! As if that's any excuse . . .'

An eruption of bangs and scuffling occurs inside the snug.

'If you think I'm going to stand here and listen to two of my boys tear each other apart then think again,' I say, tears springing to my eyes. It might sound dramatic but I refuse to lower my standards just because the lads aren't biologically mine. How was it described in that poem from the other night – perilous? Never a truer word uttered. I refuse to stand by, and I'll answer for my actions, if needs be. I wrench open the door to find the coffee table upended and the couch cushions in disarray; Emmet and River are grappling with each other in the confined space.

My hands reach out, grabbing each male's upper arm. I haven't the strength to separate them but I'm hoping the shock of my touch, my presence or my voice will ... might ... bring them to their senses. 'Stop it, both of you!' I step back from the sparring pair to find Teddy and Janie standing right behind me. I'm visibly shaking from head to toe.

There's a momentary pause, measurable by only a breath, a heartbeat or a realisation – whatever occurs, it's simultaneous in both men. Their tempers falter, fists unfurl and grasped holds release as they both fall backwards from each other, on to opposing couches. Their panting breath fills the air.

'Hello?' calls Helen, stunning us all back to reality. 'What the hell is happening here?'

I step aside, taking comfort from the fact that Helen didn't arrive five minutes earlier, but, turning to view the crowded doorway, I spy the one person who certainly isn't my flavour of the month: Annabel.

Helen

'Martha, are you alright?' I ask, tapping the kitchen table, gesturing for her to join me. I'm still processing the situation myself but at least I was spared her ordeal.

I watch as she slumps into the nearest chair, composing her features before speaking.

'I'm lost for words, Helen. And now, having realised what they were fighting about, it simply breaks my heart ... To think River could behave in such a way when Emmet has always supported him. Only two days ago I witnessed a conversation between the pair of them regarding life's morals and principles ... and now this! And as for Annabel, well ... I'm stunned. She was involved with Emmet for long enough to know how the family situation has left its mark on his life and to allow history to be repeated, well . . .' Her voice cracks with emotion. 'Sorry, seeing the lads . . . it's shocked me. I realise this must be especially painful for you.'

'There's no need to apologise. I have all the time in the world, Martha – you needn't rush yourself. I came back fearing that her presence would undermine Emmet in an instant but never did I dream I'd be walking into such a scenario. I was praying with each step I took that her motives would be good, given it's his birthday weekend as well as Christmas and . . .' I pause, allowing my own emotions to pass like a crashing wave on a beach. 'Not once did she mention River; she just kept chattering away about having remembered that the wedding reception was being held in that particular restaurant.'

'She's got some neck turning up at all, and brazen enough to walk in knowing she might be disrupting a family wedding reception! I noticed Scarlet was too shocked for words too.'

'Mmm, I expect Scarlet to be quiet for a little while, to be fair. I'm relieved that the happy couple got away when they did; can you imagine what it would be like otherwise?'

'Don't go there, please. Poor Diane would have been heartbroken if this drama had been played out between the coffee and the speeches.'

'I feel physically sick at the very thought – which I suppose is how my own mother must have felt, three decades ago, about Rupert and Janie.'

We fall silent, each absorbed into our own private thoughts.

'Where's Annabel now?' asks Martha, glancing over her shoulder towards the door.

'She and Emmet are chatting in the snug – clearing the air and discussing how to move forward, I suppose.'

'That'll be no mean feat, if River's determined to continue this carry-on.'

'This'll set Emmet back, if nothing else. I only realised this morning that he hasn't smoked as much in recent days, though he's still knocking back the whisky.'

Martha shakes her head, before saying, 'I doubt it. Fingers crossed it'll propel him forward without a backwards glance.'

'I hope so, because if there's one thing I've learnt in this fiasco of a family it's that you need to know when enough is enough. Obsessing about the past, hanging on to what might have been, never works. I could have made a life elsewhere if I'd reacted differently when our Janie did this to me. I hope Emmet's gone past the point of no return with Annabel, then he'll be free to pursue other relationships rather than . . .' I stop talking as a wry smile adorns Martha's lips. 'You know something, don't you?'

The kitchen door opens, admitting Lowry, carrying an empty coffee mug. 'Oh sorry, I didn't realise you were . . .'

Martha's gaze softens and her smile remains strong.

'No worries, we were just . . . Anyway, enough about our situation. How are you?' I ask, glancing between the two, trying to gather speed on something I mentioned the other night.

'I'm all good. Today's been slightly surreal in many ways but never mind. I'm more concerned about you guys – you've worked so hard to bring a family Christmas together, and a birthday and a wedding too, yet it all seems to have unravelled in one evening,' Lowry says, emptying the dregs of her mug into the sink and placing it in the dishwasher.

'I am upset, but it's not about me. This weekend was about others – we've been here before and we coped, so we'll support them the best we can,' I say, mindful that Martha's still grinning like a Cheshire cat.

'That's good to hear. I suppose that's the wonderful thing about family – it acts like a safety net when issues arise,' says Lowry, standing at the end of the table.

'It certainly does,' mutters Martha, still smiling.

'We try to,' I say, my mind frantically reworking the images of the weekend.

'I'll be leaving in the morning, so I'm going to call it a day. Thank you for everything you've done for my mum – she and Rupert had a fabulous wedding day. Goodnight.'

'Goodnight, Lowry,' says Martha.

'Night, Lowry,' I say, watching her retreat into the hallway. I wait until the kitchen door is completely closed before turning to Martha's beaming face. 'I'm right, aren't I?'

'If you need to ask, you must be blind,' says Martha, rolling her eyes to the ceiling.

The kitchen door reopens; I'm half expecting Lowry to have doubled back but Emmet walks in, his shoulders slumped and stubbled chin hanging low.

'Are you OK? Need anything?' I ask, half standing in my rush to tend to my son.

'A couple of pillows and a spare duvet wouldn't go amiss,' he says, reaching for the kettle.

'Are you not sleeping upstairs?' I ask, dashing a fleeting glance in Martha's direction.

Emmet heads for the sink, giving me a knowing look over his shoulder. 'Hardly appropriate given our earlier interaction. I believe Annabel may be sharing his twin room tonight.'

'They c-could have m-mentioned it to me,' I stammer, unsure how I feel about that suggestion. I bet Janie's given them the go-ahead, in Rupert's absence, without any consideration for my son.

'My God, have they no shame?' mutters Martha, her shoulders bristling.

'As you were, Martha. I don't give a damn what they do – they won't be dragging me into their situation, that's for sure,' says Emmet.

'But you're not sleeping down here?' I say, recalling my original bedroom plan.

'Yeah, I'll be snug in the snug. Anyone else want a coffee?'

We shake our heads in unison, then I correct him. 'No, Emmet. You won't get a wink of sleep lying on either couch – your feet will hang over the edge and you'll have a crick in your neck for days. The main bedroom's free now your dad and Diane have gone – let us strip the bed and remake it. It won't take long – there's plenty of clean sheets in the linen cupboard.' My tone is almost frantic, which seems an overreaction to his suggestion, but I hate to think Emmet's paying the price for their behaviour yet can still accommodate others.

'Seriously, Mum, don't trouble yourself – I'll be fine.'

'It's no trouble, we can—' I exchange a look with Martha excusing my use of the plural without asking her – 'change that bedding over in minutes.'

'Of course we can – as quick as a flash,' she adds.

'Nope. I'm grateful for the offer but it isn't necessary just for one night.' His tone is resolute as he makes his coffee.

Martha's eyes are signalling to me and she's erratically nodding at Emmet's back.

'What's with the silent conversation?' says Emmet. 'I can see your reflection in the kitchen window, you know.'

'Maybe you'd like to stay on an extra day after we've left?' I say, having understood Martha's uncanny head nodding. 'Your father's paid the rental up until the twenty-eighth. You could stay over, get some peace and quiet – and it would free me up tomorrow from having to be the last to leave. Though don't tell the others!'

Emmet turns, teaspoon in hand, and nods. 'That makes sense. In which case, I'll take you up on the offer of the main bedroom – two nights makes it worth me changing the sheets.' As soon as the words leave his lips, we both stand to crack on with the task. 'No. I'm quite capable of sorting out bed sheets, thank you very much.'

Martha

It takes all evening for my nerves to unfurl, though the kitchen is spick and span thanks to my unleashed adrenalin. I've never been one for a flurry of nervous energy but I made good use of it tonight. And now I can relax with a mug of cocoa and enjoy a little poetry before calling it a day. And boy, what a day! I raise my slippered feet, curling them beneath myself and reach for the little clothbound book. The pages open at random, and my mind is lost to a gentle world of nature and nurturing. Gone are the family issues, the tensions and the need to referee arguments as an inner peace soothes my raw nerves, refreshing my world.

There's a *knock, knock, knock* on the snug door. Now what?

'Hello?' I call, mindful of my tone.

The door opens partway as Gunner Jeffery pops his head around it.

'Only me. I was wondering if . . . I could have a chat.'

'Sure.' I close my book, pushing it down the side of the cushion. 'How can I help?' Not a line I usually offer without it resulting in a plate of something being prepared and delivered, regardless of the late hour.

Gunner Jeffery takes a seat, settles back and clears his throat.

'You may have realised that Scarlet and I are . . . well, together, as such,' he says bashfully, then pauses, awaiting my reply.

'I assumed that given some of today's conversations – overheard on the landing.' I fall silent, not sure why he's announcing this to me, the hired help. I wait, preparing myself for whatever might follow.

'Can I ask what you think Rupert will say?'

'It's not really my place to say, Jeffery. Mr C's a man of few words, and on previous occasions, he's been ... shall we say a little surprised by your actions.'

'I see. I realise that he's distanced himself over the years, and I can't blame him, but we've never argued about such matters, you understand. It's as if he's let each indiscretion be brushed under the carpet, so to speak.'

This is surreal. I can't believe what I'm hearing – a schoolboy mentality from a fully grown man. I know exactly what I'd be saying if it were Emmet, River or Teddy, but it isn't, it's Gunner Jeffery. A man I've watched come and go from Mr C's home, treated like a brother on many occasions, and who chased his best friend's ex-wives whenever circumstances suited. What the hell am I supposed to say?

'You look lost in thought, Martha.'

'I am. I hope you don't mind me saying but I've spent many years with this family watching the comings and goings. I've heard the discussions, the declarations and witnessed the divorces and never have I heard such a ridiculous question asked in all my life!' Jeffery's mouth falls wide. I continue – I wouldn't be true to myself or him if I didn't. 'Are you expecting Mr C to treat this dalliance, if I can call it that, in the same way as the others? Not on your nelly, Jeffery! If there's one thing I know about Rupert Carmichael, that is his unwavering love for his daughter – all four of his children in fact, but most certainly Scarlet. He'll see this as a personal attack which you've masterminded and implemented behind his back – and he'll hold you solely responsible for the situation, given her tender age compared to your maturity.' Gunner Jeffery's mouth is still gaping wide, but words fail him. 'I know what you'll say in reply, you'll try outlining your good intentions, reminding him of your attentive nature, your jovial personality, and you'll highlight your secure and settled position in life – which all counts from a father's point of view, but I hardly think he'll take this lying down, do you?' I fall silent, allowing my not-so-poetic words to hit home.

'Fena accepts us as a couple,' is his only response.

'Does she now!' is mine.

'You say that as if it's a bad thing.'

I incline my head, suggesting the answer is obvious. 'Given the speculation about the brief interest you might have shown in each wife, I suspect that Fena has her own agenda, a selective memory and probably doesn't give as much attention as she should to her daughter's wellbeing – maybe the situation suits everyone's purpose, shall we say?'

Gunner Jeffery looks utterly confused.

'Oh, come on, Jeffery. Surely this isn't news to you, you must have thought about these questions before you made your advances. What would you say to your best friend, or your brothers, if a similar situation arose?'

'Brian and Michael have both been happily married since their twenties – this sort of circumstance would never arise for them.'

As I feared.

He goes on. 'All I can say is that my interest in the others doesn't compare to my commitment to Scarlet. It might only be six months since we bumped into each other during one of her fleeting visits home, but we've got along fine in that time. If Rupert needs me to prove that I'm serious about this relationship, then so be it, but he'll need to hear me out.'

'He certainly will. Though I wouldn't let Janie cop you referring to her as purely an "interest",' I say, hoping this conversation is drawing to a close.

Chapter Twenty-Three

Wednesday 27 December

Lowry

My phone teases me by slowing time: it's still just 03.17. I've been watching the minutes drift past for three-quarters of an hour whilst listening for a creak on the staircase. I doubt he's able to sleep – I bet he's lying in the master suite pondering what to say when breakfast arrives. My mind loops the same set of questions, coming at them from a different angle on each approach. Will Emmet want to win her back from River? Would she be interested in reconciling? Are they actually sharing a single bed in the twin room? That's hardly romantic, given the broad shoulders on River. Annabel will spend the night clinging to the edge of the mattress for fear of being pushed out. I did it once with an ex way back in my youth, worst night's sleep of my life – never again. Then there's Gunner Jeffery, shock horror at such goings-on! And at his age too. Is that the actual issue that's giving me the ick factor, or is it the revelation about his advances towards each ex-wife? Or is it simply the age difference between them of some thirty years? That would be like Emmet marrying someone who has just been born! A girl born yesterday. Born today even. Not due to be born for another week or so! My mind does a triple somersault at the very thought. Me even, marrying someone who's yet to be potty-trained!

That's when I hear the stair creak.

I sit up, my ears straining to hear the snug door being opened, not that I know what that sounds like from upstairs, but even so, I listen. And I listen. All I can hear is the soft snuffle of a sleeping cat content in my wardrobe. I slip from beneath my duvet, grab my long cardigan and tiptoe from my bedroom. I'll die if it's Gunner Jeffery, again.

Grabbing the banister rail, I gently ease myself down over that first creaky stair to descend to the hallway. I peer through the banisters, my gaze fixed on the snug's door and the welcoming strip of light beneath it.

Rap-a-tap-tap. My knuckles softly sound upon the wooden door and I enter. Emmet is sitting, dressed in joggers and a sweatshirt, hunched forward, his elbows propped on his knees, looking decidedly miserable.

'Hi. Is it OK if I join you?'

'Sure. It'll stop my brain cells tumbling around my head some more.' He flops backwards on to the couch, his gaze stuck fast to the ceiling, and sighs.

I quietly take up position on the other couch and wait.

'The worst part of this whole scenario is that we lads have spent so long talking about the injustices we've suffered in life because of the sins of the father – yet River does me over in pretty much the same way! You know, whether it was a school disco where the girls stayed away from us, snide remarks from peers or the embarrassment every time anyone asks about family ties – the effect is never-ending, like a looming shadow which you just can't escape from.'

I get where he's coming from, but I stay silent, listening. That's what he needs from me right now.

'We were over, I accept that; but now … there's all these doubts spinning around my head, wondering if this was going on even before we actually split. When I invited my brother over, was he making eyes with Annabel across the Sunday dinner table?'

'That would be the part that would eat at me, if I'm honest. It's the perceived deception – and you know you'll never be able to believe the answer, even if you ask them outright.'

'As sure as hell. Why would they be honest? They've got this far.'

'I suppose the question is – how do you deal with the situation if they stay together and it develops further?'

'We become the next generation of my mum and Janie – that's real cool, little bro.'

'Exactly. Can you handle that?'

Emmet shakes his head. 'I won't have a choice, will I? My mother didn't. Though I feel it was worse for her, having had me; the ties linking her to my father were going to be there for ever. Thankfully, I haven't got that, but still, we have a history together – dating, living together, memories. What a mess!' Emmet rakes his hand through his curls before lowering his chin to gaze at me. 'You don't get this as an only child, do you?'

'Nope. But then you don't get a lot of things as a solo kiddy.'

'Mmm, right now, I know which I'd rather be. Though it could be worse, you could be pregnant by Gunner Jeffery! Boy, oh boy – this family's going to finish me off.'

'What?'

'Haven't you heard? That's what Annabel tells me anyway, though she might be blagging to shift the heat from her and River. Such a well-to-do family yet we can't master the basics right in life. Go figure!'

'My mum helped cast my shadows aside this weekend, so I'm not complaining,' I say. 'She actually told me who my father was.'

'And you're OK with that?' he asks.

'Yep. Fine. It's all I ever wanted to know – the basics.'

'Lucky you. I doubt my shadows will ever disappear,' mutters Emmet.

My mind is blown. There's nothing else I could hear that

would top what's happened so far in these four days. I feel as if I'm trapped inside a twisted game of Happy Families.

'I think your chances of appearing on TV's *Family Fortunes* are virtually nil,' I say, mustering a smile.

'Could you imagine it? My dad as head of the clan, alongside your mum, then four ex-wives. In fact, I think that's too many on one team, isn't it?'

'You could fill the opposing family team too.'

'My father and his offspring versus a team of your mum and ex-wives – that would work. Name something that causes chaos in life?' imitates Emmet, trying hard not to laugh. 'Mmm, let me think – my old man's addiction to wedding cake. Eh-err!'

'Stop it.'

'You're right. I should be grateful I'm no longer a small child without the ability to make decisions for myself. See, there's always a silver lining.'

'If you look for it,' I whisper, as his gaze lingers on mine and neither one of us attempts to break the connection.

Helen

'Please don't make me beg but someone needs to help me dismantle the tree,' I say, attempting to rally the troops after breakfast.

'I thought it was bad luck to take it down before Twelfth Night,' says Teddy from the armchair, not missing a pixel of the children's animation he's watching on TV.

'Nice try, lazybones, but the next guests won't be wanting our cast-off tree,' I say, blocking the screen to get his full attention. 'Especially one with a unique feature for TV viewing.'

'Oy, Helen!' chunters Teddy, shifting sideways in his seat to peer round me.

'Helen, please,' pipes up Lynette from the couch, not looking up from her magazine.

I pick up on her irritated tone and instantly begrudge her remark.

'Lynette, I'm playing with him; surely you can see that?'

'I can, but why single him out when he's relaxing? Let him enjoy his final day before it's back to the Carmichael grindstone and pressure, pressure, pressure.'

Teddy shifts uncomfortably, staring at the two of us in turn.

'I wasn't suggesting he completes the task single-handed, more just asking him to offer me a hand.'

'Please ask your own son if you need a hand – mine's enjoying some downtime,' sniffs Lynette, glued to her article. 'No wonder River and Annabel chose to remain in their room.'

'They've got good reason to and it's of their own doing, not mine!' I retort. 'They're taking cover.'

'There's never any peace around here, ever. There's always someone demanding your time, your energy ... or your attention.' She finally looks up and hard-stares me before resuming her reading.

I'm in two minds whether to answer back or simply let it go, but when you spend your own downtime organising and planning on behalf of others, such remarks feel like a kick in the teeth.

'I'm fine with helping,' says Teddy, clearly shamed into action.

'It's not necessary, Teddy. Helen can call Emmet if she needs help,' says Lynette, as if I'm not present.

'Honest. It's fine, Mum.'

'Teddy, this needs to stop. It might as well be now after yesterday's run-in.'

'What did that have to do with me? It was you and Janie who had a falling-out,' I protest, staring at Teddy since Lynette hasn't bothered to relift her gaze from the glossy mag.

'Ultimately, it involves all of you. All this co-parenting,

cross-parenting or multi-parenting you all willingly adopt – it needs to stop. They aren't children any more and they can decide for themselves what they chose to do in the presence of whoever, without additional advice from their father's ex-partners. Or the hired help, come to that.'

My jaw hits the floor. Never has something like this been said in our family. Through all the disagreements, the divorce settlements and the wrangling to secure joint custody, no one has ever argued against the principle of our blended family. Ever. As for her reference regarding Martha, well – how ungrateful can you be towards such an angel.

'Excuse me, are you suggesting that we abolish the way in which this family has conducted itself over the last three decades? Do you want to be one of those families who are literally at war with one another?'

'Not war, no. But I'm done with the likes of you, Janie and Fena treating my son as if he were yours. He's not, he's mine. He has one mother, and that's me!' So out of character for Lynette and not in the slightest bit Zen-like – maybe Janie tore a strip from that martyr mannerism in yesterday's antics.

'Mum!'

Lynette holds her hand up, silencing her son, 'No, Teddy. It needs to be said. It's gone on for long enough – it's a pretence, purely an act,' says Lynette, unconsciously adding her trademark shoulder shimmy.

I don't know how I refrain from laughing out loud, as cruelly as our Janie would, if she were present, as it totally undermines her little speech.

Chapter Twenty-Four

Martha

'Not like that!' I scold, as Scarlet jams my copper pans into their storage box.

'How then?' she retorts, her mood darkening instantly.

'As I showed you, wrap each one with a tea towel and then stack them. And make sure you include each lid – I'll have your guts for garters if I find you've mislaid one.' It's bad enough that our return journey isn't following the same arrangement as our arrival. I believe Teddy's transporting my pans and utensils back home, and I'm to accompany Helen, now that Emmet's staying on till tomorrow and locking up here.

Scarlet does her usual huff, retrieves the pans from the box and begins again, as instructed. I continue to empty the contents of the fridge, selecting items and dividing them into three groups: for binning, transporting home to Cloisters or staying to feed Emmet. I imagine he won't bother cooking for himself, so I leave a selection of cheeses, coleslaws and dips, cold meats and Scotch eggs alongside the staple basics of milk and orange juice. He won't starve, that's for certain.

'Did your mum get off OK?' I say, broaching the elephant in the room.

'Did her high-pitched wailing sound like she was OK?' scoffs Scarlet, before adding, 'Personally, I don't see why she's so shocked. She knew we were an item, she just didn't bargain on the other stuff happening so soon. But still, to leave like that proves what a drama queen she is.'

'Her reaction is hardly unjustified, though is it?' I say, sensing there's more to this story than I have knowledge of, but I can guess – without hearing confirmation from the family grapevine.

'She'll be sitting in a first-class lounge by now, so I'm sure she's happier than she was here. Though I'll never hear the end of it because you refused to sew a button on her blouse!'

'I am not a lady's maid. I'd have more free time if I were, so be grateful for small mercies.'

'Hi. Can I help in any way?'

We turn to find Annabel standing at the kitchen door, her hair twisted in a sophisticated up-do, looking a bit lost and forlorn.

'I never say no to another pair of hands,' I quip, ignoring the dark look thrown at me by Scarlet and gesturing for our new helper to grab another box before pointing towards my ceramic dishes, freshly washed and dried. 'If you could pack those, bulking them out with my tea towels, I'd appreciate it.' Scarlet gives me another mean look behind Annabel's back. Obviously there's no love lost between those two. Scarlet's prepared to cast the first stone, forgetting her own misdemeanours. Whereas I can't accept or turn a blind eye to Annabel and River's behaviour, but I do belong to the 'if nothing else, be kind' camp. 'How are you this morning?'

'Coping, I think. We're leaving in a while, so River's trying to make peace with Emmet. My innards feel like lead for hurting him so much whilst trying to stay true to myself. It sucks, to be honest.'

'I'm sure it does. But life tests us in the most extraordinary ways, and what will be, will be,' I say, trying to stay neutral despite my heart being aligned with Emmet. If he can be civil towards her, then so can I.

'Thank you, Martha. I appreciate the sentiment but this . . . is exactly what Emmet detests, isn't it?'

'Well, wouldn't you, if you'd grown up witnessing what he has?' snaps Scarlet, her brow puckered, her guard up, clearly ready to do battle.

Annabel is taken aback by the outburst, but responds instantly, 'Didn't I just say that?'

'No. What you implied by ending with a question is that you aren't quite sure what Emmet detests. So, I'll confirm it for you – you've done the dirty on him, which is exactly what he's always feared a partner would do to him. You've gone one step better by allowing Carmichael history to repeat itself, which will only prove to Emmet that no one can be trusted, not even his own flesh and blood! There, does that clarify it for you?'

Annabel purses her lips, gives a little nod towards Scarlet before glancing at me. 'I see I've hurt more than just Emmet. I'm sorry.'

'No, you're not! You're only sorry you've had to confess, and probably sorry that the family aren't going to be welcoming you with open arms any time soon – that's what you're sorry about. You're not sorry that I'll be playing piggy in the middle, adjusting my relationships with two of my older brothers. You're not sorry that you've probably stuffed up their working relationship as well as their brotherly one, and you don't care less that my father will encounter yet another drama as soon as he arrives back from his honeymoon!' Scarlet bursts into angry tears on the final line. 'Sorry, Martha, but I'm done. I can't finish this task.' She speed-walks out of the kitchen leaving me to clear up the mess.

I suppose family drama with added hormones will equal more tears and tantrums from Scarlet – Gawd help the rest of us . . . correction, the family, in the coming months. Dramas such as these can't be any good for my health – peace and quiet must be the order of the day.

'Well, that's that said and done in the Scarlet way,' I murmur, before addressing Annabel. 'Are you still OK?'

'Not really, but I probably asked for that. Will she be OK?' she asks, gesturing towards the kitchen door.

'She will be, there's plenty of people around here to dry her tears.'

'I suppose it's what everyone is thinking really. What a mess we've caused for the next generation, when the family were hoping it would be different for them.'

'You could say that, but I've a feeling there are numerous scenarios involving the next generation that are already being played out. Yours might simply be the first to come to light.' I close the fridge door and busy myself packing the food items for transporting home into my hessian shopping bags.

'I'll finish this, then leave you in peace,' mutters Annabel, stacking my ceramic dishes and bowls.

'There's no rush. I don't hold anything against you, lovey. The heart wants what the heart wants – though I didn't expect to be saying that to you younger ones.'

The kitchen door flies open and I brace myself, half expecting it to be Scarlet brandishing a clever line she's just thought of, but it's Lowry, looking pensive. Please, no more drama!

'Martha, could you do me two favours, please?' I turn to acknowledge her but she continues anyway. 'Firstly, have you any paracetamol at hand? I've got a cracking headache. Secondly, could you call Josie, the housekeeper, and ask if I could take the cat and her kittens with me when I leave? To rehome at mine, of course, not to take to the rescue centre.'

Headache? I'm not surprised with all the drama around here!

'Now favours such as those I can do without fuss or fury. Paracetamols are stashed inside my handbag – I'll fetch you two in a second. And what if Josie says no?'

Lowry ponders before answering. 'Maybe suggest she asks the

owner to come and collect them, as the mother could do with some care and attention whilst nursing the kittens.'

'I'll be on it, just as soon as I've fetched those tablets for you and finished with this packing.'

'Sure. Are you OK, Annabel? You look a bit peaky too,' asks Lowry, rubbing her aching forehead yet turning her attention to my helper.

'Not really, though I can't complain, given the upset we've caused.' I watch as a mutual acknowledgement flows from one woman to the other, despite the intense atmosphere within the family.

'Can I help with packing these pans?' asks Lowry, pointing at Scarlet's abandoned task.

'You can, and I shall give the housekeeper a call as soon as I'm done here. Are you leaving later today?' I ask, adding, 'Unless you wish to call her yourself – her contact number's inside the pantry door.'

'Yes, but nah, I'd prefer you to call. I want to dodge my job role being mentioned as people can get quite sniffy if they think they're being judged as neglectful or cruel to animals.'

Isn't that the truth? And not just animal care – human well-being too. Pity she's leaving today . . . another night under this roof without the family distractions might have been the icing on the cake.

Helen

'I'm out of here, folks,' hollers Teddy, pulling on his jacket with lightning speed. 'I'll love and leave you to lock up and bail out. Are you coming, Mum?' We follow him into the hallway to stand in a pensive semi-circle, Annabel and River, Scarlet and Jeffery, Lowry, Martha and myself attempting to obliterate certain memories by offering a united front with a fond farewell. Teddy remains jovial, acting out the necessary steps for his mother's exit. 'I'll see most of you in the coming days, so . . .'

'You'll see all of us blighters in the coming days,' corrects Emmet, shaking his head vigorously, holding the door wide.

'Not Lowry. I won't see you until . . . the Easter holidays, perhaps?' says Teddy, looking at her. I note he ignores Annabel's presence.

'Maybe,' says Lowry, blushing at being singled out, even before receiving his warm hug.

'See, Emmet? Not everyone. I hope your headache passes, but don't risk driving all that way if it doesn't,' says Teddy tenderly.

'I won't,' answers Lowry quietly.

Lynette has little to say, but falls into line following his lead as Teddy hugs his way around the group.

'Come here, you,' says Teddy, wrapping Scarlet in a brotherly bear hug.

'See you tomorrow at Dad's,' mutters Scarlet into his shoulder before escaping from his hug. 'We're driving back to Jeffery's tonight, but I'll be at Cloisters by lunchtime.' Jeffery steps forward offering the lad a firm handshake.

'Martha, will the fridge be filled with scrummy food by then, so we don't starve to death while Dad and Diane are away on honeymoon?' asks Teddy, reaching the final three people.

'When have I ever let you down, Teddy?' retorts Martha, pulling him in close before loudly whispering, 'Remember what you said – change might be needed.' What on earth does she mean by that, I wonder?

'You've never let us down, but there's always a first,' he jokes, popping a kiss on to the top of her head, as if acknowledging her message whilst covering up her words.

'Not on your nelly!' exclaims Martha. 'And you'll unload my

boxes of kitchen utensils into the house – I don't want them left in your car till I get back.'

'I promise I'll be careful while they're in my possession.'

I quickly step forward, not wanting him to leave on a bad turn of phrase and knowing Martha might take to heart his jokey food remark. I'll soothe her nerves once he's gone.

'Come here, son number three. Don't drive too fast and make sure you stop for a coffee break halfway, right? And please don't dent her copper pans, for all our sakes.'

'Right!' mutters Teddy, as I gather him into my open arms for a squeeze. Regardless of Lynette's earlier remarks, he's mine as well.

'Lynette,' I say, giving her a quick peck on the cheek, not our usual warm exchange but still, I won't be unkind. I notice she does likewise, her gaze diverted from mine.

'Bloody hell, out of the way please – some of us have got homes and sexy lovers to get back to,' groans Janie, bolting down the staircase and throwing her suitcase down the final few stairs.

'Bloody typical,' mutters Teddy, sidestepping the suitcase, which nearly knocks several of us flying. 'And you, Emmet, I'll see tomorrow.'

'Nope. I'll be off-grid for a day or so, taking some time for myself,' says Emmet, sheepishly glancing at me.

'Are you?' Teddy's tone matches his shocked expression. 'Good for you.'

'I need some space, so to speak,' explains Emmet, casually adding, 'Though you can call if you need me.'

'Wise decision,' I say, pleased that someone else is making themselves a priority in life.

'See you when I see you then,' says Teddy, grabbing his holdall and his mother's tiny wheelie case and stepping out of the hallway. 'If there's nothing more – we're out of here. See you all!'

'Bye,' waves Lynette, her timid martyrish manner returning.

'Mwah to you all! I'm not doing the kissy-kissy business

along the row, it'll smudge my lip liner,' says Janie, her car keys in hand, blowing one big kiss around the semi-circle. 'See you all soon, but not too soon! Thanks for the voucher, Helen – I'll be redeeming it in their January sale.' My sister – as brazen as they come yet I can't help loving her.

We gather around the open doorway, a mixture of waving, thrown comments and impatience awaiting the usual drive-by waves, first to Teddy's Range Rover, then Janie's car and, finally, Lynette's vintage Beetle.

'We're off too,' says River, before Emmet has a chance to close the front door. I notice he sidesteps his older brother before giving everyone else a parting embrace. Annabel stands forlornly on the sidelines before offering a meek goodbye and an almost apologetic wave to us all. They scurry along the cobbles hand in hand. Martha and I exchange a brief glance, neither of us impressed by that shoddy exit.

'Stay where you are – we're following,' says Scarlet, as Emmet goes to close the front door again.

'Bloody great, you could have timed it together,' I say, as Jeffery emerges from the dining room, having fetched their suit-cases, shrugging despondently as if unaware of his own timely departure.

'I want my own rite of departure, thanks,' says Scarlet, per-forming her round of hugs and kisses. I notice she hesitates on reaching Lowry, before delivering a polite half-embrace and adding, 'I hope your headache eases soon.' Maybe three days isn't long enough for the girls to bond properly.

The four of us stand inside the doorway, waving as necessary, as Annabel's car and then Scarlet's nippy roadster glide by the picket gate.

We finally come away from the doorstep and traipse into the warm kitchen to find a seat at the table. The hallway looks decid-edly bare without the huddle of bodies and festive decorations,

though those pesky lads haven't replaced the interior doors as
I asked them to.

'When have I ever not filled the fridges and both deep freezers
with food at Cloisters?' says Martha, as we make our way
through. I knew she'd be narked by Teddy's comment.

'Never, Martha. We'd think you were ill if that happened.
Anyone else leaving directly, or shall we have a cuppa?' I say to
the remaining three, trying to calm troubled waters. I'm pleas-
antly surprised that Lowry doesn't seem eager to leave, though
silently I'm pleased – maybe her headache is still troubling her.

'Lowry, before I forget – I called Josie, as you asked, and mentioned you'd like to take the mother cat and her kittens home.
Josie said she wasn't aware she'd had kittens but she's definitely a
stray and has been hanging around for quite a while, it appears,'
explains Martha, doing the honours by making a brew. 'She says
you're welcome to them. Though if an irate owner does come
knocking, she'd like to pass on your contact details – if you
wouldn't mind leaving them beside the keys.'

Chapter Twenty-Five

Lowry

Finally, we're alone. Everyone else said their 'hasty but huggy' goodbyes, drip by drip, over the space of an hour. Why they didn't all depart at once is beyond me; instead we kept hanging around in the hallway, repeating the same sentiments – I guess that's a side of family life that I've never experienced. In my family no one ever left, no one said goodbye and the numbers reduced only as we aged. Possibly not the kind of family life that the Carmichaels have enjoyed. Maybe that's why they're so practised at saying goodbye?

'What?' asks Emmet, sprawled on the opposite couch, cradling a small glass of red wine. The coffee table displays the remnants of our fridge raid: plates of cold meat, pickles and cheese beside a huge box of half-eaten crackers.

'What do you mean, "what"?' I ask, stretched out along my couch – he's caught me red-handed deep in thought.

'Whatever that was.' He swirls his free hand towards my face, gesturing at my expression; I'm now fully alert and probably my expression is completely different from a few moments ago. 'And don't say it was your headache, because we both know that was purely to stop tongues wagging.'

'I did have a headache!' I baulk at his suggestion that I was acting up, pretending just so I could spend time with him. He thinks he knows everything. Well, I've got him sussed, watching my every move; he thinks I haven't noticed.

'Deny it all you like, but the cogs were whirring ten to the dozen.' He sips his wine. I pretend not to notice, or care. Deep within, my intense butterflies are signalling that niggling truth that I already know but have tried to ignore: I like him. His lingering looks, the gentle touches, his attentive manner, even that brooding masculine trait which eclipses his features every now and then.

We're not doing anything wrong, there's nothing physical happening, far from it. We're each on our own sofa, sharing a half bottle of leftover wine, no hands, feet or lips touching. Just talking, or not, as the case may be. That lazy, intermittent kind of nonsense chat that only happens when you're truly comfortable in someone's presence; it's only confirmed minutes later by the deafening silence which follows, during which neither of us feels obliged to utter a word. And on occasion, though not too frequently to seem creepy, a smouldering look, full of everything you were hoping they were thinking but now know they are thinking too. This feels right, and yet so wrong!

I sip my wine, suddenly aware of my facial features giving me away. Eyebrows be still; nostrils simply be; lips sit in a neutral Mona Lisa smile ... Lowry, you ridiculous woman! I'll just be me, he'll be him. And later this evening, when I've packed my bags and tucked the cats into the back of my car for the journey home, we'll stand in the hallway and a dwindling Carmichael leaving committee will perform the farewell rites signifying my departure. After which, tomorrow, Emmet too will depart, and then there'll be none! He'll leave the door keys on the side table, along with my contact details, for the cats, and he'll go. Then that will be that. I'll have driven home to Pendlebury. He'll drive home to Todmorden. Finished. Done. No more than a forty-minute drive between us but we'll avoid each other, make no contact, and we'll arrive at the next family occasion consumed by the question of 'what if?'.

My head is thinking straight. Or is it? I won't see him, or even talk to him, until Easter. Maybe Easter, if I take time off. These past few days will become a distant memory. Faded and jaded, mentioned only in passing conversation catching up with friends and colleagues, glossed over and labelled as 'last Christmas'. Though I'm not sure I want that to happen.

'Earlier, you sounded unsure about visiting at Easter – is that so?' asks Emmet, plumping and repositioning the cushion supporting his back.

'Yeah. If I opt for time off.' I lower my head, conscious that he's watching me again. 'Work's always busy, staff rotas are always stretched and the animals always need caring for.'

'Won't you make a special effort to see your mum?'

I bite my lower lip. I don't work like that, but stupidly say, 'You know how it is, colleagues with children want to be off during the school holidays – I always feel obliged to cover and . . .' My words run short. I'm not convincing myself, let alone him. I carry on without putting my brain in gear. 'Holidays haven't been the same since my grandparents died. Returning home to Mum simply reminds me, unsettles me with painful memories.'

'It might be a fresh start, creating new memories at Cloisters?' says Emmet, calmly.

'Maybe. Mum's probably hoping for that.'

Silence lingers – talking simply isn't necessary. He's studying me intently, and I watch him watching me. Do I make a jokey comment? Look away from his dark enticing gaze, that knowing smile? Are we thinking the same thoughts? I can hear the blood rushing through my head, as if the universe is attempting to speak to me, spelling out what is happening between us. Between me and my newly acquired stepbrother. My mum's eldest stepson. Rupert's firstborn. Crying out loud, we've more backstory than a soap opera!

'Hellooo! Is anyone there?' A female singsongy voice interrupts

our peace. We both jump up from our reclined positions as if
caught by our parents, half naked in a teenage embrace, with
hickeys to hide. Shooting from our seats to stand horror-stricken,
as if caught in a compromising position. Though to any sane
outsider, we'll just be two people, adults, connected by marriage,
fully dressed, not touching, drinking wine in the snug in the
middle of the afternoon during the Christmas holidays. That is
all we are doing. Nothing more. Nothing less.

'Who's that?' asks Emmet, standing across from me like my
mirror image.

I shake my head. 'Why are you asking me? I don't know any
of the females who frequent this family.'

'There's no more wives, if that's what you're implying. All five
have been and gone.'

'Hello?' comes the voice again.

'Yes,' hollers Emmet in reply, venturing out of the snug, whispering to me, 'It's probably the housekeeper.'

'Oh God, don't say we've got the booking dates wrong,' I
gabble, straightening the sofa cushions and grabbing our wine
glasses as Emmet steps into the hallway, heading for the kitchen.
I remain in situ, clutching the glasses. I don't usually lose track
of the days between Christmas and New Year; work rotas help
to keep things neatly aligned. But today's the twenty-seventh,
isn't it? Or are we already on the twenty-eighth?

It will be embarrassing if we've overstayed our welcome.

'Hi there. Sorry to disturb you but someone called a few days
ago regarding abandoned kittens . . . I'm not sure if I've got the
right address.' I hear her opening line and instantly envision a
familiar navy uniform, silver detailing on her lapels, with clipboard and wire cat carrier in hand.

'I think this is your shout, not mine, Lowry,' Emmet calls over
his shoulder to me, stepping aside, enabling me to pass. It's as
I imagined: a woman in an RSPCA uniform identical to mine,

though not as mud-splattered. She's flashing her ID in one of our issued lanyards, her manner is pleasant but her eagle eyes are roving the spotless kitchen.

'Hi there, yes . . . I believe there was a call from an occupant here but that was the previous guests, not us. The mother and kittens are quite safe.'

'I see.' Her gaze drops to the filled wine glasses I'm clutching, before asking, 'Any chance I could . . .'

She's good, with a level of diligence which I also apply to my role.

'Sure. I'll happily fetch them. If you take a seat, I won't be a moment.' I pop the glasses on the countertop, then hesitate. Now what do I do? Ask Emmet to leave the kitchen so I can pretend they aren't upstairs but outside in the outhouse?

Emmet pulls a chair out from the table, inviting the inspector to make herself comfortable. All well and good for some.

'Well, go on then,' urges Emmet, gesturing towards upstairs.

'Sorry?'

'Can you fetch the kittens, please – from upstairs?' A wry smile adorns his lips as I attempt to cover my shock. How does he know?

I leave, darting for the staircase. My hand thwacks the mistletoe hanging above the newel post as I reach for the banister.

'Helen and Teddy forgot to take that down, didn't they?' I mutter to myself, whilst taking the stairs two at a time, heading for my bedroom and the sanctuary of the wardrobe.

'Come on, my darlings – you've got a visitor,' I say, gently lifting the cloth sacking cradling the family of three. Each kitten's tiny mouth opens and closes in protest, flashing healthy pink gums. 'I know, but I need to prove I am trustworthy.' I'm back downstairs within minutes, still flummoxed by Emmet's response.

'So, you see, it was quite a misunderstanding,' is all I hear from

Emmet on re-entering the kitchen, cradling my warm bundle in both arms.

Our visitor flushes bright pink, so I guess their topic of conversation: me.

'Ahh right, so you've mentioned it. Yes, I'm based at Salford; I expect you're at . . . Westmorland, is it?' I say, placing the cloth sacking on the table. I won't be narked if she performs a thorough check; it's what I'd do if I were her.

'I'm sorry, you never imagine . . . do you? I can't see how this call has gone astray and remained unanswered over the holiday period – something has definitely gone wrong there with the job assignments. Look at these beauties, hey?'

'My ID card. I'll show it to you so that you know we're not spinning you a yarn . . . because we both know how ludicrous some excuses are.' I leave the kitchen to prove myself quicker than I did to retrieve the kittens.

'Honestly, you don't have to . . . it isn't necessary.'

'Here you go!' I say, proudly handing over my credentials from my jacket pocket, which I know match hers exactly, apart from the name. 'Ten years in all, qualified in . . .'

'Thank you, but honestly, it's fine I've heard some tales in my time, as I imagine you have, but no one has ever pulled that line on me before. And these kittens look in fine form. Look at these podgy bellies, hey? . . . You were lucky kittens, weren't you?'

'Certainly were,' mutters Emmet. 'She's kept them in the bottom of the wardrobe, haven't you? There hasn't been a single night in which they've been outside in the outhouse as was suggested by Saturday night's caller.'

I hear his words and realise their meaning. He knew all along!

'That's good to hear. It has been particularly cold these past few nights. And your intentions are?'

'We're keeping them – taking both mother and kittens back home with us once we leave here tomorrow,' says Emmet.

'Tomorrow?' I blurt, shocked by this detail.

'Tomorrow?' asks the RSPCA inspector, glancing between us.

'Tomorrow,' confirms Emmet, eyeballing me with confidence.

'Tomorrow,' I add, for good measure. Though why he's saying this I don't know. I'd only planned to stay long enough for our afternoon tipple to pass and then set off home.

'If it's OK with you, I'll take a few details and be on my way,' says the inspector, again fulfilling her role exactly as I would. 'I'm sorry to be a stickler, but you're sure there's no legitimate owner in the vicinity who might be seeking their pet cat?'

'We've checked whilst staying here and there's no posters or signs pinned to lampposts or garden gates,' explains Emmet, glancing at me for confirmation – but I'm still stunned that he knew my secret.

It takes all of fifteen minutes, then I swiftly return the cats to their own cosy snug as Emmet waves goodbye to our surprise visitor.

I don't even wait for the door latch to click closed before I ask, 'You've known all along?'

Emmet's eyebrows shoot up, lost amongst his dark curls.

'About the kittens? Of course.'

'How?'

'Common sense. If you care enough to return them to their mother on such a cold night, there wasn't a chance you'd leave them outside in freezing conditions. Secondly, how many times have I observed you nip outside to check on them during the day? None! Go figure.'

I feel stupid. To have been play-acting while he knew what I was up to.

'You hid them well. I don't think anyone else noticed or was even bothered to check the outhouse. Don't worry, your secret is quite safe.'

I squirm under his constant gaze. 'My mum suspected too.'

'Are you actually embarrassed because I've let on that I knew?' he asks despondently. 'Would you prefer that I played along too?'

'No, but I feel stupid for being somewhat deceitful. It wasn't necessary yet I chose not to be open.'

'Don't worry about it, Lowry. You did what you did, I'm not fazed by your actions. I find them quite endearing really. And the cats were never in danger of mistreatment or neglect with you on the scene.' His words linger, softening my own inner judgement. 'It's meant as a compliment. It says more about you than you realise.' I blush profusely.

'Plus I saw you through the kitchen window on Christmas Eve, in the early hours, prowling around downstairs dressed in a cardigan and canvas pumps, carrying a cardboard box having collected something from the outhouse.'

'Where were you when I came back inside?'

'I was standing in the corridor of the scullery as you re-entered the cottage.'

A thought fills me with horror.

'You saw me standing by the snug doorway?'

'Yep, inching forward like you were trying to peer inside. Quite funny really – how I didn't give myself away I'll never know, but yep, I saw you.'

'Did you nab the midnight feast as well then?'

'Nope, that was definitely River – he's known for it.'

My gaze lifts to meet his. I feel bashful in his presence, nervous and yet joyful. If I don't have to hide anything from him, if I can truly be myself in his company . . . then maybe my own shadows might be completely chased away.

'Shall we?' Emmet gestures towards the snug.

'Maybe . . . Though you might want to grab another bottle of wine before we settle down, if we're staying for an extra night.'

'Perhaps. You might want to put some Christmas tunes on whilst I'm uncorking it. I'm liking the sound of original vinyl.

Though I'm scarred for life where "Santa Baby" is concerned, so do me a favour and choose something else.'

'Me too,' I say, as the image of Scarlet's performance replays in my mind.

Neither of us speaks but we instantly take care of our tasks. I'm as nervous as a kitten as I busy myself flicking through the vinyl for a suitable record – tomorrow I'll be back to my favourite playlists on my phone. Maybe some things are never truly outdated, like original vinyl or physical attraction, even love. I've no idea where this evening will lead or whether I should even be entertaining the idea of seeing where our chat leads. One thing's for certain, perhaps the Carmichael family trait of flirting with danger is rubbing off on me.

Martha

I pull the seat belt across and strap myself in, not that Helen's a bad driver but she does tend to take narrow lanes a little too fast at times. I think she has a tendency to imagine we're reenacting *Thelma and Louise* whenever she has to drive me. Not that I'm complaining, I'm pleased Emmet's staying put; a bit of peace and quiet and, hopefully, some nice company might make the world of difference. Though I'm worried Helen's driving might bring on my travel sickness; Emmet's driving never would.

Having kissed them goodbye, we take a slow drive past, frantically waving as we leave.

'That's another Christmas done and dusted, Martha – and we survived it. Just!' says Helen, with a gleeful giggle.

'Don't they look a picture sharing that doorstep together,' I say, turning around in my seat as far as I can, until the cottage is out of sight.

'They do, but I'm sensing there's more going on than I spotted this weekend,' says Helen, flipping down her windscreen visor to block out the low winter sun.

'Phew! You walk around with your eyes shut – a blind man could have spotted the chemistry between that pair. He didn't take his eyes off her during the games tournament, and when Scarlet pulled that stunt with her provocative dancing, by all accounts what Emmet was most flustered by was that Lowry should have had to watch such behaviour. He came in to me for two huge glasses of wine, saying Lowry was in need of medical attention having witnessed what she had,' I say, mindful of the details, it is her son I'm talking about, after all.

'Martha, could you press the satnav screen? I forgot to as we left,' asks Helen, gesturing towards the dashboard's central display panel. I raise my trembling right hand to press the green on-screen button and the details flash up: Todmorden – 92 miles, 1 hour 56 minutes. 'Thank you. We'll be there before we know it.' Then there's a heavy silence, during which Helen gives me several sideways glances before pursing her lips. She saw. She spotted my tremors. She's thinking. 'Are you OK?'

'Me? Yes, of course.' This is it. She'll either pursue her line of questioning, determined to uncover the truth, or fall back into our routine of discussing others.

'Do you reckon she's as keen?'

'As mustard, though he'll need to stay away from the ciggies and the whisky – she wasn't impressed by those. I think Diane was oblivious, which is to be expected given the wedding was at the forefront of her mind. She'll certainly notice once she returns home, that's for sure,' I say, watching the passing hedgerows fly by as Helen puts her foot down. Long lazy shadows criss-cross the road ahead, creating abstract patterns on the pristine snow.

'I'm not sure, you know. His son and her daughter – isn't that a recipe for disaster?'

'Any more so than his best friend and his daughter? Or him and his wife's younger sister, sorry to mention it.'

Helen shrugs.

'I tasted Janie's Irish cream liqueur when she wasn't looking. It nearly burnt my throat out. She tops it up with malt whisky for good measure, you know?'

'And you're surprised? I could have told you that. I knew Lynette wasn't far wrong when she spilt the beans during their fight.'

'Fight? You can't call it that!' says Helen, shocked by the word.

'It was, I tell you . . . Fisticuffs and hair-pulling was the name of the game – their actions constitute a full-blown fight. If you need it defining just ask Lowry or Emmet – you probably didn't witness it all, given your position on the lower staircase. Lynette gave as good as she got, from what I heard.'

'I don't know which was worse. Dealing with the women and then the boys taking lumps out of each other or what I had to handle in the pub. I've never walked so slowly in my life, not daring to arrive back whilst hurrying Scarlet along, knowing she needed to chat with Jeffery and her mother. Seriously, talk about being stuck between a rock and a hard place.'

'I hear there's to be an addition to the family then?'

'To be sure. Though she was swigging alcohol all weekend – so irresponsible in my opinion.'

'She'll need to stop performing those slutdrop things too,' I add.

We both tut in unison.

'What was all that between you and Teddy – that final message about change?' asks Helen, slowing to navigate a particularly tight bend in the road.

'You swear you won't tell Mr C?'

'I swear.'

'He thinks he wants a change – pastures new and such like.'

Helen sucks in air through her teeth.

'That'll go down like a lead balloon, Martha. You know how defensive Rupert is about the family business. Apparently, he tried to talk young Lowry into joining but she wasn't having any of it.'

'Really? He won't win her over on that. She's got her head screwed on tight, and she got one past him with that cat, you know?'

Helen glances at me.

'Honest, she did. It's been in the cottage all weekend, without him even knowing.'

'Never!'

'Seriously, I nipped out to the outhouse for a broom and there was neither sight nor sound of the cat or her kittens. And I thought, she's fetched 'em in, she has. Though not once did she let it slip, and she kept up her pretence by wedging the door with an old house brick. Fooled the lot of us, she has.'

'Let's hope our Emmet knows what he's letting himself in for then,' says Helen, as we navigate the tricky route ahead.

Lowry

'Stop it. I'm being serious now, Emmet. I can't reach the switch!' I giggle, my hand making half-hearted attempts and repeatedly missing the light switch as I drunkenly swipe the wall. Emmet's leaning against the newel post, calling my name, his voice distinctly slurred by the alcohol we've consumed in the snug. The whole cottage to ourselves and we stayed holed up in the smallest room, initially positioned on opposite couches, then getting closer and closer with each glass of wine. Eventually, we ended the night sharing the same couch, first sitting, then slouching, and finally lying at full stretch, wrapped in the closeness of each other. With me tucked under his arm and our socked feet entwined upon the sofa arm, we talked incessantly about everything and nothing. A physical warmth, nothing else – no kissing, no intimate touching, simply cuddling.

'You can do it, Lowry,' he hollers, from the hallway.

I lose my balance, grab the doorjamb and another fit of giggles erupts, scuppering the task.

'Come on, we'll be here all night otherwise,' cajoles a drunken Emmet.

Finally, I manage to flick the switch, plunging the snug into darkness, leaving the remnants of our cheese board and our empties on the coffee table to be cleared in the morning.

'Done it!' I proudly announce, leaning against the nearest wall for balance as I move along the hallway, partly lit, thanks to the bevelled window in the front door. I haven't felt like this for so long – the alcohol, the late night, the intoxicating company all creating a giddy feeling of immeasurable happiness.

'Ladies first,' says Emmet, stepping back from the bottom stair and gesturing with a bow, like a butler.

'Why thank you, dear sir.' My tone is coy, as is my manner. I have no idea where we're heading, apart from upstairs. I'm simply happy, for the first time in ages. It's complicated, but I don't want to think about that this evening. Though admittedly, given how much we've drunk, I'm not sure I could name all the members of this blended family, let alone recite the muddle of relationships.

I reach for the newel post and my hand, just like earlier, accidentally swipes the mistletoe hanging above it, causing it to swing.

'Look what they forgot to take down!' I say, pointing as the foliage and berries move from side to side above the notchity wooden post.

'Ha, that was Martha's doing,' blurts Emmet, swaying despite his wide stance.

'Err?'

'Teddy bought it from the Co-op. She wasn't best pleased and told him to hang it there so no one could start any trouble by kissing underneath it.' His words linger, as do we, mesmerised as the foliage returns to stillness.

Neither of us speaks; we simply stare. Mistletoe. Newel post. Mistletoe. Staircase. Possibly a wise decision by Martha but still a wasted purchase. A wasted tradition. A wasted opportunity.

The surrounding air intensifies. My shoulders bristle with the growing weight of expectation. Should I say something? Make a joke? Give him a quick peck? A comedic gesture like his butler impression? Or . . . or . . . I'm waiting for him to move, to act, to speak. But nothing. Our moment of silence is drawing to a close; I can feel it slipping by us, edging towards awkward. The final few seconds where we might steal a kiss before such an action ventures into the realm of a forced afterthought. My giddy state of happiness is gliding away towards stone cold sober.

And there it is. I blink repeatedly; the moment has passed. Gone. Kissing under mistletoe would have been a first for me.

'Dangerous territory methinks,' whispers Emmet, exiting his trancelike state.

We stand in the partial darkness of the hallway, like two strangers who haven't shared bottles of wine, who haven't shared a lifetime of stories and who certainly haven't lain on a couch, their feet entwined. My heart plummets to my feet, grounding both my senses and our reality.

Chapter Twenty-Six

Thursday 28 December

Lowry

I turn over, reaching for my phone to check the hour for the umpteenth time: 03.16. I've been awake since I climbed into bed ninety minutes ago, listening to the cottage's nocturnal rattle and groans, the heating system, the thatch creaking and yet not a sound on the staircase. Of all the nights, when we have the place to ourselves, when we don't have to creep, stealthy and silent, Emmet chooses to sleep!

I've replayed the mistletoe moment over and over in my head. We left the snug, we laughed as I'd forgotten to dowse the light, he waited while I went back, I finally found the switch and joined him. He did his butler thing and then – boom – at the mention of mistletoe the warmth and closeness that we'd achieved dissolved in an instant to leave a Lake Windermere sized void between us. We climbed the stairs as if we were physically in different postcodes, let alone trapped by our own thoughts. The landing seemed vast as we stood by the sturdy couch on which we'd tried to hide from Gunner Jeffery only the other night. How can two people be transported so quickly to a completely unexpected space in time. Not that I was anticipating anything happening. Honest, I wasn't. It hadn't even crossed my mind which bedroom I'd spend the night in. Or whether I'd be tucked up alone or . . . or sleepily nestled within the crook of his arm, my head resting on his bare chest . . . stop it!

Instead, we'd shuffled, stared helplessly at one another before he'd gently touched my cheek, moving a strand of hair to behind my ear. Then under duress we'd muttered goodnights before heading to our respective rooms. I'd closed my door really slowly, hoping to hear a last-minute call of my name, or a question, or . . . or anything. But nothing, just a solid click from the wooden door across the landing.

So I've lain here since, staring at the ceiling, recalling every minute. And listening intently, for a creak on the staircase.

Unless he stepped over the top stair. Used the banister to support his weight to avoid making it creak.

He never has before, but he might. Why would he though? Nope, he wouldn't – I must have missed it. Too busy replaying the mistletoe scene in my head to hear it. I dart from my bed, grab my cardigan and am flying down the staircase without any thought to mind the creaky stair.

Rap-a-tap-tap. I knock on the wooden door of the snug as loud as I wish. Fling open the door on the final knock and stand in darkness, staring at our debris left on the coffee table. In my hurry, I hadn't noticed that there was no mellow light showing beneath the door. Emmet's still in his bed!

I instinctively turn to view the unlit banisters, half expecting him to be peering through, watching me, making a wisecrack or teasing me about my surprise. But nothing, pure darkness. The mistletoe twists and turns above the newel post, as if mocking me.

'Now what?' I whisper, still half expecting to hear his footsteps after I made such a noise down here. Nothing. I rap loudly again on the open wooden door, just for good measure, in case he's upstairs listening for signs of life from me. Nothing.

'Bugger!' I enter the snug, switch the lamp on and flop down on to my couch. A clothbound book falls from beside the cushion on to the floor – I retrieve it and flip through. It's the poetry book Martha had been reading – I start to read to amuse myself. Emmet will be down any minute, I'm sure.

I wake freezing cold, with my head propped awkwardly against the arm of the couch, drooling into a squashed seat cushion. I sit up with a start, fearing I might have company. No one; I'm all alone but for the poetry book clutched to my chest. Great! I've had very little sleep, I've gained a knotty ache in my neck and spent the night with a couple of dead poets.

I ease myself to a standing position, roll my shoulders and slowly make my way into the hallway to be greeted by the morning light creeping through the tiny bevelled window. I stare at the cloud of mistletoe. 'It's all your bloody fault,' I mutter, snatching it and yanking it down. Then, faster than my legs usually carry me, I dart into the kitchen, across the tiles and unlock the back door before angrily launching the tied mistletoe out into the blanket of snow. The broken string looks like ribbons on a wedding bouquet as it flies through the air, heading towards the decorative archway. I hear a muted thump as it lands, instantly buried in a snowdrift. 'Good riddance to ya – for all the good you did me!'

Then I give the door a satisfying slam, lock it and return to the hallway; as I climb the stairs, I purposely stomp on the creaky one in annoyance, only to regret it seconds later.

Is it worth trying to get some sleep, or should I pack? Sort out the cat and her kittens, have breakfast and simply leave for Pendlebury? What else am I waiting for, if at the first chance we get to spend quality time together, nothing happens. Forget five days of long lingering looks, admiring glances, moments spent thinking there's a connection – it's all dissolved into nothing. All in my head, or my heart – or whatever is responsible. If a girl needed a signal, he's certainly delivered it by his absence.

I draw the curtains, reposition and plump each pillow and neaten the top sheet. 'Lost in your own head for a while there, Lowry, that's what you were,' I say, erasing all signs of my presence by smoothing the duvet. Everything will return to normal once I'm home. Washing on, suitcase stashed away and Trixie and her kittens settled in their new forever home. I might even drop by the rescue centre to see how the team spent Christmas, check on the little mite from my last working day and maybe butter up Big Boss Roger to let me to spend a couple of hours on duty. Sounds like a plan. But first, a shower, dress and pack, then my usual life can resume.

'Morning!'

I couldn't have timed it worse – the second I open my bedroom door, Emmet steps from the master suite opposite, all bright and breezy. Awkward.

'Morning, Emmet. Sleep well?'

'Like a log. And you?' he says, stepping aside to let me lead the way down the staircase. I step on the first stair and a reliable creak sounds from underfoot.

'Yes, thanks.' I want to ask questions but instead I descend in silence.

'I've no idea what goodies we left in the fridge but it'll make for an interesting fry-up,' he says, as we enter the kitchen.

'I'll probably have cereal and be on my way,' I say, heading straight for the kettle.

'You're going?'

'Yeah, I might as well.'

'But the keys aren't due till three o'clock.' He stands stock-still in the middle of the tiled floor while I busy myself: I need tea. 'Lowry, what's the rush? You're not back at work till tomorrow. I thought we could . . .' I'm taken aback by his response; he seems genuinely surprised.

'What?' I say, a little too eagerly.

'Are you OK? You seem . . . distant.'

'Distant? Me?' I blow my cheeks out and lean against the countertop. Here we go, explanation time. 'You slept like a log – well, I didn't. I came down here like a fool, thinking we'd continue the meeting-in-the-snug routine, only to fall asleep on the couch. I had a rubbish night's sleep and woke up with a squiffy shoulder.' This is as far as I go; I daren't bring up the mistletoe. I fall silent, catching my breath and allow my 'blame, blame, blame' explanation to circulate around the kitchen, weaving between us.

'Urgh!' His chin drops to his chest, and he rakes a hand through his dark curls. 'I'm sorry, Lowry. I thought it might be too dangerous.'

'Dangerous?' I mutter, verging on sarcastic.

'Just us . . . an empty cottage – wine, cuddling and mistletoe – yeah, dangerous.' He glances up, holding my gaze, and I can see the regret in his eyes.

In an instant I understand. Like a new-found hound, he's cautious, dubious yet willing to venture towards pastures new.

Helen

It takes a matter of minutes to get an economy wash on, a morning brew made and dig out my brand-new address book. It's one thing to spend a Christmas with the entire family but quite another recovering from it and resuming daily life. I could ignore the fleeting ideas buzzing around my brain, or I could take action. I could sit back and pretend that I won't be organising the bedroom plan for next year's Christmas rental, or I can figure out a way of taking a back seat and allowing others to step up. My thirty years of playing the role of the first Mrs Carmichael needs to end. And given the outbursts this weekend from Lynette, Janie and Fena, though the last was totally unrelated to me and more about her daughter's condition, I need to forge a plan of action for the New Year. What is it they say? A new year, a new me!

I open my old address book and prepare myself for the task ahead. I carefully flip open each page and, with the heaviest of hearts knowing my choice is made as fate awaits me, begin to transfer across to the new book the details of each friend to whom I'm not related by DNA or marriage. I need an address book that contains only friends. Friends I can meet up with, friends I can visit, friends I can share a day out with. Friends without the surname Carmichael. It's my own fault; I've allowed my world to become tiny, wrapped up and revolving around that one surname – now is the time to break a habit of a lifetime, to begin the fresh start I should have attempted after our divorce.

A lump jumps to my throat as I reach the details of a dear friend who died a few years ago. How quickly I lost touch when life got busy; I didn't call, I didn't visit, and now they're gone. Gone before their time, some would say. I turn the page, leaving the friend's memory to reside in the worn pages of my old life.

I might have dedicated myself to being the matriarch of the Carmichael clan but this new address book is going to be my season ticket to a new me. My new beginnings, my next chapter, so to speak, in which I'll meet new companions, seek holidays with new friends and attend more social groups. Hobbies, interests and classes will need consideration when the family make demands on my time; no more rushing to please others, I'm going to simply please myself for a change.

The children have grown up, as Lynette helpfully pointed out. Rupert is hopefully settled for good and I'm blessed to still have good health. The next generation are moving on: new relationships, babies and careers – it's time. As Emmet said at the door to Teddy, I'll be off-grid. And me, son!

I've been busying myself with everything relating to the Carmichaels and have lost myself in the process. Now, I sit in a deafening silence as the world drifts by.

I continue to transfer the contact details, having a little cry at times over a forgotten or lost friend, but eventually, I reach my final entry. One question remains at the forefront of my mind: what are my plans for Easter? It might be early but I grab my phone, speed-dial the one person who has shown their true worth for three decades, though that tense moment yesterday in the car was a first between us. I saw what I saw and didn't like to pry, given she's always been my rock and my constant companion, come hell or high water.

'Hi, Martha, it's only me. I was wondering how do you fancy a few days away over the Easter break? Just us, in a tiny cottage somewhere without fuss or favour … It'll be no trouble. I'll run it past Rupert, don't you worry – I'll tell him we're heading off-grid as a treat.'

Chapter Twenty-Seven

Lowry

'What the hell are you doing?' I scream in excitement, morphing into the child I once was, as Emmet exits the cottage manhandling an interior door to manoeuvre past the doorway and porch overhang without knocking either.

'We're going sledging.' In one effortless move, the wooden door travels from upright to horizontally resting on his head, his grip on either side stabilising the load, like a wide-brimmed hat. 'Don't look so worried – if we wreck it, I'll replace it. It's not an original door like the lounge one but borrowed from the scullery. We stock thousands of these in the warehouse, so don't fret.'

'I can't believe you've removed it to do something like this.'

'Pah! You've never lived if you've never gone sledging on a wooden door.'

'And you've removed the handle and hinges too.'

'It wouldn't glide otherwise, would it?'

'No, but . . . oh, forget it. Here, let me get the gate.' I step around him to lift the latch – he looks a right sight but my growing buzz of childish excitement eclipses my concerns regarding Rupert's rental deposit. 'Where are we heading?'

'To the top of the biggest hill we can find. Come on.'

I close the gate, securing the latch before hotfooting it to catch up with his leggy strides along the lane. His plan sounds absurd, foolhardy and possibly destructive, if we do trash the scullery door, but the thrill of acting so waywardly simply feeds my excitement. A very different vibe from our awkward start to the day, though I'm still harbouring regrets from last night's goodnight.

'What's with the name Lowry? A family tradition or something?' asks Emmet, as we walk and talk.

'No, nothing of the sort. L. S. Lowry was a local guy. My grandad liked the artist's work so he suggested it when I was born. My mum was on her own, so name suggestions were welcomed.'

'Lowry Stephens – it has a certain ring to it, I suppose.'

'You suppose?'

'Yeah, sounds OKish, I suppose.' I twig that he's teasing me and simply shake my head in response. 'What was it he liked about his painting then – his colour palette, his subject or his style?'

I hesitate, fearing Emmet might laugh if I tell him.

'He casts no shadows,' I say, watching him intently, ready to clam up and backtrack at the first sign of teasing.

'What, in his personal life? I know nothing about the chap - other than he painted match-stick people, cats and dogs – which you'd probably rescue, nurture and rehome nowadays.'

I smile at his suggested connection.

'No, in his actual paintings . . . there are no shadows.'

Emmet's eyebrows twitch, lifting high into his curls, and a slow steady smile adorns his lips. 'Is that so? No shadows, hey? I like that idea – I like that idea very much.'

We walk a little further in silence, Emmet lost to his own shadows, me pondering how our sledging might work. Do we avoid physical contact by sledging solo? Or ignore potential dangers like a couple of school kids?

'How are we going to steer it?' I ask, as my responsible adult reemerges, pushing aside my inner child.

'Our combined body weight should do the trick – if not, we'll soon find out.' Ah, that's my contact question answered.

'Combined?' I softly mutter, looking up and noticing Emmet's wry smile.

'Combined.'

'Are you comfy?' asks Emmet, as I sit in front of him, his denim-clad thighs fitting snugly around my hips – but I'm not going to complain. My heels are wedged fast against the door's panelling, my fingers attempt to grip the stained surface. Before us is a vast expanse of snow. Literally the mother of all snow hills, the biggest we could see. It took an age to climb and I suspect it will take a fraction of that time to descend. There's a smattering of mature trees around, but a clear pathway stretches before us – I'm hoping it stays that way. In a collision, pitching my bones against a tree trunk, I believe I'd lose every time. In the far distance sits Lakeside Cottage with its stone walls, nestled beside the glistening lake with an idyllic backdrop. The surrounding hills and nature provide a panoramic view on all sides. The perfect setting for a memorable Christmas, or so it appears from high up here.

'I think so,' I shout over my shoulder.

'Hold on tight then,' he says, propelling us forward with his hands along the summit's flat ground towards the descending slope. The door edges forward in a cumbersome manner as we near the point of no return. My breath snags in my throat, my heart rate lifts as the thrill and danger of our antics swirl within my chest.

'Get ready . . . and—' Emmet gives a final push – 'we're gone!' His warlike cry deafens me as the door flies down the slope, gathering pace, and the peripheral landscape blurs. Emmet wraps his arms around my shoulders, his hands resting beneath my chin. I brace my body against his chest as the door bounces and bumps along, gaining momentum. The biting wind burns my bare cheeks, causing my eyes to water. I can feel Emmet navigating, moving me from side to side in order to shift our weight. If I had time to think – which I don't – I wouldn't be placing any meaning on the physical contact we have. I can't allow myself to read anything into anything – not after last night's disappointment.

I'm jamming my heels into the panelling for fear of flying off, despite being held by Emmet. My tail bone keeps lifting and then slamming down on the door's central cross section. No doubt I'll be black and blue tomorrow and complaining loudly, but the thrill of the speed, the rush of adrenalin, more than makes up for the discomfort.

We're over halfway down, and I'm giddy from the high, when the front corner edge rises as we encounter some uneven ground; the door lifts from the snow, partially airborne, before slamming back down on to the snow slope. Instantly, my thrill turns to panic. My feet instinctively press harder attempting to press a non-existent brake pedal, my fingertips strain to grip the grain as the door reacts as physics determines, despite Emmet's masterly manoeuvring using me as a tiller.

The blurred trees are whizzing past, but all I can envisage is my broken body lying at the bottom of a tree trunk, amidst some twisted gnarly roots, the resounding pain on impact and the emergency created. I want to cry as we're thrown from side to side, the door lifting uncontrollably before slamming down, hurting my coccyx.

'Emmet!' I wail.

'Brace yourself – go with the roll!' shouts Emmet, as the door lifts on the right-hand side, tipping us both off in a thoroughly undignified manner.

I feel the shocking coldness to my face, see nothing but a blur of white, then blue sky, then white, over and over again as my body rolls. All the time, my arms are held tight to my torso by a pair of clenched arms wrapped firmly around my shoulders and back. It feels like the greatest roly-poly down a hill that any child could imagine, but I'm holding my breath, waiting for an abrupt stop at the base of a tree.

Eventually we stop, though the door continues on its path unmanned. Emmet releases me and we fall apart into the powdered snow to stare up at the bright blue sky. I'm gasping for breath, almost choking, as I scramble on to my front so I can breathe easier. Not quite the 'tumble' I'd been expecting from our time alone.

'Are you OK?' asks Emmet, looking up at me from his supine position, with clumps of snow in his hair and stubble.

'That was . . . amazing!' I gasp, between breaths. 'I thought I was a goner when we separated from the door but . . . phuh! Amazing!' I start to giggle, recalling the initial panic, enjoying the sheer relief of feeling firm ground beneath my stomach. 'How ridiculous must we have looked . . . clinging on for dear life, travelling at high speed on a door – I've never done that before!'

Emmet's gaze travels around my face, taking in my giggle, which turns into a laugh and, finally, a full-blown belly laugh. His smile broadens as my noise increases.

I fall silent, looking down at him. He's looking up at me. Silent eyes roving and lingering, drinking in every inch of the portrait before us.

I want to kiss him.

I want him to kiss me.

'Dangerous territory,' he whispers, his gaze not leaving mine before he jumps to his feet, leaving me lying face down in the snow.

Damn this man, with his commonsense values! Having spent five days slowly drawing me in, now he's bloody winding me up!

Martha

'Martha, is there any grub going begging?' asks Teddy, wandering into the kitchen literally the minute I've unpacked my copper pans and ceramic dishes. He knows me too well.

'Does it look as if I've reestablished my kitchen after a weekend away?' I say, giving him a look.

'No, but you've always got a bite or two put aside for us regardless.'

'In the fridge, there's some ham and pickles which I brought back from the cottage, though mind you don't eat it all as I won't be shopping until later,' I say, gesturing towards the fridge, hating to admit that I over-catered with certain items. 'With your sister coming over for dinner I'll be busy making a rice pudding this morning, so don't be nagging me for a cooked brunch. It'll be cupboard love until I've restocked.' Teddy knows I mean basic cupboard stocks. They all know what I mean, who am I kidding? Likewise Helen, given her quick call offering a little break off-grid at Easter. But I can't wait that long. It's a new day and I need to lay the foundations for my own plans, which, judging by the shaking of this knife blade, need to start sooner rather than later.

I begin piling my boxes ready for storage in the boot room. It never feels right until they're out of sight, much like having my suitcase emptied and clothes washed, ready for the next family jaunt. Though how I'll break the news that it won't be me filling these storage boxes with their favourite culinary delights come the next get-together is beyond me.

Teddy helps himself, making the usual mess by smearing butter over my clean chopping board, leaving a trail of bread-crumbs and half the contents of the fridge on the sideboard as he trails off towards the lounge. It winds me up a treat but then again, it's great to be back to the usual routines of home, sweet home.

'You can get yourself right back in here and sort out that mess,' I call after him, knowing full well the reminder isn't necessary but he'll never be too big for me to correct him. Over thirty years I've learnt my place in this family; it's evolved with each passing year and I know what Mr C expects of me. Along with Helen, I'm a constant within this family, come good times and bad, relied upon to provide what I can, when I can, for this family, as willingly as I would have for my own. Though after this weekend, I know I need to dive between the pages of my glossy Hawaiian brochures and make firm decisions about specific dates. I know exactly what I'd like to experience, given their weather and climate, but whether the pennies can stretch that far is another matter.

I quickly pop the kettle on, before collecting the cake boxes and selecting my knives for the task ahead. Not that I need another job to entertain me, but the sooner I get this one done the better. Thankfully the wedding cake made it back from the cottage in one piece so I collect the assortment of tiny boxes, pre-prepared and addressed before I left five days ago, and carefully measure out the portions. Personally, I think a sliver of cake this size is no good to god nor man, but it's what Diane and Mr C have chosen to do, so I'll follow their instructions. They could be in the post as early as tomorrow.

I'm certain there'll be plenty more wedding cakes to be made for this family, but I sense I won't be making them, or a christening cake, unless Jeffery gets his act together pretty sharpish.

It feels good to be home, in my own kitchen alongside my faithful Aga, my well-stocked store cupboard and every cookery gadget imaginable close at hand.

I position myself at my scrubbed table, gently scoring the royal icing with the tip of my quivering knife, gauging where to cut through. A calculated process, where each faint indent determines the eventual cut – after which, correct or miscalculated, it can't be erased once performed. Much like my forthcoming announcement to the Carmichaels. Get the wording or the timing wrong and I'll risk losing the only family I've ever known and loved. I need to be brave, for my sake and theirs.

An image of Lowry flashes before my eyes. Diane's girl's a welcome addition to the family, because surely if you can stand up for yourself with Mr C and nurture something that isn't truly yours, you won't go far wrong in this family. Having such principles has served me well in the last thirty years.

A lump jumps to my throat. Thirty years, where has the time gone? More importantly, what will the next few bring for me? I pause, my knife wavering, before making the first cut and ruining the layer of icing on the cake. I can't think in years, I need to think in steps ... and the first step is to share my secret. With Helen. She's been my trusted companion through thick and thin – she's the right person to lean on. And she phoned me not more than an hour ago. I'll phone her back once this cake is sliced. I'll apologise and explain that I can't possibly wait till Easter, before taking her back to our satnav moment and my shaking right hand, and explaining about my Parkinson's. Strange how I rarely repeat the word 'disease' but it makes it sound almost infectious or contagious, which it most certainly isn't!

'Wedding cake? Is there a slice going spare?' asks Teddy, reappearing with an empty plate and hopefully, a full belly.

'I won't know until I've sliced it all, but you can sort out that countertop in the meantime,' I say, ensuring he gets from under my feet.

'Go on, Martha. Let me pinch a bit of the corner icing – you know it's the best bit!' I wave aside his fingers, fondly remembering the boy of seven.

Memories, ahhh – long may they remain. I've a head full of memories and a heart brimming with love. Together, like almond marzipan and caster sugar, they're a winning combination. Providing a solid foundation and the final flourishes in life. Simply the icing on the wedding cake!

Chapter Twenty-Eight

Lowry

It takes a matter of minutes to rehang the cottage's interior doors, uniting their hinged couplings perfectly. Whereas it felt like it took a month of Sundays for us to regain our composure, to brush ourselves down and endure a lengthy walk in silence back to Lakeside Cottage. With every step I wanted to speak – I simply couldn't. The aftermath felt like that stomach-dropping moment when you tell someone you love them but they don't say it back. A moment of regret, berating yourself for your honesty, for revealing your true feelings. You wish to reap something in return, be it a look, a garbled phrase – anything but silence. Lord knows why people pay top whack to experience silent retreats in far-flung locations around the globe; mine was free of charge and deeply uncomfortable. It isn't so much an icy silence between us, more a 'I daren't speak because I can't truly explain' silence. Though I'm not sure which is worse.

With each stride, I wanted to conjure the niceties of small talk about the chill in the air, the clear blue sky, or comment on the passing hedgerows or the lakeside view, but nothing came to mind other than a continual replay of our missed opportunities: last night and now today too! What was the point of me spending an extra day at the cottage if we were to just skirt around each other? I might as well have headed straight home alongside the others. Once our sledging moment had passed, Emmet's only concern was to locate the scullery door and assess whether it was damaged or warped! I can certainly name someone whose inner self is feeling damaged and slightly warped in this moment!

And now, having rehung the two interior doors in the hallway, we're yet to achieve a comfortable interaction. We're both so wooden, our staccato speech silently practised before airing, and neither one can look the other in the face, as we begin rehanging the scullery door.

'A hinge is a highly underappreciated piece of engineering – it might be unseen but it's vital for a smooth operation,' I say to Emmet, his pursed lips lined with a row of screws, as he aligns the first hinge plate against the doorjamb before working a screw into the existing hole with a long-handled screwdriver. Emmet raises his eyebrows in agreement, as he can't speak. I continue the thought. 'Probably no different to marriage, I suppose; two halves securely joined together, working as one to perform a purposeful but vital task when nestled together or apart.'

Emmet's screwdriver arm stops pumping. He inclines his head to stare at me as if my musings have hit home somewhere in his psyche.

'What?' I ask. Emmet shakes his head and continues to work the screw head.

I wait until he's replaced each screw and is free to speak.

'Is it damaged in any way?' I ask, scanning the outer side of the scullery door, which we'd reclaimed from the overgrown hedgerow at the bottom of the hill.

'Nothing that a wipe over with a damp cloth won't remove,' says Emmet, running his fingers over the wooden panelling, picking off the odd deposit of flaky mud or twig here and there. I don't hesitate but leave the scullery to fetch a damp cloth from the kitchen sink, anxious to be done with the task and hopefully move on. Though my nerves are clearly not prepared for either more interaction or a discussion about our previous ones.

I return, handing Emmet the damp cloth to perform the honours.

'I was half expecting to have to replace it but it seems fine. If we can realign the handle, no one will ever suspect it's ever been removed, let alone spent a wild afternoon proving itself worthy of an alternative existence.'

Wild afternoon? Does that include us, or is he simply referring to the door?

'I suppose that statement hardly fits with our maturity and constraint,' adds Emmet, as if reading my thoughts.

'Mmm.' I flash a coy smile in his direction as my stomach lurches with anticipation.

'So now what?' he asks, briskly wiping each panel, leaving a trail of clean damp wood.

Not a question I was expecting. I don't answer; I haven't exactly thought this through. I wasn't seeking a relationship when I arrived here. Wouldn't say I intended to kiss him before I actually wanted to. Didn't think I liked him enough to consider such a move, and yet . . . I felt rejected when it didn't happen.

'Are you blatantly ignoring my question or simply stalling for time?' asks Emmet, stepping backwards to inspect the door but switching his gaze to me.

'Er, kind of both. I don't know what to say, Emmet. I've been doing what felt right in the moment and now you're asking me questions I have no answers . . . so yeah, that.'

'I see.' I'm waiting for him to fill the silence, come up with a suitable solution, provide an excuse for our behaviour – meaning I won't have to. Hardly mature, but it's been so long since I connected with anyone that this feels huge. Add in our family circumstances, and it feels monumental. 'Could you pass me the door fittings from off the countertop, please?'

I'm glad of the opportunity to busy myself, easing the tension, though it appears to be affecting only me, not him. I collect the dismantled handles, back plates and numerous gold screws.

'Here,' I say, offering the jumble of metal.

'Cheers.'

We resume our silence. I need to get going in a while – it'll take two hours to drive home. I could pack my car while he finishes this task. I could strip the bed ready for the housekeeper's arrival. I could even . . .

'So, what now?' Emmet asks again, peering at me momentarily before continuing to attach the handle.

I give a nonchalant shrug, as my heart leaps from my chest.

'I reckon it might be complicated given the circumstances.'

'Perhaps,' I mutter, unsure whether to air my thoughts.

Emmet continues to focus on the door handle, but a wry smile adorns his lips.

'You're not too bothered then? Is that it?'

'No!' My response is immediate, giving the game away.

'Oh, you are bothered?'

'No.'

Emmet's face cracks into a smile.

'Careful, Lowry, for a minute there I thought you might be playing it cool.'

'No,' I whisper. 'I'm not used to this . . . I'm no good at having to explain my actions.'

'So back to my original question . . . what now?'

'It depends.'

'Mmm, depends whether I'm going to continue to act like a scared cat caught in a damned corner,' he says, rattling the attached handle firmly. 'Or actually admit that I'm interested.'

'Interested?' I scoff, falling silent before I do further damage.

'Yeah, interested. You know, for someone who works with

animals and has studied their behaviour – you're definitely slow on the uptake when it comes to human beings.'

My mouth falls wide. His eyebrows merely twitch in response.

'I'll put it to you plain and simple. I like you – you're a decent sort. Given our relaxed manner last night, I assume that the feelings are mutual. So as long as I continue not to smoke, which you said you dislike, I assume you'd be prepared to spend an evening out with me once we've finished this Christmas holiday. If not, then I'm way off the mark!'

'Phuh!'

'Don't worry, I can get past the fact that you're Diane's daughter. Likewise, you've discovered that my family don't define who I am. There, I think that sorts it.' Emmet stands tall, tapping the screwdriver on his open palm.

'I don't think so,' I say, saucily implying me.

'I was referring to the door handle.'

I blush profusely. 'Oh, yes ... good job.'

'And?' His gaze is intense, as if searching for an answer.

'A scared cat caught in a damned corner, are you?'

'After recent events, yeah – I am.'

'It's a good job I'm an expert in my field then. As most animal behaviours can be successfully addressed with a little patience and oodles of kindness,' I say confidently, before adding, 'And I have both in abundance.'

'Shouldn't they be in a box for added safety?' asks Emmet, holding the car's passenger door open for me while I access the rear seats, clutching my feline family in their cloth sacking.

'Give me two seconds and you'll see my plan in action.' It's a tight fit but I manage to unzip my suitcase, scoot my belongings over into a jumbled pile in one half of the case and gently ease the cloth sacking into position. The mother cat eyes me calmly, while her kittens squirm in protest at being disturbed. 'They'll be content lying in the empty half until I arrive home, I promise. That's me done then.' I back out of the car and close the passenger door. 'What time are you off?'

'As soon as I've handed the keys to Josie.'

Emmet lingers, watching my every move. I'm waiting for his goodbye, be it a warm embrace, a peck on the cheek, even a robust, 'Cheerio, see you at Easter!' – but nothing. I'm shifting from foot to foot as the cold is nipping at my hands, but Emmet's not moving. He's had three opportunities to kiss me and he hasn't acted on any – letting the mistletoe, the sledging and even our last discussion pass without igniting the passion.

'You've got enough screenwash to get you back home?' he asks.

'Yep.'

'You know where you're going?'

'Yep, I've programmed the satnav already.'

'OK, that's good.'

'Emmet . . .'

'Yes?' His expression is eager to please.

'Call me,' I say, gesturing to my ear.

'I certainly will. We'll grab a drink, maybe a meal and see what's what.'

'Before Easter . . .'

His smile beams, chasing away any shadow of doubt. 'Drive safe now.' With this final line, he gives me a peck on the cheek and a last smile before striding back towards the picket gate.

Is that it? No passionate embrace? No lingering kiss to remember him by? A quick peck, in a 'be gone' kind of fashion. I watch him go through the gate, close the latch and head for the cottage door – his head's bowed, there's no last-minute glance over his shoulder. Has he misunderstood my comment about patience and kindness in abundance? I was hinting that we can take it slow, but if this is anything to go by, I'm surprised we even managed to end up sitting on the same sofa in one evening. Has he even realised I haven't jumped into my car yet?

So I do just that.

I fasten my seat belt, activate the satnav, turn the ignition and we are off! I perform a nifty U-turn in the lane, fuelled by my frustration, and drive by the cottage to see an open front door and Emmet standing on the step, shoulders slumped, expression nonplussed. A replica image of the brooding Emmet I met that first night. He raises one hand solemnly as I wave a flourish of goodbyes. In an instant, I've left. The cottage is behind me, Emmet's presence is no more. I don't get it. How can we cross that distance between two sofas in the space of an evening, helped by a bottle of wine, yet separate in the space of a minute whilst standing at the bottom of a staircase thanks to some mistletoe?

What the hell is wrong with him? Have I totally misunderstood? Read the room incorrectly? Forced myself into his line of vision when actually . . .?

Walking along the roadside towards the cottage is a mature lady, dressed in a tweed skirt and sensible shoes – I assume it's Josie, making her way to collect the keys. I drive by knowing that in a few minutes Emmet will have completed his task, have jumped into his car and be gone. Gone until whenever? Maybe Easter, if he doesn't bother to call me. Could be longer if I don't get time off at Easter due to the work rota. Or if he chooses not to attend the family gathering at Easter, despite what he's suggesting now.

I jam the brakes on, causing everything in the car to lurch forward.

'Sorry!' I call to the cats on the rear seat. What the hell is wrong with him? But deep down, I know. I know because I've seen that expression before . . . several times a week, actually, for the last decade at the rescue centre. Emmet's got the exact look of a dog who doesn't want to be where they are, is watching his

potential companions leave without him and allowing the hope
that fuelled his earlier excitement to wane, fearing the reality
won't live up to his expectations.

Oh my God! It's he who doesn't believe *my* words, not the
other way around! He's said goodbye to so many people that
he believes he knows the outcome, just like the old-timer dogs
never chosen for rehoming.

I perform a second natty U-turn and drive back towards the
cottage. I'm hoping against hope that the Josie-lady isn't there
yet, but just like the families choosing a stray dog to rehome, I
need to make sure he knows he's wanted. I am as good as my
word, always.

I arrive to find the cottage door closed.

I draw my Mini to a halt, jump out and secure the doors to
prevent my cats from escaping, not caring that I've abandoned
the car in the lane. I'm nipping through the white picket gate
and along the cobbled pathway before my brain can find a gear,
let alone apply the brakes. I lift the latch on the front door and
march in. I cut straight through the hallway, into the kitchen
and head for the back door. Emmet is nowhere to be seen, not
that he's my priority at this very moment, but he will be. Soon.

I cross the patio and am gingerly ascending the garden steps
to the snow-covered lawn, searching left and right as I near the
decorative archway. There's an irregular crater, beside the arch,
ruining the blemish-free snow – in which lies a discarded bunch
of hand-tied mistletoe.

'Lowry! What are you doing?' calls Emmet, from the back
doorstep, as I retrace my path down the garden steps.

'I . . . I . . . just wanted to do this.'

And without another thought, I lean forward, holding the
retrieved mistletoe above our heads, as best I can being much
smaller than him. My lips are on his, which are soft and surpris-
ingly warm. The slightest pause occurs before his lips respond to

mine. Not in an urgent way but in a soft sensual manner; our lips move naturally, automatically fitting together as if they always have, while his palm sweeps along my jawline to slide beneath my ear, disappearing into my hairline to gently caress the base of my neck, igniting joyous shivers along my spine. Our first kiss!

I sense his surprise but there's more, much more. As I draw back, slowly retreating to view his dark features staring down at me, I see the relief in his eyes – an acceptance that I am being true, he can believe in me and I won't create shadows in his life.

'Do you usually kiss men out of the blue?' says Emmet.

'I don't make a habit of it, if that's what you're suggesting.'

'Honoured, am I?'

'You should be. That's a first for me, under mistletoe,' I say, waving the foliage excitedly.

Emmet peers at me momentarily before a smile adorns his lips. 'And me, in more ways than one!'

'Must dash – I've left Trixie and her kittens unattended in the car. Mwah!' I blow him a kiss as I quickly sidestep his frame and retrace my steps through the cottage, clutching my bouquet of mistletoe and heading for home.

Epilogue

Tuesday, 31 December 2024

Lowry

What a difference a year makes! I'm the first to arrive, which is a novelty for me regarding any holiday, plus Big Boss Roger didn't have to shoo me from the Salford rescue centre this time. I park my old brown Mini in front of the drystone wall, knowing a convoy of vehicles will arrive in the coming hours. For once, there are no delays or alternative arrangements; everyone is arriving on the same day. Boy, how much has changed in one year!

Leaving my suitcase and belongings in the car, I lock the driver's door and admire the view before me. Thankfully, the cottage looks exactly the same as it did. Its white picket gate, the well-worn cobbles and the bare winter branches – which Helen insists are wisteria – framing the quaint front door are picture perfect. The cottage looks cosy and welcoming with its upper windows peeking from beneath its traditional thatched roof. The image matches my memory of last Christmas, and for that I'm grateful. Not that I would complain if the owners had altered anything but we dreamt of a return to our special place, especially for this celebration.

The front door springs wide open and a spritely lady, in a tweed skirt and sturdy walking shoes, smiles from the doorstep. Very different to my previous arrival, when a box of kittens was thrust upon me on a dark and chilly night.

'Hello, I'm Josie . . . housekeeper for Lakeside Cottage. Lowry, is it?' she asks.

'Yes, it is. Nice to meet you,' I say, stretching out a hand in appreciation. 'Arriving ahead of our large party, as advised.'

'A wedding party, I understand.'

'Yes. We get married tomorrow at St Michael's.' I stupidly gesture into the distance, as if she's unaware of her local church. Though I forget, on purpose, to mention the accompanying angels.

'New year – what a wonderful time for a wedding!' gushes Josie enthusiastically.

'We tried to separate it from Christmas as the Carmichael family already has a birthday and an anniversary around then,' I say, brimming with excitement at the mention of our big day. 'We spent last Christmas here when our parents were preparing to marry.'

Josie's brow furrows a little, but I let it go without explanation. I'm getting used to spotting this kind of reaction when particular details about the family are mentioned. It only confuses people if you provide too much detail and they attempt to join the dots together.

'I remember . . . amidst the snowdrifts too, magical but it complicates matters. I thought I recognised the surname as a rebooking, though wasn't it Helen who was the designated key-holder last year?'

'Well remembered. Thankfully, they haven't forecast snow this year. Helen's coming but I've taken over her role – there've been lots of changes in recent months, though I doubt I'll have thought of or planned for every eventuality as well as Helen always did.'

'I'm sure you have. I've booking details for a party of fourteen adults and one baby,' she says, stepping aside and allowing me to step inside. Seeing the familiar hallway, the central staircase, the solid beams overhead and the polished floorboards feels like returning home after a long absence. My heart flutters on seeing the notchity newel post and remembering the mistletoe sprig hung as decoration during last year's stay.

'Yes, that's right. I requested a cot to be available in one of the double bedrooms.'

'You did, that's been arranged. Though with a choice of nine bedrooms they might prefer a different room, but the cot's light enough to be moved between rooms.'

'Thank you, the parents will appreciate that.' I can breathe, the request has been sorted eliminating an excuse for a family drama.

'I'll run through the basics quickly then, given you've stayed here before,' says Josie, opening the first panelled door on the left.

I smile, knowing the guys will lift the lounge door off its hinges in no time.

Helen

For the first time in years, I'm nervous about conducting the family introductions. Since Rupert's last wedding, I've taken time for myself, with hobbies, new interests and even off-grid adventures to far-flung destinations. I've stepped back from the family fold – passing much of my involvement on to others or allowing certain aspects, such as leading the introductions, to fade. It's not that I've forgotten how, despite it being a year since I ran through the protocol on Lowry's arrival, but this introduction is personal to me. It matters to me that Adam understands the foundations of our blended family, because if he doesn't, I may lose someone who's becoming increasingly special in my world.

'Adam, this is the family. Here is my only son, Emmet – soon to be married to the lovely Lowry,' I say, gesturing towards the couple sitting on the couch before moving along to the next couple, standing beside the roaring fire. 'This is my nephew, River, Emmet's younger brother, and his girlfriend, Annabel.' A chorus of chirpy hellos fills the air after each name. I sneak a quick glance at Adam; he seems unfazed at present so I bravely continue. 'Rupert's third son, Teddy, stands beside the doorway, and the mother and baby are Scarlet and Elijah, Rupert's daughter and grandson.' Another quick look confirms Adam is still following and politely exchanging hellos with each new person. 'Sitting next to them is Jeffery, who is Scarlet's partner, Rupert's best friend and Elijah's father.' At that point, Adam's brow furrows.

'Ah right, quite complicated there, but hello,' says Adam, a wry smile adorning his clean-shaven features.

'You've done well to reach that point before the brain cells questioned what's being said,' offers Emmet with a chuckle, earning a swift nudge from Lowry.

'This dear lady here is Martha, who looks after us in the most beautiful way, despite retiring from service after thirty years. She's part of our family, when all is said and done. Rupert has renamed her "his angel who still bakes, sometimes".' I pause. I could say a lot more about our dear friend Martha, feeling I've undersold her qualities, but I won't as she'll not take kindly to her struggles being highlighted. 'The next lady is my younger sister, Janie – who is River's mum . . . and finally we have Rupert and Diane Carmichael, my ex-husband and his new wife, who happens to be Lowry's mother.' I pause for breath, cautiously taking in Adam's puzzled expression.

'Thank you for that. I was expecting a name or two but not so much the family titles, which have probably bamboozled me into the middle of next week, if I'm honest,' says Adam, looking around the sea of faces all staring at him. 'Is anyone missing?'

'Yes, Lynette and Fena – ex-wives number three and four, but neither one is attending this get-together or the wedding,' I answer, fairly confidently.

'As far as we know!' adds Rupert. 'But that doesn't mean they won't show up unexpectedly.'

'My mum, Lynette, won't be coming – she's on a silent retreat in Goa,' offers Teddy, leaning against the doorjamb. I can't help but frown in his direction, not because of the information he's relayed but because of his stubbled chin, which now matches his older brothers'.

'Her shoulder shimmy might come in handy after all!' mutters Janie, cradling one of her festive coffees, causing the women present to turn and stare. 'What? Just saying.'

'Who knows where mine is – she could be anywhere mid-flight between here and Nippori, Japan,' explains Scarlet, rocking a swaddled Elijah on her lap.

'Wow, I'll apologise now for getting your names wrong, but please correct me when I do otherwise, you'll be renamed for ever!' jokes Adam, talking to the assembled group. I feel I could burst with happiness – we didn't scare him off.

Martha

'I assume you haven't brought the cats with you?' I ask Lowry, as we prepare the vegetables for a roast-beef dinner.

'Hardly an option, given Rupert's initial response. I swear they remember, because on every visit to ours all three cats launch a full-scale protest with much hissing and spitting, which is entirely embarrassing for him and for me. Jenny, a colleague from work, is house- and pet-sitting so no doorstep drama this time.'

It feels good to be back in the realms of the family, having officially retired from service back in January to focus on my Hawaiian adventure. I was all of a dither making that initial phone call to Helen, but within a handful of sentences she knew where I was heading and the importance of such a trip. Though never in my wildest dreams did I expect such an eager companion. Not to mention the generosity of Mr C with a retirement gift of first-class accommodation, plus air tickets!

'No plans to join the family firm then?' I ask, knowing it's been a hot topic in recent months.

'Nope. I love what I do with the RSPCA. I'll thank you for not stirring the pot on that one at the dinner table, Martha.' She gives me a knowing look, before adding, 'Teddy seems happier, doesn't he?'

'He certainly does. It just goes to show that a stint away can work wonders. Supporting youngsters from disadvantaged areas has brought out the best in his nature, which is quite remarkable,' I say, sensing that others aren't so complimentary about his recent success. 'Though if he sports that stubble for much longer, Helen will be on a mission to scrape his chin bare.'

'She has mentioned it. A change of career has been the making of him – he can always return to the fold in the future, that's how I see it.'

'You and me both, lovey,' I say, pausing before asking, 'And Emmet and River – how are things?'

'Still dicey where trust is concerned. Emmet seems to have accepted his relationship with Annabel but that brotherly bond, well, that's broken. Emmet can't get his head around River repeating their father's moral lapses when they've endured the repercussions of Rupert's actions. I can see both sides – the heart wants what the heart wants – but for Emmet, the shadows cast by Rupert affected so much and too many. Thankfully, Rupert seems settled and happy now.'

'Oh yes, definitely. I couldn't agree more. Pity he didn't meet Diane years ago . . . but then, well, that would change things for you and so many others too.'

'Don't complicate matters, Martha . . . please. And you? Are you glad to be home after your dream holiday?'

'It seems a lifetime ago and yet only yesterday. It was all I'd ever dreamt it would be, the beautiful sights, the volcanoes and the food ... don't get me started talking about the cuisine we tasted.'

'And now, back home – were you surprised?'

I get a little choked every time I have to address this issue, but I plod on, my quivering hands busily peeling the vegetables. 'I was ... very shocked by the gesture. I've lived in that granny annexe for decades, but it never crossed my mind that they would allow me to stay on after my retirement. It's such a blessing to have the family so near, just across the lawn, to be able to attend meals whenever I choose and welcome visitors to my own little home. I'm very grateful to Mr C and Diane for allowing that. Plus, my replacement, Sophia, is very obliging and lets me into her domain if I fancy a little baking session.'

'And you seem ... well.'

Bless her for asking so politely. 'I'm doing OK, Lowry. My right hand is worse than it was, but I can't complain because my left remains unchanged. My walking has slowed as my muscles get stiff nowadays, but I can still bake and ice a wedding cake like no other!' I say proudly, anticipating her delight on viewing her cake tomorrow.

The kitchen door opens and a tentative Adam makes his way through.

'That's fantastic news, Martha. Hi, are you OK?' asks Lowry attentively.

'Yes, thanks. I was wondering if I could put the record player on that's in the hallway without disturbing you in here, Lorna.' He gestures behind him whilst speaking. 'It's been years since I saw vinyl records.'

'Forgive me for correcting you, but it's Lowry. I remember how it was for me, with so many names, but you'll get there. And yes, some music would be wonderful ... though can I suggest you don't put on "Santa Baby" – my wedding nerves couldn't handle another rendition and the associated memories from last Christmas.'

'Apologies, and thank you, Lowry,' he says before heading out.

I stifle my laughter, knowing it would come across as rude towards Adam and require a detailed explanation, which I'm not willing to provide.

'He seems nice,' whispers Lowry, once the door is closed.

'A good match for Helen. I understand she's cautious but smitten.'

'As smitten as Gunner Jeffery.'

'Mmm, though how ironic that Scarlet's rendition of "Santa Baby" still affects you, given that her Santa baby was already on the way!' I say, giving a cheeky wink.

'I know, I still cringe to think she performed so seductively despite the audience being her father and brothers! Martha, that after-dinner treat still haunts me.' We continue with our vegetables as the opening bars of U2's 'New Year's Day' fills the cottage.

'A day early, but never mind,' I mutter, relieved he took Lowry's advice.

Wednesday, 1 January 2025

Lowry

Ting, ting, ting! Rupert stands up from our top table, tapping his empty wine glass with his coffee spoon, causing all of us in the reception room at the Queen's Head to fall silent and pay attention. 'Thank you. I've been described by some as a man of few words but today I'd like to prove them wrong. Diane and I are delighted that you could all be here to celebrate the wedding of our children, Emmet and Lowry. To friends newly acquainted with the dynamics of our unique family, I do sincerely apologise for the confusion about to follow. It isn't every day your son gets married, let alone to your wife's daughter, my stepdaughter but also his stepsister. Though since the vows, she is now officially his wife, my daughter-in-law and Diane's . . . well, whatever the family title is . . . this is getting more complicated by the minute. I'm not sure whether our attending guests would benefit or be hindered by a family tree in support of these speeches. But what I wanted to say, and I speak on behalf of us all, is welcome to the family – both of you, from either side of the in-laws. May you both be very happy with many years of love and laughter ahead of you.' Rupert raises his champagne glass, and our guests follow suit, as he proudly declares, 'To the bride and groom!'

Rapturous applause, accompanied by much laughter, fills our wedding reception, and I'm instantly choked by the genuine warmth and love that flows in our direction from our small party of guests. I couldn't have asked for more.

Once silence resumes, Emmet pipes up. 'Thank you, Dad – I'm sure we will be. Though from now on, I'll be insisting that the term "stepsister" be deleted from the family's terminology.' Emmet shakes his head vigorously, adding to the comedy. 'A somewhat unappreciated and inappropriate label, I think.' A titter of polite laughter laps each of the ten dining tables. I take hold of his nearest hand and give a gentle squeeze.

'Hear, hear!' replies Rupert, raising his glass again, in agreement.

I blush instantly, and avert my teary gaze towards my bridal bouquet, a sumptuous cloud of mistletoe adorned with white roses, sharing pride of place beside our beautiful tiered wedding cake. I can't believe how perfect today has been. Me in a simple classic gown of white silk trimmed with faux fur, and Emmet, suited and booted in a navy suit with a rosebud buttonhole.

I look around the sea of happy smiling faces belonging to devoted family and close friends. There's no bickering, no drama or ill-will – simply joy. A far cry from the 'blended family' I met last Christmas, providing many more relatives than my tiny Pendlebury family. Thankfully, there are no longer unanswered questions about my dad, no lingering secrets casting obscure shadows over my daily life. Instead, I've found a safe new home alongside Emmet, my trusty companion and lover. And now husband. Despite him being dubious and slightly mistrusting at the onset, much like a rescued hound who's been let down by previous owners, Emmet's welcomed me into his life with open arms, enabling the shadows of his own childhood to fade away.

Through the tall windows, I see a fluttering of snow begin to fall, gentle at first but within seconds much heavier.

'Look,' I whisper to Emmet, gesturing towards the windows. 'Just as it was on your thirtieth birthday – when we first sat alone on the garden bench, talking, and I pretended to sip strong whisky.'

Emmet squeezes my hand tightly and doesn't let go.

'Lowry, is there anything you'd like to say?' asks Emmet, pulling me back from our moment and gesturing towards our guests.

'Only that I'm delighted to become the latest Mrs Carmichael,' I say coyly, igniting another round of joyous laughter topped with some applause. 'And together, as a family, over the coming years, we'll be creating many more Christmas wishes at the Lakeside Cottage!'

Acknowledgements

Thank you to my editors, Nicola Caws and Celine Kelly, plus everyone at Headline Publishing Group for believing in my story-telling and granting me the opportunity to become part of your team.

To David Headley and the crew at DHH Literary Agency – thank you for the unwavering support. Having a 'dream team' supporting my career was always the goal – you guys make it the reality!

Thank you to my fellow authors/friends within the Romantic Novelists' Association – you continue to support and encourage me every step of the way. Special thanks to Bella Osborne, a treasured writing friend, who inspired me to write a 'family Christmas' book having read her delightful festive book *One Family Christmas*, some years ago.

A daily thank you to The London Writers' Salon at www.writershour.com and the thousands of writers from around the world with whom I sit alongside in silence and write numerous times each day. We may not be together but something magical occurs at each session!

A lifetime of thank yous to L. S. Lowry for capturing the ordinary scenes of everyday life and making them extraordinary, minus the shadows! Your matchstalk men are still loved by this little girl.

A heartfelt thank you to a naughty little rabbit in a blue coat with brass buttons – who led me to the delightful villages of Near Sawrey and Hawkshead, inspiring a new series of books!

Unconditional thanks to my family and closest friends, for always loving and supporting my adventures – wherever they take me. Amy Peel, nee Yates – (my maternal great-grandmother) you now have a headstone, albeit within the pages of my book.

And finally, thank you to my wonderful readers. You continue to thrill me each day with your fabulous reviews and supportive emails. I'm truly humbled that you invest precious time from your busy lives to read my books. Without you guys, my characters, stories and happy-ever-afters would simply be daydreams.

Don't miss Erin's perfectly uplifting read
of fresh starts and warm friendship!

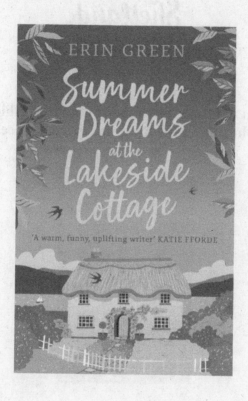

Available now from

from Shetland, with love

An uplifting novel about how friendship
can blossom in the most unexpected places . . .

Available now from

REVIEW

from
Shetland,
with love at
Christmas

Spend the holiday season in glorious Lerwick!

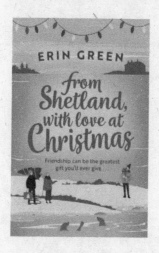

Available now from

REVIEW

a Shetland Christmas Carol

Curl up this Christmas with the new feel-good read for the holiday season from Erin Green!

New Beginnings at Rose Cottage

Don't miss this perfect feel-good read of friendship and fresh starts from Erin Green, guaranteed to make you smile!

Available now from

Taking a Chance on Love

The perfect feel-good, romantic and uplifting read –
another book from Erin Green sure to warm your heart.

Available now from